Teacher Trouble

Alexander McCall Smith

illustrations by Ian Bilbey

BLOOMSBURY

Published in Great Britain in 2006 by Bloomsbury Publishing Plc,
36 Soho Square, London, W1D 3QY

First published in the UK by Young Corgi Books, 1994

A CIP catalogue record of this book is available from the British Library

ISBN 0 7475 8039 1
9780747580393

Printed in Great Britain by Clays Ltd, St Ives Plc

1 3 5 7 9 10 8 6 4 2

All papers used by Bloomsbury Publishing are natural, recyclable products
made from wood grown in well-managed forests. The manufacturing processes
conform to the environmental regulations of the country of origin.

www.mccallsmithbooks.co.uk
www.bloomsbury.com

CHAPTER 1

First Day at School

Jenny was very tall. She had always been tall, right from the very beginning, and now that she was ten she was almost as tall as most grown-ups, and a good deal taller than some. This was often very useful. She always came first at high jump, and in libraries she was able to reach books from the shelves that nobody else could reach. The best books were always to be found there, she thought.

But there were times when it was certainly a bit of a nuisance being tall. It was sometimes quite difficult to get clothes that were just the right size, and the desks at school often didn't have quite enough knee-room. And then there were occasions when being tall led to quite remarkable things, as happened with the great mistake.

It all started when Jenny had to change schools. Her family had moved to a new town and Jenny and her brother had to go to new schools. Her brother was older than she was, and so he was to go to one school while she was to go to another. Jenny, in fact, had a choice of two schools.

The schools wrote to her mother and sent their brochures. Each had a picture on the front page and inside you could read about what the schools were like. There was nothing particularly unusual about these schools, but there was a very curious thing about their names. One was called the Pond Street School and the other was called Street Pond School. This was very strange, as they were not far from one another and Jenny thought that it must have led to lots of mix-ups.

And she was right. There had been lots of confusion. For example, the mail for the Principal of Street Pond School often went to the Principal of Pond Street School, and the other way round. Sometimes Pond Street School got a bill which was meant for Street Pond School – and paid it – which meant that when the mistake was discovered, Street Pond School had to pay Pond Street School back.

Sometimes Street Pond School won a competition, but the papers announced that Pond Street School had won. This made Street Pond School furious, and there would have to be an announcement in the papers that Pond Street School hadn't won anything at all, which made Pond Street

School furious – because they sometimes won things anyway. So it was all very confusing.

Jenny could not make up her mind which school she preferred, and so her mother chose for her and Jenny agreed with the choice.

'Pond Street School looks fine,' said her mother. 'I think you should go to that one.'

Jenny agreed. The name sounded quite nice and she was sure that she would make new friends there.

On her first morning at the new school, Jenny got everything ready in good time. She packed her bag with the new pencil case she had bought and with all the other things that she was bound to need. Her mother had insisted that she dress as smartly as she could on her first day at school, and had made her wear a dress which Jenny didn't really like.

'It's such an old-fashioned dress,' Jenny complained. 'It makes me look so old.'

'Nonsense,' her mother retorted. 'You can't
go to your new school wearing jeans and a
scruffy T-shirt. You look very good in that
dress.'

Jenny knew that it was no good arguing with her mother when she had made up her mind about something. So she put on the old-fashioned dress and went down to breakfast. Then, when she was finally ready to leave the house, her father and mother both wished her good luck.

'I'll drive you to school,' her father offered.

'No thank you,' said Jenny. 'I know the way . . . I think.'

Jenny waved to her parents and began the short walk that would lead her to the front gate of her new school. She felt very excited, and a bit anxious, as you always do when you are about to start a new school and aren't quite sure what everybody will be like. She wondered whether she would meet many new friends there. She had had very good friends at her last school and she had been sorry to leave them. She hoped that the pupils at her new school would be as nice, or at least almost as nice.

As she drew near to the new school she began to walk more slowly. It was far bigger than her last school, she thought, and there were many more pupils milling about. And where was she meant to go? Should she walk straight in the main entrance and try to find the office, or should she look for some children who were about her age and just follow them in? She could always ask somebody to help her, of course, but she didn't know anybody and everyone except her seemed to be busy talking to their friends.

Jenny arrived at the entrance to the school and looked about her. Nobody was taking any notice of her and so she decided just to stand there for a little while and see what happened. Perhaps one of the teachers would come and ask her her name and then take her to her classroom.

'Good morning.'

Jenny spun round. One of the teachers had come up and was standing right behind her. Jenny noticed that she was taller than

11

the teacher, who was smiling at her in a friendly manner.

'So there you are,' said the teacher. 'We've been expecting you.'

'Oh, good,' said Jenny. She was pleased to hear that they knew she was coming. This meant that she wouldn't have to ask her way after all.

'If you'd like to come along with me,' said the teacher, 'I'll show you where your classroom is.'

Jenny followed as the teacher led the way. They went into the building and walked along a long corridor past the open doors of several classrooms. Jenny noticed that most of the classrooms had now filled up with pupils and that lessons were just about to begin.

'By the way,' said the teacher. 'I didn't introduce myself. My name is Alison.'

Jenny was rather surprised. Alison sounded like a first name, and it was rather odd for a teacher to give her first name to a

pupil. Perhaps this was a very friendly school, where everybody called the teachers Mary, or John, or whatever their first names might be. Jenny had heard about schools like that before, but she had never actually been in one.

They stopped outside the door of the last classroom in the corridor.

'Here we are,' said the teacher. 'This is your classroom.'

Jenny looked through the door. The classroom was full, and all the pupils were seated at their desks, looking at her. She wished that she had arrived earlier. Nobody would have paid so much attention to her if she had arrived at the same time as everyone else.

They went into the classroom and everybody stopped talking.

'Good morning class,' said the teacher.

As the class replied, Jenny glanced nervously about the room. She was surprised to see that everybody looked younger than she did – at least one or two years younger. *But perhaps I am imagining it*, she thought. *Perhaps it's just because I'm not used to them.*

She looked around the room again. Every single desk was occupied and there did not appear to be a single seat left. She looked at the teacher.

'Excuse me,' she said. 'Where do I sit?'

The teacher looked at her in surprise, and then smiled.

'Yes,' she said. 'I'm sorry. The school is a bit crowded. But don't worry, we've kept your seat free.'

And with that she pointed to the chair behind the table facing the class. The teacher's seat!

CHAPTER 2

Taking the Register

For a moment, Jenny did not know what to think. The teacher had definitely pointed to that chair, and her ears had not been deceiving her when she heard her tell her that she was to sit there. But where was the teacher going to sit herself? Would she walk about the classroom or just stand in the same place all day? Surely she would need to sit down some time.

'Well,' said the teacher. 'I'll leave you to get on with it. I've got to go and teach my class. But I'll come back when the break bell goes and show you where the staff room is.'

Staff room? Why should I need to know where the staff room is? Jenny asked herself. *Perhaps I might have to run an errand for a teacher some time.* But there was still the problem of the chair. Perhaps she should do as she was told and sit in it after all.

Jenny went towards the teacher's chair and sat in it, feeling very embarrassed as she did so. Yet although everybody was staring at her, nobody was laughing.

'By the way,' said the teacher as she left the room. 'You'll find the register in the top drawer of the desk. The principal likes it to be called first thing every morning.'

Jenny was astonished. Usually teachers

called the register, but perhaps this school was different. Well, if that's what they wanted her to do, she could do it for them . . .

The teacher now left the classroom and Jenny opened the top drawer of the desk. There was a large brown book, which she took out and opened at the first page. There was a list of names, written out in alphabetical order, and against them neat lines of ticks and crosses had been put in.

Everybody was quiet as Jenny called out the first name.

'George Apple,' she called.

'Yes,' said a boy from the front row. 'Yes, I'm here.'

Jenny put a tick after George Apple's name.

'Caroline Box,' she called.

There was no reply, so Jenny called out the name again in case Caroline Box had not heard.

Still there was no reply. Then a girl sitting at the front put up her hand.

'Please, miss,' she said. 'Caroline Box isn't well. She lives next door to me and her mother said she had a bad cold.'

'Oh, I see,' said Jenny, putting a cross against the name. Then she stopped, her hand frozen where it was. The girl had called her 'miss'! Why on earth should she do that? It was not as if she was a teacher.

Suddenly, and with a terrible bump, it all fell into place. No! Surely the teacher couldn't have mistaken her . . . for a teacher! It was quite impossible. And yet, everything seemed to point to this. She had been shown the teacher's chair. She had been told about the staff room. She had been asked to call the register.

Jenny's mind raced as she thought about the terrible mistake that had been made. She was tall, of course, and people often said she could be mistaken for a grown-up. But nobody had ever actually made that mistake, and certainly nobody had ever mistaken her for a teacher!

They must have been expecting a new teacher, she thought. *Then, when they saw me standing at the gate, they must have thought that I was the person they were waiting for.*

It was an awful mistake to have been made, but it had been made and here she was in charge of a whole class, calling the register! The very thought made Jenny's skin come out in goose-bumps. It was the most embarrassing, terrible thing that had ever happened to her. It was a complete and utter nightmare.

Without really thinking of what she was doing, Jenny continued to call the register. Then, when all the names had been called, she replaced the book in the drawer of the desk and took a deep breath.

The simplest thing to do would be to get to her feet and to rush out of the room. She would run out of the school and all the way home and tell her parents all about the terrible mistake.

She looked at the people in front of her. They were all sitting quite still, waiting for her to begin. Somehow it seemed impossible to rise to her feet and run out of the room.

Her legs just would not carry her that far, she thought.

'Well,' she said suddenly, her voice sounding very small and far away. 'What lesson do you normally have at the beginning of the day?'

'Maths,' said a boy in the front. 'We do mathematics on Monday, Wednesday and Friday. On Tuesday and Thursday we do history.'

Jenny thought quickly. At least she was quite good at mathematics – it was her strongest subject in fact. But would she be able to teach it? It was hard enough to be able to do complicated sums, but it must be even more difficult to teach other people how to do them.

'Get out your maths books, then,' she said. 'Start where you left off and do the whole page.'

Desks were opened and maths books were fished out. Then, with a busy murmur, the class got down to work. Jenny sat in her chair and looked about her. *Perhaps I could dash out while they were all working*, she thought. *I could tell them that I was going to get something from the staff room, and run away once I was out of the door.* Yes. That was the way to do it.

She rose to her feet.

'Carry on with your maths,' she said, trying to sound as firm as possible. 'I've just got to get something from the staff room.'

'Please, miss,' called out George Apple. 'I'll go and fetch it for you.'

'No,' said Jenny. 'You stay here and work. I'll just be a moment.'

Not looking behind her, she walked across to the classroom door, opened it, and went out into the corridor. Nobody was about and so she started to walk purposefully towards the door at the far end.

She had got about halfway when she heard footsteps. Somebody was coming round the corner and, in an awful moment of panic, Jenny realised that there was nowhere to hide. She would shortly come face to face with the person who was coming around the corner – whoever that might be.

CHAPTER 3

Sent Back to Class

It turned out to be a rather severe-looking woman, a little bit taller than Jenny, wearing small round glasses and with very short, red hair. When she saw Jenny, she fixed her with a firm gaze and walked quickly towards her.

'So,' she said. 'You're the new teacher. I'm very glad to see you.'

Jenny swallowed hard, wondering what to say.

'I'm Miss Ice, the principal,' said the woman. 'And may I ask where you're going? We normally don't leave our classrooms unattended at this school.'

Jenny looked down at the ground. She was completely terrified of this severe-looking woman and, even if she had known what to say, she doubted whether her tongue would work.

'Well?' said the principal. 'Are you going back to the classroom?'

Jenny nodded miserably and, under the principal's suspicious stare, she walked quickly back to her classroom. Everybody was still working on their maths when Jenny got back. The classroom was quiet – rather unusually so, and Jenny wondered whether something was going on. Nobody was whispering to one another and every head was bent over a book. Jenny sat down at her table and looked down at the class. What was the reason for the quiet? Was the maths all that difficult? Surely not.

Suddenly she heard a noise. It was not a loud noise – more of a scuffling sound. She strained her ears to hear it better. It had gone, but then it came back – an odd, scraping sound, rather as if something was scraping at a bit of paper.

Jenny looked behind her. There was nothing there. She turned to face the class again, and she saw that several people were looking up at her. One of them was George Apple, and he was grinning broadly.

'Is there something wrong, miss?' he said.

Jenny shook her head.

'No,' she said. 'I thought I heard a noise, but I think it's gone.'

Everybody looked up now, and Jenny noticed that most of the class was grinning. This was a trick of some kind – she was sure of it.

'I heard a noise too, miss,' said George

Apple. 'I thought it was coming from the drawer in your desk.'

Jenny looked down. The noise was there again, and yes, it did seem to be coming from the drawer.

'Why not open the drawer and take a look,' suggested George Apple. 'Just to check.'

Jenny reached out and opened the drawer, and the moment she did so out jumped the largest brown rat she had ever seen. Jenny pushed her chair back as quickly as she could, letting out a scream that made the windows rattle.

'A rat!' she shrieked. 'A great big rat.'

The rat had now landed on her table and was scurrying around, wondering what all the fuss was.

'You've got a rat on your table, miss,' said George Apple helpfully. 'Should I take it away for you?'

Jenny nodded miserably. She had always been scared of rats and when it had popped

its head out of the drawer her heart had almost stopped. She sat quite still as George Apple sauntered up to her desk, picked up the rat by its tail, and took it back to his desk. Then he slipped it into his bag, and sat back at his desk.

Every eye was on Jenny. Some people were trying not to laugh, and succeeding. Others were giggling under their breath. Everybody thought it very funny – except Jenny. She had no idea what to do. Should she report George Apple to the principal? If she did that though, she would have to face Miss Ice again and that was the last thing she wanted to do. So she decided to get back to maths and to forget about rats for the time being.

'Will you give us the answers now?' asked one of the girls. 'I hope I've got everything right!'

Jenny took the girl's book and looked at it. The work seemed rather difficult to her, and she was not sure if she would be able to do it.

'Well, let's see,' she said. 'I'll call out the answers and you can all mark your own work.'

Reading out from the girl's book, she called out the answers.

'Problem number one – the answer is two thousand three hundred and forty-two.'

Nobody said it wasn't, so Jenny moved on to the next problem, and the problem after that. Each time she called out the answer she saw in the girl's exercise book, and each time, it seemed to her, she had the good luck to be quite correct.

'Thank you,' she said to the girl as she handed her book back. 'You're obviously very good at maths. Well done.'

Now what? They had finished their mathematics, and Jenny did not fancy the idea of doing any more. She might not be so lucky this time, and it would be terrible not to be able to do the sums she was meant to be teaching.

An idea came to her.

'Let's do some geography,' she said. 'Can anybody tell me what the capital of France is?'

'That's easy,' several voices called out. 'Paris.'

'Good,' said Jenny. 'Now what about Italy? Who knows the capital of Italy?'

Several hands went up, and Jenny pointed to a boy at the back.

'Cairo?' he said.

Everyone roared with laughter.

'That's in Egypt,' said George Apple, in disgust. 'Everyone knows it's Rome.'

Jenny thought quickly. Perhaps she should try something harder.

'What's the capital of . . .' she paused for a moment, trying to think of a country. 'Yes, that's a good idea. What's the capital of Australia?'

The word Australia just slipped out, because Australia had somehow come to her mind. But no sooner had she said it than she realised, with a shock, that she had no idea at all what the capital of Australia was. There was a hope, of course, that somebody would know. If only somebody came out with the right answer, then she would not be shown up.

There was a silence. People looked at one another, and one or two scratched their heads. Then a girl in the middle row raised her hand slowly.

Jenny felt a surge of relief.

'Yes,' she said. 'You look as if you know the answer.'

'Sydney,' the girl said. Then she added 'I think.'

Jenny had been very happy to hear 'Sydney', but was less pleased to hear the 'I think' added on at the end.

Was Sydney the capital city of Australia? Surely it must be, now she came to think of it. It was so big and it had that great big bridge and that wonderful white opera house. When you thought of an Australian town you always thought of Sydney. It must be the capital.

'That's right,' she said. 'Well done. That was not an easy question.'

She was about to ask another question, when she saw George Apple's hand go up.

'Yes, George,' she said. 'Do you have a question?'

'It's not Sydney,' he said simply.

Jenny looked at him. Was he trying to be troublesome, or could he possibly be right?

'Of course it's Sydney,' she said. 'We all know it's Sydney, don't we everybody?'

'Yes,' said a lot of voices. 'Of course it's Sydney.'

'It isn't,' said George. 'I've been there, and I know.'

Suddenly everybody became quiet. Jenny stared at George Apple for a few moments. Had he really been there, she wondered, or was he just pretending?

'Well,' she said after a while. 'If you're so clever and you've been there, you tell us what the right answer is.'

'Canberra,' said George simply. 'Canberra's

the capital of Australia. And look, I've got an atlas here to prove it.'

Nobody said a word. The whole class stared at Jenny, who said nothing, but just stood there, becoming redder and redder.

Just at that moment, the door behind her opened and another teacher walked in.

'Is your class ready for gym?' she asked. 'You're late already.'

Jenny heaved a sigh of relief. Sydney, and Canberra, and even Australia itself could be forgotten now. Thank heavens for gym!

CHAPTER 4

Trouble in the Gym

The gymnasium was a large hall with a creaky wooden floor and all sorts of exciting equipment arranged around the walls. There were wooden horses for jumping over; ropes to swing on; and wooden bars for climbing up. Jenny was delighted. This was very much better than mathematics or geography.

She could really teach gym, she thought, even if she wasn't a real teacher.

The pupils all changed into their gym outfits and stood waiting expectantly for Jenny's instructions.

'Can we play with the sand bags?' one of them asked.

'No,' said another. 'Can we get the trampoline out?'

Jenny clapped her hands, just as she remembered her last gym teacher doing. Everybody fell silent.

'We'll do some vaulting first,' she said, in a firm, gym-teacher-type voice. 'Make a long line and jump over the horse one by one.'

The members of the class quickly fell into line and started to jump, one by one, over the wooden horse. Most of them did it quite well, although there were one or two who got stuck halfway and had to be helped across.

After everybody had jumped over the horse twice, Jenny decided it was time for something a little bit more adventurous.

'We're going to climb the bars now,' she said. 'Everybody will climb right up to the top and then climb down again.'

They started, one by one, to climb the bars. The first girl went up very quickly, and then shot down again in no time at all. The second was almost as fast, but not quite, but the third was best of all. She climbed up and down so quickly that you could hardly see her. Then it was George Apple's turn.

He was much slower, and clearly felt rather nervous about the whole thing. He took a lot of time to reach the top and then, when he did, he stopped.

'Come down now,' Jenny called out. 'The next person wants a turn.'

George looked down at the floor of the gym and turned quite pale.

'I can't,' he said, his voice shaky with fear. 'I'm stuck.'

'Come on,' urged Jenny. 'Just climb down the same way as you climbed up. It's simple.'

George gulped and slowly lowered a foot to the rung below. There was a creaking noise and then the sound of snapping. Jenny caught her breath as a large section of the bars gave way beneath George. If he had not been properly stuck before, he certainly was now.

George let out a wail.

'I can't,' he shouted out. 'The bars have gone!'

Jenny dashed forward and looked up at George. He was right — he was absolutely stuck.

'He's going to die, miss,' said George's best friend. 'That's the end of him. So sad. Goodbye, George! Can I have your rat?'

'Oh, miss!' wailed one of the girls. 'Poor George! He's not all that bad. It'll be an awful pity to lose him!'

Jenny looked about her. She was the teacher, and she would have to save George. But how?

Her gaze fell on the ropes tied up against

the opposite wall. Yes, that was the way to do it! She could use the ropes. It was exactly what Tarzan would do, if he were there.

Wasting no time, Jenny ran to the other side of the gym and untied the thickest rope. Then she tucked her skirt up, climbed a short distance up the rope, and pushed herself away from the wall with all her might.

Like the pendulum of a great clock, the rope, with Jenny clinging to it, swung all the way across the gym. There was a gasp from the pupils as Jenny sailed her way across the void, and a sigh as her outstretched hand narrowly missed the terrified George. But Jenny was not put off by failure, and when she swung back to the other side she pushed herself off again.

This time she reached George with no difficulty, and, taking him quite by surprise, wrenched him off the bars with one hand. Then, holding on to him with all her strength, she sailed back on the rope to the

other side and then slid down to the ground, George and all.

As her feet touched the floorboards, a great cheer arose from the class.

'Well done!' they shouted. 'Well done! You've saved George's life!'

George stood up on his rather shaky legs and dusted himself down.

'Thank you,' he said to Jenny. 'I'll never forget that. You're a real heroine, miss!'

'Oh, it was nothing,' said Jenny, casually. 'That's what teachers are for, aren't they?'

George looked down at the floor. He was clearly feeling ashamed of himself.

'Sorry about the rat, miss,' he said. 'I was just having a bit of fun.'

Jenny smiled. 'Don't worry about that,' she said. 'It *was* quite a good joke, I suppose.'

Everybody was too excited after that to do much more gym, and so they all changed back into their ordinary clothes and began to go back to the classroom. Jenny told them to go in twos, with each person having a partner, and for some reason this seemed to please everybody.

On the way, they saw the principal, or rather, she saw them. She was standing in the doorway to the library, and she frowned crossly as Jenny walked by.

What a horrible person, thought Jenny. *She's obviously very cross about something. I wonder what it can be?*

CHAPTER 5

Miss Ice is Taught a Lesson

Jenny was soon to find out why Miss Ice had looked so cross. Just as the class reached their desks again, with everybody talking in an excited way about how George had been rescued by the new teacher, the bell went for break.

As she had promised, Alison, the teacher

who had been so friendly earlier on, came back to show Jenny to the staff room. Jenny had to give up any thought of running away now – it would have been very rude to Alison to do that.

She was very worried about going into the staff room, because she thought that she was bound to be found out there. But Alison was very helpful and poured out a cup of tea for her, also giving her first choice of biscuits. Then Jenny sat down, with Alison at her side, and began to drink her tea.

The other teachers were all looking at her, and Jenny felt very awkward about it. But they all seemed quite friendly too, and Jenny soon relaxed.

But not for long.

'Where were you teaching before you came here?' asked one of the other teachers politely.

Jenny had been about to take a sip of her tea, but her hand froze halfway to her lips.

'Er . . .' she began. 'Where was I a teacher?'

'That's what I asked,' said the other teacher.

Everybody looked expectantly at Jenny, but her mind was a complete blank. Then a place came into her mind, and she blurted it out, relieved that at least she could give some answer.

'Canberra,' she said.

'Oh!' exclaimed one of the other teachers. 'How interesting. Please tell us all about it.'

Jenny felt her cheeks burning red.

'It's in Australia,' she said.

Everybody laughed.

'Oh, we know that,' said somebody. 'But what's it like?'

Jenny looked at the floor. This was terrible. Why had she not run away on the way to the staff room? At least then she would have been spared this terrible nightmare.

'It's very nice there,' she said. 'What with the sea and everything.'

There was a silence. Then one of the teachers sitting at the far end of the room said something.

'Sea?' he snorted. 'Canberra's hundreds of miles from the sea.'

Jenny looked at him.

'I didn't say it wasn't,' she said defiantly.

'But you did,' he said. 'You said the sea was what made Canberra a nice place.'

Jenny shook her head.

'That's not what I meant,' she said, trying to sound slightly cross. 'I meant that if you don't like the sea, and you want to be far away from it, then Canberra's a good place to be.'

A few of the teachers looked a bit puzzled by this, but, to Jenny's great relief, it was at this moment that the Principal came in and everybody turned in her direction. She did not look very happy, and Jenny noticed that for some reason the principal was glaring straight at her.

Jenny's heart sank.

'She must know,' she said to herself. 'She must have found out!'

The principal helped herself to a cup of tea. Then she examined the plate of biscuits, took the largest, most chocolatey one left, and bit into it with a resounding crunch. As she did so, she shot a furious glance at Jenny.

'I saw your class going back after gym,' the principal said frostily. 'I noticed that they were walking in pairs.'

Jenny looked about her for support, but

everybody was looking at the principal.

'Yes,' she said after a while. 'I think they were.'

The principal swallowed the last of her biscuit and cleared her throat.

'In this school,' she said, her voice still cool, 'the pupils always walk single file. That's the way we do it.'

'But that's silly!' Jenny blurted out. 'That means that they must take twice as long to go anywhere.'

As Jenny spoke, some of the other teachers drew in their breath loudly. They seemed to be shocked that anybody was daring to tell the principal that she was wrong and they were watching closely to see what would happen next.

The principal put down her teacup with shaking hands.

'I beg your pardon?' she said. 'Did I hear you correctly? Did you say it's actually better to let the pupils walk in pairs? Is that what you're saying?'

Jenny shrugged her shoulders.

'Yes,' she said simply. 'That's right. After all, it does seem more sensible, doesn't it?'

The principal let out a sound which was half a snort and half a puff of rage.

'That's not the point,' she hissed between clenched teeth. 'If I say something is to be done a certain way, then that's the way it is to be done!'

'But what if it's better to do it another way?' said Jenny, feeling and sounding very miserable. 'Surely you should do something the best way rather than do it another way just because that's the way it's always been done.'

The principal stared at Jenny, her mouth open in astonishment that anybody would actually dare to talk like this.

Then, from the other side of the room, one of the teachers spoke out.

'She's right,' he said. 'I don't see why we should always do things the way they've been done in the past. And anyway, why don't we vote on it?'

'Good idea,' said another teacher.

'Yes,' said another. 'Let's vote.'

So the teachers all voted, and everybody, except for the principal, voted to allow the pupils to walk from classroom to classroom in twos, or even threes. The principal was dumbstruck and, after she had finished her tea, she slunk out of the room, looking quite confused and unhappy.

'Thank you,' whispered one of the teachers sitting next to Jenny. 'You've done what we've all been itching to do for years. You've put Miss Ice in her place! Well done!'

'Let's all celebrate by having another chocolate biscuit,' said Alison, reaching for the biscuit plate.

'But Miss Ice said we can only have one a day,' said somebody else.

'I don't care,' said Alison. 'In fact, I'm going to have three!'

All the other teachers agreed, and as they sat around finishing off every chocolate biscuit on the plate, they smiled warmly at Jenny.

'You haven't been here a full day,' said somebody, 'and already you've changed things for the better.'

Jenny didn't know how to reply. She had not meant to offend the principal like that and she hoped that everybody, including Miss Ice, would forget about it as soon as possible. All that she wanted now was to get home and to ask her parents to come to the school to sort out the mistake. But there were still several lessons left to be taught, and she would have to survive those before she could get away. Would it be easy? She had a dreadful feeling it would not.

CHAPTER 6

An Unexpected Reaction

The bell went and everyone returned to their classrooms. Jenny found all the pupils in her class already in their seats, looking at her expectantly. They had been most impressed by her rescue of George Apple, and they wondered what this exciting new teacher would have in store for them next.

It was chemistry. Jenny had not planned to have a chemistry lesson – she had not planned to have any lesson, in fact – but when she saw the box marked *Chemistry* she thought it would be a good idea.

Everybody agreed. They watched carefully as she placed the box on her desk and took out the various bowls and bottles inside. There were also jars of chemical powders – red powders, white powders, blue powders – and these she put neatly to one side.

'I shall now teach you some chemistry,' she said to the class.

Picking up a jar of white powder, she opened it and peered at it carefully. The powder looked a little bit like sugar, but it smelled quite different. In fact, it smelled like rotten eggs.

'I'm going to mix a bit of this powder with the red powder,' Jenny explained. 'Then we'll add a bit of the blue powder, just to be on the safe side.'

'Why?' called out a boy from the back.

'Why are you mixing the powders together?'

Jenny looked at him scornfully.

'Because that's what chemistry is all about,' she replied. 'And anyway, have you got any better ideas?'

The boy shook his head.

'Well, then,' Jenny went on. 'Here goes!'

She poured some of the white powder into a dish and then, standing well back, poured a small quantity of red powder in and mixed them up. Nothing happened.

'You've got to put in much more, miss,' said one of the girls at the front. 'Our last teacher used to put in loads and loads of powder.'

'I know,' said Jenny crossly. 'I'm just testing it to see if it works. I'm going to add much more now.'

She took up the jar and tipped the rest of the red powder into the mixture. Then she stirred it a little with a long glass rod.

Something was happening now. The mixture was beginning to sizzle a bit. Jenny stood a bit further back. You never knew with chemistry – odd things could happen.

And they did. Suddenly there was a puff of smoke and a bang. Jenny gave a start, and a few people let out whistles of surprise. A cloud of green smoke was now rising up from the dish and beginning to fill that corner of the room.

'There,' said Jenny triumphantly. 'You see, that's chemistry. It works.'

The cloud of smoke seemed to be getting bigger and bigger, and every now and then it made a rather strange, popping sound. It was really rather alarming, thought Jenny, but at least it could not go on for ever. Sooner or later the chemicals would calm down and the cloud of thick green smoke would disappear.

It was while Jenny was thinking this that the door of the classroom opened. Jenny turned round to see Miss Ice standing in the doorway, a look of outrage on her face.

'What is happening here?' the principal

demanded. 'What is the meaning of this . . . this green cloud?'

'Chemistry,' called out one of the boys.

'Silence!' hissed the principal. 'Miss . . . Miss whatever your name is, what do you think you're doing filling the classroom with green smoke?'

She did not wait for an answer. Striding forward, she went straight into the middle of

the cloud of green smoke, waving at it with her arms.

'I shall put a stop to this,' she spluttered. 'I have never seen anything as disgraceful in my . . .'

Her voice broke off. The principal had disappeared into the swirling cloud of smoke and now there was not a single sign of her.

'She's dissolved!' shouted George Apple. 'Miss, you've dissolved the principal!'

Oh dear, thought Jenny. *I really shouldn't have tried chemistry. If only I'd stuck to geography.*

Suddenly there was a coughing sound and the principal reappeared from the cloud, holding the dish of chemicals, which she had now covered with a cloth.

'This is a disgrace!' she stormed. 'You could have blown us all up!'

Jenny was about to say how sorry she was, but stopped. There was something funny about the principal, and all the class noticed it too. Her hair, which had been red when she came into the room, was now quite green!

'Excuse me,' Jenny said. 'I'm very sorry, but your hair . . .'

'Don't you talk about my hair,' said the principal. 'There's nothing wrong with my hair. You just open all these windows and get the smoke out of the classroom.'

Jenny did as she was asked, but as she did so everybody else started laughing. They had tried to conceal their mirth over the principal's funny hair, but it was just too difficult. Soon everyone was holding their sides, tears of laughter streaming down their faces.

Miss Ice stormed out of the classroom, holding the dish of chemicals in her hand. But just before she left, she stopped and turned in Jenny's direction.

'You're dismissed!' she said. 'You will leave the school immediately!'

The laughter stopped. Now everybody sat as quiet as mice, looking at Jenny.

'That's not fair!' said George Apple. 'You saved my life!'

'You're the best teacher we've ever had,' said another. 'Please don't go.'

Jenny felt touched by these kind remarks, but at the same time she felt very pleased that she had been sacked. Her being a teacher could not last, and she was relieved that it was all over.

But before she went, she thought she would do one last thing.

'Let's have a picnic,' she said. 'It's far too nice a day to sit inside and do lessons.'

CHAPTER 7

A Double Mix-up

Out into the school garden they all trooped, taking with them the sandwiches they were meant to have for lunch. They found a good place, and they all sat, enjoying the sunshine and munching sandwiches and crisps. Everybody was very happy.

Jenny sat next to a girl called Lucy, who

told her how much she had enjoyed the school day.

'Our last teacher was very nice,' said Lucy. 'But not nearly as much fun as you are.'

Jenny smiled and thanked Lucy. Then Lucy took two lollipops out of her pocket and offered one to Jenny. Jenny was very pleased. Lollipops were her favourite sweet, and red lollipops were her favourite of favourites.

And that is what she was doing, sucking a

red lollipop, when the principal stormed out of the building, her green hair waving in the breeze, and came over to stand indignantly in front of Jenny.

The principal looked down at Jenny, her mouth wide open in astonishment.

'I can't believe my eyes,' she said at last. 'I never thought I'd see the day when a teacher – a teacher, mind you – would be sitting out in the school garden sucking a lollipop!'

Jenny took the lollipop out of her

mouth and was about to say how sorry she was. But she had no chance to say anything, as just at that moment the school secretary came running across the grass.

'There's a telephone call for you,' she said to the principal. 'And it's urgent.'

The principal gave Jenny a withering look, and turned on her heels. Then, together with the school secretary, she strode off in the direction of the office.

The telephone call turned out to be a very strange conversation indeed.

'I'm so sorry about not being there today,' said a voice at the other end of the line. 'I seem to have put the wrong day in my diary. I thought I was starting tomorrow.'

Miss Ice frowned in annoyance.

'I have no idea what you're talking about,' she snapped at the caller. 'Where are you? And why do you think you should be here, rather than there? And *who* are you, anyway?'

'I was meant to be there today,' said the

voice. 'I thought today was tomorrow. I mean I thought that tomorrow was today. I thought that . . .'

'But why do you think you have to be here tomorrow, or today?' said the principal in a voice that was by now becoming extremely vexed.

'Because I told you that I was going to be here, or rather there, today. I mean, that today was when I was going to start, rather than tomorrow.'

The principal drew in her breath.

'Let's start at the beginning,' she said coldly. 'Who are you?'

'I'm your new teacher, of course,' said the voice. 'I was meant to be starting today.'

'But you have,' said Miss Ice. 'You're here.'

'No I'm not,' said the voice. 'I'm not there. I'm here. And that's the problem.'

'But I've just seen the new teacher,' protested Miss Ice. 'I've just been talking to her. She was sucking a lollipop . . .'

'A lollipop?' asked the voice at the other end, sounding very surprised. 'I don't eat lollipops. I used to, of course, but that was a long time ago. Chocolates, yes, that's a different matter . . .'

Miss Ice cut her short. It was now becoming clear to her that something very strange was happening.

'Very well,' she said in her steeliest voice. 'Very well. You don't eat lollipops and you're not here. Just come along as soon as you can.'

And with that she put down the receiver and stormed out of the office.

Jenny was still sitting with her friends when Miss Ice returned. They had not noticed the principal return and they all got a shock when they heard the angry voice bellowing out behind them.

'Now I know,' cried the principal, her voice cracking with anger. 'You're not a teacher at all!' She paused. 'You're a . . . you're a girl!'

Jenny dropped her lollipop. She could not deny it. It was all over.

'It wasn't my fault,' she said. 'I didn't want to be a teacher at all. I didn't start it . . .'

The principal, who was now quivering with rage, took a step forward, and stood on the lollipop. She looked down at her right shoe, which now had a lollipop stuck to it. Then she bent down to scrape off the sticky mess, and that was Jenny's chance.

'Run!' whispered Lucy. 'Quick!'

Jenny leapt to her feet and ran across the garden towards the school gate. The principal started to give chase, but Jenny was far too quick for her and had soon disappeared round the corner. She had made it!

After a while, Jenny stopped running and began to walk. She looked over her shoulder to see whether she was still being chased, but there was no sign of anybody following her. She breathed a sigh of relief and turned the corner into her own street.

As she did so, she almost bumped into a woman who was walking in the opposite direction.

'I'm sorry,' said the woman, looking

anxiously at her watch. 'I wasn't really looking where I was going.' She paused. 'Could
you help me? I'm very late, and very lost.'

'Of course,' said Jenny. 'Where are you
going?'

'Well,' said the woman. 'It's rather a long
story. I put the wrong date in my diary. I
thought today was tomorrow, or the other

way round, I'm not sure. I'm trying to find the school near here. Street Pond School. I'm the new teacher there and I'm terribly late. I've just been speaking to the principal on the telephone – Miss Frost I think she's called – and she sounded terribly hot, I mean cold, about it all.'

Jenny listened to this carefully, and as she did so she began to smile. This was the real teacher, the teacher whose place she had taken for the day.

'You're not far away,' she said. 'If you walk down that road, turn left, and then carry on all the way up the street you'll reach the school.'

'Thank you,' said the woman gratefully. 'I do hope that my class has been looked after this morning.'

'Oh I think they had quite an interesting morning,' Jenny said. 'They studied rats, I mean maths. And then they did gym. I shouldn't worry about that if I were you.'

The real teacher thanked her and went off

on her way. Jenny watched her as she went, pleased that they had bumped into one another. She liked the sound of the new teacher and she was sure that the pupils would too.

But Jenny had not yet solved all her problems. Although she had managed to get away from the school, she would have to go back there the next day. And what would happen then? How could you go back to a school where you had dyed the principal's hair green? Miss Ice would not forget something like that in a hurry.

Jenny was thinking of this, feeling quite miserable, as she walked in the front door of her house. So she paid very little attention to her mother's calling her until her mother rushed out of the sitting room and gave her a big hug.

'There you are!' her mother said. 'What a relief! I've been so worried about you! Where were you?'

'At school,' said Jenny simply.

'But the school telephoned,' said her mother. 'They said that you hadn't arrived this morning. You can imagine how worried I was!'

Jenny sat down and sunk her head in her hands. It was going to be very difficult to explain.

'I *was* at school,' she said. 'Or rather, I went to school. But there was an awful mistake, you see. They thought I was a teacher.'

Her mother looked at her in astonishment.

'Do you mean they put you in charge of a class?' she exclaimed.

Jenny nodded.

'It was terrible to start with,' she said. 'But then it got better. In fact, I think that all the children enjoyed themselves very much.'

'I see,' said her mother. 'Well, I shall be able to phone Mr Brown now and tell him not to worry.'

Jenny was puzzled.

'Mr Brown?'

'The principal of Pond Street School,' said her mother. 'I spoke to him on the phone this morning. He was very puzzled as to why you weren't there.'

'But the principal isn't Mr Brown,' protested Jenny. 'It's Miss Ice. She's a lady with green . . . I mean, red hair.'

Jenny's mother looked surprised. Then a smile spread slowly over her face as she realised what had happened.

'Jenny,' she explained, her voice breaking into a laugh. 'You went to Street Pond School, didn't you? That's the other school! You were due to go to Pond Street School.'

Jenny began to laugh too.

'So I don't have to go back there,' she said. 'What a relief!'

She was very pleased that she would not have to face the principal again. She was also pleased that she would not have to explain to all her pupils at the school that she may have started off as a teacher but was coming back as a girl. That would have seemed very odd to everybody.

So she went to school the next day – to the right school this time – and she was very happy there. She didn't have to sit at the teacher's desk and she did not have to conduct any lessons. It was wonderful to be able to sit there, not having to know the answers to everything.

And as for Street Pond School, well, her day there had changed things in more ways than one. A few weeks later, while she was helping her mother with her shopping, she met Alison, the friendly teacher, in the supermarket.

'There you are!' exclaimed Alison. 'I'm really glad that I saw you. I wanted to thank you for making things so much better at the school.'

Jenny was puzzled, but Alison explained everything to her.

'You see, after what happened in the staff room, we all decided that we would stand up to Miss Ice and not let her push us around quite so much. So we started to vote on all the important things. And since there were far more of us than of the principal, the school began to be run the way we had always wanted.'

'I'm glad,' said Jenny. 'I thought that I had just caused trouble that day.'

'Not at all,' said Alison, smiling. 'And another thing – Miss Ice got used to the new way of doing things and became far, far less bossy. She's really quite nice now!'

'I'm very pleased,' said Jenny.

'But the oddest thing of all,' said the teacher, 'is what happened about Miss Ice's hair. She decided that she rather liked her hair the colour you made it – green. So now she has it dyed green permanently, and it suits her very well!'

'So everybody's happy?' asked Jenny.

'Yes,' said the teacher. 'Everybody is very happy. What's more, any time you'd like to come back as a teacher for a day or so, please do!'

Jenny thanked her warmly. She did not think that she would go back, but it was nice to know that the invitation was there. She thought back on her day as a teacher. She hadn't done so badly after all. She had sorted out George Apple, and saved his life as well. She had stood up to Miss Ice, and made her much better while she was about it. And she had given the whole class something to laugh about. Perhaps she would go back now and then, just to make sure that things were still going well. *After all*, she thought, *I was really quite good at it*!

Bernardine Kennedy was born in London but spent most of her childhood in Singapore and Nigeria before settling in Essex, where she still lives with her husband Ian. She also has a son, Stephen, and daughter, Kate. Her varied working life has included careers as an air hostess, a swimming instructor and a social worker. She has been a freelance writer for many years, specialising in popular travel features for magazines. Her previous novels, *Everything is not Enough*, *My Sisters' Keeper*, *Chain of Deception* and *Taken*, are also available from Headline.

Bernardine Kennedy's website address is
www.bernardinekennedy.com

Bernardine Kennedy

Old Scores

headline

First published in 2005
by HEADLINE BOOK PUBLISHING

First published in paperback in 2006
by HEADLINE BOOK PUBLISHING

A HEADLINE paperback

8

ISBN 978 0 7553 2247 3

Typeset in Bembo by
Palimpsest Book Production Limited, Polmont, Stirlingshire

Printed and bound in Great Britain by
Mackays of Chatham plc, Chatham, Kent

Headline's policy is to use papers that are natural, renewable and
recyclable products and made from wood grown in sustainable forests.
The logging and manufacturing processes are expected to conform to
the environmental regulations of the country of origin.

HEADLINE PUBLISHING GROUP
A division of Hodder Headline
338 Euston Road
London NW1 3BH

www.headline.co.uk
www.hodderheadline.com

2004 was a complex year for me with even more highs and lows than normal. As it was the year of writing this book, I'd like to dedicate it first and foremost to Ian, whom I married in 2004 after many, many years of being best friends. I think 43 years was long enough for us to decide that it would work out! A big 'thank you' must also go to all the family and friends who came along to help us celebrate and make it a day to remember.

It was also, sadly, the year my mother Rosemary died, aged 94, after a long and mostly good life. I think she was proud of my books in her own way although she did berate me for the 'bad language' and would wrap each book in brown paper and hide them under the sideboard away from visiting eyes. That way she could boast that her daughter was an author without having to show them the finished product!

My father George died many years before, in 1973, but it is he whom I thank for my lifelong interest in reading and writing. He was a prolific reader and his books all travelled the world alongside us so I was certainly never short of something to read. I know he would have been delighted to have an author in the family.

RIP to them both.

Prologue

A large bulbous tear grew slowly and conveniently in the corner of her right eye and threatened to roll down her professionally made-up cheek as, demurely, the woman looked down at her perfectly manicured fingers which were loosely held together; almost in prayer, but not quite.

The emotional break in her voice as she introduced herself made Tallulah, the presenter and star of the afternoon help programme *Tallulah Talks*, smile sympathetically at her.

Maria Harman glanced up through her thick, dark eyelashes, well aware of the soulful expression that she needed to fix on her face.

The banks of stage lights shone down brightly from above, lighting up not only the two women on stage but also the excited audience who had been bussed in from different parts of the country to watch, and maybe even participate in, their favourite soul-baring television programme.

Maria had dressed carefully, taking on board all the advice given to her beforehand by the programme researchers. She knew she had just the one chance to make the viewers feel for her and want to help her. She had bought a navy blue linen suit with a skirt that just skimmed her knees, emphasising her long legs without being overtly sexy. To add just a touch of glamour she had teamed it with an emerald-green silk blouse and a thick silver choker that glittered under the lights.

When she had arrived at the studio, her thick chocolate-brown hair had been newly straightened and trimmed to just skim her shoulders but the stylist behind the scenes had straightaway scooped it back with a couple of over-large combs and then pulled a few tendrils out to curl gently around her jawline.

Her instant reaction had been to resist but Maria quickly realised the new style softened her features and would look more appealing on camera.

'I know this is hard for you, my dear,' murmured Tallulah as she moved across the stage and perched on the edge of an empty seat, 'and I understand only too well that this has caused you a lot of heartbreak in your life, but the more information you can give the viewers, the more chance we have of finding your birth father. The birth father you have never met. The birth father you desperately want to find before it's too late.' Tallulah emphasised the last two words dramatically and, on a prompt, the audience gasped and looked at each other. Tallulah waited for the noise to die down.

'So, Maria, tell me how you came to be adopted;

in fact tell me everything you know about your background and about this man . . .' The presenter paused again and smiled intimately at her other audience, the enormous one tucked away inside the camera, 'This man who may be watching as we speak, this man who has a daughter he doesn't even know exists. We're going to do all we can to help our guest here find her long-lost birth father.' She looked at the studio audience. 'We're going to do that, aren't we, audience? And how are we going to do it? Because we know that *Tallulah Talks* has the most generous audience and viewers in the world!' Tallulah worked the audience expertly and then smiled triumphantly at her guest as they all cheered and clapped in agreement.

Maria wanted to stand up, to move towards the all-important camera, but she had been given strict instructions to stay seated because, at over six foot tall in her heels, she would tower over the tiny Tallulah.

Raising her eyes once again, just as she had practised in front of the mirror at home, she looked sadly into the lens of the camera with the red light glowing on top. As luck would have it, just as she opened her mouth to speak, the tear started its journey down the side of her nose and coursed down her subtly blushered cheek. Determined to take full advantage of her moment in the screen, she didn't try to stop it.

'This is so hard for me,' she took a second to sweep a glance in Tallulah's direction before focusing back on the camera, 'but the man I'm looking for is, as far as I know, called Joseph Samuelson but he was always known as Samson.' She looked out at the audience and grimaced, holding her hands out to them, palms up. 'I don't know if there's any relevance to the name Samson, but that's what I was told. It's the only name I have and, as he was known by it, that's all that matters really.' Again she made full use of her dark, curling lashes and blinked a few times as she hesitated coyly and bit her bottom lip. 'Samson Samuelson was, is, of mixed race. His father was allegedly Egyptian, but he had lived in England all of his life. I was born in nineteen sixty-nine . . .'

Maria carried on telling the presenter, the camera and the audience as much as she could about her conception, her birth and her subsequent adoption. Or rather as much as she wanted them to know she knew.

Maria was actually enjoying the experience despite having been dreading it for weeks, ever since the first follow-up phone call from the TV company that had set the whole thing in motion. She wondered if she might have been an actress in a previous life as she discovered performing skills she never knew she had. Tallulah may have thought she was orchestrating the show and her guest but in fact it was Maria who was in charge.

Tallulah herself was a hyperactive tiny blonde with heaps of tumbling hair subtly streaked and backcombed, and size two and a half feet tucked into the highest and strappiest shoes she could buy to add some height.

Her wide mouth was carefully outlined and painted with her trademark red lipstick that accentuated her straightened and whitened teeth to perfection. At first glance, she looked like a bit of a bimbo but Tallulah was actually a highly motivated career machine with her eyes firmly fixed on the top rung of the highest ladder. Her daily show, *Tallulah Talks*, was merely a stepping stone to bigger and better in the world of television.

The basic facts Maria had shared were correct and easily corroborated by the researchers who had interviewed her when she had first approached the show. Now she hoped she was fooling the viewers into giving up the information she needed to find Joseph Samuelson.

The man she was searching for was indeed her birth father and more than anything in the world she wanted to find him, to meet him and to ask him why.

And then her intent was to kill him.

Chapter One

1985,
Colchester, Essex

Maria turned her head and listened with relief to the temporary sound of silence that flowed up the stairs towards her. It was a welcome break from the constant bickering and backbiting that usually echoed around the walls of the thirties semi. It was especially nice not to have to listen to her mother constantly snapping away at her father like a bad-tempered terrier worrying at a rabbit hole.

Maria admired him for being able to successfully turn a deaf ear to most of the sniping, for the way he could rise above all the put-downs and insults that were aimed at him with such accuracy. But at the same time it infuriated her that he let his wife talk to him as she would to a naughty child, with the same tone, the same words, even the same disapproving expression on her face that Maria herself had grown up with. Much as she loved her father she often thought things might have been better for everyone if he had occasionally retaliated and asserted his authority in the family home.

The next sound she heard was the front door beneath her bedroom window clicking shut as he quietly let himself out of the house.

She wanted to scream after him, 'Stick up for yourself for once. Just once. Just once tell her to shut the fuck up . . .' but the words echoed silently in her throat because despite her youth Maria had a good understanding of the situation in the Harman household.

She knew that custom and practice meant that Sam Harman's time for asserting himself with his wife had long since passed and now that the children were all grown, he just let his wife's vicious tongue wash over him and quietly got on with his other life away from the family home as much as possible.

Looking out of her bedroom window Maria watched intently as, with his head on one side and his lips down-turned, her father climbed into his car and drove off. It struck her for the first time that he was starting to look older. The once bright sandy hair was dull and flecked with grey and thinning slightly on top and there was an aura of sad disinterest about him when he was in the house. Yet when he was heading away from home his shoulders straightened and the corners of his lips twitched upwards again and he turned back into the man that Maria adored. She guessed where he was heading and she certainly didn't blame him. In fact she wanted to go with him to the discreet bolt-hole that only she knew about. To the place that was bright and happy and where her father could relax and be himself.

Sighing deeply, Maria turned away from the net-draped window and slumped onto her bed in angry frustration.

Once again her mother had clamped down heavily and confined her to her room for a relatively minor misdemeanour and also put her on punishment duties for a whole week. On slave rota was how Maria described it.

At just sixteen and about to leave school, she hated her situation and her mind was totally focused on her future freedom and what she would do with it. Constantly she fantasised about life away from the claustrophobic presence of her mother and the oppressive atmosphere of her hated family home.

'Maria!' The familiar angry voice interrupted her thoughts, reverberating up the stairs and through the bedroom door. 'Maria, you still haven't done the dishes, I'm getting so tired of telling you, you know you have to do them every day this week after every meal.'

Maria ignored the command and waited expectantly, knowing just how frustrating her mother found it when she didn't jump to attention.

'Maria, just for once listen to me and move yourself.' The voice was getting closer. 'Get downstairs now and get the washing-up done, you know I should be up at church by now, there's a requiem tomorrow and all the flowers have to be done for the vigil.'

The bedroom door flew open and Finola Harman appeared in the doorway, hands on broad hips and sensibly shod feet planted firmly apart.

'Oh, wow! How absolutely wonderful, bet you can't wait!' Maria muttered drily without looking up from the book she had grabbed at random. 'A lovely uplifting funeral for you and your holy cronies to get your teeth into, I don't know how you can take all the excitement.' She paused before continuing. 'Maybe I'll do the dishes later, maybe I won't. Then again, I might just wait until the golden boys get in so they can help me.' Unable to stop herself, she smirked slightly and continued to focus on her book, knowing it was a sure-fire way to send her mother into orbit.

'After all,' Maria continued, sarcasm oozing from every word, 'they're *soooo* much cleverer than me, *soooo* much nicer than me, I'm sure they can do it *soooo* much better. In fact they're so bloody marvellous I don't know why you don't frame them and put them on the wall for everyone to admire.'

Finola's face visibly darkened as she responded angrily through gritted teeth. 'Leave your brothers out of this, my girl. Get yourself downstairs right now and do as you're told, I've had enough of your eternal defiance.' Finola wagged her finger up close to Maria's face. 'Do you want to spend the rest of your life in punishment? I never had this with your brothers, they're such good boys.'

Raising her eyes to the ceiling, Maria unwrapped

herself from her blanket and stood up, revelling in the fact that she stood a good nine inches taller than her mother.

'OK, I tell you what.' She sighed theatrically. 'I'll do the washing up if you stop going on and on about it. It's only a few lousy pots and pans after all, hardly a matter of life or death. I doubt that poor old sod who's going to be buried tomorrow cares about the dishes.'

Finola pursed her lips and gave what Maria had always called 'the glare'. Her eyes narrowed until the furrows between her eyebrows sank into crevices and the lines around her mouth bunched together as she pursed her lips. It fascinated Maria that any woman could deliberately make the worst of themselves and yet that was how Finola Harman looked. Her greying hair was self-cut straight across the bottom at chin level and pushed back off her face with a thin plastic Alice band and her chin nestled uncomfortably on the tight collar of her plain white blouse which was buttoned right up to the neck. Her only concession to femininity was a floral apron fixed round her expansive waist, and tights.

'You have a vicious streak in you, girl.' She paused and shook her head. 'One day you'll get your comeuppance. Then you'll come running to me for help and what will I do? Nothing, nothing at all, that's what I'll do because you're—'

'Yeah, yeah, I know,' Maria interrupted. She looked her mother straight in the eye, 'I'm no good, in fact

I'm completely useless at everything, as you keep telling me. Well, as soon as I'm out of here, which will be soon, I promise, I'll sink or swim on my own, thank you very much. I wouldn't ever come running back to you for help. I'd sooner die.' She pushed past and loped off down the stairs three at a time to the kitchen. Finola stomped purposefully after her.

Maria watched as her mother, still tutting and muttering to herself, whipped off the apron and put on her all-encompassing and well-worn coat before picking up her leatherette shopping bag and leaving the house without saying goodbye.

After a dismissive glance at the carefully stacked dishes waiting for her, Maria reached for the telephone.

'Hiya, it's me. Coast is clear for a couple of hours, she's off to do the flowers at church and the golden boys are gonna meet her there. See you on the corner in five?'

She licked her fingers and ran them through her hair and under her eyes before grabbing her key and hot-footing it down the road to meet Davey Allsop, the local bad boy who was like a magnet to her.

Maria and Davey had been drawn together when the Allsop family had moved across the town and he had transferred to the same school. The pair had quickly formed an unholy alliance of rebellion that caused problems both at home and at school. Unlike Davey, Maria never did anything really bad but somehow it was always just bad enough for Finola to be informed and for

Maria to be confined to barracks, as Davey laughingly called it.

It hadn't taken Finola and her friends long to hear the whispers that Davey had been expelled from his previous school. That, along with several other rumours about the family that got bigger in the telling, was enough for Finola to form her own judgement on the Allsops.

Suddenly the family was the talk of the parish and Maria had been banned from having anything to do with Davey. Predictably, Finola's disapproval had made Maria even more determined to stick with him. The fact that the stereotypical bad boy was good looking and sexy and flattered her like mad was a bonus.

Maria walked quickly down the road to the intersection at the end of the street, checking occasionally over her shoulder, to make sure no one was around. Her eyes scanned the street not only for her mother but for her dreaded older brothers as well. She knew she could deal with any of them if she had to but she really didn't want a confrontation with the volatile Davey. She especially didn't want him face to face with her mother, the woman he hated with a terrifying intensity. Finola Harman had, with mission-like zeal, made the Allsop name mud in the area and he had sworn he would get even with her somehow. Maria hoped it was all talk and that he would never actually do anything, but she didn't want to tempt fate.

Tall and voluptuous and looking more confident than she felt, Maria strode quickly along the tree-bordered crescent of sturdy old houses where she had lived all her life.

King's Crescent looped round in a semicircle off the busy main road which was lined with shops and led straight into the Essex town of Colchester. The crescent was generally quiet and peaceful because it didn't go anywhere other than back to the main road so no one bothered to use it unless they either lived there or were visiting.

As Maria approached the corner she heard a loud whistle followed by the stuttering roar of an engine. Davey was on the opposite side of the road astride a rickety old motorbike.

'Whose is that, for God's sake?' she shouted as she skipped across the main road, weaving in and out of the stream of traffic. 'Surely it's not yours.'

'No, it's me brother's, he let me borrow it in exchange for a tank of juice. He's completely skint as usual. This is one mean machine.' Davey laughed as he twisted the throttle. 'Fancy a spin?'

'Not a chance, and that's no mean machine, that's a death trap on wheels. Anyway, you've not even got a licence, have you?'

'A licence?' Davey crossed his eyes and faked a big cheesy grin. 'Who needs one of them? This is a piece of cake, even a five year old could ride it.' Davey turned the throttle as far as it would go and revved the sickly sounding engine even louder. Throwing back his head he took off into the traffic and, tugging the handle-bars up into the air, sped away on just the rear wheel.

Maria watched and laughed as he disappeared round the corner in a haze of blue fumes. Two minutes later he appeared from the other direction.

'Sure you don't want a spin?'

'No way, I don't want to die just yet. Let's go and have a burger. My shout, Dad slipped me a fiver when he got in from work.'

'Fucking hell, you're one lucky bitch, the only thing my old man ever slips me is his fist on the earhole. And that's on a good day!' Davey swung his leg over the motorbike and parked it at right angles to the pave-ment before grabbing Maria's hand and pulling her along the road.

They both looked considerably older than their six-teen years as they skipped and jostled their way along, cutting through the other pedestrians. They received a host of disapproving glances but no one actually said anything to them. Davey Allsop could intimidate almost anyone with his well-practised, cold-eyed stare.

Maria laughed when she saw people shy away from him because she knew the other side of Davey. His quick-witted, mercurial temperament had amused and attracted her the first time she had clapped eyes on him. She was aware of the underlying hint of violence in him but had never seen it first-hand. She simply empathised with his desperation to get out of his circumstances, though his reasons weren't the same as her own.

Both were dressed from top to toe in faded denim and they wore identical Doc Martens. But while Maria was olive-skinned and dark-eyed, her deep brown hair cropped as close to her head as it could be without being actually shaved, Davey's black hair was almost on his shoulders and lively green eyes shone out from his fair skin. His Celtic ancestry was strikingly obvious to any observer. Visually they complemented each other perfectly.

'Your mum still giving you grief?' Davey asked as he stuffed a handful of chips into his mouth and then greedily licked the ketchup off his fingers.

'Yep, it never stops. Never has done. Fuck knows why she ever adopted me in the first place, the golden boys are all she cares about.' Maria carefully opened her bun and removed the onion, passing it to Davey. 'Dad's OK in his own way, and I adore poor Eddie, he gets flak from the golden boys as well because he's not as bright,' she paused and grimaced, 'or as vicious and two-faced. Fortunately!'

Davey looked at her curiously. 'Do you know anything at all about your real parents? Maybe you should look for them, maybe you've got a dad with pots of cash and a fucking great mansion.' His speech became faster in his excitement and he started gabbling. 'Maybe he's a famous rock star, maybe he's on telly. Imagine, you could be set for life.'

'You're talking shite, give it a rest,' Maria snapped. 'I've told you before, I don't give a toss about all that sentimental claptrap, I'm not at all interested in family, birth or otherwise. I just want to get away and do my own thing in peace.'

'Mmmm, I guess that'd be OK.' Davey looked at her thoughtfully. 'But how can you do that? How would you know where to go? We've both spent all our lives here, furthest I've ever been is Petticoat Lane twice with me uncle and then we got lost coming home.'

Maria laughed. 'Isn't that a good enough reason to get out? Christ, this is Colchester, Davey, hardly the epicentre of fun, is it? No, I want a decent job. I've always fancied being a hair stylist but I don't care what I do so long as I can earn enough to not have to live here, near them!' She pushed the table away sharply and stood up. 'I'd better get back before the dragon lady returns from church and decides to call the Old Bill again. Not that they take much notice of her but it gets our names around and I know you can do without that.'

'I couldn't give a flying fuck what they think or do.' Davey straightened his shoulders and bristled with bravado.

'Don't give me that crap,' Maria sniped with a laugh. 'You know you don't need any more hassle from them or your dad. Don't forget, I know all about you and your really bad habits, Davey Allsop!'

He grinned. 'Yeah, OK. I've got to get the bike back anyway.'

When they got to where Davey had left the motorbike he pulled her towards him. As Maria responded and wrapped her arms round his neck, she spotted two policemen heading towards the bike.

'Don't look now,' she whispered without moving, 'but there are two coppers eyeing up that old pile of junk you call a mean machine. You go slowly off the other way and I'll distract them.' She pecked his cheek and quickly disentangled herself from him, then marched up to the officers, looking wide-eyed and tearful, putting herself between them and the motorbike.

'Excuse me, officers,' she murmured pathetically, 'I don't know what to do, I've lost my purse. I don't suppose anyone has handed it to you?'

'No, love. Where did you lose it?' the older of the two asked while the younger one eyed her appreciatively.

Sucking in her stomach and pushing her well-developed chest towards them, she pointed away from the motorbike and Davey. 'Somewhere along there, I think. I've looked for it as best I can.' She blinked rapidly, making her eyes look watery. 'It's got my mum's money in it, she asked me to get some bits from the shop. She's going to kill me if I don't find it. I don't know if I dropped it or if someone filched it out of my pocket.'

Looking at the ground she started walking in the direction of her pointing finger and they instinctively turned after her. Maria carried on walking and talking tearfully until she heard the roar of the motorbike that Davey had pushed silently round the corner. Turning back to policemen she shrugged.

'Oh well, I suppose I'll have to go home and face the music. Thanks anyway, I really appreciate it.'

Before they could say anything, she turned and, with drooping shoulders, walked away from them. As soon as she reached her own street she broke into a run and legged it home, laughing to herself all the way.

Men were just so easy to manipulate, she thought as she put her key in the lock.

Chapter Two

Maria had just dunked the last plate into the soapy water and slammed it on the draining board when her mother arrived home with Patrick and Joe.

Soapsuds ran down the sink unit and splattered the floor and the sink was blocked with soggy peas but she didn't care. Maria knew that even if she'd scrubbed and polished the dishes to perfection and left the kitchen pristine, it wouldn't have been good enough, she would still have been in trouble.

'Oh, you stupid girl, just look at the mess you've made,' her mother started as soon as she marched into the large, old-fashioned kitchen but Maria had already decided she wasn't going to be baited. She just shrugged her shoulders, laughed drily and ran up the stairs to her bedroom. As she closed the door behind her she could hear Joe and Patrick joining their mother in vocal disapproval.

'She's such a slut, look at this mess, this is disgusting,' Patrick's voice mocked her from a distance. 'And did you see that T-shirt? It's so low, she looks like a tramp, you should do something about that, it's disgusting.

Imagine what Father Richard would say if he saw her out like that.'

'And she's out all hours, probably with that lowlife Allsop creep, even when she's supposed to be indoors. You don't know the half of it, Ma, we've seen her with him,' Joe joined in.

Maria turned her stereo on and ignored them. She had given up wondering why the three of them despised her so much.

Most of the vitriol was aimed at Maria and her father, although young Eddie, who had a learning disability, came in for some of it. It seemed that as far as Finola was concerned, father and daughter were both as useless as each other, with Eddie not far behind, while Joe and Patrick, those devious, sly and underhand brothers who trotted along behind their mother to church and hung on her every word, could do no wrong in Finola Harman's eyes.

As quietly as possible Maria opened her door and sneaked along the narrow landing to Eddie's room.

'Hi there, Ed.' She smiled as she put her head round the door. 'Want a can of Coke? I brought one back for you.'

Eddie Harman looked up and smiled widely. Although nineteen he looked a lot younger than his sister and he was the polar opposite in looks and temperament. Enormous blue eyes looked out from under a wispy, ginger fringe and he smiled what Maria called 'Eddie's smile', a big open grin that spread readily across his whole face and exposed his over-large and slightly protruding teeth.

Eddie had suffered meningitis as a very young child and it had affected his learning capacity and left him progressing several years behind his chronological age. Despite being an adult, his comprehension was more in line with a ten year old's.

'Thanks. What are they shouting about now?'

Maria handed him one of the cans and they snapped them open in unison.

'Oh, just the usual, I didn't wash up properly, I look a mess, blah blah blah.'

'I can't wash up properly either.'

'Well, you're all right this week, you won't have to do it, I'm on punishment duties again, remember?'

'Did Mum hear you go out earlier?' Eddie's forehead creased with concern.

'Sshhh, she'll hear you or else one of the golden boys will. That's our secret, Eddie. I don't tell when you stop off at Jenny's on the way home from the centre and you don't tell when I go and meet Davey. That's the deal, right?'

Eddie grinned again. 'Right. I'd never tell on you, Maria, you know that. And I like Davey, he makes me laugh.'

'I know, Ed, but—' Maria stopped and turned her ear to the door. 'I can hear footsteps, I'd better get back to my room or we'll both be in the doggy doo doo again.' Maria blew a kiss and left him giggling.

She sneaked back into her room and closed the door just as the footsteps reached the turn in the stair.

As her backside hit the bed, the door flew open and Patrick lumbered in with a spiteful smirk pasted across his wide face. Maria's stomach lurched.

'Mum says you're to get your lazy fat arse down and make us all a drink as you're on kitchen duty.'

'Fuck off, I'm not on any duty and I'm buggered if I'm going to wait on you.'

The smirk turned to a sneer in an instant and Patrick reached forward and grabbed her wrist. Twisting it at the same time, he pulled Maria off the bed and dragged her out onto the landing.

'Mum,' he shouted, 'Maria just swore at me again.'

'Tell her to get down here this instant if she doesn't want to get in any more trouble. I will not have foul language in this house.'

As Finola's voice floated up over the banisters, Patrick looked victoriously at his sister. 'Well? Are you going to go willingly or do I have to make you?'

Maria thought about it and then gave in. She knew that if there was a fight Joe would race up to side with his brother and then Eddie would join in and take her side and certainly come off worst.

Maria snarled quietly at Patrick, 'You're a fucking bully and one day I'll get my own back on you big time. One day you're going to regret your life. I hate you so much.'

Patrick laughed and an intense feeling of hatred

surged through Maria. She knew that if she could have laid her hands on a sharp instrument she would certainly have stabbed him. The strength of her emotions scared her.

He twisted harder on her wrist. 'Naughty, naughty, now off you trot and do as big brother tells you!'

As Maria waited for the kettle to boil she looked around the room with a sense of detachment and wondered anew at her strangely dysfunctional family. The two elder brothers jostled and shoved each other at the table like infants fighting for their mother's attention as Finola watched over them affectionately. Meanwhile Eddie, who had followed her down, sat silently opposite, desperate not to attract the attention of any of them.

The three brothers were all born within just over two years of each other and there was no doubting their parentage. All three had inherited the red hair and freckles of their father and the pointed features of their mother. Patrick at twenty-one was the eldest and the tallest and could easily have been the best looking but Finola Harman's obsession with putting enormous meals on the table for her sons, combined with Patrick's natural greed, had left him bordering on obesity. His round, ruddy face was framed by droopy jowls and several chins and his ever-expanding paunch flopped over his waistband.

It fascinated Maria to watch his stomach moving independently of the rest of his body.

Joe, a mere eleven months younger, was obviously his brother's brother but he was half the width because he was sports mad and very active. He wasn't as inherently nasty as Patrick but he was equally self-serving when it came to ingratiating himself with his mother. Both boys had learnt from a very early age that their mother was the most powerful person in the house and that she was the one they had to please if they wanted an easy life.

Eddie was an open book who just wanted to please everyone and Maria felt an almost maternal protectiveness towards him.

'Come on, are you deliberately taking as long as possible? It's not that hard to make a bloody pot of tea for us all, is it?' Patrick's sneering voice jogged her out of her reverie.

'Just warming the pot for you.' She smiled sweetly. 'Why don't you get the biscuits out and put them on the table.' She looked at him quizzically. 'Unless of course you've pigged the lot again.' She looked him up and down and smiled. 'Yep! It looks like you have, Paddy Potbelly!'

Eddie sniggered none too subtly behind his hand.

'Shut up, thicko.' Patrick glared poisonously at Maria and leaned across the table to pinch his youngest brother hard on the arm.

Finola looked up from the newspaper she was reading and her face instantly softened as she looked at her beloved firstborn. 'Now leave your brother alone,

Patrick love, it's not Eddie's fault, he doesn't understand. And as for you, Maria, you weren't brought up to speak to anyone like that. Now apologise to Patrick.'

Maria looked at Eddie and spoke to him with her eyes only. He understood what she meant and instantly lowered his head and kept silent.

Finola Harman genuinely adored her two elder sons and made no secret of the fact that they were her favourites and they could do no wrong in her eyes. Whenever they were in any trouble it was always someone else's fault and they were forgiven in an instant. She had a kind of affection for Eddie but her irritation at his limitations was never far from the surface, along with her shame that he was less than perfect. Finola always made a point of telling people about Eddie's illness as a baby, so terrified was she of having any blame attached to her for his disability. It was the same with Maria. Her failings, real or imaginary, were laid firmly at the door of, 'Well, it's only to be expected, she's adopted, you see.'

The years of emotional neglect had hardened Maria but she still wondered why her mother, who had willingly adopted her because she wanted a daughter, appeared to dislike her so much.

'Oi, you! You're supposed to be apologising to me,' Patrick said nastily.

Maria ignored him so he reached across and flicked her ear. She shrank away, as she did every time he touched her unexpectedly. It flicked a switch in her brain and reminded her why she hated Patrick so much.

'Don't touch me, you disgusting creep,' she spat at him. 'Don't ever touch me.' With tears of anger prickling behind her eyes, Maria pushed back her chair and ran out of the room, the sound of Patrick and Joe's laughter echoing behind her.

'Leave Maria alone,' she heard Eddie shout as she rushed up the stairs. 'You're both pigs!'

'Enough of that, Eddie, I don't want to hear you copying your sister's foul mouth,' Finola snapped.

Maria closed her door and leaned against it. Her breath came hard and fast as she tried to calm herself and smother her swinging emotions.

She hated Patrick, despised Joe, adored Eddie, loved her father and wanted to be loved by her mother. It was all too much and she pummelled her pillow in frustration as the tears flowed. At that moment all she wanted was to be out and about with Davey Allsop, having fun, being reckless and stupid – doing anything, in fact, to make Finola sit up and take proper notice of her.

Chapter Three

Ruth Easter, large glass of red wine in hand, was about to settle down for a lazy evening in front of the television when she heard a key rattling in the already double-locked front door. She jumped up and ran out into the hall but before she could get to the door, the intercom jumped into life.

'It's only me,' a disembodied, apologetic voice echoed around the inside lobby.

'Sam! Hang on a sec, I've got all the bolts on already.' Quickly she slid the bolts back and disconnected the security chain.

Sam Harman smiled sheepishly as Ruth stood back to let him in, proffering her cheek to him at the same time.

'Sorry, Ruthie love, I know I should have phoned but you know how it is.'

'It's not a problem, Sam, you know that.' A wide attractive smile spread from her mouth up to her eyes. 'Although if I had known I might have waited a little longer before I slobbed out so completely. Just look at me!' She cocked her head to one side and looked closely at Sam. 'On second thoughts, never mind me, you look worn out. Come on through and I'll put the kettle on, unless it's something stronger you want?'

Sam pursed his lips and shook his head regretfully. 'I wish I could but I have to get back tonight, the usual hoo-hah chez Harman and Maria is in the thick of it once again. I've left it simmering away like Mount Etna and I've no doubt it will all erupt again.'

'You should have brought her with you. You know I like Maria, she's a good girl at heart, just a bit strong-willed. Reminds me of myself at her age.'

'I suppose I could have brought her, I didn't think of it, I must admit.' Sam sighed and then shook his head. 'But I'd like it to be just you and me for a while. I need a breather before the next round.'

Taking his hand, Ruth led Sam through to the sitting room. Gently she pushed him down into a well-worn green leather armchair, one of a pair that were placed in the wide bay window, with matching footstools close by.

'Have you eaten?' Ruth rumpled his hair affectionately. 'I'll make you a sandwich if you like. I've got cheese, ham or sliced beef, take your choice.'

Pottering around, making idle conversation and keeping Sam comfortable was never a chore to Ruth. She knew that there were friends and family who thought she was crazy letting a married man become the centre of her life, especially a married man who had always made it clear that he could never leave his wife. But she had made her choice many years before and it was now a way of life to which she had adapted without any resentment. In her eyes that didn't make her a silly, weak woman. She was simply in love, a woman prepared to wait and take second place in her man's life until one way or another the time was right for them to be together.

Ruth saw herself as independent and self-supporting, with a good life that she lived happily on her own most of the time. Her time spent with Sam, whom she loved unconditionally, was an extra. She called him her partner and thought of him as such, even if was only part-time.

When he'd eaten a couple of beef sandwiches Ruth placed her hands on his shoulders and started massaging. 'So, do you want to talk about it?' She rubbed his neck gently. 'You know you don't have to if you don't want to but I'll listen if you want.'

'I probably don't want to talk about it, if you don't mind. Anyway, you've heard it all before, it's just the same old nonsense.' He laughed wryly. 'Same nonsense, different day.'

Ruth smiled as he closed his eyes, visibly relaxing.

'I'll make coffee.' She spoke softly and then kissed the top of his head. She padded barefoot across the stripped pine floor to the modern kitchen that was separated from the sitting room by a wide, mosaic-tiled dining bar. Casually dressed in a light grey jogging suit and with her shoulder-length lightened hair pinned up on top of her head, Ruth looked a lot younger than her actual age. In fact, because her face was scrubbed and clear of her normally perfectly applied make-up, she looked more like a teenager than a woman nearing forty.

'Can you get away for a few days at the end of the month?' Sam asked as she poured the freshly brewed coffee into cups the size of soup bowls.

'Not sure, why? Have you got something in mind?'

'I'm going to a conference, a three-day residential conference up north, and partners can go as well. I'd love you to come with me. Who knows? We might be able to stretch it to a week. I'm sure we're both in need of a decent break.'

Ruth placed the cups on the table beside Sam's chair before perching on one of the footstools.

'Let me have the details and I'll check at work. Depends on Maggie of course but it sounds good to me, be nice to spend some real time together. We haven't been able to get away for a couple of years now.'

'I'm sorry, it's not easy . . .'

Ruth raised her eyes to the ceiling and made an exaggerated tutting sound. 'I know that, you dope, and there's no need to sound so defensive. I've never made any demands on you, I just agreed with you and said it would be nice to get away again.'

Sam reached across and gently touched her arm. 'Sorry, I'm just jumpy at the moment, take no notice.

31

As soon as I get sorted at home I'll be able to relax again for a while. I don't know, I seem to lumber from one crisis to another. I don't know if I can carry on like this much longer without having a bloody heart attack or something.'

Ruth sat quietly without responding. Although she would listen and make the right noises, she really didn't want to get too caught up in Sam's other life, the life that he had committed himself to many years before he had met her.

'It's so difficult trying to keep the peace,' Sam continued. 'Maria just can't seem to keep her head down and stay out of trouble, she has to fire up Finola and then the boys get in on the act. It's like living in a battle zone.'

Still Ruth didn't respond so he carried on, almost speaking to himself.

'Now Maria's in trouble again. I wish I could do something but there's no point in going head to head with Finola over something that Maria often brings down on herself.' He looked at Ruth. 'I'm sorry, you don't want to hear all this. I don't know why you put up with me.'

'Yes you do.' Ruth's deep laugh filled the room. 'It's because I love you, Sam. Now shall we watch a movie or did you have something else in mind? Have you got time?'

Sam smiled widely and nodded. 'Something else sounds good.'

They had barely reached the bedroom door when the phone rang.

'Leave it.' Sam continued walking through.

'I can't, you know my mother isn't well, I have to answer it just in case.'

Ruth went back to the lounge and picked up the receiver and instantly recognised the young, hysterical voice at the other end.

'Ruth? It's Maria. I'm sorry. I'm in a phone box. Patrick has just beaten Eddie up, I've had to run out. Tell Dad he has to come home. I'm sorry but I'm so scared for Eddie, Patrick is really mad this time . . .' Maria's stuttering sobs echoed down the line.

Pressed into the corner of the telephone box down the street and positioned so that she could see back towards the house, Maria shivered. She guessed it wouldn't be long before Patrick stormed out looking for her. She felt guilty at having run out of the house, leaving Eddie.

It wasn't that she had abandoned him, she told herself, she knew that her mother would eventually call a halt to the fighting, but she also knew she had to get her father home to deal with Patrick. She hoped that he could maybe protect Eddie once and for all. She wanted him to know what was really going on instead of him getting the pro-Patrick, sanitised version from Finola after the event, when the furore had died down. Her brother was getting out of control and someone needed to stop him.

The adrenaline rushing through her made Maria feel as if her whole body was palpitating. When Patrick unleashed his temper it was inevitably directed at her or Eddie and usually when their mother was not around.

As she scanned the street impatiently for her father, Maria wondered again why Patrick hated her so much, why Finola despised her and why her father wouldn't or couldn't do anything about it. It kept her mind off what had sent her running out of the house.

Maria had still been lying on her bed idly plotting her fantasy future away from home when Patrick had barged in again.

'Get out, you're not allowed in here.' Maria had jumped up from the bed and backed up to the wardrobe that took up most of the spare space in her tiny box room. The rest of the room was filled by Patrick's bulk.

'I can go anywhere I want in this house and there's nothing you can do to stop me, slut!' He shut the door and leaned against it, arms crossed. 'Paddy Potbelly, eh? You're going to regret saying that, you little bastard. And I mean bastard literally, 'cos that's what you are, a fucking little bastard.'

Maria didn't have time to flinch before his huge hand clipped the back of her head. The impact of the swipe made her feel as if her brain was bouncing around and for a few seconds she couldn't focus.

'You're a bastard, a fucking cuckoo in our nest.'

Patrick's face screwed up as he spat the words at his sister.

'Get your hands off me, you fat pig.'

The second blow followed quickly but glanced off her shoulder. The connection wasn't as fierce as the first because she managed to duck her head.

With an angry roar he leaned over to take aim again but the door was suddenly pushed open and hit Patrick full force on his backside, causing him to stumble forward across Maria's bed.

'Get off her, leave her alone!' Eddie screamed hysterically as he hurled himself onto his brother's back. But he was no match for Patrick's bulk. Patrick spun round and threw Eddie against the wardrobe then viciously kneed him in the stomach.

Eddie dropped like a dead weight, clutching himself, and Maria shot out of the room and hung over the banister, screaming.

'Mum, Mum, Patrick is beating Eddie up, you've got to help him!'

Maria watched as Finola marched up the stairs like a woman on a mission and with a quick flick of her wrist clipped Patrick around the ear. It was a practised flick, the same wrist action that she had perfected on them all when they were young children.

'Patrick! Get off your brother, you're old enough to know better, fighting like two little guttersnipes.'

'Eddie started it,' Patrick started to whine but his mother's face quickly made him change tack. 'But it was Maria's fault, she kicked me and then called for Eddie to back her up. You wait, she'll be blaming me in a minute.'

'Oh, do stop it, all of you. You're not children any more, even if you act like it.' Finola's voice had cracked through the air as she glared from one to the other. 'Eddie, go to your room. Patrick, go back downstairs.' She looked around angrily. 'Where's Maria?'

It was at that point that Maria had fled down the stairs and straight out of the front door.

Chapter Four

As Sam's car screeched through the narrow gates onto the cracked concrete driveway, Maria saw him and rushed out of the phone box.

'Dad!'

'What's going on now, Maria? Where are the others?' Sam's expression as he looked at his daughter was a mixture of exasperation and concern.

'You're going to blame me, aren't you? Why do you always think it's me?' Maria's accusatory tone was the same one she had used when she was a little girl. Instead of waiting, she had always gone in on the attack.

'Because, Maria, there was trouble bubbling away between you and your mother earlier and you can't deny you were goading her and looking for a row.' He hesitated and looked towards the house. 'But that's by the by at the moment, I'm concerned about Ed. Now tell me what's going on, what started it. Quickly, though, before we get indoors.' Cupping his hand under her elbow he steered her towards the front door.

'It was Patrick again, he came into my room and

hit me, he hit me round the head and then Eddie followed and jumped him and all hell was let loose. By the time I ran out, Patrick had kicked Eddie on the floor and Mum was trying to break it up.'

Sam put his arm round his daughter's shoulder. 'Come on then. Let's go in and sort this out.'

'Dad, I was so scared, really bloody scared. Patrick is a maniac. You have to do something this time, you really do. I thought he was really going to hurt me and Eddie . . .' Her voice rose and Sam tightened his arm.

'OK, OK, just leave it to me.'

Sam was as non-committal as always. He wanted to hear all sides before making judgement but he knew instinctively that Maria was telling the truth. Sadly he was well aware of his eldest son's unpredictability. He himself had been on the receiving end of it.

'Does Mum know you phoned me?'

'No, of course not, I just did a runner to the phone box. Patrick scares me when he's like that. I wanted to stay for Eddie but I knew it was useless. Mum's the only one who can deal with Patrick, he's a bloody psycho.'

As father and daughter walked into the house together, Finola appeared from the shadows in the dingy hall, her face a mask of fury. She reached out to try and grab Maria by her arm.

'How dare you run out of the house like that? You know you're not allowed out.' Ignoring her husband, Finola focused all her anger on Maria.

'I can go wherever I like when that thug is hitting me,' Maria yelled back. 'He's a big fat bully!'

'Don't tell such lies, Maria. Patrick has already told me what happened, he never laid a finger on you. I wish you'd stop doing this all the time, it's not fair on your brothers.'

'Of course he *laid a finger on me*, as you so nicely put it.' The pitch of Maria's voice rose hysterically as she stood face to face with her mother. 'He hit me round the head and he kicked Eddie in the stomach, but then of course he told you it was all my fault. And Eddie's, I'm sure.'

'Don't you try and blame Eddie.'

'I'm not blaming Eddie, it was Patrick . . .' Despite her best efforts, angry tears ran from the corners of her eyes and her chin wobbled furiously as she fought to keep control.

Sam watched helplessly as mother and daughter squared up to each other. A part of him wished that Maria would back down sometimes. He knew that if she could give in on the irrelevant issues then he would have more chance of supporting her successfully over the things that really mattered. But another part of him was envious of the way Maria didn't let Finola grind her down. He wished he could be more assertive but she intimidated him in a way that even he couldn't really understand.

The hard-faced Finola Harman standing in front of him bore little resemblance to the girl he had married nearly twenty-five years before. Now in her mid-forties and several stone overweight, she looked like the caricature of an ageing spinster in a nineteen fifties timewarp.

'Enough now, Maria,' Sam interrupted mildly, not wanting to inflame the situation any further. 'You just go through to the kitchen and leave this to me, maybe put the kettle on.'

'Dad, she believes Patrick, it's always the same.' Maria looked at her father despairingly.

'Who's she? The cat's mother?' Finola snapped. 'And why do you blame Patrick for everything? Always making yourself out to be the little angel to your father but you're nothing but a spiteful alleycat.' She paused and turned her attention to Sam. 'And as for you,' she looked him up and down dismissively, 'you take no responsibility for anything in this house. I have to do everything, deal with everyone, and all you do is slope off at the drop of a hat to that club of yours.'

Without answering, Sam swiftly stepped round Finola and moved to the bottom of the stairs. 'Eddie?' he called up. 'Eddie, come down here, I want to talk to you. It's OK, lad, you haven't done anything wrong.'

Sam did his best to sort it all out and ensure a truce of sorts in the family but he was only too aware that it was temporary. It was almost as if two feuding families inhabited the same building, with Finola, Patrick and Joe on one side wielding all the power, and Sam, Maria and Eddie on the other wading through treacle.

Later that night, as he lay wide awake in his single bed which was permanently separated from his wife's by an imposing old-fashioned tallboy, he turned over the events of the evening.

With hindsight, Sam blamed himself.

He blamed himself for not standing up to his wife in the beginning and he blamed himself for allowing her to raise their children her way, without intervening. Because of his own volatile upbringing he had done everything to keep the peace but instead of valuing his gentleness, Finola had seen it as weakness and now he didn't know what to do.

Many years before, when Sam had had to make the biggest decision of his life, he had done what he thought was the right thing and had promised Finola he would always stand by her. But as time went on and she became even more bitter and twisted, he found it increasingly hard to keep that promise and often wondered whether their chosen option had been the wrong one for all of them. And then of course there was Ruth. The love of his life and his true other half. Sam tried hard not to think about how different his life would have been if only he'd met her first, but sometimes the thought would sneak up on him and catch him out, usually in the middle of the lonely nights he spent in King's Crescent.

Gently he pushed back the heavy old blankets and candlewick bedspread and crept out of their bedroom, trying his best not to wake Finola. Lifting his dressing gown from the hook on the door he tiptoed barefoot along the landing to Maria's room, tapping lightly on the door.

'Maria? Are you still awake?'

'Is that you, Ed?' Her voice was sleepy and disorientated.

'No, it's Dad, I want to talk – if you're awake.'

'Well, I'm awake now. Hang on while I move the chair.'

It had been a long time since Sam had had a late-night chat with his daughter. It had started many years previously when Maria suffered terrible nightmares and Sam would sit and talk to her to calm her. After that it became an occasional ritual with hot cocoa and digestive biscuits, but one night Finola had got out of bed and found him in there, sitting on the end of Maria's bed. Her rage had been terrible to witness. She had tried to attack both her daughter and her husband, claiming that they were perverted and declaring her hatred for both of them.

Mortified more for Maria than himself, Sam had never set foot in her room again.

Now Maria sat in bed. Shivering and slightly disorientated, she pulled the covers up to her neck, hugging her knees.

'I wish you'd get some bloody heating in this house, it's stupid having to shiver like this all the time.'

'Of course it's cold, it's the middle of the night,' Sam whispered conspiratorially as he perched on the chair that had previously been propped under the handle to her room.

'Yeah, I know,' Maria shivered theatrically, making her teeth chatter, 'but there are icicles on the windows and my fingers and toes have frostbite.'

'Don't exaggerate, Maria, it's not that bad. A bit nippy perhaps but hardly sub-zero!'

They laughed quietly, both savouring this secret and peaceful time with each other.

'Maria . . .' Sam hesitated, wanting to pick his words carefully. 'I know life isn't a lot of fun here for you sometimes but you do know that I love you, don't you? That I'd do anything for you?'

Maria grimaced. 'Anything except stand up to Mum.'

'It's hard.' Sam shrugged in the half light. 'She means well in her own way, it's just that she's so set. It's the way she was brought up. The husband goes out to earn a living and the wife rules the household. It would be almost impossible for her to change.'

'Yeah, well, I don't believe that. Granny Bentley isn't like that so it isn't because of how she was brought up.'

'Maybe not entirely, but sometimes lots of different events come together at the same time and—'

'Surely if you'd stood up to her in the beginning, not let her use you as a doormat, then she wouldn't be the way she is. I don't mind for me so much, I can see why she treats me differently, but I hate the way she is to you and to Eddie and I don't understand it.

How can she be so nice to Patrick? Can't she see what a disgusting animal he is to everyone?'

Sam reached out and touched his daughter gently on the hand. 'Your mother is very complicated, there's a lot of things that you will never be able to understand, reasons why she is as she is, why she treats Patrick and Joe as she does. I'm not saying it's right, because it certainly isn't, not at all, but—'

'Reasons?' Maria interrupted brusquely. 'Such as? Mother or not, she's a bully, Dad, we've got them at school like that. Come on, we've had this conversation before. What is there to understand?'

Sam smiled sadly. 'A lot, Maria, a lot, but I can't talk to you about it so now I'm going to change the subject. I'd like to talk about your future plans. I'd like to know what you're going to do when you leave school. I know you're set on leaving as soon as you can but shouldn't you stay on and maybe go to college or university? You're bright, you could really make something of yourself.'

Maria sighed. 'I just want to get out, out of school, out of this house and out of this deadly town. I want a life, Dad.'

'OK, my sweet, I can understand that, but it seems a shame to cut off your nose to spite your face. In just another two years you could have your A levels and then go away to university.'

Maria threw up her arms in exasperation and wrapped them over the top of her head. 'I don't want

A levels, Dad, I don't want to go to university,' she whispered fiercely. 'I want a job, I want money, and I want independence. I want to be like Ruth, she's got it sussed just right.'

'Yes, but you only see her as she is now. Ruth had to work hard to get where she is, to have her own company.' He paused and smiled thoughtfully. 'But I suppose if you need a role model then she's a good one. She really likes you, you know, she's a good one to advise you if you won't listen to me.' Sam shook his head at the irony of the situation. Daughters weren't supposed to get along with secret mistresses.

'Shall we tiptoe down and have a cuppa?' Maria looked affectionately at her father. She could see that he was being pulled in all directions. Finola complained constantly and vociferously that he was weak and lazy. Ruth spoke endearingly of him being kind and gentle. In actual fact he was somewhere in the middle.

Sam smiled and touched his daughter's cheek. 'Why not?'

Chapter Five

Davey Allsop was doing his best to be inconspicuous as he hung around King's Crescent, hoping to make contact with Maria as she headed off to school. His shoulders hunched, hands deep in his pockets, he meandered along the road with his head down.

He had, once again, been suspended from school after being caught huddled in the far corner of the playing field with another boy, trying to barter a stolen half-bottle of vodka for a couple of ready-made joints. They had been in the process of discussing their respective booty when a suspicious teacher who had circumnavigated the perimeter had suddenly appeared silently behind them.

Davey had got off relatively lightly with a two-week suspension and an irrelevant letter to his parents, but the other boy, who unfortunately still had the incriminating joints in his hand, was expelled and reported to the police. Drugs were far higher up the school disciplinary scale than cigarettes or alcohol. Davey had laughed it all off as usual, he wasn't in the least concerned about either his punishment or the other boy's;

he had already decided that it was going to be his last suspension. He had no intention of ever going back to school and wasting any more time there. In fact he had already discovered a talent for making more than enough spending money by wheeling and dealing on the side.

As he scanned the road, Davey noticed Maria's brother Eddie ambling in his direction and stepped forward.

'Hello Eddie,' he smiled.

Although initially startled Eddie smiled back.

'Hello, Davey, I'm going to work at the centre. I look after the gardens there and I'm training to be a gardener. I'm meeting Jenny first and we're going in together but don't tell Mum, she'll kill me! I'm not allowed to have a girlfriend, same as Maria isn't allowed to have a boyfriend.'

Davey slung his arm loosely round Eddie's shoulders and, in step, they carried on walking round the crescent.

'I'm going in that direction so I'll walk some of the way with you, Ed. Where's Maria? I thought you two always walked together.'

'We do, but Maria's not well today, she's got a headache so she's staying in bed. Dad said she could. He said I could stay home as well 'cos Patrick hit me in the belly last night but I like going to work and seeing Jenny.' The words tumbled out so quickly, that Davey had trouble keeping up.

'Hey, slow down a bit, mate, you're making me tired just listening to you.' He smiled to make sure Eddie didn't take offence before continuing casually, 'And is your mum staying home today to look after your sister?'

'Er, I dunno. Sometimes she stays and sometimes she goes out, she didn't say. She might go to church.' Eddie looked puzzled. 'Why? Do you want to talk to my mum? I thought you didn't like her.'

Davey laughed and pulled him closer. 'No, Eddie, it's Maria I want to talk to, not your mum. But I want to see her alone, without your mum there.'

'Oh my God, you mustn't go to my house, no, you mustn't.' Eddie's voice was deadly serious as he took in what Davey was saying. 'Mum might catch you and then she'll boot you up the backside.'

Davey made a sound like laughter but his eyes froze, his fists clenched and he had to fight with himself to stay calm. Keeping his voice light, he said, 'Oh, come on, Eddie, that's not you talking, is it? That sounds more like your mum. Is that what she said about me?'

'Yep, she said if she saw you in this street she'd boot you up the backside and kick you all the way to the police station.' Eddie's smile was as wide and innocent as Davey's was tight and furious. 'Mum doesn't like you, but that's OK because she doesn't like Maria either, or me or Jenny. But she likes Patrick and Joe.' Eddie's face creased into a frown as he thought about

48

what he was saying. 'And Maria says Mum doesn't like Dad much, which is funny, isn't it?'

'Well, I like you, Eddie,' Davey said quietly, his tone conspiratorial, 'and I like Maria and I'm sure I'll like Jenny when I get to meet her. We'll all have to go for a drink sometime, really get to know each other. We could all go to the pub.'

'Oh, I couldn't.' Eddie gasped and his hand flashed up to his face, showing his gnawed fingernails. 'I'm not allowed in pubs, Mum would kill me.'

'Never you mind your mum, she needn't know. Come on, you're old enough and I won't tell. It can be our secret.' Davey loosened his grip on Eddie and pushed him away gently. 'Go on then, off you go to meet Jenny. When you get home tonight will you ask Maria to ring me?'

'Mum won't let her.'

Again Davey had to force himself to stay cool. 'I know that, Eddie, so you won't tell your mum, will you?'

'OK, I won't, not if you don't want me to.'

'No, I don't want you to.'

'Are you Maria's boyfriend?'

Davey smiled at the guileless young man with his eyes wide and questioning.

'Well, Eddie, I'm a boy and I'm Maria's friend, so what do you think?'

'I suppose you are. I have to go this way to meet Jenny.'

'See you later then, Ed. Don't forget to tell Maria to ring me, will you?'

Eddie smiled and waved as he trotted off in the opposite direction, turning back occasionally to wave again at Davey who waved back with a cheery smile, but as soon as he turned out of sight, Davey's face changed. His lips thinned into a straight line and his already pale complexion whitened with anger. How dare the sanctimonious old bitch talk about him like that? Just who did she think she was?

His first reaction was to spin round and head towards the house but after a few steps he thought better of it. It wasn't worth causing a scene right now. No, Davey decided, he would bide his time and calmly figure out the best way to get his own back on Finola Harman.

Davey turned in the opposite direction and made his way to the town centre where he knew he'd find something or someone to amuse himself with for a while.

Even walking alone he couldn't help but swagger and glare at anyone in his direct path. It was a game to him to hold their gaze until they looked away; he would stare arrogantly as they slowly submitted, lowering their eyes and then moving to one side to let him pass.

The precinct was always the best fun, especially when there were three or four of them and not too many pedestrians about. They would march side by side and force the shoppers and bystanders to slide out of their way. He could almost smell their fear as their eyes widened and they looked around for support and found none. It empowered him to be able to make others feel the same fear that his father had instilled in him all his life, the crippling terror that had overwhelmed him as a child when his father's hand had reached out for the wooden walking stick propped by the back door. He didn't use the stick to walk but he did use it regularly to impose his authority on the whole family.

'Davey Allsop!' called a voice 'Over here, Davey.'

Davey glanced across and spotted the Farrell brothers. They were the last people he would have chosen to meet but now he had no choice but to join them where they lounged against a long brick wall, their booted feet planted deliberately in the carefully laid out flower beds that were the pride of the local shop-keepers. But no one said a word to them, no one argued with the Farrell brothers unless they wanted to suffer serious injury and public humiliation.

Fixing his smile for the second time in an hour, Davey marched over confidently.

'Tommy! Tel! Man, good to see you. How ya doing?'

'Fucking great, Davey! Fucking great! And you?'

The usual insincere but ritualistic hugging, hand-shaking and back-slapping took place. Davey was younger than both of them but he was the tallest, an advantage he made the most of by pulling back his shoulders and stretching his spine. It made him feel just a little less threatened.

The Farrell brothers could have been twins, they were so similar; both were short and stocky with collar-length, dirty brown hair and taut, spiteful jawlines. Despite their lack of height they exuded a permanent air of menace because they were both broad-shouldered and muscular, with swarthy complexions that boasted a permanent five-o'clock shadow.

'Not at *school* today then, Davey? Been allowed out on your own?' Tommy Farrell oozed the words with a sneering smile, the insult veiled behind a baring of teeth and a dismissive top-to-toe glance.

'Oh hey, man,' Davey laughed nervously, 'left that dump yonks ago. I don't need all that shit any more, got my own business now, doing my own thing.'

'Doing what?' Tel asked suspiciously. As he frowned his furry eyebrows joined together like two mating caterpillars.

'This and that, got a few projects on the boil. You know what it's like, anything to earn a quid or ten. Gotta eat, drink and smoke.'

'Anything we should know about?'

Davey mentally kicked himself for showing off and tried to backtrack a little without making it obvious.

'Nah, just buying and selling, a bit of pirating here and there, you know the sort of thing. Nothing big.'

'If it's good then you'll remember to count us in, Davey, won't you? We've been mates a fucking long time.'

Again the unspoken threat, but Davey wasn't as stupid as the lads the Farrells usually intimidated; they were only one step up the evolutionary ladder from pond life and he reckoned he was probably brighter than both of them put together.

'Sure I'll count you in. Jeez, be great to have you along with me but it's fucking small beer for you, just a bit of knock-off. You're into bigger and better shit than I can even dream about. I heard about the . . .' Davey paused and scanned for listeners before continuing, 'I heard about the raids. Fucking spot on! I don't know how you did it.'

The brothers preened visibly.

'Wish I could put something like that together,' Davey went on, enjoying himself. 'I'd kill to be in on something like that but then I'm not as clever and experienced as you two.' He started to move away. 'Oh well, better go now, lads, things to do.'

'Hold up.' Tommy's hand shot out and grabbed Davey's forearm, stopping him in his tracks. 'You can stay with us. We're off to the Horse and Groom for a meet. We might even let you be a part of it, you said you fancied it.'

Davey felt his mouth go dry. He had gone too far. The last thing he wanted, needed, was to get caught up with the Farrells and their dealings.

'I'd fucking love to, Tommy, but I'm meeting the girlfriend and she'll go ape if I don't show. You know what these birds are like.'

Tel, the older of the two, looked at his brother and nodded at Davey.

Tommy took the hint and moved closer. 'But, Davey, we've given you an invite, it'd be bad manners to turn us down.'

Davey knew he'd backed himself into a corner, so he just grinned broadly while cursing himself for trying to be too clever with them. 'Yeah, you're right, stuff the girlfriend, she's getting to be a pain in the arse and I'd sooner be with you two anyway. Horse and Groom it is then. Who else is going to be there?'

Chapter Six

The two women in the crowded restaurant were laughing as they relaxed at the small bistro table. It was obvious to anyone watching that they were enjoying each other's company over a long and sociable Saturday lunch.

Although both were blonde, attractive and casually but fashionably dressed in slacks and sweaters, that was where the similarity ended. Ruth Easter was quite short with a well-rounded body but, with lots of strawberry-toned hair tousled around her face and nape, and wearing high boots, she gave the impression of more height than her mere five foot and a bit. Maggie Crowley, her best friend since their very first day at secondary school, was tall and broad with ample curves in all the right places and she wore her much darker but natural blonde hair pulled back into an elastic band at the nape.

Ruth could best be described as bubbly and girly whereas Maggie was elegant and sleek but both exuded self-confidence and waved their hands about as they talked quietly but intensely.

'Well, I don't know what to do, what do you think I should do?' Ruth puzzled as the waitress placed steaming dishes of pasta in front of each of them.

'I reckon you should listen to your Aunty Maggie, dump Sam and his troublesome family and take up with someone like that delicious young man from the office upstairs! He's charming, irresistible and unfettered by wife and children, and of course besotted with you. A much better bet than Sam the Man and his crazy encumbrances.'

Ruth poked her tongue out at her friend and colleague. 'Not a chance. Can you imagine Mr Smoothie as a permanent appendage? And anyway, that wasn't what I was talking about, as you well know.'

Maggie smiled and Ruth continued, 'No, I'm just thinking out loud really, wondering what to do, if anything, and hoping to benefit from your years of experience of kids.'

Maggie nearly choked on her garlic bread. '*Moi?* You jest of course! I no longer have any comprehension of kids at all, especially in the dreaded teenage years. They're not like we were as teenagers, you know, they're like a whole different species that exist in a parallel black universe, seeing but not noticing, listening but not hearing, touching but not feeling . . .' Maggie rambled on light-heartedly, making fun of her life as a mother and feigning despair.

Maggie was in fact the perfect mother who understood her children completely. She was the epitome of a successful business woman by day in her partnership with Ruth, and at home in her sprawling old rural farmhouse with Jason, her husband of nearly twenty years, and their three teenage children, she was a natural earth mother. The power suits and immaculately applied make-up that were necessary in the world of property management were ditched as soon as she walked in the door and on went the battered jeans and green wellies suited to the country life she loved so much.

Ruth knew from experience that Maggie's home was a no-go area for any talk of work, even with her husband, and that weekends with her family were usually a sacrosanct time but on this particular Saturday she was in town helping Ruth celebrate her thirty-eighth birthday.

'Give over,' Ruth snorted. 'If anyone lives in a parallel universe, it's you, Maggie. I can honestly say, hand on heart, you're the only person I know with a pet pig, let alone a pig called Angelique who trots into the kitchen and whose best friend is a chicken called Amelia-Anne!'

'Angelique belongs to the children,' Maggie protested. 'Nothing whatever to do with me, I just look after them all.'

'You wrapped that pig in a pink baby blanket when you brought her home from the farm.'

Maggie sucked in her cheeks and tried to appear nonchalant. 'Yes, but it was the children who really wanted her, they persuaded us to let her stay permanently, she was the runt, no one wanted her.'

'And naturally you took a lot of persuading.'

'Well, she was so cute and of course once they put the bow round her neck I suppose I couldn't resist.'

Ruth laughed. 'I give in on the pig.'

'But seriously, Ruth,' Maggie went on, 'you've been with Sam for – what? Ten years? I just don't know how you do what you do, I really couldn't put up with it. I could not be second best no matter how I felt about someone.'

'But I'm not second best.' Ruth leaned across the table earnestly. 'At least not in that sense. Second best to his family as a whole maybe but that's only to be expected. Come on, I didn't get sucked into this like an infatuated teenager, I went in with my eyes wide open.' She pulled a wry face. 'Well, sort of. I didn't set out to fall for a married man but I did so I take it as it is. I'm happy with the situation.'

Maggie grimaced and rolled her lively green eyes expressively. 'I'm not entirely convinced. Are you telling me that if Sam upped sticks from the holy Finola and turned up on your doorstep with a change of underwear in his little spotted handkerchief you'd kick him into touch?'

'No of course not, but that's not going to happen in the near future and I really am fine with it. I enjoy my life, I have a business that I love and a jolly good social life, considering. But to go back to what I was saying about his daughter—'

Maggie held up one hand. 'No, no, no. You'd be

mad, Ruth. Sorry, but you did ask. I think it would be a recipe for disaster. Help the girl out if you feel you must, give her as much tea and sympathy as she needs, but to have her live with you? What would happen if you fell out with Sam? No way! Dangerous territory.' Maggie shook her head hard and fast but Ruth continued to plead her case.

'But I like her, Sam adores her and her mother treats her like shit. And anyway, I'm hardly likely to fall out with Sam after all these years.'

'Then help her get a job and a flat, give her a few quid to get her started if you feel that strongly about her.'

'But she's barely sixteen. I can remember when I was sixteen, I couldn't have coped away from home for five minutes.'

'Yes, but we were spoiled rotten. God, I didn't even know what a vacuum cleaner was, let alone how to use it. If this girl is treated as Sam says then she must have an independent streak to have survived unscathed.'

Suddenly serious, Ruth shook her head. 'No, Maggie, I don't think the girl is unscathed. I think she has been badly damaged by it all. It's all very strange and I try not to delve. I don't want to know too much about Sam's home life but Maria is different. I feel an affinity with her, she was so much younger when Sam and I first started our relationship and she's the only one who knows about us.' She paused and looked out of the window. 'Oh, I don't know what to do!'

'Then while you think about it, take my advice and do nothing, it wouldn't be fair to get her hopes up, would it? Or Sam's, for that matter. Please don't do anything hasty. I know it's none of my business but you did ask.'

'You're probably right, as usual. I'll keep the idea to myself and chew it over for a few days.' Ruth stopped and frowned slightly. 'Maggie . . .' Ruth's sudden change of tone from lively to hesitant registered instantly with her friend.

'Uh huh?'

'If I tell you something, do you promise not to tell a soul? Only I haven't decided what to do yet.'

'Of course I wouldn't say a word to anyone, you should know me better than that. What is it? Is something wrong with you? You're not sick, are you?'

'Well, yes and no.' Ruth hesitated and looked down at her perfectly manicured hands. 'Maggie, I'm pregnant. I did the test today. I've been trying to pretend it's not happening because I don't want to think about it today of all days. I mean, for God's sake. Pregnant at my age is bad enough but an accident is pathetic!'

Maggie's hand flew to her mouth and Ruth knew it was to cover the fact that she wasn't sure how she was supposed to react. Whether to congratulate or commiserate.

'Have you told Sam yet? Does he want another child?'

'No I haven't told him, I can't tell him. The poor

man would go into respiratory failure. He's got four kids already!' Ruth laughed and pulled at a stray strand of hair that hung in front of her ear. 'No, it's my problem, I'll decide what to do about it. I'll probably have a termination. I can't imagine me with a baby, can you?'

'But surely you don't want that, not at your age, this might be your last chance at motherhood.'

'Oh, come on, Maggie, thirty-eight might be a tad aged for a first pregnancy but it's hardly the stuff of world records, is it?'

'You know what I mean. But you have to tell Sam, surely he should have a say in what you do?'

Ruth shook her head slowly. 'In a way I agree with you but he's got enough going on at the moment. I can't lay this on him, especially if he doesn't need to know. What he doesn't know he can't fret over, can he?'

'Oh, come on, you're always making excuses for him. You didn't manage to get pregnant all by yourself. If you have to make a decision like this then he should definitely be part of it. Jeez, Ruth, it takes two to tango!'

Ruth laughed out loud. 'OK, point taken, but still I'll have to give it a lot of thought before I say anything to him. I mean, once I've said it then the genie's out of the bottle and there'll be no putting it back. Metaphorically speaking. The decision then has to be mutual. Supposing we disagree? No, I have to really think about this.'

'Oh Ruth, your first pregnancy especially should be a time of such joy and happiness, a time to be shared with the father. This seems such a shame.'

Ruth leaned towards her friend and took her hand. 'Good old Maggie, always the idealist, but I can't be like that. My life is so completely different to yours and, rightly or wrongly, I'll have to deal with this in my own way. I mean, I am an independent business woman, am I cut out to be a single mother?'

Maggie laughed wryly. 'If that is what you decide then you won't be a single mother, you'll have me! Still, I think this answers your question about Maria. It has to be a no, doesn't it? Can you imagine the backlash if she found out that you're pregnant?'

Chapter Seven

'I'm sorry.' Eddie stopped and looked down at his feet, mumbling apologetically into his chubby chin. 'I forgot to tell you something. I should have told you something but I forgot.'

'What was that, Ed?' Maria asked half-heartedly, not really concentrating as Eddie had been chattering on for ages as they walked their usual morning route together, he to the training centre and she to school.

'I forgot to tell you that Davey wanted you to ring him, he asked me on Friday, he wanted me to give you a message.'

Maria was suddenly alert. The thought of Davey speaking to Eddie alone and actually asking him to pass on a message made her feel unusually nervous.

'But it's Monday morning now, how could you forget about it for that long?'

'Sorry, I just forgot and you were in your room with the door shut and Mum was shouting and Patrick—'

Maria put her finger to her lips. 'OK, OK. Now don't get upset, Ed. I certainly understand what it's like at home. I'm not cross with you, just tell me what he said and where you met him.'

Eddie relaxed visibly and continued speaking in his usual speedy staccato manner. 'I was on my way to the centre, he was up the road and we just bumped into each other. He said that me and Jenny and you and him could all go out to the pub together and be friends. I told him Mum would kill us!'

Maria smiled. Although it was an expression he used all the time, she knew Eddie wasn't far wrong. Finola would probably burst a blood vessel if she found out Davey had even set foot in the crescent, let alone talked to Eddie!

'You're not far wrong there, Ed. Mum certainly wouldn't be too happy about you having anything to do with Davey.'

'But I like Davey.'

'I'm sure you do.' Maria thought quickly. She needed to phrase her words so that Eddie understood what she was trying to say without being alarmed. 'I also like Davey, but I know him very well and he can be a bit naughty sometimes. He's a bit of a bad boy.' She laughed and nudged her brother in the ribs. 'You're much more sensible than Davey. To be honest, Mum's opinion of him is about right but I'd never tell her that. Please, Eddie, promise me you'll not have anything to do with him if I'm not around.'

'But you're always with him, he can't be really bad.'

Eddie looked puzzled and Maria could see he was trying to figure out her contradictory message.

'I didn't mean he was bad as in nasty and horrible, he just does things he shouldn't do sometimes. If you were there he might accidentally get you into trouble so please don't see him without me, will you?' Maria put on her most serious expression.

'Not if you don't want me to.' Eddie walked a few more steps and then stopped and turned towards his sister. 'But we can still go to the pub with him, can't we? Davey was really nice to me, it was like he was my friend and friends go to the pub together, don't they? I told Jenny about it and she wants to go.'

'I doubt Jenny's mother would let her go out with you in the evening to the pub with us. It's not the same as going to the centre, you know.'

'But Jenny's mum likes me.' Eddie's lips turned down and he dropped his chin to his chest.

'I know she does,' Maria reassured him, 'and that's why I think going to the pub with Davey isn't a good idea, you don't want to upset Jenny's mum, do you? Then you might not be able to see Jenny any more.'

'OK, but Davey wants to meet Jenny. Can he do that?' Eddie smiled again, accepting what Maria was saying but still wanting to push the point.

'Maybe another time, Ed, we'll think about it another time. Now tell me about the craft fair you're having at the centre.' Maria looped arms with him and smiled widely. Knowing how easily Eddie could be distracted, she hoped that would be the end of it.

Maria knew only too well how much Davey hated Finola. He could be quite ruthless when crossed and she was scared he would use Eddie as an easy route to putting one over on her. Davey could quite easily treat Eddie as his best friend if it would annoy Finola and then drop him just as soon as he'd served his purpose.

As they reached the traffic lights, Maria leaned over and kissed Eddie affectionately on the cheek. To any passer-by they looked like an attractive young couple; visually there was nothing to set Eddie apart from any other young man of his age apart from the slightly formal, old-fashioned clothes that Finola bought for him. While his peer group were all in jeans and sweat-shirts, Eddie always wore grey trousers with knife creases down the front and perfectly ironed white shirts, topped with V-necked jumpers. Old man's clothes, Maria called them, but Finola wouldn't budge and it would never occur to Eddie to rebel.

'Go on then, off you go and find Jenny. I'd better get my arse in gear and head for school, I'm supposed to be in early today. See you tonight. Be good.'

'Yep, see you tonight. You be good too!'

Eddie almost skipped off. Maria could see that in his eagerness to see Jenny their conversation was already forgotten; she hoped he would forget about Davey just as readily. Waving until he disappeared out of view, she envied him his uncomplicated take on life.

His girlfriend Jenny was, at twenty-nine, considerably older than him. Small in stature and very round, her learning disability was greater than Eddie's but each of them was blissfully unaware of the other's limitations. Bouncing happily through their lives, they took everything in their stride but Maria worried about Eddie, and that took her thoughts straight back to Davey Allsop and her relationship with him.

It was fun, he was fun and the fact that he irritated the hell out of her mother was the best fun of all but for all her rebelliousness Maria was, deep down, sensible and mature beyond her years. If Eddie was being drawn in by Davey, that could put a different slant on everything. She had no illusions about Davey, his habits and hobbies. It was the element of danger that attracted her to him but now it made her wary of him on Eddie's behalf. Davey Allsop would manipulate anyone if he thought it was good for him.

On the spur of the moment Maria turned in the opposite direction. She decided to take a chance on bunking off school to go and seek him out, just to put her mind at ease.

'Can I speak to Davey please?' Maria guessed it was one of his brothers who had answered the phone with an aggressive 'Yeah?' She heard the receiver clunk down on a hard surface and a voice shriek, 'Davey! Get out that fucking bed, there's some bird on the phone.'

'Maria!' After she had identified herself his voice took on an eager tone. 'Why did you take so long to get back to me? I thought the wicked witch might have locked you up in the attic for ever. I was going to look for you this morning, check you were OK, but I overslept.'

Maria was instantly flattered by his concern so when he invited her round to his house for the first time, she didn't hesitate, all her reservations went flying out of the window. Running from the phone box she jumped on a passing bus even though it was only a couple of stops to where Davey lived.

The street of small, identical semi-detached houses was long and narrow, with cars parked up on the pavements on both sides. Maria negotiated her way along until she reached number 52, but as she was about to turn off the pavement, she paused and looked around in horrified fascination.

A piece of rusty ironwork that she guessed was once the front gate was lying on its side in the front garden which was choked with overgrown grass and weeds and littered with all manner of rubbish. There was a path of sorts that led to the front door but it was more a well-trodden route of flattened brown grass that had grown up and over the flagstones. Maria tried not to look too hard as she tiptoed up to the door but it was hard not to notice the rusty car parts under the front window, surrounded by soggy black rubbish sacks. Their contents were hanging out of rips where animals had been scavenging and the pungent smell made Maria feel quite nauseous.

She didn't get as far as the door before it flew open and Davey stood grinning widely, wearing just a pair of baggy boxer shorts. Bleary-eyed and grubby, his hair was a dishevelled mass of curls and black stubble spread over half his face. Despite his welcoming smile, Maria felt a tinge of apprehension.

'Welcome to the Allsop family home,' he smiled, 'or should I say the Allsop shit hole! Not quite King's Crescent, I know, but it's home for us. Come in. You'll have to take us as you find us, we're not too great at housework.'

She was stunned to see that the interior was just as bad as the outside. She had to resist the urge to walk on tiptoe across the grimy carpet that stuck to her feet as he led the way through the small hallway to the kitchen-diner at the back of the house.

'This is Maria,' he announced to the faces sitting around a small oblong table that was overflowing with mugs and plates and an assortment of newspaper pages. In the centre, almost in pride of place, was an over-large ashtray full to overflowing with cigarette butts and ash. A haze of smoke hovered over the people grouped at the table.

'Hello.' Maria looked around sheepishly, completely out of her depth and unsure what was expected of her in this alien environment.

Five pairs of eyes glanced in her direction and looked

her up and down before carrying on their conversation as if she wasn't there.

'Coffee?' Davey asked with a grin.

Maria looked around at the mountain of dirty crockery piled on every surface, along with dirty saucepans and a frying pan full of congealed fat.

'No, I'm all right thanks. Can we go somewhere private to talk?'

'What? In this gaff? In your dreams, unless you fancy cramming into the bog with me. Privacy don't exist here, nor do secrets.'

Everyone in the cramped room sniggered and Maria felt an involuntary shiver of discomfort run down the back of her neck. She had to banish the thought that maybe her mother had been right about the Allsops after all.

'In the garden then? I can't stay long, I have to get to school. I daren't muck about any more.'

'Come on then.' He grabbed her hand and pulled her behind him to the back door and then out into the area at the back that looked more like an industrial scrap yard than a domestic garden. The smell was rancid and Maria tried to steer away from the fly-infested pile of yet more rubbish sacks that had been systematically shredded open.

Davey turned back and reached inside the door to grab a filthy old raincoat and a raggedy pair of plimsolls.

'Who actually lives here?' Maria asked as nonchalantly as she could while trying not to stare around her.

'Me and three brothers, two sisters and me dad.' Davey pushed his feet into the plimsolls which were noticeably too small and shrugged into the grubby old coat.

'What about your mum?'

'Oh, she pissed off years ago after Sy was born, couldn't cope with us all. Haven't seen her since the day she left. The bitch ran off with a bloke old enough to be her father. Allegedly he had cash and she went to live in a bungalow in Clacton.' He paused to roll a cigarette.

'I'm sorry, I hadn't realised.' Maria shook her head. 'Why didn't you tell me before when I kept going on about my mother? I'd have been a bit more tactful.'

She felt strangely embarrassed by Davey's revelation. He made it sound so irrelevant yet at the same time there was huge hurt in his voice.

'Hey, we don't give a toss, none of us. She never bothered to contact us again.' Davey laughed harshly. 'She wasn't a mother worth having. She was just a pis-shead who only kept on having kids because she couldn't be bothered not to. We all get on great without her.' He kicked a piece of metal that lay near his feet and flipped it into the air like a football. Maria watched it fly through the air and land with a crash near a feral-looking black cat that hissed, raised its hackles and fled over the broken fence.

'Where do you fit in the age range?' Maria asked curiously. 'Are you the eldest?'

'Almost in the middle. There's Steve, Phil, then me, then Karen, then Sharon and then Sy, the baby of the family. He's eight. Mind you, there'll soon be more 'cos Karen's got herself up the duff. Fuck knows where that's going to fit in here.'

Maria gasped, unable to disguise her amazement any longer. 'But how old is she? If she's younger than you then she can only be—'

'Nearly fifteen,' Davey interrupted quickly. 'Daft bitch, but she wouldn't get rid of it so we just have to wear it. Another fucker in the house!'

Maria didn't know what to say so she just grimaced and nodded silently as if she agreed with him.

'Anyway, how's it all going back in the house of horrors?' Davey asked and for a split second Maria wanted to defend her family. She thought if any family was dysfunctional it was certainly the Allsops but she couldn't bring herself to say anything.

Suddenly she felt very sheltered and grateful for her own family and their comfortable circumstances. There was no way she could imagine living the life that the Allsops had. In fact she almost felt grateful for having Finola as a mother.

'Oh, not too bad, considering,' she replied nonchalantly. 'Weekend was bearable, Patrick and Joe were out a lot, so was Dad. Mum was back and forth to the church as usual so that just left me and Eddie.'

'Yeah, I saw Eddie last week, he's a great kid. Makes me laugh.'

'He's not a kid actually, he's older than you,' Maria snapped defensively. 'He's nineteen, he's just a bit behind his years, that's all. It's not his fault he was brain-damaged as a baby.'

'Yeah, I know.' Davey looked at her as if trying to understand her sudden defensiveness. 'I'm sorry, just saying it like it is. He is a great guy, so open and friendly, really cool.'

'I know, Davey, and now you mention it I wanted to say something about that. Eddie can be a bit naïve and he takes everything at face value so he really thinks you're his mate now and that you really intend to take him to the pub for a drink.'

'I do,' Davey said sharply. 'I just said I think he's great.'

'No! That isn't going to happen. Eddie isn't your kind of friend, I know that, so don't try and put one over on me. I can't let you use Eddie to get up my mother's nose. Anything else you want to do I don't give a toss about, but don't use Eddie!'

Davey looked at her quizzically for a moment and then, leaning his head on one side, he twisted his mouth and chewed on his bottom lip.

'You're taking the piss, right? You're not really standing in my garden giving me a fucking bollocking, are you?'

Maria stood her ground and looked directly at him. 'Yes, actually, I suppose I am. Eddie is the most important person in my life and I will do anything to protect him so don't push it!'

'More important than me?' Davey's eyes suddenly lost all their expression and Maria was unable to tell whether he was really mad at her or whether he understood her feelings. A part of her instantly regretted her vehemence but it was too late, she'd gone for the direct approach and hoped that Davey would appreciate the protectiveness she felt for her brother.

'That's not the same thing, it's not what I meant.'

'OK. So is that all you came round for? To warn me away from your precious Eddie?' He smirked and there was a sneer in his voice.

'Of course not. I phoned because you asked me to and I came round because you invited me. I wanted to see you, Davey. You're the one who brought up the subject of Eddie.' She paused and looked at him, not too sure that she still liked what she saw. 'Anyway, it doesn't matter 'cos I'm off now. I've got to get to school, I'm already on report.' Maria picked up her school bag and looked around the side of the house, seeking an exit route that didn't involve confronting his family again. 'I'll go this way. Your family didn't seem that impressed with me being here.'

Davey didn't say a word. He just turned as she stumbled across the debris littering the sideway and went back indoors.

Maria paused and glanced back through the curtainless window. She watched him chuck the raincoat and plimsolls into the corner, then, dragging a chair across to the crowded table, he spun it back to front and swung his leg over to sit astride it, wearing just his boxer shorts.

'Any tea left in that pot?' He rubbed his hands together and laughed. 'It was fucking freezing out there with me kit off!'

Chapter Eight

Despite what she had told Davey she didn't go back to school; it was actually easier to stay off for the whole day than go in late and explain.

Zipping her coat all the way up to her neck she covered up her school uniform and headed across town on the spur of the moment to visit her sick school friend Annalise Carson.

'What are you doing here? Not bunking off, are you?' Annalise grinned as her mother shepherded Maria into the large room at the back of the house that had been transformed into a light and airy bed-sitting room.

Maria shrugged sheepishly, hoping Mrs Carson hadn't heard. 'No, I've got a couple of free periods so thought I'd come over and check you out, fill you in on all the news and gossip.'

'OK,' Annalise's mother smiled, 'I can take a hint so I'll go and make us all a snack. What would you like, Maria? Lizzie can only have something very light but I'm sure I can tart it up to make it palatable for you.'

'Gee, thanks, Mum.' Annalise screwed up her face in mock distaste. 'She gets her grub tarted up and tasty and I get bland and boring. Rub it in, why don't you!'

'I'm sorry, sweetheart, it won't be long before you can enjoy the tarted-up version as well, just get this week over with and you'll start to feel human again.' Carrie Carson gently ran her fingers back and forth over her daughter's forehead for a few seconds. 'Right, I'm going to leave you girls to it.' She looked over to Maria. 'I'm so pleased you're here even if it is in school uniform in school time.' A knowing smile flickered around the edge of her lips as she turned to leave the room. 'But I won't ask any questions!'

Maria had been friends with Annalise since the beginning of senior school when everyone wanted to be friends with the popular Annalise Carson. She was the one all the girls wanted to be, and all the boys wanted to go out with. She had an unusual combination of personality traits; she had heaps of self-confidence but there was not a shred of nastiness in her despite being the most popular girl in class. Annalise was like the fairy off the Christmas tree, dainty and blonde with a big smile and a hypothetical wand with which she tried to make everyone happy.

And then, a year or so previously, after she had been off from school for several weeks, the news had filtered through.

Annalise Carson had cancer. To all her schoolmates,

especially a group of young teenage girls, that meant just one thing, their friend was going to die. Their teacher had tried to dissolve the ensuing rising hysteria and rumours by explaining the situation to them but still they thought Annalise was unlikely to survive. Now, seeing her frail body leaning back in the chair, Maria wondered how she could have survived so long. The shoulder-length blonde curls were long gone and in their place was a covering of dark beige down; her baby blue eyes were circled with smoky panda-like rings that were so pronounced they looked like bruising. Despite her natural reticence at being confronted with such physical signs of illness, Maria smiled and gently grasped Annalise's hand.

'How's it going? You look better than when I last saw you.'

'Oh, you liar! How can you sit there and lie like that? I look absolutely bloody awful.'

'No you don't.'

'Come on, I do and you know it, but no matter. It's not going too bad, my last chemo session has just finished so I just have to wait and see. Next week I'll look and feel a lot better. I'm really looking forward to having a bloody good meal and not chucking it up again.'

'Pizza! As soon as you're up and about we'll go out for pizza. All the toppings and as much from the salad bar as you can eat!'

'Sounds great, and ice cream as well, please. Do you

know,' she looked at Maria wistfully, 'I'm even gagging to get back to school!'

'You're not, are you? I'm leaving at the end of the term and I'm also leaving home as soon as I can. My mother is driving me completely bananas!'

'I've got to catch up a bit. Well, quite a lot actually, so I'm going to stay on. This has made me think about everything differently. If I've been given a second chance then I want to make the best of it. Not only for me but also for Mum, for everything she's done for me. I think it was worse for her than for me.'

Maria felt a wave of embarrassment wash over her as Annalise's words hit home.

'You must think I'm such a selfish bitch,' Maria started.

'Of course I don't. Now don't go all morose on me, I want you to be entertaining! So, tell me all the news. I heard on the grapevine that you've got it together with that new lad you've got the hots for.'

'Do you mean Davey Allsop?'

'Yes, of course I mean Davey Allsop.'

'We're just friends.'

'Double liar! He's too cute to be just a friend.'

'OK, OK, I'll tell!'

The two girls laughed and chatted for a couple of hours until Annalise started visibly to tire. Maria saw her eyelids droop gently and what little colour there was left in her fragile face slowly faded, leaving her skin looking almost translucent.

'Right,' Maria stood up, 'I'd better go and let you get your beauty sleep. I've got to go home and pretend I've been at school all this time. Oops! Mum will take off into orbit if she finds out I've been bunking again, but it was worth it to see you looking better.'

Annalise smiled weakly and pulled herself up from the chair. 'See that over there? That big shiny glass thing on the wall?' She pointed. 'That's called a mirror and I can see myself in it so don't give me bullshit!' She managed to raise herself enough to slide across onto the bed. 'I won't come to the door, I'm just going to have a lie-down. God, I hate being so weak and useless.'

Maria reached across and hugged her lightly. 'Just think pizza and ice cream. It's a date as soon as you're ready.'

As she made her way home, Maria found it hard to shake off the feeling of intense guilt and also envy that washed over her every time she visited Annalise. Guilt because she had her health and still wasn't happy, and envy at the closeness between Annalise and her mother. Each time she would try to imagine how Finola would be in the same situation and always she came to the same conclusion. She guessed she would still be a disliked nuisance in her mother's eyes.

Flicking away the tears with the back of her hand, Maria sniffed and reiterated to herself that as soon as possible she would leave home, be independent and make the very most of her life.

★

She let herself into the house quietly and held her breath, waiting for the sound of her mother's irate voice to rush down the hall towards her. But there was silence so instead of scampering straight to her bedroom she dumped her bag on the floor and went to the kitchen. Again all was quiet and Maria sighed aloud with relief when she saw the note propped up against the kettle.

Back late tonight, Mrs Callaghan is sick so I'm covering her duties.
1. Maria. Casserole in the oven. Potatoes in the saucepan. Cook potatoes and heat up casserole so it's ready for everyone at 6.30 and then clear everything away. I don't want to come home to a mess.
2. Sam. Post is in the top drawer. Your mother rang. Feeling poorly.
3. Patrick/Joe. Will one of you come to the church at 10 and walk me home?
Everyone behave.
Mother.

Maria was irritated that she would once again have to wait on her brothers but at least Finola did not seem to know about her bunking off – not yet, anyway. Maybe she would even get away with it completely for a change.

She looked at the clock. Ten past four. Maria punched

the air and danced around the kitchen. That gave her two clear hours before Patrick and Joe came in. Time to put her feet on Finola's table, watch Finola's TV and work her way through Patrick's biscuits and chocolate milk in peace.

Two and a half hours later Patrick banged the handle of his knife on the table.

'That's it, we've waited long enough. Come on, Maria, dish up. Brainless can have his cold whenever he finds his way home.' Patrick laughed and looked at Joe who at least had the grace to look sheepish.

'Don't talk about Eddie like that.' Maria glared at Patrick. 'Something must have happened to him, he's never late.'

Patrick laughed again. 'Yes he is, and because Mum's out right now he'll be hanging around with that silly girl he was going on about. Don't be such a drama queen.'

'He didn't know Mum would be out, none of us did.'

'Yeah, of course, you wouldn't be here for a start if you'd known, would you?' Joe interjected with a knowing grin. 'We all know where you'd be!'

'Stop it, all of you,' Sam intervened, his voice weary. 'Maria, look, Eddie has probably lost track of time, so let's all have our dinner and then I'll heat Eddie's up if he's not here in a few minutes.'

'But Eddie's never late.'

'To be fair, it has been known,' Sam smiled affectionately at Maria, 'and he is an adult, you know, it's good that he's feeling his feet!'

Maria silently slapped the dinners on the plates and put hers to one side, along with Eddie's.

'I'll have mine later when Eddie comes in. I'm just going up the road to see if he's around anywhere.'

Patrick laughed nastily. 'You're an interfering bitch. What business is it of yours?'

'That's enough, Patrick. You might get away with that with your mother but not with me. You either show your sister some respect or leave the table. Now!'

There wasn't a sound and all eyes swivelled and focused on Sam who had uncharacteristically raised his voice.

After a few seconds the silence was broken by a loud snort from Patrick and a snigger from Joe.

'I mean it,' Sam warned. 'I've had enough of you all acting like children. Joe, Patrick,' he pointed at them, 'you're grown men. Start acting like it. Now, Maria, you sit down and have your dinner with us, Eddie will be here soon, I'm sure, and he won't thank you for being a mother hen.'

His words to Maria were softened by a smile and Maria smiled back before taking her dinner over to the table and sitting down.

It was another half-hour of strained silence before the door opened and Eddie appeared.

'Eddie!' Maria jumped up. 'Where—' She stopped

83

as her father caught her eye. 'You're late, your dinner's getting cold.' She smiled at him.

'I'm sorry, I was at the . . .' Eddie stopped. As soon as his face reddened and he started mumbling, 'I was at the . . . they wanted me to . . .' Maria knew without doubt that he was lying.

Fortunately Patrick and Joe weren't interested in what Eddie had been up to. As soon as he sat down, they stood up in unison and walked out of the room without a word.

'Mr Manners not at home today then?' Maria shouted after them.

'Leave them be, Maria.' Sam sighed. 'All you'll do is annoy them and then they'll show off as soon as your mother gets home. You sit down and I'll put the kettle on then the three of us can have a cup of tea in peace.'

Maria looked at Eddie. 'Where were you?' she whispered. 'And don't lie to me because I'll know.'

'I was with Davey.'

Maria suddenly felt quite sick and dizzy. She knew instinctively that Davey didn't want to be friends with Eddie so he had to have an ulterior motive and the thought scared her witless.

Chapter Nine

As Finola Harman vigorously polished her way through the silent church she savoured the familiar smell of old-fashioned beeswax polish blending gently with the lingering smoke of recently snuffed candles. The old building, with its high ceilings and classic stained-glass windows, was her sanctuary and she loved every moment she spent inside, away from the harsh realities of life and her own hyperactive conscience. Finola was all too aware of her failings in both her personal life and her religion and her time spent within the confines of the church and its congregation helped her to feel more worthy as a person.

Running the duster along the highly polished and age-pitted pews, she wondered if she would have felt the same if St Bede's had been a modern church like St Angela's across town, a box-like building crafted in clear lines of new timber and shiny glass. To her mind they just didn't have the same feel to them, there wasn't the same sense of reverence that the old churches commanded.

'Are you OK there, Finola? You were miles away.'

Deep in thought, she hadn't heard the elderly priest making his way down the aisle towards her and his sudden presence made her jump.

'Yes, Father,' she whispered respectfully. 'I've nearly finished now. Are you waiting to lock the doors? I just have to finish mopping out the vestry.'

'Oh no, no, no, you must leave that, you've done more than enough for us, Finola.' He paused and smiled. 'You're working too hard here, my dear. Why don't you get off home to the family? I'm sure they'll be missing you and I know their need is greater than mine.'

'Oh no, Father,' Finola said quickly. 'They can all manage perfectly well without me and, anyway, this isn't work to me, I enjoy it, it's restful and calming.' Smiling hesitantly at the gentle man beside her she tried to sound upbeat. 'Actually it makes a peaceful change from life at home with a husband and four children who all want different things at different times. Having such a diverse family really is a challenge at times.' She knew he was looking at her, his eyes ready to see into her soul, but she couldn't quite meet his eye. Father Richard had been in the parish for so many years that he was one of the few people who knew almost everything about her but still she felt compelled to put up her defences and pretend all was well in her life.

'I know. And you're doing a grand job with them all.' He patted her arm gently before continuing, 'So whenever you're ready, either to go home or to stay and talk—'

'Oh no, I'm fine, Father, you know me.'

'Yes, Finola, I do know you, so bear in mind that my door is always open but in the meantime when you're ready to leave, let me know. I'll be next door washing my socks.' He raised his eyes and sighed heavily, pretending exasperation.

'Oh Father,' Finola said quickly, 'you don't want to have to do your own washing. Go and get it and I'll take it home with me.'

'Oh no you won't! The day that I can't manage a simple task like doing a bit of washing will be the day that I hang up my cassock and head for the hills.'

Finola smiled. 'I'm sorry, Father. I forget how independent you can be. Actually I will make a move now. Maria was going to prepare the dinner for the boys so I can only imagine the mess I'm going to have to face when I get back. That girl would try the patience of a saint. She's such a trial to me.'

Father Richard put his head on one side and made a gentle tutting noise. Despite his seventy-odd years, he still had a full head of silver hair that was always just a fraction too long, giving him a dishevelled and slightly eccentric air. Many years of kneeling in prayer had sent arthritis coursing through his joints, resulting in a limping, sideways gait, and small children were often scared of him despite the fact that he was one of the kindest, most caring men Finola had ever met.

Without him she knew that she probably would have rolled over all those years ago and given up on everything. It had been the thought of letting him down that had stopped her hand as she was about to take the handful of pills that would have ended it all.

'Don't be too hard on your daughter,' he counselled gently. 'I know you think she's deliberately wilful but I think she's a rather spirited young lady and in this day and age, spirit is no bad thing.'

'But she's so difficult and so rebellious, I find her hard to manage. The boys weren't like that. I feel as if she's my cross to bear. She won't even attend church any more. Everything I hold dear she tramples underfoot.'

Father Richard shook his head. 'Please don't see her like that. Maria is your daughter, a gift from God, and you should see her as a gift, not as a burden to be shouldered. Right now she is seeking herself and, with the right guidance, in time she'll take the right road, I'm sure.'

Finola had had the same discussion with Father Richard many times but she couldn't make him understand how she felt. How every time Maria defied her, disobeyed her or offended her, it was as if it was her punishment for past sins. She found it impossible to see Maria as her daughter, as a gift from God. To her mind Maria had been sent by the devil to be a constant reminder of her biggest, most unforgivable sin.

The priest smiled acceptance of her lack of response.

'One day, Finola Harman, you'll see that I am right. Maria really is a good girl deep down. Rejoice in that and forget the rest. It does no one any good for you to be constantly punishing yourself. Now go.' He pointed towards the doors dramatically, his cassock flapping wildly at the sudden movement.

'Yes, Father.' She smiled. 'I'll see you tomorrow. And if Mrs Callaghan is still unwell then I'm happy to help out, I don't mind, really I don't.'

'Go.'

Finola went over to the small cupboard at the back of the church and squirrelled away her polishes and dusters before slipping into her coat.

'Goodnight, Father, and thank you.'

'Goodnight, Finola. Now you take care on your way home. Do you want me to get you a taxi? It's late.'

'It's OK, I enjoy the walk and one or both of the boys is coming to meet me.'

'That's good. Give my regards to the rest of your family and I offer them my apologies for not sending you home sooner.'

'They won't have missed me.'

'Stop beating yourself up, Finola Harman. That's a direct order from above! Savour your family, there are many who would love to have what you have.'

Father Richard saw her to the end of the path before turning back towards the church to lock the doors.

'Mum . . .'

At the sound of Patrick's voice Finola felt her mood lighten instantly. There was no question that out of all her children, he was her favourite.

Her firstborn and her first son.

Her first true love.

Before Patrick had been born, Finola had never experienced that emotion. She and Sam had known each other nearly all their lives, they had met at church and gone to the church socials as part of the same group before predictably gravitating towards each other as individuals. They had courted formally for a year, become engaged and then married two years later, by which time Sam was well into his accountancy career and Finola was working in the local Inland Revenue office. Their respective parents had been church acquaintances for many years and were all in favour of the match so there was no question that it would not go ahead.

A perfect match in the eyes of the family and the church.

But although Finola loved Sam and enjoyed his company, she knew she had never been in love with him. She also knew that it had been the same for him. They had both drifted into marriage because it was easier than breaking up and upsetting both families. When she was with him, or even away from him, she didn't experience that overwhelming, all-encompassing feeling that she read about in books and watched at the cinema with Sam by her side, holding her hand affectionately.

But then she had given birth to Patrick and suddenly she had been engulfed in a wave of pure love and had, in that instant, understood exactly what love was all about.

Now Patrick came up to her and kissed her cheek before putting his arm round her shoulder.

'What's up with old Ma Callaghan then? Not croaked it, has she?'

Finola slapped his chest playfully. 'No of course she hasn't, you naughty boy. You mustn't talk about the poor old dear like that. She's got a cough and cold and at her age it's best not to take chances.'

'Yeah, but I bet you wish she would give it all up, move over and let you take over the crown as Father Richard's right-hand woman.' Patrick sniggered and Finola slapped his chest again with the back of her hand.

'It's not like that at all, as well you know. I think it's wonderful that she's still working away for the good of the church at her age, she's well into her seventies, you know. We all do what we do for the church and for Father Richard not for glory for ourselves and certainly not for financial gain. Anyway, Mrs Callaghan lives in, I couldn't do that, I have to stay home and look after you all.'

'You're too right about no financial gain, you hardly ever even get a cup of tea, do you? Mind you, I bet old Ma Callaghan does all right shacked up in the house on a salary, albeit a pittance. They're like an old married couple, Father Richard and her!'

Finola felt guilty because she knew that if Maria had spoken like this she would have been punished but it was hard for her to take offence with Patrick, she loved him so much. In fact she loved him so much she ached when she was away from him.

'I'm happy with what I'm doing, it fits in around all of you and I know I'm fulfilling my duty as a good parishioner. I just wish the rest of you were more involved in the church. Just going to Mass isn't enough, you know. If you do still go to Mass as often as you should. I'm never sure who does and who doesn't now you're adults.' Finola didn't look at her son. She had her suspicions that none of them went as often as she would like but if they elected to go at a different time to her then she couldn't keep track of them. In fact she didn't want to keep track of them because then she would have to confront the issue and maybe be disappointed.

'We do what we're supposed to do. Maria bunks off, I know, but Joe and I don't, we do our duty, we always have done.'

'How was dinner?' Finola asked to change the subject. She didn't want to think about Patrick possibly telling lies.

'Oh, the usual. Dad was being a pain and siding with Maria, and Eddie came in late. I bet he was with that daft Jenny girl.'

Finola's head spun round. 'No! He wouldn't dare. I've told him I don't want him hanging around with her, she'll get him into trouble, I just know it! Eddie may be a little slow but he's not like her.'

'Well, stop him then.' Patrick grinned slyly. 'But you'll have to talk to Maria. She encourages him to think he can do whatever the rest of us do, she doesn't have a clue about what's really best for Eddie.'

'I don't know about that, Patrick. She really does love Eddie, in fact I think she prefers him to any of us.'

'No she doesn't, she uses him. Just like she uses Dad. I know it's too late now but just think how much better we'd all get on if she wasn't around. If you'd never adopted her.'

Finola hated to hear her son talk like this but at the same time she always found it hard to remonstrate with him.

'Come on now, Patrick, I know you and Joe don't get on with her but Maria is your sister, your sibling. We're family.'

'Sorry, Mum, but she's not our sister and never will be. And never ever will I be able to understand why you had to adopt her when you already had three of us.'

Finola once again felt cornered by her beloved son. He always kept going back to it, as if he was hoping for a different response.

Her favourite son had been irrationally jealous of Maria from the very first day she and Sam had brought her home and, even after sixteen years, no amount of reassurance would shift him from his position of total resentment.

'I've told you before, it was the right thing to do at the time and your father and I agreed that it was the right thing to do. Maria was just a tiny baby with no family and no future. We had no choice. Now,' she linked her arm with his, 'tell me about your day. How was work?'

Together they meandered home, Finola savouring every moment alone with her favourite son and Patrick enjoying every moment that he kept his mother to himself and away from the rest of the family.

Chapter Ten

Davey Allsop and the Farrell brothers were ensconced in the corner of the pub plotting their biggest coup to date. Although Davey really didn't want to be involved with them he had been backed into a corner by his own cockiness. Despite the fact that it had worked to his benefit and he had more cash in his pocket than he could have imagined a couple of weeks previously, deep down he was still scared.

'Now, you've got it all straight, have you, Davey? Know exactly what you've got to do?'

'Yep,' Davey replied eagerly. 'I've got it dead straight. I won't let you down.'

The brothers exchanged amused glances.

'Don't you go getting too excited, punk.' Tommy rapped his knuckles on the table. 'That's when you'll make a mistake. Cool and calm is what makes for success and if this is a success then, trust me, you'll earn fucking well out of it. If it all falls apart then you'll get something but it won't be what you want.' Tommy looked at Davey through narrowed eyes and shook his head knowingly. 'Now we've got other business, confidential business, so piss off, shut the fuck up and keep out of sight for the next few days.'

'Right.' Davey stood up obediently and forced a wide grin onto his face in an attempt to hide his nervousness and look confident and winning. 'See you Friday then, and thanks again for bringing me in, I won't let you down.'

The Farrells didn't respond, in fact they didn't even look at him again. They had already dismissed him from their presence and their minds. So Davey turned and strutted out of the pub, trying to look important and also old enough to actually be in there in the first place.

Once outside, though, he heaved a sigh of relief and hot-footed it away from the pub as fast as he could, his heart thumping. The last thing he had wanted was to get caught up with the Farrells but suddenly he found he was up to his neck in it.

A bit of wheeling and dealing was one thing but the brothers and their cronies were bad news and Davey palpitated at the thought of his father finding out, let alone getting caught by the law.

All the Allsop boys had been brought up to believe that the petty stuff was a legitimate way of life and that so long as no one got hurt too badly it was fine. His father had always lived happily off every state benefit he could claim on account of his bad back and had no qualms about earning whatever he could on the side. A touch of shoplifting here, some smuggled tobacco and knocked-off gear there, along with the occasional insurance scam were perfectly acceptable activities that made life more comfortable for them all, but none of them had been involved in anything much more than that. But the Farrells were out and out thugs with neither morals nor scruples. They were way out of the Allsops' league and Davey knew he had to at least try to find a way out of the corner he was backed into.

He headed to the town centre where he hoisted himself onto the brick wall and rolled a cigarette. He wanted to talk about it to Maria but because she had gone off at him about Eddie, his pride had been hurt and his ego demanded that she should apologise first.

Deep in thought, he didn't see Sam Harman hustle Ruth Easter into a nearby café.

'See that lad on the wall out there? The one with the long hair swinging his legs?' Sam nodded his head in the direction of the wall. 'That's Davey Allsop, the one I told you about, the one that Maria has been hanging around with for the past few months. It sends Finola into a frenzy, she can't stand him or his family.'

'Well, I can certainly see the attraction for Maria.' Ruth smiled as she studied Davey from a distance. 'He's a very good-looking lad. Just the type of boy the young girls seem to go for, I'm afraid. Pretty with just a hint of danger. We've all had one of those at one time or another, all lithe and sexy.'

'Pretty?' Sam looked stunned. 'How can you call a boy pretty and then say that's what the girls want? Good job he can't hear you. That would damage him for life.' Sam looked at Ruth askance. 'Pretty?' he repeated, shaking his head in amazement.

'Well, he is pretty in a macho kind of way and looking at him there he might as well have the word trouble tattooed on his forehead. Not that the girls would be put off. Look,' she pointed, 'look at that group of giggly girls over there, they can't keep their eyes off him and they're all several years older than him.'

'Hmmm. He shouldn't be hanging around town on a weekday. I wonder why he's not at school today.'

'Ooh, Sam, now let me think. No, I couldn't possibly imagine why he's not at school.' Ruth laughed and reached out her hand to touch him lightly on the cheek.

'No need to be sarcastic, madam, you know exactly what I mean. Maria seems to be attracted to trouble and if Davey Allsop is playing truant then I'd bet she's probably not far behind.' He leaned forward in his seat to get a better view from the low Georgian bay window of the café and was scanning both ways when Ruth grabbed his arm and pulled him back.

'Well, if she turns up you can go out and drag her

in here but in the meantime I'm starving and I haven't got long for lunch. Maggie's going off early today, school play or something similar.'

Sam pursed his lips and faked a sharp intake of breath. 'Ugh! Rather her than me. I'm glad I'm past all that. It used to be a nightmare trying to co-ordinate all the plays, open evenings, sports days and the like. Though now it's mentally time-consuming worrying about them all. At least when they're babies you know where they are, who they're with and what they're doing.' Sam raised his eyes towards the ceiling. 'I wonder at what age all that ends?'

Ruth thought about his words for a moment and nearly blurted out her pregnancy but the thought of saying it in a public place stopped her.

'Didn't you enjoy having children around? You had four so I assumed you must like them a bit.'

'Yes, I did actually, at the time, but now I'm glad it's all over, all that eyes in the back of your head business, although thinking about it, the way mine are always at each other's throats it is still a bit like having four toddlers around.' Sam laughed and cut his chunky baguette in half, completely oblivious to the hidden agenda behind Ruth's casual words.

'If you had your time again, what would you do? About children, I mean. Would you still want to have them?'

'Probably not! No, that's not fair. Patrick and Joe aren't exactly a barrel of laughs but then Finola ruined then completely. But Maria and Eddie . . .' He laughed but at that second a movement caught his eye and distracted him; he looked back to where Davey had been sitting. The wall was empty.

'He's gone. Did you see where he went? I wonder where he is now. I should have kept an eye on him, I could have followed him.'

'Sam! Please, I haven't got a long lunch hour today, you're not listening to me and you haven't answered my question.'

'Sorry, what question was that?' Sam frowned absent-mindedly.

'Oh, never mind, it wasn't important. How's your baguette?'

Ruth watched her lover as he concentrated on his lunch. She had yet to decide what to do about her pregnancy and, despite her attempt a few moments before, was once again in two minds about involving Sam in the decision.

Decisions had to be made, she knew that, and they had to be made soon because as each day passed Ruth knew that, despite her best efforts at detaching herself, she was starting to feel maternal and becoming emotionally attached to the baby growing inside her. The rational part of her brain told her that her circumstances and her relationship were not conducive to family life and she herself wasn't cut out for single motherhood. But at the same time her emotions told her to take the opportunity that was on offer. The opportunity to have a child of her own. Sam's child.

'Penny for them.' Sam's voice broke into her thoughts.

'Sorry?' She looked at him, unsure of what he had just said.

'I said penny for them. You were miles away just then. Something on your mind, love?'

'No,' Ruth smiled, 'just work. Bit buried at the moment and there's not enough hours in the day. We're interviewing tomorrow for another assistant, which is good of course but it can be a little distracting. In fact I need to get going. Are you going to be able to make the dinner tonight?'

'I certainly intend to, I'm looking forward to it. I like your friends, they're so open and accepting of me and the situation.'

'I know. That's because they like you and as far as they're concerned we're a couple.'

'So I'm not just some dirty old lech with a young gorgeous mistress?'

Ruth laughed out loud. 'Young? I'm not that much younger than you, and gorgeous went out the window twenty years ago!'

'You're still absolutely gorgeous, especially to me.' Sam looked directly at her, his face suddenly serious. 'In fact you're even more gorgeous than when I first met you. I love you, Ruth, always have and always will.'

Smiling, Ruth blew him a kiss and leaned down to

pick up her handbag. 'I really have to go now, Maggie will be panicking if I'm late back. I'll definitely see you tonight then?'

'Mmm,' Sam responded distantly as he looked out of the window again.

'Sam! I said I'm going now, I'll see you tonight. Nine o'clock at mine with a bottle of red wine and an empty belly.' Her assertive tone brought Sam back to her.

'Sorry, Ruth, sorry. But that Davey Allsop is back. I'm just wondering whether to have a word with him about Maria.'

Ruth laughed and shook her head. 'If you really want your daughter to never speak to you again then by all means go out and waylay the lad, but I would suggest leaving him be. And to be honest, you won't get anywhere with him anyway, I can see that just by looking at him. That's a lad who abhors authority, likes breaking rules.'

'Mmmm,' Sam responded.

'Don't bloody *mmmmm* at me again. Do whatever you like but think first!' Ruth kissed him on the cheek, it was her public kiss, the one she used for all her friends. Just in case anyone relevant was around and unseen. 'I'm really off now. See you tonight. Don't be late.'

Sam smiled up at her and then, glancing back out to the wall, disappeared back into his thoughts.

★

Davey was also immersed in his thoughts but he was thinking about himself, and the fix he was in.

He was terrified. Terrified of getting caught by the police for something so big, terrified of doing something wrong and having to face the wrath of the Farrells, but mostly he was terrified that he wasn't up to the job and would lose face.

Swinging his legs nervously back and forth, Davey turned the plan over in his mind. There were so many things that could go wrong.

He had been told to be outside the designer sports shop on the main road at midnight that night. If the street was clear and there were no late-night revellers to witness the events, he had to make a sign to the Farrells' driver who would be parked up the road in an already stolen four-by-four, with the full array of bull bars on the front, and he would then simply ram straight through the plate-glass shop windows. The Farrells would be right behind in a large van and all four of them would fill it up with everything they could grab and be away within minutes before anyone could respond to the alarm.

In theory.

Easy, Tommy and Tel said. They had done it before in Romford and Basildon and not been caught but this time it was on home territory. On Davey's home territory, and he was really scared.

Maria was stretched out on her bed pensively chewing

over the previous few days. Her thoughts, usually focused on herself and her future, were suddenly in a whirl because of her visits to Davey and Annalise. It was as if a hand had appeared in front of her holding a big STOP AND THINK sign, forcing her to re-think her life and her relationships.

Despite experiencing everyone's worst nightmare, Annalise seemed as comfortable as she could be with her life and had a good family relationship with both her parents and her only brother. Her thoughts for the future were focused on staying alive as opposed to Maria's which were solely about getting away from her family and earning lots of money.

Maria wondered how her family could be so different from Annalise's, how they could bicker among themselves all the time when in fact there really was everything to be grateful for. They were all fit and healthy, unlike poor Annalise, and there always seemed to be sufficient money to live comfortably. None of them had ever gone without the basic necessities and they lived in a reasonable house.

Unlike Davey and the rest of the Allsops. As she thought again about Davey's home and family she realised that things could be a lot worse for her.

The guilt that washed over her made Maria decide then and there that she would make more of an effort with her mother. Patrick was a different issue but she determined that even he would no longer be able to rile her so successfully.

In the half-light of dusk she looked out of her window at the sky and promised herself that everything was going to change. She would make every attempt to get on with her family and be grateful for everything she had.

Chapter Eleven

Davey had given in and was once again hovering around the turning to King's Crescent. He wanted, needed, to speak to Maria even if it meant actually forcing himself to apologise for his previous surliness.

Although his macho pride would never let him admit it in a million years, Davey looked up to Maria and respected her common sense. A common sense beyond her years, combined with an insight that he knew he didn't have. Nobody with any common sense would have got themselves into the mess he was in with the Farrells.

In order to save face he didn't intend to approach Maria about it directly; he planned to bump into her and then throw it into the conversation casually as an afterthought. Just mention that the Farrells wanted him in with them. He knew that as soon as he did mention it to her Maria wouldn't be able to resist telling him exactly what she thought and then he might, in a roundabout way, be able to ask for her help in getting out of it. One of the first things about her that had attracted him was the fact that she wasn't shy about voicing her opinions and sticking up for herself. Others called her self-opinionated and arrogant but Davey knew better.

As he continued to pace up and down and scan the street, his mind wandered back to the first time he had come across her.

It had been his first day at yet another school after yet another family eviction and his reputation as a hard lad from an even harder family had preceded him. The tormenting had started almost instantly. It had been subtle to start with but Davey's lack of response had soon inflamed the situation until, during a lunch break, the circling had begun in earnest.

Like hungry sharks they had slowly closed in on their prey but just as Davey was flexed and ready to fight all-comers, a tall, leggy girl who stood a head above everyone else had pushed her way through to the front of the spectating group of schoolchildren. Her air of authority was such that the group parted willingly to let her through.

'What the fuck are you morons up to?' Placing her hands on her hips she slowly surveyed the crowd and laughed sarcastically. 'You stupid dumb bastards, all ganging up on one poxy new boy? What's that going to prove? That ten of you are stronger than one of him? Wow, that'll impress us all, won't it, girls?' She had looked them over disdainfully, turned on her heel and then shouted back over her shoulder, 'Shit for brains, the lot of you!'

A silence had gradually descended over the baying crowd. The girls had started to snigger and take the piss, and the boys had deflated and then moved away as if the energy had been sucked out of them.

Davey had run after her. 'How did you do that? Or rather why did you do that? I had it under control, I could have smashed every fucking one of 'em all into oblivion, no problem.'

The girl had stopped and turned towards him with a sneer. 'Oh, come on, don't tell me you're thick as well. I did it because I knew I could!' Throwing back her head, she laughed. 'I love to divide and conquer. Make the boys look stupid in front of the girls and it's all over because we have the brains and the power! Anyway, I loathe cowards and people who run in packs are just fucking cowards. But it's OK, you don't have to thank me for it.'

'I wasn't going to. Why did they listen to you?'

'I don't know, why not ask them?' Maria had smiled enigmatically and turned away.

'What's your name?' he had shouted after as her long legs took her across the playground in a few strides.

'I'm sure you'll find that out if you want to!' she had shouted without turning back.

And of course he had.

Davey shook himself back to the present and looked around for her impatiently.

Yes, Maria would have a better idea about how to get out of the raid that was arranged for that very night. Just the thought of it had had him walking the floor all night in desperation. He could almost hear the cell door slamming shut on him while the Farrells walked away unconcerned and unmarked by the episode.

As he nervously stepped from foot to foot, he stayed right back from the kerb, trying hard to be inconspicuous, but his mind was so absorbed with thoughts of the Farrells that he didn't notice Eddie Harman suddenly appear beside him.

'Hello, Davey.' Eddie smiled delightedly. 'Are you looking for me?'

'Erm . . .' Davey hesitated for a moment. 'Well, yes, I thought I might just say hello to you and also to Maria as I was passing this way. I really wanted to see both of you. Just to say hi of course, see how you're both doing.' Davey didn't want to upset Eddie or hurt his feelings. Not for any deep charitable reason but because he didn't want to upset Maria again. Even so, it amused him to think of Finola Harman breathing fire at the thought of him befriending another of her children.

'So, Eddie, me old mate,' he slapped the smiling young man on the back in a phoney show of affection, 'how's it all going with you? And how about the lovely Jenny? Not with her today then? Cor, she's a bit of all right, that one, you're one lucky bugger, you are, wish I could grab meself an older woman!'

Eddie glowed with happiness and for a split second

Davey felt a gentle wave of guilt. He knew that he wouldn't normally give someone like Eddie the time of day, let alone get into conversation with him but because he was Finola's son, Davey got a perverse pleasure out of it.

'Jenny wasn't at work today,' Eddie said, unaware of Davey's wandering train of thought. 'Her mum said she's got a cold. That's why I'm back early. I'm bored now though, I don't want to go home. Can we go to the pub again?'

'Not a good idea today, Eddie. Did anyone find out about last time? You didn't get in trouble, did you?'

'Not really. Maria found out but she said she wouldn't tell if I promised not to do it again without telling her first. So we could go to the pub and I could tell her this time and then it would be OK, wouldn't it?' His eyes opened wide in eager expectation, making Davey feel as if he was about to kick next door's cat back over the fence.

'Maybe another time, Ed. Anyway, where's Maria now? I haven't seen her come home yet.'

'Dunno.' Eddie shrugged his shoulders rapidly several times.

'Come on, Eddie, don't fuck me about, you must know.'

'But I don't, honest, she never said. She might be at her friend's house.'

'Which friend?' Davey's rising panic was making him snap harder at Eddie.

'Dunno, she didn't tell me.'

'Think, Eddie, think hard. Which friend?'

'I dunno! Don't shout at me, Davey, I don't like being shouted at. Patrick shouts like that and it scares me, Maria says—'

'I'm sorry, Eddie, I didn't mean to, it's just the way I speak sometimes.' Davey knew he had to make a concerted effort to calm him down. 'Nothing to do with you at all. Me and my mates shout all the time, it doesn't mean anything, honest. Want to come for a Coke with me?'

'Oh wow, yes please, Davey.' Eddie's face positively glowed with pleasure.

'Come on then, mate, let's go. The café up the road do you OK?'

Davey smiled as he walked along the road with Eddie. Suddenly he had a plan. If he couldn't get out of the raid then he might as well take the opportunity to score some points off Finola Harman.

'Mum, can I talk to you? Please?'

Finola's head spun round to look at her daughter, her expression showing such suspicious disbelief that Maria smiled.

'I mean it, Mum, I'd like us to sit down and talk, like mother and daughter, like friends, like whatever. I just want us to talk, not fight. I'd like us to be friendly to each other.'

Finola looked genuinely puzzled as she turned back

to the ironing board and ran the iron up and down it furiously.

'Have you got yourself in trouble? Heaven forbid, you're not pregnant, are you? That's all I need, you to get in trouble with that Allsop boy. I told you he was no good, didn't I? Didn't I tell you?' Finola's expression as she spoke the words was one of sheer panic.

'No. I'm not in any trouble and I'm certainly not pregnant.' Maria breathed deeply and forced a smile. 'Did I tell you I went to see Annalise? Do you remember her? The very pretty girl from school who came round here. Patrick and Joe were nearly struck dumb when they saw her.'

'Don't talk about your brothers like that and pull your skirt down, you look like a tart.'

Maria uncrossed her legs and tugged at her skirt, mentally forcing herself not to react. 'I'm not talking about them like anything, it's just conversation. I was actually making a bit of a joke. Anyway, I don't know if I told you but Annalise has been really sick, she has cancer, leukaemia. She's just finished her last course of chemo and everyone hopes she'll be all right now but it started me thinking.' Pausing for a response, Maria looked expectantly at her mother but Finola was still feigning concentration on the ironing and staring uncomfortably at a shirt collar.

'I was trying to figure out why you and me don't get on. Why I annoy you so much. I don't mean to

but I seem to be able to annoy you just by being here.'
Maria paused again but the iron moved furiously along
the body of the shirt and Finola's lips were so pursed
she looked as if she was about to start whistling. 'Mum,
please, I'm trying to make some amends here. Seeing
Annalise so ill made me think how lucky we all are
really. I know we fight but deep down we all love each
other, don't we?'

The grip became so tight Finola's knuckles whitened
but the iron slowed and Finola looked around in
Maria's general direction although she didn't meet her
eye.

'You don't love anyone, Maria, apart from yourself,
you've only ever thought of yourself. You take no notice
of me, you never do anything I ask you to, or not with
a happy face.'

Maria gritted her teeth and tried her best not to
go down the blame-throwing route that she and her
mother usually took. But she found it hard. Finola had
always had the knack of chucking every past misdemeanour back into Maria's face.

'That's not true! Look, please will you talk to me?
I would just like to figure out what's wrong between
us. Annalise and her mum get on so well, it's like they're
friends, they have a laugh together.'

'Parents aren't meant to be friends, Maria. Parents
are parents, our job is to teach you the right road in
life and if that means discipline, as it always does with
you, then so be it.' The first shirt was transferred to a

hanger and another dragged from the laundry basket in the time it took Finola to finish her sentence.

'Yes, but you get on with the boys and they're not perfect. Why don't you get on with me?'

Finola didn't say anything and her eyes were firmly fixed back on the ironing board.

'Mum, why do you hate me? I'm your daughter, even if I am only adopted. You must have wanted me in the first place so why do you hate me now?'

'I don't hate you, Maria, hate is a sin. But I don't like what you have become, I don't like the way you behave and I certainly don't like the way you undermine us all and our religion, but mostly I don't like the way you treat Patrick and Joe, especially Patrick. There,' Finola shook her head vigorously, 'you asked so I'm telling you. You don't fit in this family, you're not the kind of daughter I would have expected to give birth to.'

'But you didn't give birth to me,' Maria said sharply. 'You allegedly *chose* me. Dad has always told me that you both chose me, he makes it sound positive, so why don't you feel like that? I didn't just fall out of the sky and land in your lap unasked. Why did you decide to adopt me if you didn't really want me?'

'I've had just about enough of this psycho babbly nonsense. You watch too much television.' Finola's voice echoed angrily around the kitchen walls. 'I don't have to explain myself to you, Maria, you're just a child. If you want to make amends then the best thing you can do is go and see Father Richard in the confessional but in the meantime do something constructive and put the dinner on. Patrick and Joe have been at work all day and so has poor Eddie in his own way.'

Maria thought that if she was asked to describe her mother she would say 'permanently angry'. Her speech was angry, her face was angry, even her body language shouted angry. The only respite from her anger seemed to be when she was with Patrick and Joe.

'And Dad?' Maria tried to keep her voice neutral. 'What about Dad? I don't understand why you always ignore him. He's the one who supports everyone.'

Finola snorted. 'He does nothing and deserves nothing. You think I don't know what he gets up to? You think I don't know that you and him are joined together in secrets like Siamese twins? Talking me down? He deserves nothing from me.'

For a second Maria thought she was referring to Ruth. With her heart in her mouth she quietly let Finola continue.

'He doesn't want to spend any time here with us so why should I want to consider him? Your father is weak willed. He prefers to scuttle away to his so-called club or whatever you both choose to call it and hide away from any responsibility. I get more support from Father Richard than I ever do from your father.' The iron stopped moving and Finola stared into the middle distance, her lips pursed, as usual, in thoughtful disapproval, but then it was as if she suddenly realised what she was saying to her daughter and she shook herself back to the present. 'I told you to start the dinner!' She fired the words like bullets at Maria before crashing the ironing board away and marching red-faced out of the kitchen.

But rather than feel disappointed as she watched her mother disappear through the doorway, Maria actually felt quite satisfied. At least she had started the communication even if it had only been fleeting.

She promised herself she would try again.

But as the evening progressed and events started to spiral out of control, all hope of any kind of reconciliation between Maria and her mother faded away and by the time it got to eleven o'clock the Harman house was in a state of uproar.

'I told you to go and look for him earlier,' Finola shouted, targeting her frustration at Sam. 'All this *he's an adult* nonsense. Eddie is not an adult, he needs looking out for.'

'But he is an adult,' Sam intervened gently. 'We can't keep watch on him all the time. I'm sure he'll show up soon. Maybe he's forgotten the time, missed the last bus . . .'

'Nonsense. He's with that Jenny girl somewhere.'

'No he's not.' Sam's voice was getting an edge to it. 'I told you already, I've phoned there, Jenny is at home with her parents, she hasn't been to the centre today, her mother said she's not well.'

'Stuff and nonsense, the woman's lying. Go round there now and bring him home,' Finola snarled. 'I've had enough!'

'I'll go,' Patrick volunteered gleefully. 'I'll sort them out, lying lowlife. He came in late the other night when you were at church, you know, and he looked really smug about it.'

'You will do nothing, Patrick,' Sam ordered. 'Jenny's mother certainly wouldn't lie about something like that. Maybe there's something going on at the centre. Maria, any suggestions who we could ring?'

'You're joking, aren't you?' Patrick sneered. 'She's enjoying all this. She knows exactly where he is, same as she always does.'

'But I don't!' Maria was struggling to keep her emotions under control but finding it hard. Her worst nightmare was unfolding in front of her. Not only was she worried sick about Eddie not coming home, she was also terrified that he was with Davey and that her mother and brothers would find out. 'I'm as worried as everyone else and I really don't have a clue where he could be. I hope he's just lost track of time. Maybe he's with someone else from the centre.'

'It's OK, we know this has nothing to do with you,' Sam touched her shoulder reassuringly, 'but he's never been this late without us knowing where he is. I'm going out in the car to have a look around. You can come with me.'

Maria knew her father was trying to get her out of

the house away from the others and she gratefully accepted.

She had such a bad feeling about Eddie that she felt physically sick.

Chapter Twelve

'Come on, Eddie, this is going to be fun. You said you were up for a laugh earlier. You're not going to bottle on me now, are you?'

Eddie looked on bewildered as Davey, high as a kite after popping a couple of uppers for Dutch courage, ran along the top of the high wall that edged the main road and jumped off the other end with an acrobatic flourish and then took a bow to the passing traffic.

It was eleven thirty at night and obvious, even to Davey in his heightened state of excitement, that Eddie should have gone home hours before. But Davey was enjoying himself now and Eddie, who had never done anything like it in his life, was scared of upsetting him. He was also absolutely terrified of being in trouble when he got home. Despite his lack of ordinary perception, he realised that he was in big trouble whichever way he turned, with Davey on one side and his mother on the other.

'I didn't have you down as a wimp, Eddie. Come on, live a little. I've got a surprise for you. We're going shopping.'

'But all the shops are shut and I don't have any money.'

'I know but I'm going to get one opened up especially for you, Eddie, 'cos you're my mate. And you can choose whatever you want. We'll get you out of that fucking school uniform gear and into something really trendy, something the girlfriend will just *lurve*!'

'Davey, I think I ought to go home, it's really late. I'll get in trouble with Mum and Maria will be worried.'

'Crap, Eddie. You're a man, you can go home whenever you want.' Davey looked at his watch. 'Come on, let's go or we won't be on time. Now listen hard to what I'm saying and do as you're told. We're going to meet my other mates and then we're going to hit the shops.' Davey stopped and roared with laughter at his own joke as the pills combined with a couple of cans of strong lager really took effect. 'But, you have to stay right behind me all the way and keep schtum.' Now that he had accepted the inevitability of going on the raid, Davey was delighted with the cleverness of his plan.

He figured that if he took Eddie with him on the raid and they got caught then Finola Harman would be mortified with shame, but if they didn't get caught then he would have a secret weapon that he could pull out and use at any time. Holy Finola wouldn't be able to slag him and his family off any more because her own would be just as bad.

'Davey, I really want to go home. I'm scared, I don't like being here so late.' Eddie was shivering with a combination of cold and fright.

'Well, you can't go home. It's too late now so fucking pull yourself together and let's get going. My mates are waiting. Now do exactly as you're told because if this goes wrong you're in serious trouble; in fact, we'll both be up to our necks in it. With everyone.'

Eddie's eyes widened in panic as he watched Davey jumping about manically in front of him, darting back and forth across the pavement, laughing wildly. Then just as suddenly Davey slowed and smiled. Wrapping an affectionate arm round Eddie's shoulders, he led him gently forward.

'Fun, Eddie. Remember, this is going to be fun like you've never had in your life before.'

Eddie didn't utter another word. His terror consumed him so completely he simply couldn't speak but Davey was too hyped up to notice his lack of response as they cut through narrow side streets and alleyways to their destination. When they reached the deserted main street, Davey pulled him into a doorway.

'Just do what I say. When the car hits the glass don't worry about it, it's a game, so just follow me closely into the shop, grab everything you can and stay behind me, OK?'

Still Eddie couldn't speak but he nodded fearfully.

At a couple of minutes to midnight the stolen four-by-four drove by for the first time as arranged, past the shop then down to the roundabout and back again, giving everyone time to assess the situation.

On the second lap it pulled slowly into the side of the road but the engine stayed running. Further up the street Davey could see the van that he guessed the Farrells were in, waiting by the kerb.

Stepping forward he carefully scanned the street, checking for any movement this way and that, making sure it was all clear. All the pubs were at the other end of town and the Farrells had chosen a Monday night when the streets were virtually dead at midnight.

Seeing nothing moving, Davey signalled at the driver of the four-by-four and stepped back.

The driver pulled a scarf up over his nose, revved full throttle, turned the wheel and then hurtled full speed straight at the plate-glass shop window.

As the engine roared, Davey pulled Eddie over the road in readiness.

'Don't make a fucking sound, Eddie,' he snarled at the terrified lad behind him.

The explosion when the vehicle crashed into the glass was like a bomb going off. The nearby buildings shook and several of them suffered shattered windows as well. The four-by-four ploughed on into the shop itself, to be followed by the van which spun round on the pavement and backed up through the smashed window, debris crunching under its wheels.

'Right, Eddie, in the shop and grab as much as you can, anything and everything, and chuck it in the van. Come on, move it.'

But Eddie was frozen to the spot, completely traumatised by what he had just witnessed and by the deafening sound of several burglar alarms all triggered at once.

'Eddie, move it! Now!'

Grabbing him by the hand, Davey roughly dragged him forward. Stepping carefully through the demolished shop front, he tried to pull Eddie through with him but Eddie held back.

Adrenaline pumping, Davey tugged at him even harder. Eddie instinctively reached out and grabbed the window frame to halt his progress. The sharp movement loosened a couple of large pointed shards of glass that were still hanging in the frame like stalactites in a cave. The pieces of glass twinkled eerily in the van's headlights and then dropped straight and fast towards the ground. The larger piece pierced Eddie's chest like a sharpened sword.

As his knees slowly crumpled beneath him, he fell back onto the debris, the weight of his body pulling his hand away from Davey.

'Eddie, get up, stop fucking about and get up.' Without looking round, Davey reached out to grab at Eddie. 'Come on, Ed, we haven't got time for this, just get up and get on with it.'

But Eddie didn't move, he lay exactly where he had

fallen, his eyes wide open with shock as dark red blood spread out from around the piece of glass sticking out of his chest.

'What the fuck?' Tommy Farrell, laden with boxes of designer trainers, stepped over the prostrate figure. 'Who's that? What's he doing here?'

'I dunno.' Davey sobered instantly as the enormity of what had happened suddenly hit him full force. 'He just appeared from nowhere and got in the way. He must have been following us. I didn't see him in the street, he just appeared and slipped on the fucking glass.'

'OK, shut up and get the stuff on the van. We've got to get out of here. We can do without this crap. Come on. One more armful each then everyone in the van and let's go.'

Without a second glance at the young man lying hurt on the bed of broken glass they threw in as much as they could through the rear doors of the van then three of them piled in on top of the haul and Tel jumped back into the driver's seat and they sped off.

It had taken a mere three minutes for them to steal half a million pounds' worth of clothes and shoes, and a couple of mountain bikes.

Davey looked back out of the small window in the van door at the nineteen year old they had left bleeding to death on the pavement and felt sick. It had been a stupid, spur-of-the-moment idea to take Eddie along and now it had all gone wrong. Suddenly sober, Davey could see Eddie was in mortal danger but there was nothing he could do for him without alerting the Farrells to his stupidity.

Chapter Thirteen

Maria and her father were in the car driving on the outskirts of town en route to Jenny's house when they heard the muffled sound of a crash in the distance.

'Sounds like there's been a bit of an accident. Bloody joy riders again no doubt, they all think they're invincible but every week there seems to be another tragedy reported in the paper.' Sam glanced briefly at his daughter sitting in the passenger seat beside him. 'Without being callous, I hope this doesn't hold us up, we have to find Eddie before your mother does. She's likely to spontaneously combust any minute now.'

'Yeah, or else she'll combust me.' Maria shrugged and pulled her duffel coat tight around her body. 'I promise, Dad, I really don't know where he is, and I'm really fed up with getting the blame for everything. Nothing I do is ever right. I did try talking to Mum earlier, you know, tried to make peace with her.'

Sam smiled. 'That's good to hear, but what brought it on?'

126

'Seeing Annalise, my schoolfriend who has cancer. I wish me and Mum could get on the way Annalise does with her mother. They're so close.'

'Yes, but I can see why they are. Tragedy has that effect on people. Makes them realise what the important things in life really are.'

'I know, that's what I thought when I left there, that's why I tried to talk to Mum. I thought it had gone quite well and then Eddie goes missing and again I get the blame.'

'I don't think you did really, she's just worried and lashing out without thinking, as usual. That's the problem with Eddie, we all want him to live a normal life but then when he does we panic. Anyway, let's hope we find him quickly. Jenny may at least have some idea of where he might be.'

They both looked ahead at the road.

'If we don't find him you know we're going to have to call the police.' Sam sighed. 'It's really late now.'

'Yeah, I know, I don't understand why he's done this, his sense of timing is usually spot on.' Maria's eyes darted back and forth across the road in front of her, desperately hoping that they might see Eddie, loping along with his hands in his pockets and a big grin on his face.

'Damn and blast,' Sam suddenly uttered. 'I've just remembered I was supposed to be somewhere tonight. I'm just going to make a quick call. I'll stop at the next phone box.'

Maria shook her head and sighed. 'Why don't you just move out, Dad? Go and live with Ruth? You love her, no one would blame you – apart from Patrick and Joe, of course, but they're both stupid, ignorant pigs without a nice bone between them.'

Sam grimaced and looked quickly at his daughter. 'And what about your mother? How could I do that to her? Anyway, I never said it was Ruth! Oh Maria, I wish you'd never found out about us, I hate the idea of you knowing that your father is . . . is a . . . is a . . .'

Maria completed the sentence for him. 'That my father is too soft for his own good? Oh Dad, I understand all this only too well, I am sixteen, I could be married by now, for God's sake. I can smoke, have sex, do whatever I like except go into a pub – legally, anyway.'

'You'd better not be spending time in pubs, my girl!' Sam smiled and shook his head as he pulled into the layby next to the phone box and jumped out, leaving Maria in the car. 'Back in a sec. Lock the doors until I get back.'

The sirens of police cars and ambulances wailed in the background, rapidly coming closer, and then in a blur they flashed past, making Maria jump in her seat.

'Right, let's go and find that erring brother of yours.' Sam spoke purposefully as he jumped back into the car. 'He can't be too far away'.

★

When Finola answered the phone she assumed instantly that it would be Sam with news of Eddie. But it wasn't.

The voice at the other end of the phone was efficient and to the point. Eddie's ID bracelet, the one Maria had bought him, had told them his name and next of kin. Eddie was seriously injured and his family should get to the hospital as soon as possible. Finola could feel her heart thumping fit to burst. Her worst nightmare, something happening to one of her boys, had become a reality.

'Patrick, Joe, quickly, I have to get to the hospital, Eddie's been in an accident. I don't know what's going on. I'll take a taxi, one of you try and get hold of your father. He was going to that Jenny's house, try and ring him there.'

Patrick, taking charge as always, grabbed his mother's coat and handed it to her. 'Joe, you try and get the old man, I'm going with Mum. You can follow when you've found him.' Patrick looked at Finola. 'What's happened to him? Did they tell you how he is?'

'No, nothing more than that it's serious, he's in a bad way. I knew it, I just knew it. When he didn't come home I knew, it's a mother's instinct, I'm telling you . . .' Her hands flapped about as she tried to get to grips with what was happening.

'Don't panic, the taxi is on its way, we'll be there soon.'

'What about your father?'

'I'm trying now,' Joe shouted over his shoulder. 'I'm waiting for someone to answer that bloody Jenny girl's phone.'

The taxi arrived. As it sped through the deserted streets to the hospital, Finola remembered back to when Eddie was a baby and he had contracted meningitis. No one had thought he would live through the night but Finola had got down on her knees at his bedside and prayed like she never had before. The first critical twenty-four hours had dragged into forty-eight before they had been given a glimmer of hope by the doctor. Her relief at his survival had been tempered slightly by the news that he may have some brain damage but that was manageable in her eyes. He was going to survive, she wasn't going to lose her youngest son.

For a while after that Finola had lost some of the self-control that had got her through the worst. It was as if she had been suddenly plunged into the depths of despair and then languished there for far longer than the time it took for Eddie to recover. It was during that time that she made the mistake that would change the rest of her life forever.

Now she wondered if she had just delayed the inevitable with Eddie, maybe he had always been destined to be taken from her as punishment.

The taxi pulled up and they jumped out and ran through to the casualty department.

'Where's my son?' Finola demanded of the receptionist. 'My son has had an accident, you phoned me, I want to see him now, where is he? Take me to him.'

Patrick pulled her back slightly by the arm. 'His name's Eddie Harman.'

'I'll call a doctor to see you, just take a seat.'

'We're not waiting while you meander through your bloody bits of paper,' Patrick said loudly. 'We want to see him and we want to see him NOW.'

'Don't do that, Patrick.' It embarrassed Finola when Patrick showed off in public. 'We'll take a seat and wait for the doctor. I know the procedure. But we need to call Father Richard, he'll want to be here.'

'I'll phone him in a minute. Let's see what's going on first. Eddie might be perfectly OK.'

Finola shook her head. 'No, he's not. A mother knows these things. Eddie isn't OK and he isn't going to be OK. Call Father Richard now, Patrick.'

She watched, her hands together in prayer, as he marched over to the public phone that afforded so little privacy under its small plastic bubble that she heard every word of his abrupt message to the priest.

Patrick had just returned to her side when a doctor appeared in front of them.

'Mrs Harman?'

Finola nodded and stood up expectantly.

'If you'd like to come through here please.'

He led them into an empty cubicle. 'I'm really sorry to have to tell you this but your son has been

in a serious accident and he is very badly injured.'
The doctor, who Finola thought didn't look a lot
older than her sons, gazed at her sympathetically.
'I'm afraid his injuries are so severe it's going to be
touch and go. I have to warn you, this is a life-
threatening situation although we're doing everything possible.'

'What happened?' Finola asked, not really wanting
to know the answer. How it happened wasn't as important as what was going to happen.

'No one really knows. I think the police will want
to speak to you about that, they found him, but he
has a severe injury to his chest area, many of his internal
organs are damaged.'

'By what, for heaven's sake? Has he been attacked?
How could it have happened?' Patrick fired the questions. Finola stood stock still, her face pale and expres-
sionless, the only movement a tic under her left eye
that pulled at the skin around her cheekbone.

'You really have to ask the police the details but a
large piece of glass appears to have fallen on him and
pierced right through his chest. His wound is similar
to a stab wound. I'll take you through to see him but
we're taking him down to surgery just as soon as
you've seen him, we have to move quickly now that
he's been stabilised.' The doctor's voice was kind
enough but his sense of urgency was apparent. Finola
could see that he wanted to get Eddie away for his
operation as quickly as possible but she knew she had

to see her son before they took him away. In her heart she was convinced she wouldn't get him back a second time.

'You can't take him until Father Richard gets here, he has to be seen by the priest, and what about his father? He's not here yet.'

'I'm sorry, but every second is vital if we're to have any chance of saving him. This way, please.'

Finola could feel her legs becoming weaker as they went through the doors to the resuscitation area and she saw her son. Tubes and machinery seemed to be entering and exiting every part of his body and his unmarked face was distorted by breathing tubes.

'Oh dear God, how can this have happened to my boy? Patrick, just look at him.'

'Mrs Harman, I'm really sorry but we have to take him now. We'll do our best.'

Finola leaned forward and as a solitary tear fell from her eye onto his naked shoulder, she touched Eddie carefully on his hand.

'See you soon, son. God will take care of you, whatever happens He'll look after you, one way or another.'

Patrick pulled her back and within seconds the staff were back round the trolley, getting ready to move him.

Almost in a trance she watched the group as they disappeared through the doors at the end of the corridor.

'Say goodbye to your brother, Patrick, say goodbye.'

'He'll be fine. You know Eddie. Don't worry, he'll be fine.'

A policeman appeared beside them.

'Mrs Harman? Could we have a word somewhere please? I need to talk to you about the events surrounding your son's accident.'

As they turned towards the privacy room, the two heavy plastic doors flapped wide and Sam and Maria ran forward.

'Where is he? What's happened?'

Slowly and purposefully Finola turned to face them. 'They've taken him away. They've taken him to the operating theatre but it's a waste of time, Eddie is going to die.'

Maria gasped out loud. 'What do you mean he's going to die? He can't die, he can't!' Her voice was high-pitched with terror and echoed down the now empty corridor.

'I mean exactly what I said. Now you just get out, get out of my sight. I want you out of this hospital, this is all your fault. For the rest of your life you will have this on your conscience. You made that boy go off and do things he would never have done without you egging him on. You are the spawn of the devil and I never want to see you again.' Finola could feel the anger rising inside her, an anger she had suppressed since her time in the abyss.

'No, Finola,' she heard Sam say. 'I know you're upset but you can't blame Maria.'

Suddenly Patrick swelled himself up to his full size and moved between his mother and Sam. 'You heard what she said, now get her out of here. She's not wanted.'

'One more word from you, Patrick, and I swear I'll flatten you,' Sam snarled. 'We're all staying here, all the family.'

'Mum doesn't want her.'

'I'm warning you, keep out of it. Your mother's upset and you're making it worse.' He turned to Maria and pulled her towards him. 'Maria stays, I stay, we all stay and that's an end to it. Where's Joe?'

Finola looked around at them all but the focus for all her emotion, all her hatred, was Maria. It was almost as if she didn't recognise her daughter. She stared at her as if she was an alien interloper in the family.

'Finola,' a familiar voice said from behind her. She turned and saw Father Richard striding towards them with Joe alongside.

Now they were all there.

Finola looked around at the group. Sam, her weak-willed husband who could have turned her life around for her if he had made a different decision. Patrick and Joe, both reminders of a happier time in her life. Father Richard who had helped her through the worst time of her life. And of course, Maria, the inter-loper she had never wanted in her family but who in her confusion she had been persuaded to take in.

As she looked, Finola felt herself becoming more detached, as if she was floating away from them all, far away.

Without another word she slumped to the floor.

Chapter Fourteen

'Harman! Look at me, Harman, you bastard!' Davey's father shouted across the narrow side street outside the court. 'Just wait till we get our hands on your fucking daughter. She got my boy sent down, she grassed him!'

Sam Harman, his face taut with anger and hurt, took a step off the pavement opposite, leaned forward and stared back at Davey's father, Charlie.

'You've got some nerve. Our son is dead. Just remember that. Eddie is dead because of your son, but your boy is still alive and kicking. Two years? Two years in a juvenile holiday camp, less if he manages to behave himself. That's *nothing*.' Sam's hands were tightly clenched in his jacket pockets as he continued. 'You'll get your son back but we won't ever see ours again. Our Eddie won't get his life back after two years because, just in case you've forgotten, we've buried him.'

Charlie Allsop, his other sons only a few steps behind, also stepped forward but he hesitated when he noticed two police officers walking sharply in their direction.

Charlie was a lot shorter than his sons but he was stocky and he had a full black beard and moustache that covered half his face. A black T-shirt stretched across his broad shoulders and showed off his heavily tattooed arms. He was by far the most intimidating of the family.

Sam, in contrast, was clean-shaven, his face pale, dressed for the occasion in a sober dark grey suit and tie.

Charlie's dark and angry eyes pierced Sam across the road. 'She didn't have to spill her guts, she didn't have to put Davey in the frame. It was a fucking freak accident, the coroner said so. She didn't have to ruin our Davey's life. Your precious Eddie went with him by choice. Do you hear me? By choice, he went by choice, why should my boy carry the can for that?'

Sam looked the man up and down and turned away but Patrick, also suited, continued to face up to the Allsops, almost encouraging them to take that extra step that would lead to a physical confrontation in front of the watching police.

Davey's family had shown up at the court en masse via the pub and obviously spoiling for a fight, their sense of injustice bubbling away, ready to erupt into violence at the slightest encouragement.

It had been clear to everyone right from the start that the actual sentence would be irrelevant. The Allsop family wanted to fight the Harmans whatever the outcome because it was Maria who had gone to the police.

With his guilt at Eddie's death overwhelming him, Davey had immediately held up his hands to the ram raid but he kept resolutely quiet about the Farrells' involvement. He had taken the full blame and denied vigorously that anyone else was involved but the police knew from the scene that there was no way Davey Allsop could have done that on his own. They were certain who the brains were behind the raid but the Farrells had used their criminal know-how to ensure that there was absolutely nothing to connect them to the raid, and their alibi for the whole night was watertight. They could somehow prove they were both in France with close friends.

Maria had confronted Davey. Without hesitation he had admitted that he had taken Eddie along with him on the raid as a way of getting back at Finola. Demented with both grief and anger, Maria had gone straight to the police. She risked bringing the wrath of both families down on herself, the Allsops because Davey was one of them and the Harmans because she then had to admit she knew that Davey had been hanging around the crescent and had befriended Eddie.

Now Davey was going to be locked up for his involvement in the raid. In a way, Maria already was, except she had locked herself away in Ruth's apartment.

As the Allsops continued to make threatening noises

outside the court, Patrick carried on snarling and aggravating the situation.

'I'm going to kick his brains in, I'm going to be waiting for that little shit when he comes out. As for the rest of you, a whole fucking family of deadbeats and losers, that's what you are,' Patrick ranted. 'Lying, thieving tinkers—'

'Oh, shut up, Patrick,' Sam snapped. He tried to grab Patrick by his arm. 'You sound like one of them. Isn't what's happened bad enough? Isn't your mother going through enough?'

Patrick spun round and for a split second Sam thought his son was going to hit him.

'And whose fault is that, eh? That bitch Maria, she's ruined this family, and you. You ruined this family the day you brought her into it. Well, now you can keep her out of it. Forever.'

'None of this is Maria's fault, as you well know,' Sam retaliated angrily. 'Davey Allsop used her the same way he used Eddie. She didn't have a clue about any of it!'

'Of course she knew. They're sick, the pair of them, they were in it together and now she's got off scot-free.' The hatred in his voice made Sam take an instinctive step back.

'I'm sick of you making mileage out of this tragedy and I'm not going to have you talk like that, Patrick. You'll keep a civil tongue in your head when you talk about your sister, about anyone in fact.'

Patrick stared his father in the eye. His upper lip twitched into a sneer.

'Bollocks to you, old man, you're nothing to me,' he spat.

'How dare you.' Despite his determination not to let his son get to him, Sam couldn't disguise his shock. 'Don't you ever talk to me like that, I'm your father.'

'Not any more, you're not. Why don't you and Maria just piss off and leave the rest of us in peace? Mum doesn't want either of you. Go get the bitch and then get out of our lives.'

Sam couldn't believe what he was hearing. He had always tried to be as fair as possible to Patrick because he knew that Finola had brought him up to believe he could do no wrong. But despite knowing why Patrick was as he was, Sam still found his attitude hard to take. He was so angry it was on the tip of his tongue to justify himself but he stayed silent, he didn't want to give Patrick any more information with which to taunt the already splintered family.

Drawing on all his reserves of self-control, Sam shook his head and turned and walked away, leaving Patrick to make his own decision whether to fight or flee the Allsops. In a way Sam hoped he would fight and that the Allsops would beat him to a pulp.

'It'll be OK in time, María love, you really did do the right thing. You know that, don't you?' Ruth Easter looked sadly at the distraught girl curled up in front of her. 'It seems worse again today because you know Davey's in court, it's brought it all back.'

'How could it be the right thing when I've caused Eddie's death? Patrick is right, I've torn my family apart, I might just as well have stabbed Eddie myself.' Maria cried, great big sobs that racked her body. Her damp hair clung to her scalp and her face was blotched and ruddy from the constant crying.

'Sshh, come on now.' Ruth crouched down beside her, wrapped her in her arms and rocked her back and forth like a baby. 'You didn't tear the family apart and you certainly didn't cause Eddie's death. Did you know what Davey was planning to do? No you didn't. Did you know Eddie was with Davey? No. It was a terrible, terrible accident brought about by a combination of circumstances. And, to be fair, Davey himself wouldn't have known what was going to happen, it was a freak accident.'

'But why did it have to be Eddie? Out of all the people he could have chosen, why Eddie? Why did he have to take him along with him? Poor Eddie who wouldn't have known what to say, he wouldn't have had a clue what was going on.'

Ruth thought carefully before she answered, she didn't want to lay all the blame on Davey Allsop but at the same time she didn't want Maria taking all the blame for it on herself.

'Sadly that's probably why he got caught up in it. No one else would have gone along with it. Davey was being a smart-arse thinking he could upset your mother. He obviously didn't think about the things that could go wrong. He was a stupid, stupid boy who just didn't think.'

'What do you think he'll get? Do you think they'll send him to jail?'

'I hope so. Maybe if Davey learns his lesson now it'll set him on the right course for the future. I know you liked the lad but let's face it he was definitely on the way to a life of crime.' Gently she carried on stroking Maria's hair as if she was a small child. 'Maybe just a little good will come out of this eventually if Davey Allsop realises that there are consequences for doing the wrong thing and learns from it.'

Maria leaned back and rested her head on the soft leather that had the comforting smell of her father engrained in the wings.

Being cooped up with nothing to do except watch TV, eat comfort food and read magazines, she had put on a lot of weight and looked pasty and dishevelled. The tight jeans and skimpy tops that she used to wear had been replaced with baggy tracksuits and oversized T-shirts that covered up everything. She didn't care, in fact she felt better when she looked a mess, and when she thought about it she could understand the biblical sackcloth and ashes.

'Do you think Eddie knew he was going to die? Do you think he realised what was happening? Maybe he didn't see the glass. If he didn't look up he wouldn't have seen it . . .'

Ruth looked at Maria sadly. Her reddened eyes begged for reassurance. It had been six months since Eddie had died but the pain and guilt eating away at Maria was getting worse rather than better. In the beginning a natural numbness had made it easier to bear but as that wore off, it uncovered a gnawing pain that was a constant reminder.

'You're torturing yourself now and there's really no need. You know what the coroner said. Exactly what you just said. He would have passed out instantly as the glass hit him, he wouldn't have known what happened, he wouldn't have seen it coming.'

'But he must have known he was doing something wrong, out that late and with Davey. He knew, I'd told him not to go near Davey, I'd told him . . .'

'Maybe he was actually enjoying himself and forgot everything you had said.' Ruth tried to choose her words carefully. 'Maybe he thought it was all just a laugh. Eddie didn't have the same take on life as the rest of us. He was uncomplicated and could never have analysed the situation. He thought he had a new friend and was happy. You have to focus on that, Maria, you have to believe it, because I know it's true and so does your dad. The rest of it is nonsense and your mother knows that, she's just grieving and saying things she doesn't mean. And Patrick, well. He's just being Patrick. If he can get mileage out of this then he will. That's his style.' Ruth pushed herself up and walked over to the kitchen. 'I'm having a cup of hot chocolate, do you want one? It'll help you relax.'

'Do you think Mum will ever forgive me?'

'Give her time,' Ruth murmured comfortingly, 'give her time. She's hurting as well and looking for a reason for what happened to Eddie. She wants someone to blame but she'll come round, I'm sure she will.' But Ruth knew these were empty words. Finola would never forgive her daughter.

'I can't stay here, can I? I have to move away.'

'You don't have to go anywhere. It'll all blow over eventually and you can stay here until it does. Once the pain of the grief has eased a little your mother will realise. The Allsops will be dealt with by the police and they'll have to leave you alone.'

'That's crap, Ruth,' Maria spat. She jumped up and started pacing back and forth like a caged cat. 'You don't know my mother, do you? She really hates me, she always has and this was just the confirmation she's been looking for, that I am no bloody good.' Maria ignored the burning tears running down her cheeks onto her jumper and pulled back her shoulders. 'No, I have to get away. I want to go to London and start out on my own, make my own way now. Will you help me, Ruth? Please? I don't know who else to ask.'

The shrill ringing of the phone made them both jump.

Maria looked at Ruth. 'That'll be Dad at the court.'

Ruth went to the phone. 'Are you ready for this, Maria love? The case must be over, Davey will have been sentenced. Maybe this will bring an end to all the nastiness and we'll all get back to normal.'

Chapter Fifteen

Ruth Easter stretched out on the sofa and shook her head to try to stay awake. The tiredness she felt after twenty-four hours with only catnaps was threatening to overwhelm her but she knew she couldn't go to bed.

Apart from the brief phone call from outside the court the day before to tell them about Davey's sentence, they had heard nothing from Sam and as time had gone on Maria had become progressively more hysterical. The fact that Davey had been sent to jail had terrified Maria and it had been left to Ruth to calm her down. She had been convinced that the Allsops would try to get to her as they had threatened to do if Davey was sent down.

Despite being fond of Sam's daughter, who Ruth felt had been given a rough deal by both the Harmans and the Allsops, she resented not having the support that she felt Sam owed her in her condition. Twirling her fat, puffy ankles in the air, and automatically massaging her swollen belly, Ruth felt her baby kick back at her hands. Savouring the movements from inside her belly, she contemplated everything that had happened since Eddie's death.

It seemed a lifetime ago that she had agonised over whether or not to tell Sam. Just as she had decided to have a termination and not tell him anything about it, Eddie's accident had happened and everything went on hold.

Until the day she had found herself in a position with no choice but to confront it.

'I don't know how you're coping with all this,' Maggie had sighed as she took a gulp from the long-stemmed glass. 'I don't think I could deal with it, what with everything going on here and trying to keep on top at work, it's mad!'

'You don't have to tell me.' Ruth shook her head and smiled ruefully. 'From just having myself and of course our business to look after, suddenly I have a bereaved teenager living in my spare room who blames herself for the death of her brother, and her father, my occasional boyfriend, is so overwhelmed with guilt himself that he's hardly ever here to help.'

Maggie glanced sideways at her friend and then carried on looking silently ahead as Ruth carried on.

'I can understand their terrible grieving, really I can, but the rest of it is so very tiring. And of course in the middle of it all my other little problem still hasn't been resolved.'

Ruth and Maggie had been on the balcony for most

of the afternoon, with their feet up on the railings, drinking a bottle of wine and talking over everything that Eddie's recent death had thrown up.

'Where are they both now?' Maggie asked curiously. 'It all seems peaceful enough here right now. Are they both out?'

'Yep. That's why I begged you to come and join me. Don't get me wrong, I feel so bad for both of them, it is such an unimaginably terrible thing to happen. I'd never met Eddie but I know he had problems and according to Maria was the nicest person in the whole family.' Ruth paused and looked out over the perfectly laid-out communal garden below where the elderly gardener was pottering in the flower beds. He looked up and waved. Ruth smiled and waved back.

'But . . .' Maggie prompted her.

'But somehow I'm in the middle of it all and I really don't want to be. Finola won't have anything to do with Maria because she blames her for everything but meanwhile she suddenly wants Sam there. She never bloody wanted him before, yet now, when his daughter needs him so much, he goes off and leaves her with me.'

'Mmmm. Dodgy one that. I suppose in fairness to Sam he feels he must support Finola, they were both parents to Eddie.'

'I know. I just feel so helpless in the face of it all. Hormones, I suppose, they're making me look for complications and confrontations.'

Maggie laughed, causing the gardener to look up again. 'Oh, I don't think so. The whole situation is a bit bizarre and I don't doubt it will get worse before it gets better, it's only been a few weeks.'

Ruth leaned back in her chair and turned her face towards the sun. 'I know, and I could cry for them, really I could, but I still have my own life to consider, and of course the business. I'm self-supporting and need my income, as I know you do.'

'Oh, we can manage a few lousy weeks without you up to speed, I'm sure. Anyway, what about your other problem, as you call it?' Maggie asked. 'Have you reached a decision yet?'

'I thought I had. I was going to have a termination and not tell Sam about it but now I'm in such a quandary.'

Maggie didn't say anything, she just looked into her glass and waited for Ruth to continue.

'Maggie, how can I possibly toddle off to a clinic and abort Sam's child when he's just lost a son? How can I do that? And yet, how can I tell him at this moment in time that I'm pregnant with his child?'

'I don't know. Why don't you try?'

Maggie and Ruth both jumped. They looked round to see Sam standing close behind them just inside the open plate-glass doors that separated the sitting room from the balcony.

'I didn't hear you come in, I wasn't expecting you back yet. Where's Maria?' Ruth muttered, her face bright red with confusion and embarrassment. She couldn't believe that she hadn't heard Sam coming up behind them.

'Maria's with Annalise for a couple of hours, and yes, I can see that you weren't expecting me. I think there are things we should be talking about, don't you?' Sam's voice was cool and calm but his face was pale and his demeanour rigid. 'I know what I'm going to do, I'm going to pour myself a large brandy and wait for you in the kitchen – until you've finished confiding in your friend instead of me.' He turned sharply and left the two of them looking at each other aghast.

'Oh fuck!' Maggie grimaced. 'Now you've really done it.'

'I know. I wonder how much he heard.'

'Oh, pretty much everything, I'd reckon. Still, at least you don't have to torment yourself any longer looking for the right moment.' Maggie smiled wryly.

'One way to look at it I suppose. You stay here, I'll be back in a while.'

Maggie stood up and shook her head. 'Not a chance. I'm off now to let you and Sam sort this out on your own. Not for me to be involved. You know what I think, this is how it should be – both of you talking it through.' She had grabbed her friend by the shoulders and kissed her affectionately on both cheeks, whispering in her ear as she did so, 'Good luck, but remember, darling, it's ultimately your decision, don't be railroaded either way just because you feel guilty.'

As soon as Maggie had left, Ruth had found Sam lying on the bed, with his hands under his head, just staring at the ceiling.

'Sam, I'm sorry—'

'No. It's OK,' he interrupted. 'I can see why you didn't tell me.' Smiling sadly, he reached out to her. 'I can't say I'm not shocked, but maybe this was meant to be.'

Ruth sat on the edge of the bed but didn't make eye contact. 'What shall we do?'

'What do you want to do?'

In that instant, Ruth knew exactly what she wanted to do. 'I want to have our baby, Sam.'

'I was hoping you'd say that.'

The sound of the front door opening snapped Ruth sharply back to the present. She hurried through to the lobby, reaching it just as Sam stepped over the threshold.

'Sam! Where the hell have you been? It's been a whole day since I heard from you.'

With a crash, she slammed the door and marched into the sitting room with Sam close behind. 'You told me to tell Maria you wouldn't be long. The poor kid's been tearing her hair out and I'm totally shattered.'

As she turned to face Sam, he leaned forward to kiss her but she backed away; she wasn't in the mood to be kind and understanding.

'I'm so sorry, love, but I really had to go and tell

Finola what had happened in court. It was only fair, especially after Patrick got himself embroiled in a set-to with the Allsops. I despair of him, he was just looking for a fight.'

Ruth shook her head. 'And I despair of you. If you want to talk fair then it was only fair that you should come back here and tell your sixteen-year-old daughter exactly what was going on. She's been up all night terrified that the Allsops are going to come after her and it's not been a barrel of laughs for me either, I'm so very tired.'

As she looked at Sam's bewildered expression, Ruth could feel her exasperation reach boiling point.

'You don't realise, do you? Sam, I'm sorry but I'm fast getting to the point where I just want to say fuck Finola! She chose her route, she chose to shut Maria out of her life. I mean, let's face it, holy Finola doesn't know or care where her daughter's been these past six months, yet you toddle off straight back there when she whistles you up like a bloody Border collie. Maria shouldn't have had to hear all about it second-hand from me. That was your job. You should have been here with her.'

Sam moved towards her apologetically, his hands outstretched in the gesture that she usually reciprocated. But she stood resolutely still with her arms crossed over the top of her bump.

'You're right, I know you're right and I should deal with it all differently perhaps, but Finola—'

'But Finola nothing.' Ruth was so angry she was bordering on hysteria. 'You could have left it to Patrick to tell her. You're going to have to decide exactly what you want. You can't keep splitting yourself in pieces over a woman who doesn't love you and two sons who despise you. I am having our baby any day and it's time to look to the future.'

'I had to speak to her face to face. Eddie was her son as well, this has been so hard for her.'

Ruth shook her head in despair at his almost innocent lack of comprehension. 'Not so hard that she couldn't use the situation to torment Maria even more! Look, I know the timing isn't good but you have to make up your mind. You can't keep two families on the go like this.'

'I know, but things should get back to normal now that young Allsop's been dealt with at last.'

'No, Sam. I've been thinking about this all night while I've been trying to stay awake to care for your daughter. Things are not going to go back to normal, as you put it. It's all going to change.'

Sam looked stunned as Ruth spoke the words she had always promised herself she would never say.

'I mean it, you have to decide how you're going to play this long term. Finola or me. You have to choose.'

'How can I choose with things as they are? Finola needs me.' Sam's shoulders were hunched and the corners of his mouth drooped and Ruth suddenly thought he looked older than his years; in fact in the previous few months he had probably aged five years, but she knew she had to harden herself, she had their child to consider.

'Sorry, but you're going to have to. We're over six months down the line since the accident and I'm nearly nine months pregnant and in limbo, I don't know whether I'm coming or going.'

Again he reached out for her but she turned away.

'Please, Ruth, I can't do anything at the moment, I really can't.'

'Well, I can do something. If you continue to live at King's Crescent then we can't carry on as we are. What I want you to do now is go home, go back to Finola and your single beds and think about it. Then, when you've made a decision you can come back and let me know.'

He gasped in surprise and took a step back. She hardened herself to look directly at him, her expression deadly serious.

'Sam, you wanted me to have this baby and you promised you would be there, that we would be together, but it's not happening, is it? Now Maria wants to move away and, to be honest, I'm seriously thinking of going with her. The only thing keeping her going right now is looking forward to the arrival of our baby. She could live with me.'

'You can't move away, your life is here and your job. I'm here.'

'No, Sam, my life is wherever I choose to live it.

Many years ago I chose to stay near you but I can just as easily choose to stay away from you.'

'You don't mean this, do you, Ruth? What about the baby?'

'Wrong question, Sam. You'll have to do better than that.'

Chapter Sixteen

Finola Harman had obsessively cleaned the house from top to bottom. Every nook and cranny in every room had been dusted and polished, every drawer and cupboard emptied and tidied. There was not a single thing left to be done in the whole building but instead of putting the vacuum cleaner back under the stairs and the polish under the sink she prepared to start all over again.

Anything to take her mind off her discovery.

Finola had known, and accepted, many years before that Sam had a mistress. She had never spoken about it to him or in fact to anyone, but she knew. She guessed that he thought it was a well-kept secret and had gone to great lengths to try to keep it from her but it actually hadn't bothered her. She had even accepted that Maria was party to her father's infidelity and friendly with his mistress. In a strange way she had even been grateful when she had found out for sure about Ruth because it had instantly justified the single beds that she had had installed just after they brought Maria home to King's Crescent. The single beds that had signalled an immediate end to her unsatisfactory and unwanted sex life.

Once everything had settled down, it hadn't taken Sam long to bond with his adopted daughter, but no matter how hard she tried Finola just couldn't accept her. Every time she looked at the strange baby in her crib who bore no resemblance to her other three children, her precious sons, she felt nothing for her other than resentment and guilt. Bringing home and bringing up the baby had been Sam's idea and also his decision, although there had been considerable pressure brought to bear on her by Granny Bentley, her own mother. Finola knew she should have resisted but at the time it had seemed easier to agree, especially when Sam had promised he would always be there for her and Maria and their sons.

If only things had been different. Maybe if Maria had been their child—

The ringing of the doorbell interrupted Finola's thoughts. Briefly she wondered if she could get away with ignoring it but then she remembered she had left the door on the latch.

Peering round the kitchen door into the hall, she thought she recognised the large outline visible through the stained-glass panel at the top of the front door. It looked like Mrs Callaghan, Father Richard's unbearably nosy and gossipy housekeeper.

Before Finola could slide out of sight, the letterbox rattled open and a pair of eyes blinked at her.

'Hello there, Finola. Finola? I heard the news about that Allsop boy, I've just come to see how you are . . .'

Reluctantly Finola opened the door and Mrs Callaghan lumbered past, talking nonstop, and headed straight towards the kitchen.

'Oh Finola, I was so worried about you, how's the family coping with all this upset? Still, it's a good thing that troublesome Allsop hooligan is locked up. Please God they'll thrash the living daylights out of him in that Borstal-type place and teach him a lesson.' She lowered herself carefully onto the chair with a groan, pulled up her voluminous skirt and rubbed her swollen knees.

'The pain I have to put up with; this arthritis will be the death of me. Anyway, as I was saying, I always knew he was no good, and as for that girl of yours,' she paused and rolled her eyes meaningfully, 'I'm sure you won't mind me saying but, well, she's not much better. I hear she's run off now. You're best rid of her, if you ask me, something rotten in her no doubt, but you must have known that when you took her in . . .'

There was no let-up until a pot of tea had been made, brewed, poured and the cup actually at Mrs Callaghan's lips.

'I'd rather not talk about it if you don't mind,' Finola eventually said when she had the opportunity to speak. 'It's finished now and I just want to get over it all and get our lives back to normal. Anyway, Father Richard has been a tremendous help to me, I really don't need—'

'Oh, I'm sure he has in his own way but he has no idea really, he's a man.' She leaned forward on her elbows towards Finola and despite there being no one else in the house said in a stage whisper, 'And of course he's a man who's never known a woman. He doesn't understand the way another woman does, but I know what you're going through, my dear.' She reached across and patted Finola's cheek as if she were a child. 'Father Richard is so concerned about you and how you're coping, he asked me to visit you. He trusts me, you know.'

Edna Callaghan was well into her seventies but she hung on to her job as housekeeper to the priest because it was all she had in her life and he felt sorry for her. A widow with a daughter who was married and had emigrated to Australia, she had been left embittered and lonely.

She carried on talking nineteen to the dozen.

Although her obesity and dodgy joints made movement slow and difficult, her face remained remarkably unlined for her age and she still had her hair permed and coloured platinum blonde. She wore flowing and flowery clothes and with her strangely flamboyant swipe of red lipstick she actually looked quite good for her age.

Finola shook herself back to the conversation and jumped in quickly.

'Did you say Father Richard asked you to visit? Now that's very strange, he knows I'm OK, Mrs C, because I spoke to him only this morning. But enough about me, tell me about your Angela. How is she and that handsome husband of hers? In Australia, aren't they? What a shame you can't get to see them more than once every few years.'

A snort echoed across the table. 'That good-for-nothing wastrel, he'll see her off, I'm sure. He only married her to get his hands on my money. Well, he won't get it, mark my words, all he'll get is his come-uppance. Can you believe that a man would do that? That he would take a daughter away from her wid-owed mother? Take precious grandchildren away from their grandmother? That is so wicked . . .'

Finola had long learnt that the best way to stop Mrs Callaghan prying and digging was to ask about her Angela. Everyone knew that Angela and her husband had emigrated to Australia because it was the furthest they could get away from her constant interfering.

Nowadays her interference was limited mainly to Father Richard himself and any of his parishioners that Mrs Callaghan either took to or against. Finola knew she was one of the few people that the woman had taken to and was unsure whether it was good or bad. At least if she took against someone then she would talk about them behind their back rather than turn up on their doorstep.

As Mrs Callaghan went on and on about Angela

and her no-good husband, Finola's thoughts drifted to where they had been before she had been interrupted. In fact she was so far away that it took a few seconds for her to register exactly what Mrs Callaghan was saying.

'Mrs Callaghan, would you repeat that please? What did you just say?'

'Repeat what?'

'Repeat what you just said about my daughter.'

Mrs Callaghan sighed. 'I said that Bridget Hudson had seen her walking along by the river and, noticing that she looked pregnant, wondered if that Allsop boy was the father. I mean I know it's none of our business and to be fair it was probably expected with Maria being as she is . . .' She paused just long enough for the words to sink in before continuing with a compassionate expression on her face that didn't match the words coming out of her mouth. 'Still, I suppose if you don't know where the child is even living then you wouldn't know she was pregnant, would you?'

Finola, unable to believe what she was hearing, jumped up and shook her head vehemently. 'Maria most certainly is not pregnant, Mrs Callaghan, and I'm surprised at you spreading rumours like that. Father Richard would be horrified if he knew you were in here gossiping, especially under the circumstances.'

As soon as the words were out and she saw the expression on Mrs Callaghan's face, Finola could have kicked herself. She had instantly handed the woman an even better piece of gossip to add to the Chinese whispers.

Maria Harman is pregnant and her mother didn't even know.

The news, true or false, would spread like wildfire across the parish, thanks to Mrs Callaghan.

Despite the fact that her heart was thumping in her chest and her knees were feeling weak, Finola forced herself to smile at her visitor. 'Nice as it's been to see you, Mrs Callaghan, I have to get on now. Sam and the boys will be home soon and I still have to get the dinner prepared. There's not enough time in the day when you've got a family to care for, a family that still lives with you.' Edna Callaghan's face dropped as Finola, now standing really close to her, turned the knife and reminded her viciously of everything she had lost. Finola didn't care in the least. All she wanted was the woman and her words out of her house so that she could think what to do, how to find out if there was any truth in the rumour.

Maybe it was true, she thought as she closed the door and retreated back to her duster. Maybe bad blood will always out as they say and Maria really was bad through and through. Maybe she really did take after her natural parents.

Finola sank to her knees in the middle of her hallway, clasped her hands and bowed her head.

'Dear God, don't let this be true, please God, let

Maria not be pregnant, please don't let her heap any more shame on this family. And that woman also. Please don't let her be having Sam's bastard, that would be too much for me to bear,' she repeated over and over again.

When Finola had first realised that Sam was seeing someone else she had made a point of finding out as much as she could about the woman and the relationship. She knew she could easily turn a blind eye to Sam sleeping with someone else, it relieved her of the duty she never wanted to be part of again, but she needed to know if her marriage, her security and her reputation would be at risk.

It hadn't been too difficult to find out all she needed to know and not once did she let slip to Sam or anyone else what she discovered. Only the private investigator she had employed knew.

Ever the pessimist, Finola had always saved as much money as she could each week from the house-keeping. In her eyes she felt entitled to it, she called it her insurance policy and kept the building society book tucked away under the lining of her under-wear drawer, her favourite hiding place for anything she didn't want seen. It had cost her some of this insurance to pay the private investigator but it had been worth it.

As a result Finola knew Ruth's name, her age, where she lived, where she worked, even where she shopped. She knew everything except the person herself. Many times she had thought about going into the office in town to ask about renting a house but had decided against it. There was no way she wanted Sam to know that she knew.

She had watched and waited and as time went on and everything stayed the same at home, she had relaxed and trusted the words Sam had spoken all those years ago when he had promised he would always be there for them all.

Until this week, when Finola had gone into town for the first time since before Eddie's death and out of habit had detoured past Ruth's office. Her timing couldn't have been better, or worse, because just at that moment Ruth walked up the street. The sight of Sam's mistress walking towards her with an advanced pregnancy on show had hit Finola between the eyes like a flying brick. Quickly she had ducked into the nearest shop and, breathing deeply, stayed hidden until Ruth had disappeared from sight.

The thought of Sam fathering another child so soon after Eddie's death made Finola want to chase after the woman and rip the baby from her body. Instead she focused on Maria who was now living with the woman and was party to it all.

What if Edna Callaghan was right about Maria?

Finola carried on praying almost maniacally. A part of her desperately wanted to love her daughter and be loved back but the brick wall of shame and guilt that had been built up over so many years was too high.

When Maria had gone and stayed gone, Finola had felt nothing but relief at not having to see her every single day of her life.

Chapter Seventeen

'What do you want really? A boy or a girl? Come on, tell me, I won't tell anyone.' Maria nudged Ruth's elbow playfully.

'In all honesty? Cross my heart and hope to die? I don't mind at all. Just healthy, that's all I ask. I know everyone says that but I really mean it.' Ruth smiled and Maria watched affectionately as she dipped her fork into the over-large slice of coffee gateau.

'Hormones,' she muttered. 'I didn't order this, my hormones did.'

'Yes, I know, but don't change the subject. Come on, you must have a preference. Mum and Dad had three boys and then really wanted a girl so they adopted me . . .' Maria resisted the urge to carry the sentence to its usual end. She had promised Ruth she would try to look forward.

'Well, I can understand that,' Ruth murmured. 'If you've got three of one sex then maybe you might fancy a change but I really don't mind. This is my first and probably my last, I'm certainly too old to start producing a football team.'

It caught Maria unawares to hear herself laugh spontaneously. Her misery had been so profound for so long she had thought she would never be anywhere near normal again. Yet here she was in a swanky coffee shop on the opposite side of town well away from the Harmans and the Allsops, talking about something other than Eddie and Davey and actually enjoying herself. A wave of gratitude and affection swept over her; she knew that it was only thanks to Ruth who had reiterated over and over again that Eddie's death was not her fault.

Much as Maria loved her father, she was becoming even more aware of how weak he could be when it came to his wife. He just couldn't seem to stop himself from rushing back to Finola every time she tweaked the invisible but oh so strong thread that joined them. Neither she nor Ruth could figure out why the bond was so strong when the relationship had been a disaster for so many years.

'Thank you, Ruth.' With a grin Maria suddenly leaned across and kissed her on the cheek.

'What was that for? A coffee and a piece of cake? And thick gloopy fattening cake at that, but then again, who cares? I'm eating for two.'

'You are so you've got an excuse but I really need to cut down. I've put on about two stone since you know when and I look as pregnant as you!' Maria rubbed her belly the same way she had seen Ruth do and made a silly groaning noise.

'Cut that out, you, you're laughing at me!'

'What I meant was thank you for everything. For doing everything you did for me.' Maria looked intently at Ruth. 'You'll be such a good mother to your baby, I wish you were mine.'

Ruth blinked rapidly and smiled. 'Do you know, that's the nicest thing that anyone has ever said to me. I think you're a cracking daughter.'

'Mmmm, my mother wouldn't agree with you on that—'

'Come on now,' Ruth interrupted sharply. 'We're definitely not going to go back to that, we agreed. None of us is perfect so we have to take the good with the bad and accept that some things won't change immediately. Now you've got to look ahead to your new life. A new home and a new baby brother or sister.'

'I know, and I am looking forward to it but I really, really wanted to move to London and have a life of my own away from everyone who knows about Eddie and Davey, everyone who blames me. I could just imagine myself in somewhere like London earning loads of money.' Her voice had taken on an involuntary pleading edge as she thought about all the fantasies she had had about making it on her own in the big city. Living in a village with a sort of stepmother, a half-brother or -sister and an occasional father certainly wasn't what she hankered after.

'One step at a time. You'll soon be seventeen and

you've got all your life ahead of you to do weird and wacky things. Right now you can't afford to support yourself and pay rent in London so this is a compromise just for the moment, till you have some qualifications.' This time it was Ruth who nudged Maria. 'And the house is fantastic, isn't it? Go on, admit it!'

'Oh God, yes, I love it, it's gorgeous, but—'

'No buts,' Ruth interrupted. 'I know it probably seems a bit isolated to you but you can soon have driving lessons and now she's so much better you could have Annalise to stay for the odd weekend.'

'Do you think Dad will come and live there as well?'

Ruth chewed her lip thoughtfully 'It's difficult, Maria. Your father has other commitments as you know. It's a hard time for him right now but we'll see after the baby is born – if it's born! It's overdue and I'm beginning to think I'm not pregnant at all, it's just wind.'

'Maggie lives near the new house, doesn't she?'

'Fairly near but she lives further out in the sticks with lots of mud and animals and children. I don't think I could do that. I'm not a country person. No, this is a happy medium, it's not in town but it's not in the middle of nowhere. I couldn't bring up a child in the apartment in town, prams and stairs don't go together naturally.'

Maria leaned back in her chair, folded her arms and then looked down, wondering how to phrase her real concern without sounding sorry for herself; but she had to know.

'Ruth, I know you said I could live with you but I'm scared I'll be in the way, you and the baby or you, Dad and the baby, you'll be a real family. Because I was adopted Patrick always called me the cuckoo in the nest. Well, we're not even a little bit related so won't I still be the cuckoo?'

'Patrick's a prat of the first order as you well know,' Ruth snapped, 'and he certainly won't be part of this family – not that he'd want to, mind. But you are welcome to live with us as long as you want, whatever the circumstances. I want my baby to know his or her big sister.' She paused and smiled. 'And anyway, I need you for a bit of grown-up conversation else I'll go baby ga-ga very quickly. I'm not like Maggie who thrives on riotous children.'

Maria looked out of the window at the passers-by racing along to beat the black thunderclouds gathering overhead. She hadn't heard the words that had been exchanged between Ruth and her father the day after Davey Allsop's trial, but she had immediately noticed the tension and the fact that, despite the impending birth, Ruth was suddenly house-hunting out of town without Sam. Then had come the announcement, 'I've bought a house in the country!'

Sam's face when she had broken the news had told Maria that he hadn't been a part of the decision and the ensuing stilted conversation told her he wasn't at all happy about it either.

But Maria was ecstatic as soon as she had seen it. Compared to the house in King's Crescent, which hadn't been modernised in all the years they'd lived there, the new house was a palace. It wasn't huge and because it was only a few years old, it didn't have much character but it was detached and set way back from the road which meant the front garden was larger than the back, and the lawn, edged with climbing roses that disguised the fence, encircled the house on all sides. But best of all was the ultra modern bathrooms and full central heating.

'Are you still with me? You look miles away all of a sudden.' Ruth nudged her again.

'Sorry, just thinking about the house. Can I really have the bedroom at the back? The one with its own bathroom? Won't you want that for the baby?'

Ruth rubbed her distended belly ruefully. 'I know this bump here looks huge but it is really only a tiny baby. It will sleep with me to start with and after that it won't take up much room for years. It certainly won't need its own bathroom for many years.' She pushed back her chair and stood up clumsily, using the table and the back of the chair as props. Once up, she kept a hand on the table and sighed loudly. 'This is getting impossible, one day I won't be able to get up at all! Come on, we'd better get home before the rain really starts, it's black as pitch out there for this time of the day.'

After quickly paying the bill, Ruth looped her arm through Maria's for support and they headed off through the light drizzle in the direction of the car park which was set back from the road behind a high brick wall.

'Well, I'll be fucked! Look at that, everyone, it's that Harman slapper who got our Davey sent down! The one who grassed him up to the Old Bill!'

Maria physically jumped as she heard the shrill voice close behind her. Spinning round she found herself face to face with Davey Allsops's sister Karen, along with half a dozen other teenage girls.

Karen Allsop stepped forward until she was as close as she could be without actually touching Maria. The eldest Allsop girl had a reputation as a spiteful street fighter and Maria could feel herself trembling. Not so much in fear for herself but for Ruth who was standing beside her looking bewildered but with an arm instinctively wrapped across her unborn baby.

'Here, you lot, look at her. A big fat squealer pissing her pants now she hasn't got Daddy to protect her. Where have you been hiding out? In the pig trough?'

The gang of girls all screamed with laughter and started making oinking noises.

'Leave Maria alone and get out of my way, please, there's no need for this.' Ruth grabbed Maria's hand and tried to pull her forward but the girls slowly closed in until they were in a tight semicircle with Maria and Ruth backed up against the inside of the car park wall.

Maria looked for the best route to the car but there was no easy way to get past them with a very pregnant Ruth unable to run.

'Let her go to the car, please.' Maria looked at Karen Allsop and nodded her head towards Ruth. 'You can see she's pregnant and due any minute, just let her pass and then we'll sort this out between the two of us.'

Karen's face twisted with hate. 'Fuck off, Harman. I've got you now. You really think I'm going to let her go and get help for you?' She laughed and then stared at Ruth. 'Who is she anyway?'

Quick as a flash Maria answered before Ruth could open her mouth. 'She works in the café, I was making sure she got to her car OK. She's having pains.'

'Who gives a fuck?' Karen sneered. With one quick movement of her eyes she mobilised the girls who were with her and in a moment Maria was on the wet ground flat on her back, her arms and legs pinned down by an array of hands and Karen's booted foot on her throat.

'Now you're going to find out just what happens to anyone who crosses the Allsops. You fucked up our Davey and now I'm going to really fuck you up.'

Very slowly she moved her foot almost gently from Maria's neck and slid it down to her stomach before raising it high and then stamping it down as hard as she could just under Maria's ribcage. Maria screamed in agony and as the girls loosened their grip on her limbs she rolled over, pulling her legs up and wrapping her arms over her head. She knew exactly what they were going to do next.

The last thing Maria remembered before all the feet surrounding her thudded into every inch of her body was hearing Ruth's high-pitched scream in the distance.

It sounded as if she was far, far away.

Chapter Eighteen

Sam was angry, in fact he was absolutely furious.

Once again Finola had called him at his office, saying she needed to speak to him, that it was urgent and couldn't wait. Once again, after apologising profusely to his assistant for leaving her in the lurch, he had raced to King's Crescent, worried that there really was an emergency. Once again it was yet another gripe about Maria.

In the months after Eddie's death Sam had become increasingly concerned for his wife's mental health. She was at church every day, sometimes twice a day and for hours on end; he knew that although all her anger was directed at Maria, it was really herself she blamed. She saw Eddie's death as inevitable, something that was destined to happen as a punishment for her past sins.

Under the circumstances, Sam felt responsible for his wife despite the pressure he was under from both Ruth and Maria to break away. He had done his best to be detached and to get help from the church but his half-hearted attempts to talk to Father Richard always failed. Their conversations were stilted and nonproductive as the two men warily skirted around the problems, each not sure how much the other knew.

'Maria? Pregnant?' he shouted in disbelief after Finola had greeted him in the hall with the news. 'You're really talking nonsense now, Finola. Where on earth did you get this latest piece of rubbish from? Patrick?'

'No, not Patrick,' she snapped. 'Mrs Callaghan said someone had seen her and that she was pregnant, she said she was huge already. Now I want to know, is this to do with Davey Allsop? I know you know about this so tell me the truth, I have to know.' Her eyes blazed with anger. Make-up and hairstyles had never been her thing but in the past few months even the touch of crème puff had been forgotten and her hair hung lank and unkempt. As he looked at her huffing and puffing and working herself into a frenzy, Sam felt embarrassed for her.

Trying his best to be calm and reasonable, he spoke forcefully but quietly.

'Listen to me, she is not pregnant. Do you understand me? Not pregnant! She's put on some weight, yes, because she's hardly been outside her friend's front door in months, but she is *not* pregnant.'

'Are you covering up for her again?'

Sam sighed and shook his head slowly. 'You're obsessed, Finola. You have to stop focusing everything on Maria. It's not healthy.'

Finola stared at him. 'Of course I'm obsessed, you stupid man. That child is bad, she killed Eddie as sure as if she had picked up a knife and stabbed him in the chest herself. She has bad blood, you know that better than anyone, and I don't want any more shame heaped on this family by her or for that matter by you and your—' She stopped abruptly, suddenly aware that her mouth was running away from her. 'By you and your stupidity in protecting her. Why do you do it? Why do you always support her and not me? Send her away, just send her away and then we can get back to normal.'

'And what is normal to you? Me spending all day every day with my nose in other people's boring tax returns so that I can provide for you all and as payback I get treated like dirt by you and those boys? Call that normal?' Sam made his way through to the kitchen with Finola right on his tail screaming at him.

'We're a family and you promised me that was how it would stay. Nothing has been right since Maria came into this house, it all changed, but we could go back to being a family now she's gone.' A pleading tone had entered her voice but Sam knew where she was heading and was determined to head her off.

'That wasn't Maria's fault, it was yours. You never tried to love her like you did the boys. Maybe we shouldn't have brought her home but I never expected you to treat her like an outsider all her life. No wonder she got caught up with the likes of Davey Allsop.' Sam paced the floor trying to get through to Finola, 'She was just a helpless baby who had done nothing to deserve her situation. How could we have just left her? Really, how could we?'

'So what are you going to do when she has a baby? Offer to take that on? Look after it yourself? Make me a complete laughing stock? Bring up another devil child? Just imagine it, Sam, the child of Maria and that Allsop boy.'

The phone started to ring in the hall and Sam turned towards the door and shouted at it, 'Shut up, damn you.'

'Don't be ridiculous, Sam, shouting at the telephone. Mind out of my way, it might be Father Richard. He must have heard that Maria is pregnant, it'll have gone round everywhere by now. The shame of it . . .'

Sam threw his hands up in defeat and started to walk through to the sitting room. With Finola's irrational behaviour on one side and Ruth's pregnancy on the other, he felt as if he was walking a tightrope over the top of Mount Etna.

'Sam,' Finola called, her voice impatient, 'come and take this phone call, it's about Maria apparently, obviously it's of no interest to me.'

As Sam took the phone from Finola she turned and walked away, her lips pursed and her hands clenched. For a moment Sam thought she was actually capable of attacking him.

'Mr Harman? It's about your daughter. I'm afraid there's been an accident . . .' Sam's stomach lurched and a nightmare feeling of déjà vu enveloped him.

*

Maria woke up with a splitting headache, a sore throat and aching all over. Momentarily she wondered if she had flu but then she cautiously opened her eyes and looked around.

She couldn't get her bearings, she couldn't move and she could feel something blocking her throat, suffocating her and stopping her from closing her mouth. Completely disorientated she tried to grasp whatever it was but a hand took hold of hers.

'Maria, Maria love, can you hear me? Maria . . .'

She tried hard to focus on the blurry but familiar face of her father who was leaning over her. She moved her head tentatively and looked around. Slowly the fug started to clear.

Karen Allsop. Davey's sister.

She tried to speak but no words came out.

'Excuse me,' Sam called across the room. 'My daughter's awake.'

Maria's eyes were wide and wild as the doctor gently pulled the tube out of her throat and checked her vital signs, reassuring her at the same time.

'Ruth! Where's Ruth? Did they touch her?' It hurt her to speak but it was all she could think about and the panic soared through her as she started to remember what had happened. Karen and her buddies kicking the crap out of her as Ruth screamed at the top of her voice.

'No, she's OK, just worried for you. She's in a cubicle outside being checked over. I'm sure you'll see her in a while.' Her father sank onto the hard plastic chair beside the trolley before reaching over to take hold of her hand. 'She's still very scared though, and quite rightly by the look of it. They seem to have really laid into you. I don't understand anyone behaving like that, but especially girls. Oh Maria, I was so worried, especially when they said you were unconscious.'

'How long have I been here?' Maria whispered carefully, her voice hoarse and her throat tender.

'A few hours. I've only just got here, the traffic was a nightmare and I had to get from King's Crescent – another sickening dash to the hospital because of the bloody Allsop family.'

Maria winced as she tried to move and get more comfortable on the narrow trolley. 'God, everything seems to hurt. Do you know what's wrong with me? Have they told you?'

'Not yet but I don't think anything is actually broken. You look a bit of a mess but, according to what they said, nothing is broken. You're lucky after what those girls did. They need locking up.' Sam stood up and started pacing at the end of the trolley.

'Don't!' Maria tried to sit up but only made it onto one elbow. 'Don't you dare tell anyone about this. It's been bad enough because of Davey, I can't do that again. Don't you dare even think about involving the police!'

Sam leaned forward and grasped her shoulders, gently pushing her back down onto the trolley.

'OK, OK, don't get upset, we'll talk about it later but don't try and sit up yet, sweetheart.'

Maria closed her eyes. She wanted to think but it wasn't long before the medical staff started checking her again and, as the painkillers took effect, she gave in and let herself drift off.

The next couple of hours passed in a blur of tests and X-rays until eventually she was taken to the small observation ward that lay at the back of the accident and emergency department.

Still slightly disorientated, Maria screwed up her face and looked at Sam who was still glued to her side.

'What about the baby? Is it OK?' Maria asked hopefully. She couldn't believe she had actually forgotten about it, but as she looked at her father she noticed him visibly pale. 'What's happened?' Maria asked feeling a wave of panic. 'What's happened to the baby?'

Sam stood up and turned away, and Maria was convinced that Ruth had lost her baby. She started to cry, big heaving sobs that were a combination of pain and delayed shock.

'Why didn't you tell me, Maria?' Sam asked sadly. 'If I'd known we could have sorted something out. Why couldn't you have confided in me?'

'About what? I don't know what you mean?' Maria asked, still trying to get her head clear.

'You know what I'm talking about.'

'No I don't, I haven't a clue, I just want to know if the baby is OK.' Maria paused, feeling the nausea making its way from her stomach up to her throat. 'I'm going to be sick . . .'

The nurse appeared beside her with a bowl but slowly the nausea subsided and Maria looked again at her father.

'What are you talking about, Dad?'

'That you're pregnant, of course! I didn't believe your mother when she told me, I thought you and I didn't have secrets. And even if you couldn't tell me, then what about Ruth? After everything she's done for you.' Maria could hear the sadness in his voice.

'What did Mum tell you?'

'That someone had seen you and noticed, one of the women from the church. Your mother is really distraught.'

'But you didn't notice?' Maria tried hard to keep her voice calm despite her anger.

'No, I just thought you'd put on a bit of weight. You kept complaining about getting fat and I believed you.'

Maria didn't respond, she just turned her face away from her father so he wouldn't see the tears.

'Don't worry, we'll sort this out. I'll deal with your mother.' Sam's voice was gentle as he spoke to her but Maria kept her face away from him.

A few minutes later the doctor who had first treated Maria appeared at her bedside. 'How are feeling? Like you've been kicked by a horse?' He smiled.

'Something like that,' Maria muttered, looking

directly at him and avoiding the gaze of her father.

'The bad news is that for a couple of weeks you're going to look as if you've gone a few rounds with a prize fighter.' He patted her arm reassuringly. 'The good news is that there's no lasting damage anywhere. But we'll keep you in overnight because of the concussion.'

'What about her baby?' Sam asked.

The doctor looked puzzled and turned back to Maria. 'You're not pregnant, are you? Only if you are then I must have missed something.'

Maria smiled at him then grimaced at the pain that shot up the side of her bruised head. 'No of course I'm not bloody pregnant. I told you that when you asked me earlier.' She turned her gaze to her father and her expression made him feel like a reprehensible schoolboy.

'I'm sorry, Maria, I thought—'

'Don't worry, Dad, I know just what you thought. But I never slept with Davey, in fact I've never slept with anyone. Now if you don't mind I'd like to rest but can you just tell me how *Ruth's* baby is?'

'Ruth and the baby are fine, she'll be in to see you . . .'

As soon as she heard that Maria switched off. From as far back as she could remember she had accepted that her mother would always think the worst of her but she had never expected her father to think the same.

Sam carried on speaking, his tone alternating between soothing and apologetic, but she didn't listen to his words. Her body ached and she felt sick but it was nothing compared to the feelings of complete betrayal she felt.

'Get out!' The words flew out of her mouth. 'Get out get out *get out* . . .' Anger and hysteria mingled and grew.

The nurse appeared beside her. 'Maybe you ought to go, Mr Harman, and let Maria calm down. You can come back later. Go on, I'll talk to her.'

Maria watched her father leave the ward, his shoulders stooped and tears glistening in his eyes but she didn't care. He had betrayed her. Same as her mother had. Same as Davey Allsop had.

It was the final straw for the emotionally fragile Maria and it pushed her over the edge. Turning into her pillow she started sobbing.

When she was still sobbing twenty-four hours later, the psychiatrists were called and she was immediately sedated before being taken to a psychiatric ward.

Chapter Nineteen

2005,
London

'Answer my mobile, will you, sweetie, it's driving me nuts and I'm buried out here.' Maria, waving a set of curling tongs in the air, called through from the main salon to the smaller, more intimate room at the back where Ali took his favoured clients, charging them considerably extra for the privilege.

'Contrary to popular opinion I'm not your slave,' a disembodied voice shouted, 'so shift your cute ass and answer it yourself.'

'You selfish git! It's only a phone, for God's sake. I'm not asking you to redesign the Sistine Chapel in your lunch break.'

'Selfish git? You should have it in your pocket, you silly mare, and then you could actually answer it yourself.'

'Don't call me a silly mare . . .'

The ringing stopped.

'Ooops.' Ali laughed and looked round the stainless-steel door jamb. 'You spent too long whingeing. They've hung up on you!'

'That could have been important.'

'Then you should have shifted a bit quicker and answered it.'

The clients and other stylists dotted around the expanse of stark white minimalism smiled at the familiar exchange of insults between Maria and Ali, the couple who jointly ran the exclusive hairdressing salon. Their arguments and backbiting were notorious and all part of the expensive experience at 'Head Start'. The good-humoured bickering continued until the last customer finally exited the plate-glass doors.

Maria locked the door with a flourish and flopped down into one of the huge leather floor cushions that were scattered around the lounging area.

'Jeez, I must be getting old.' Maria sighed. 'I swear that was one of the busiest days ever. Isn't it time we retired and took off to the sun? We could buy a super-yacht and go off cruising around the Caribbean, soaking up the sun, sipping rum punch at sunset.'

Ali grinned. 'Hey, we're still young and energetic, why would we want to laze around all day sunning ourselves on the deck of a million-pound yacht when we can slog our guts out here day in and day out?'

Ali and Maria were wearing matching outfits, white, loose cotton trousers and long-sleeved shirts that were so fine they were almost transparent. It was a pseudo oriental style Ali had contrived, at the same time as he decorated the salon throughout in white with just the occasional flash of black. All the other staff, regardless of height or size, wore exactly the same outfits, black designer jeans and tight white T-shirts, all provided by the salon. The only concession to individuality allowed was instantly apparent in the choice of hairstyles.

It was a clever concept because all the staff, from the trainees and receptionists right through to senior stylists, went out of their way to find the most outrageous and colourful hairstyles imaginable in order to assert their personality and liven up the monochrome black and white.

The carefully selected flamboyant staff, along with Ali and Maria's bickering, had become a bit of a legend in the successful East London salon and even those who couldn't afford to cross the threshold would stand and gaze in from the pavement outside, fantasising about the day they might be part of the whole experience.

Maria laughed as she reached down and grabbed a soggy towel and threw it in his direction. 'You're a selfish asshole, you know. I'm constantly at your beck and call, catering to your every whim and you reckon I'm not worth a measly little million-pound yacht?'

The door at the rear of the shop suddenly opened and a small face appeared.

'Mummy, the phone was ringing upstairs. I didn't answer it but there's a message for you.'

'Thanks, honeybun. I'll be right up. Just as soon as

your tight old git of a daddy here agrees to buy your mummy the new toy she deserves.' She laughed, waiting for her son to join in but his face remained serious.

'Mummy, I think it's important. It's a message from Grandpa Sam. He wants to talk to you now. He sounded sort of cross.' The little boy looked at her intently, his disapproving expression telling her that she was not taking him seriously enough.

'Grandpa Sam cross?' Maria laughed. 'Never, Merlin. Grandpa's never cross!'

'Honest, Mummy. If he isn't cross then he's upset. It didn't sound like Grandpa Sam, he sort of spoke quickly and he didn't leave a message for me.'

Maria felt a shiver of apprehension flutter down her spine. Her father rarely sounded anything other than gentle. She jumped up from the beanbag and pulled her mobile from the depths of her handbag to check the missed call. It, too, was from her father. 'Maria, it's Dad here. I need to talk to you urgently, please call me right away. It really is urgent. As soon as you can.'

Maria tried to shake off the unease that was beginning to grip her.

'I'm just going up to call Dad on the home phone,' she said to Ali. 'He says it's urgent so I'd better do it now.'

'OK. I'll sort out the clearing up and then I'll be with you.'

Maria hurried through the door and up the stairs to their private apartment.

'Good luck. I hope there's nothing seriously wrong,'

Ali called after her as her feet clicked up the wrought-iron spiral staircase.

After a few moments of deep breathing to calm herself, Maria hesitantly dialled Ruth's number to speak to her father.

After she had finished the call and put the phone back into its cradle she sat stock still in the chair looking straight ahead until Ali appeared in the doorway, his concern apparent on his frowning face.

'Hey there, what's wrong? Honey, you don't look good. Bad news?'

'Dad says that Finola's seriously ill, she's suddenly gone downhill. Her cancer has spread and she's not got long to live, weeks at the most apparently, maybe only days.' Still she didn't move but an involuntary pained expression swept across her face.

'What are you going to do?' Ali asked. 'I can manage here if you want to go. I could even run you up there tonight if you like. We can leave Ollie in charge for a few days. Finola is your mother . . .'

Maria's head spun round and she glared at Ali. 'No she isn't. She's Finola Harman, the woman who did her best to fuck me up and nearly succeeded. With a bit of luck this will really be the end and she'll be out of my life forever.'

Ali walked over to where Maria sat frozen to the spot but, sensing the invisible barrier that was Maria's trademark when she was upset, he made no attempt to touch her.

'Don't say that, Maria. You know you don't really mean it. What does your dad want you to do?'

'To go and visit, make my peace with her and say goodbye. He's always been too soft on the old cow. I think now that she's dying she's worried she's going to rot in hell for her sins. I wonder what she'll say in her last confession? "I was a bitch to my daughter. I adopted her but I didn't want her." Do you think she'll confess to that?'

Ali sat quietly for a moment before responding to the venomous words.

'Are you going to go and see her before she dies?' he asked gently.

'Am I fuck going. The golden boys will be there, won't they? Patrick no doubt wondering where his dinner is and Joe with his smug little family alongside, and they'll all be in a huddle wringing hands and weeping and wailing. Nope. I said I would never, ever go back and I mean it. I'm not putting myself into that firing line again. No way. No. I can't do it, I don't want to do it.' Pulling her already folded arms even tighter, Maria shook her head vehemently.

'Won't you regret it at a later date? And what about Merlin? Maybe he needs to meet his grandmother just once before she dies. As I said, I'll come with you if you want me to. I can understand how you feel.'

'Ali,' she snapped without looking at him, 'you don't have any fucking idea how I feel so just leave it. Instead of trying to sort out my life why don't you go and sort out your own? That's far more complicated than mine. At least I can walk away from mine.'

'That's not fair,' Ali protested. 'There's no comparison between your mother and my . . . my family.'

'Life isn't fair. I found that out long ago. Now leave me alone and let me think.'

'OK, but think about this.' Ali reached out and rested his hand on the very edge of her shoulder. 'You may not want to go for Finola's sake, but think about yourself. Maybe this will be the last chance you will have to say goodbye and make peace with yourself. Not peace with your mother but peace with Maria Harman. Maybe you need this closure.' Before she could respond, Ali turned and disappeared off in the direction of their son Merlin's room.

Maria stared into space as she sat on the upright chair in the lines of shadows caused by the half-light filtering eerily through the blinds. Unbidden, her mind went back twenty years to the last time she had seen Finola and her brothers Patrick and Joe. The golden boys.

She had tried not to think of them over the years, tried to delete them from her memory but it had been hard.

After the tragedy of Eddie's death and the beating she had received, Sam and Ruth had taken over her shattered life and arranged everything. They had saved her life, she knew that now. Not from the Allsops who everyone had thought were going to be the problem but from herself. If Ruth hadn't given her the mothering that she was in dire need of, she knew with certainty that she would have killed herself, or died of grief.

Now Finola was dying and wanted to see her. Maria tried to work out her mother's age. Around sixty, she reckoned. Certainly not old in years but in Maria's eyes Finola had always been old. Finola and her own mother could, at first glance, have passed for sisters. Except that Granny Bentley smiled more often than her sour-faced daughter and possessed a wicked sense of humour. It flashed through Maria's mind how awful it must be for Granny B to know that her daughter was going to die before her, but almost as quickly she dismissed the thought. The last time Maria had seen her grandmother the old lady had been slowly sauntering towards happy senility. Confusion was taking over her mind but it was a happy confusion, interspersed with strange flashes of perception. The unpredictable thought processes coupled with a lack of inhibition had made for an entertaining visit. No one ever knew exactly what she would say next.

Maria frowned. Maybe she ought to go back and give Granny Bentley some support. She certainly wouldn't get any from the golden boys and there was no one else.

'Ali,' she called. 'Ali, can you come through here a sec? I need a hand with the dinner.'

He appeared in the doorway and looked around, bemused.

They were an unlikely couple. She was tall and slender, bordering on thin, with her shoulder-length chocolate-brown hair lightened and streaked through with several different lighter shades. He was a good couple of inches shorter than Maria even when she was barefoot and his slight and boyish build disguised his oncoming middle age. His poker-straight black hair hung thick and heavy almost down to his shoulders and had electric-blue highlights. Despite being Asian, Ali looked more like a native American, a look which was contrived and guaranteed to attract attention. Yet another part of Ali and Maria's long-term business plan.

'Dinner?' He raised one dark eyebrow and pretended to frown. 'Since when did you cook dinner on a Saturday?'

'I wanted you to come through but not Merlin. I knew he wouldn't want to come and help with dinner.' She smiled. 'You were right and I've decided I will go home. Just once for one visit to Finola for my sake and also to see Granny Bentley for her sake. It must be hard for her.'

'Sounds like a good idea.' Ali spoke neutrally. 'Do you want me to come?'

Maria leaned forward and kissed him full on the lips. 'It's entirely up to you, I really don't mind if you don't. I've told you what they're like. But I will take Merlin I think, although they're all such fucking loons, I don't want him to be upset.' Maria looked at him and laughed. 'Or you for that matter. The golden boys will hate you and won't try and disguise it.'

'I can live with that, in fact I might actually enjoy it.' He laughed and started jumping around the room, swinging his legs and chopping with his hands. 'I'm sure I can match them both verbally and physically, I could take their legs out with a touch of karate. How about that?'

'Not a good idea because they would just love that. No, we'll go, but I don't want them to find out about your situation. OK? I'd hate them to have that information.'

Ali shrugged. 'OK, if that's the way you want it. It's your family.'

'And we'll stay in a hotel. The best we can fucking find. Let's really screw the minds of the golden boys. It will piss them off so much to know that I've done better than either of those dumb bastards!'

Chapter Twenty

As Sam's car pulled up outside the house in King's Crescent, Maria stiffened in the passenger seat as she felt the panic rising. It had been nearly twenty years since Eddie's death. Nearly twenty years since she had gone to Ruth's apartment, never to return to her home again, and yet still she could feel the same overwhelming sense of inadequacy washing over her. The same insidious feeling of not being good enough to belong to the Harman family that had plagued her life.

Sam reached across for her hand. 'It'll be OK, Maria, I promise. There's no one else around. I didn't tell them you were coming, they're at work.'

Maria knew he meant Patrick and Joe.

Ali and Merlin had stayed at the hotel. Maria had thought about it and decided that she wanted to see Finola alone to start with. She wanted to gauge her mother's reaction and she also wanted to gauge her own feelings. She wondered if Finola thought about her as she lay on her sickbed, if she regretted her rejection of her daughter, if she regretted never having met her grandson, and most importantly if she regretted ever having brought Maria home in the first place.

Sam helped her out of the car in his genial, gentlemanly way and Maria looked up and down the quiet leafy road, surprised to see that it still looked much the same as it had throughout her childhood.

He stood back as she opened the gate, an unfamiliar and obviously new gate, and walked up the path. The front door was exactly the same, as was the open redbrick porch and the polished brass doorknocker and matching letterbox. The dark green wooden door with the stained-glass panel across the top was the original door from when the house had been built. Maria could see it had been painted but the colour, bottle green, remained exactly the same. The only thing different was the doorbell which Sam rang before he put his key in the lock and turned it.

'Why did you ring the bell?'

'Out of politeness and habit.' He smiled. 'Don't forget, before your mother was ill I spent very little time here. Just enough to keep up the façade in front of the neighbours and the old biddies at the church, for your mother's sake.'

'When is she going back to the hospice?'

'At the weekend, all being well. It's a hard one to call, she needs more care than we can give her, but . . .'

His words faded and Maria knew exactly what he meant: Finola would go back at the weekend if she was still alive then.

The unexpected smell that assaulted her nostrils as Maria entered the familiar hallway made her want to gag. It was different, unrecognisable and sickening, a combination of disinfectant and air-freshener vying with the unmistakable smell of terminal illness. Maria found it hard to associate it with her family home which used to smell of beef dripping, cabbage water and scouring powder.

'Mum's in the front room. We've turned it into a bedroom for her. She hasn't been able to manage the stairs for quite a while and this makes it easier for the nurses.' Sam took her arm and turned her towards him. 'I know you're angry, I know you've got a lot of things you want to say, Maria, but please remember how very ill she is. She doesn't deserve this pain and indignity. No one does. Life can be very unfair.'

His voice was soft and gentle and in that moment Maria loved her father more than she had ever done. Her longstanding anger at him for being weak and indecisive dissolved in an instant.

'Can I go into the kitchen first? I know it sounds silly but I'd like to reorientate myself with my surroundings. It is all so familiar yet at the same time so unfamiliar, I feel as if I know the house from a dream as opposed to having lived here.' She ran her hand along the edge of the hallstand with the decrepit mirror that still housed hats, coats and umbrellas; then she touched the handle of the ancient basket on wheels, standing to attention at the side.

All the old signs were there, the signs that Maria used to look for when she got in from school to see if her mother was in.

'OK, sweetheart, you go through and take your time. I'll just let your mother know you're here.' He paused. 'If she's awake, that is. She drifts a little. It's the morphine.'

As soon as her father used the word morphine the reality of the situation hit Maria in full.

Her mother was dying. It was the first time she had seen her in all these years. It might be the last time she would ever see her. There was so much to say and so little time to say it in.

The kitchen was much as she remembered it apart from the folded wheelchair in the corner. It was still old fashioned and impractical with a collection of wall and base units that didn't match and the old multi-purpose pale blue Formica table and chairs. Maria looked around. The wallpaper was different and there was a microwave on top of the fridge but that was about it. It was more or less as she had remembered it. Finola had never believed in spending money on something new if the old still served its purpose. The same old saucepans that Maria had scrubbed many a time as punishment were in the same corner on the same plastic-coated rack, and there was still no electric kettle.

Maria walked over to the gas stove and picked up the blackened whistling kettle just as her father appeared in the doorway.

'Will she want a drink?'

'Who's she? The cat's mother?' Sam smiled wryly at his daughter.

Maria was just about to snap at him when she saw his expression and smiled back. 'I wouldn't mind a fiver for every time she said that to me in this room. I wonder where the silly saying came from?' Maria could feel herself becoming emotional and that was the last thing she wanted. 'And why is there still not a decent kettle in this place?' she growled to take the heat off herself.

'You know your mother, she hated what she called gadgets. Electric kettles came into that category. In fact anything with a plug was called a gadget. Do you remember when I wanted to buy an electric toaster? God, you'd have thought I was about to splash out on a Ferrari!'

Maria smiled. 'You got so much grief. And do you remember when I wanted some electric curling tongs for my hair?'

They both laughed, and for just a few seconds they were back in the past, away from the reality of that moment in time.

'Sam? Are you there, Sam? Is that you?'

Maria stopped laughing and looked round to see who was calling her father.

'Just coming, Finola,' he called back and Maria realised that the barely audible pleading voice belonged to her mother, the woman whose voice they used to joke could shatter mirrors three streets away and whose strident tones would set her daughter's teeth on edge.

Maria and Sam locked eyes.

'Do you want to go through? On your own maybe, best not to crowd her.'

Maria nodded despite the urge to turn and run out of the house forever.

Glancing at herself as she passed the hallstand mirror, which had lost most of its silvering, Maria gently opened the door.

Ever since Sam had so readily believed she was pregnant, Maria had been obsessed with keeping her weight down as far as possible. Despite being nearly six foot tall and naturally voluptuous, she was stick thin and always perfectly groomed but that morning she had taken even more care. Her hair hung sleekly round her oval face which was dominated by her perfect jawline and high cheekbones. Her favourite, and very expensive, trousers and jacket clung tightly where they touched.

'Hello, Mum, it's me.' Maria had determined beforehand that she would call her mother by her Christian name, she had had no intention of calling her Mum but the word came out automatically.

Walking slowly into the dimly lit room she glanced around to get her bearings in the once familiar lounge that was now a sickroom.

'Who's that?'

Maria stepped forward. 'It's me. Maria.'

'Oh yes, your father said you were coming. Have you come to watch me die?'

Maria had been prepared for her mother to reject her, she had also been prepared for the spiteful comments that were always Finola's trademark but what she wasn't prepared for was the skeletal body that barely registered under the sheets, and the unfamiliar hollow eyes that looked at her.

'I knew you'd have to say something like that and I knew you wouldn't really want to see me but that's tough because I'm here.' Maria struggled to keep her voice light and emotionless as she perched at the end of the bed. 'Tomorrow I'm going to bring your grandson, if you'd like to meet him.'

'Haven't changed much, I see.' Finola's voice was weak and her breathing laboured as she turned her head to look at the daughter she hadn't seen since she was a teenager. 'Still sharp as a razor, not so scruffy though.' She spoke slowly, taking deep breaths between words. 'You look like you've done all right for yourself.'

'You sound surprised. Come on, don't pretend you know nothing about me.'

Finola managed a smile. 'I hear it but I don't get to see it. You, Merlin, Sophie . . .'

Maria didn't know what to say so she stood up and moved towards the door. 'I'm just going to make a drink. Would you like one? A cup of tea?'

Finola nodded her head weakly as if even that was

too much effort and suddenly all Maria's fight flew out of her. The strong and aggressive woman she had spent so many years despising and resenting wasn't there any more, there was someone else in her place. A sick, thin, harmless old woman.

'I'll just go and make one then,' Maria muttered and quickly stepped through the door back into the hall, determined that there was no way her mother was going to see her cry.

Tears streaming down her face she hurled herself into the kitchen where Sam sat at the table with his head in his hands.

'This is so unfair of you, why did you make me do this? Why didn't you leave me to think of her as she was? It's horrible seeing her just lying there.' Maria slumped into the chair opposite her father and glared at him.

'Because time is fast running out and I knew you would hate yourself if you didn't say goodbye to her.' Sam pulled a handkerchief out of his pocket and passed it to her. 'I know that deep down your mother loved you, there were just things that got in the way and you were the scapegoat. That was wrong, but we're all human and we all screw up.'

'Don't give me that "she loved you really" crap, Dad. I'm a grown-up now, I don't need mollycoddling. You of all people knew what went on all those years. She didn't even like me, let alone love me.'

'Yes, I do know what it was like, but it takes two

to make a war and I just feel that if you haven't built at least one bridge by the time your mother passes away you'll regret it for ever.'

Maria gave a watery grin. 'That's actually what Ali said.'

'Then he's a perceptive man.' His voice was light and Maria was grateful to him for taking the edge off the situation. 'The nurses will be here later and then Patrick will be back at tea time, as will Joe, I suppose, and of course the priest and the biddies from the church. Sometimes I think it's too much but that's the routine and it's hard to cut it down without offending anyone.'

'What about Father Richard?'

'He's so old now, he must be creeping towards ninety. He phones occasionally but he's very frail. Shame, he was one of the few who your mother really cared for.'

'What will you do? Will you marry Ruth after . . . after she goes?'

'This is hardly the time or place for that question, is it? You know there are reasons why your mother and I didn't divorce but in time it'll all be right for Ruth and Sophie.' He paused and smiled at the thought of his daughter, a close intimate smile. 'If, of course, she'll still have me after all the water that's passed under the bridge.'

'I eventually forgave you for being a complete prat so I'm sure Ruth has too!'

Comfortable in each other's company, they laughed together.

'Where's my tea?' The voice wavered painfully but the demanding tone was exactly the same although it no longer had the power to upset Maria.

'Just coming,' she called as she poured her mother's milky tea into a feeder cup. 'Is there anything else you want?'

'Come and talk to me.'

Sam and Maria exchanged glances.

'What are you going to do?' Sam asked cautiously. 'Please don't upset her, please, she's not got long.'

'As in the distant past I'll tell her what I want her to know. No doubt it'll be the Spanish Inquisition all over again.'

Maria picked up the cups and headed back to Finola's room.

Chapter Twenty-one

The effects of the high dose of morphine that was being administered by a pump meant that Finola kept drifting in and out of sleep and when she was awake she could be disorientated. Maria sat and talked for a while, telling her a little about her life but after sitting beside her in silence for over an hour as her mother dozed, she crept back out to her father.

Eventually, needing to escape the invasive smell in the house, she left Sam and walked round King's Crescent the way she used to every day before Eddie's death, the last day she had ever spent in the house that had been her home for the first sixteen years of her life.

A few of the sturdy old houses in the crescent still looked the same but most had changed as they changed owners. A new driveway here, some double glazing there, but on the whole it was still familiar territory and the old wounds that she thought had long healed felt as fresh and painful as ever.

She thought about her last walk with Eddie and, for the first time in years, she wondered about Davey

Allsop. Silly, silly Davey who had done so much damage because of an ill-thought-out whim to annoy Finola Harman.

Contrary to what she had expected, Maria had soon grown to be content in her life with Ruth away from Colchester and her family.

She adored her young sister from the very first moment she had seen her. Ruth had been rushed into hospital for an emergency caesarean section with a general anaesthetic so Maria had actually seen the baby before anyone. Even before Ruth and Sam.

Ruth had hung on for over three weeks after the incident with Karen Allsop, by which time Maria had been allowed home under the supervisory eye of a community nurse. Screaming and red, the wrapped infant had been briefly waved under Maria's nose as she waited outside before being taken off to the special care unit for observation. Maria had never seen a newborn before and she had been enthralled from that first moment on.

It was baby Sophie who had brought Maria back to life again and the bond between them had stayed strong over the years, regardless of the ups and downs between Sam and Ruth.

Slowly but surely Maria had realised she actually might have a future to look forward to even though the first year had been difficult to get through, not only because of the rift with her father but also because he remained living at King's Crescent to look after his increasingly obsessive and paranoid wife.

Because of that, and despite having a new baby as well as her career, Ruth had once again stepped into the role of surrogate parent and pulled all the stops out to support Maria and help her get her life back on track.

Now, slowly retracing the last steps she ever took with Eddie, Maria realised she had much to be grateful for and that set her wondering whether Davey had gone on to bigger and better things after his spell in prison or whether he had followed the route of crime that they had all predicted for him. She thought of him walking beside her, confidently planning his future, so handsome and full of life. She had really thought they were two of a kind. Both of them had been desperate to get away from their families and make something of themselves. Despite everything, she had succeeded, but she knew nothing of Davey.

On the spur of the moment she decided she would go to see Granny Bentley, the oracle of local gossip. If anyone knew anything about the Allsops, it would be her.

Maria quickly turned and walked the short distance to the nearby new estate which housed an eclectic mix of both buildings and residents and where her grandmother now lived. Her small first-floor flat, in a sheltered housing block close to the newly built shopping complex, was easy to look after and she had lots of company. Maria knew that Granny B loved it there but she also knew the time would eventually come when the old lady was going to need more help than they could provide. In the meantime she muddled amiably along with the help of the warden and her wide circle of friends.

Granny B peered curiously at Maria through fogged-up glasses as she opened her door.

'Hello, dear, have you come to take me shopping?'

'It's me, Gran. Maria, your granddaughter. I've come to see you.'

The old lady smiled at her in vague recognition, and Maria kissed her on the cheek. She peered over her grandmother's shoulder into the flat. 'Have you left something on the hob? It looks a bit steamy in there.'

'I'm cooking a boiled egg for my tea.'

Maria went through the dividing curtain into the tiny kitchenette.

The blackened saucepan had boiled dry on the bright red electric ring and the bullet-hard egg was bouncing around in the bottom of the empty pan: Maria ran it under the tap and waited for the hissing to stop before getting another egg out of the tiny fridge that sat squarely on the short stretch of worktop.

'I'll cook you another one. This is more like beach pebble, it's so hard.'

Pottering around and chatting, she could see Granny B trying hard to stay focused but she was inclined to jump about in her conversations and occasionally she would forget who she was talking to so Maria talked about nothing in particular as she boiled the new egg and carefully buttered some bread.

Maria thought she looked even smaller than the last time. Always compact and wiry, the old lady now looked positively tiny as she sat hunched over the tray on her lap. Her sparse white hair barely covered her scalp and faded blue eyes peered out from a weather-beaten face that was criss-crossed with deep wrinkles.

As her grandmother munched her way through her lunch, Maria looked around at the flat. It seemed like a doll's house, especially compared to the old stone terraced house in Clacton-on-Sea that had been her family home until five years previously.

'And how are all your boys?' she asked Maria.

'I only have one, Gran. Merlin, he's seven now. You saw him when I came up for Annalise's wedding. Remember Annalise, my friend from school? The one who was so ill.'

'Of course I do!' The tone was sharply defensive. 'Do you think I'm losing my marbles? Just because I forget some things doesn't mean I'm completely ga-ga you know. You're like your mother, she thinks I'm ready to turn my toes up.'

Maria smiled reassuringly. 'I know you're not ga-ga and I'm sorry. Anyway, Merlin is great, he's growing up fast. I'll bring him over to see you tomorrow if you like, and my boyfriend Ali, remember him? We're staying a couple of days.' She paused and looked at her grandmother, wondering exactly how much she had taken in about Finola's condition. 'I'm here to see Mum, she's very poorly.'

'Mmm. I don't know how long she's got left. I never thought she'd go before me but it looks like she will. I bet that upsets her, the thought of not seeing me off.' She smiled smugly and then looked deep into Maria's eyes, her mind suddenly clear. 'Have you sorted things out with her? All that nonsense between the pair of you?'

Maria couldn't help but laugh, her grandmother had never been anything other than direct.

'In a way, yes. As best we can with so little time. Yes, I think we're as OK as we're going to be. Sadly too many things have happened for us ever to kiss and really make up.' Maria smiled affectionately at the old lady who had often fought her corner for her when she was a child. 'I was thinking about taking Merlin to see her tomorrow, but I'm not sure, she looks so ill it might frighten him.'

'You should take him. As I always told your mother, a child has the right to know its background, life's too short for secrets and they always come out in the end, but your mother never agreed with me, that's why we were never allowed to tell you . . .'

The words took a few seconds to register, and when they did Maria bit her tongue and did her best to keep her face neutral, letting her grandmother chatter on.

'But at least she's told you now and made her peace

so that's OK. I knew it would all come out in the wash one day.' The old lady suddenly looked puzzled and glanced around. 'Would you like a cup of tea? Or how about a glass of sherry? You know when I was a child my mother used to let me sip her drink when no one was looking, I got quite a taste for sweet sherry. Mind, I also like a bottle of Guinness now and then, did you bring me one?'

Maria reached out and patted her arm. 'Gran, we were talking about Mum. And the family secret. I'd like to know what you really think about it all.'

'Oh that.' Her eyes flickered back to the present. 'Well, I think your mother should have told you years ago but she said it should always stay a secret so that's what we all did, kept it a secret. Me, Finola and Sam.' Granny B carefully ticked the names off on her fingers as she spoke. 'It's a good job your grandfather wasn't alive then, he'd have horsewhipped her, married or not. Sam was such a saint over it all and your mother was always so ungrateful. It seems strange under those circumstances that you were always his favourite.' Carefully taking the strain on her skinny arms the old lady pushed herself up from her chair and grabbed her walking stick. 'Just need to flex my knees a bit, they lock if I sit for too long. I like to take a walk around the furniture now and then.'

Maria itched to move her along with the story but she didn't want to distract her so she continued to stay quiet and let her ramble in and out of the story.

'Where was I? Oh yes, your mother came to ask me for help and then everything changed for everyone. Secrets do that, don't they? And of course it was such a terrible thing to happen to her but as I said at the time, she put herself in that situation and that's when men will be men.'

'Mum didn't tell me all the details, she said to ask you.' Maria felt guilty as she lied to her grandmother but her instincts told her that this wasn't just a confused old lady rambling about the past. 'Every word is such an effort for her as she is, it was hard for her to tell me everything.'

Granny Bentley's eyes misted over and she looked into the middle distance. Her mind was back in the past where it functioned best.

'It was a bad time for her then, what with your father working abroad. It was hard for your mother alone with three young boys and her feeling as she did. But she managed mostly and they really needed the extra money, they knew it would make all the difference to them. And that's when it happened, when he was away.'

'And?' Maria prompted.

Granny Bentley looked bemused. 'And? And your mother got pregnant with you, of course.'

'Do you mean Finola?'

'Of course I mean Finola. Your mother, I just said so, she got pregnant with you while your father was away. Well, he wasn't your father then, was he?' Granny

Bentley raised her eyebrows and laughed at her own joke while the room spun round Maria and claustrophobia enveloped her like fog.

'Then of course we came up with the story. We couldn't pretend you were Sam's, everyone could add up and know it wasn't possible, particularly as your real father was half Egyptian. Sam was out working in . . . in . . . oh, I don't know, somewhere in Africa. So we all pretended you were adopted.'

'Gran, I have to go and get something out of the car,' Maria muttered as, with legs like jelly, she headed for the door. 'I'll be back in a sec.'

She fled the flat as fast as she could, gasping for breath. Outside, feeling sick and dizzy, she fumbled in her pocket, pulled out her mobile and pressed in a number.

'Dad? It's me. I want you to come to Granny Bentley's now. She's told me!'

'Told you what exactly?' Sam's overly cautious tone told Maria all she needed to know.

'You know exactly what she told me. Meet me here. Now.' Without giving him a chance to respond she clicked the phone off and, almost in a trance, wandered over to one of the wooden benches outside the building. She sank down onto it and tried to come to terms with what Granny Bentley had said.

Finola Harman, the woman who had constantly treated her as an unwanted interloper in the family, was actually her birth mother. And if Sam wasn't her birth father and she had been born after all the boys, then it could only mean that her mother, her ever judgmental and obsessively holy mother, must have had an affair!

Chapter Twenty-two

Maria was still sitting on the bench with her elbows on her knees and her head in her hands when Sam's car pulled in just a few minutes after her phone call. He got out and ran over to her, leaving the door swinging open in his race to get to his daughter.

'What's she been saying to you?'

Maria didn't look at him, she just gazed down at her designer boots and let her hair shield her face.

'That Finola is my mother, that the bitch actually gave birth to me but you're not my father. That's all. Not a lot to get stressed out about really. Is it true?'

Sam's head drooped to his chest and he slumped down beside her on the bench. He stretched his legs out in front of him and crossed them at the ankles.

'I'd like nothing better than to deny it but I'm ashamed to say it is true. Where do I start?'

'At the beginning but first I have to go and make my excuses to Gran. I told her I'd only be a minute. And then we're going back to King's Crescent.'

'Don't go storming in and telling your mother that you know.'

'Telling her that I know what? That my whole life to date has been a lie? Mustn't I ask her why she treated me the way she did when she knew I was as much a part of her as her golden boys? Oh, and what about my birth father? Was he just someone she shagged to pass the time while you weren't around? Holy Finola thought she'd like to get down off her pedestal for a bit, did she?'

Without looking at her Sam leaned his head back on the bench and folded his arms. 'Don't be angry at her, not now, especially when you don't know the whole story. It's nothing like as basic as that.'

Maria jumped up and stood in front of her father, hands on hips and blazing with anger. 'You are joking, I assume? Don't be angry? I'm absolutely fucking furious at her and you as well. Why did no one tell me? How could you all do this to me? Did Ruth know?'

'No. No one else knew except me, Granny Bentley and Father Richard.'

'Oh, Father Richard was in on it as well. Gran didn't mention him. Anyone else?'

Sam sighed and reached out to take her hand but she pulled back as if she had been stung.

'Look, go and say goodbye to your gran and then we'll talk. But remember, she's an old woman and quite fragile, don't go off at her.'

'You really think I'd do that? Still, I shouldn't be surprised, you were more than ready to believe I was pregnant at sixteen because Finola said so. The same woman who didn't mind shagging around herself!' She turned on her heel and stormed off, too angry and stunned to cry.

As he waited for his daughter Sam thought back to that far away time when he had returned from a lucrative twelve-month contract working as an accountant for an oil company in Nigeria. It had been the chance of a lifetime, it paid more than four times his normal salary, accommodation was rent free and there was a bonus payment at the end. So he had left his wife and three young sons at home, flown out to Lagos and lived for a whole year as a single man in single accommodation.

He had returned to be confronted by the news that his wife was four months pregnant with another man's child.

They had all thought that he was being positively saintly in his acceptance of the situation and also in the way he had let Granny Bentley organise everything but none of them knew of his own secret guilt that had made the circumstances a little easier to accept. How could he tell Finola that he had been unfaithful himself when he was away? Taking on baby Maria had helped him feel a little better about himself.

'OK, let's go!'

Maria's voice made Sam jump but when he got up and headed towards his car, Maria didn't follow.

'I'm going to walk back.' She spoke quietly and without making eye contact. 'I don't want to be that close to you right now. I want to walk, think and calm down before I see her again.'

'Please come in the car with me.'

'No. I told you I have to think. I'll see you back at the house.'

As she started walking towards the path that cut through to the main road, she knew Sam was watching her but she couldn't bring herself to look round.

Much as she tried, she couldn't get her head around the fact that Finola had actually given birth to her and then spent all her life denying the fact, pretending that she had been adopted, even going so far as to blame every little hiccup in her behaviour on the fact that she was adopted.

'Daughter of Satan', 'spawn of the devil', 'bad blood' – all had been hurled at her over the years, and then there had been Patrick and his constant 'cuckoo in the nest' jibes. Never once had Finola stood up for her; in fact she had actively encouraged his almost paranoid dislike of her. *'It's because she's adopted, you know.'*

Why? The question repeated itself over and over again in her head as she walked, her pace quickening until by the time she got to King's Crescent she had broken into a run. She arrived at the house out of breath at the same time as Sam pulled up in his car.

'You go through to the kitchen and I'll send home whoever is in there with Finola. It could any one of half a dozen of her self-appointed angels of mercy.'

Normally Maria would have smiled at his description of Finola's friends from the church but she couldn't bring herself to respond so she walked in without saying anything. She heard him talking to Finola's visitor and then she heard the front door open and close.

'That was easier than I thought. Your mother's asleep so Angie left quite happily. I'll just put the kettle on.'

Maria shook her head slowly. 'I don't think this is something a hot drink and a few kind words will resolve, do you? It's the sort of thing you always said: "I'm sorry Mummy's been nasty to you, she doesn't mean it, have a mug of hot chocolate and forget all about it."' She turned and leaned against the draining board. 'I came to visit her because Ali thought, and I thought, that it would bring some closure to the past, but instead it's a hundred times worse than it was to start with.'

'That's why we never told you, the implications were too great. I wish I'd known you were going to see your gran, I could have come with you.'

'And shut her up, I suppose.'

'Probably, yes. For your sake, no one else's.'

Nervously tapping her foot on the floor and pulling at her hair, Maria asked the question she wasn't sure she wanted an answer to.

'Tell me about my biological father.'

'I can't.' Sam looked at her sadly. 'Not really.'

'You're going to have to, I want to know.'

'You were never interested in your birth father before, why should this make any difference? I'm your father.'

'I want to know,' Maria said forcefully.

'I can't tell you because I don't know. He was long gone by the time I got back and found out. He never even knew your mother was pregnant. Look, Maria, do you really want to know everything? It's none too savoury but if that's what you want then I'll give it to you, you're old enough and I want you to have just a little compassion for your mother.'

'Forget compassion, I want the truth, all of it. I've had enough of being lied to.'

'OK. But it's not a truth that you'll like and it certainly won't resolve anything for you.' Sam looked directly at her, an expression of genuine sadness on his face. 'I'm sorry, sweetheart, I'm really sorry, but I can't let you think so badly about your mother. She became pregnant with someone else's child because she was raped.'

Chapter Twenty-three

That night Maria lay rigid in her bed, staring up at the ceiling. The hotel bedroom had two large double beds and Ali and Merlin were curled up fast asleep in one, while Maria lay alone and wide awake in the other. She had wanted to be on her own, insisted on it, and Ali hadn't questioned her wish, thinking it was because she was upset after having seen her mother.

She couldn't bring herself to tell Ali about the revelations of the day, she hadn't been able to bring herself to speak out loud the words that were reverberating in her head. She didn't know how she would ever be able to tell him the shameful secret that she was now a part of.

Maria clenched her fists in the darkness. Even on her deathbed and drugged to near oblivion Finola had still been able to reach out and stick a knife into her heart.

I am the product of rape. My mother was raped. I really do have bad blood in me.

As is said to happen at the moment of death, so it happened to Maria: her early life flashed past her eyes at breakneck speed and suddenly everything fell into place. Her mother's constant disapproval and resentment, her obsession that her daughter had been born bad. Suddenly Maria could understand why her mother hated her. Every single day she was confronted by a reminder that she had been raped and that her child had the bad blood of her attacker coursing through her veins.

Sam had done his best to explain everything but Maria wasn't in the mood for reasons or reasoning. All she wanted were the hard facts. She wanted, needed, to know every detail. But Sam claimed to know very little and remember even less. All he could tell her was that the man had been staying in digs in the same street where Granny Bentley had lived. His name was possibly Joseph and he was mixed race. His nickname was Samson and that particular summer he had a job at the nearby holiday camp.

Finola had left the boys with a babysitter one afternoon and gone to visit her mother. Samson, whom she knew slightly, was on the same bus back to Colchester so they had sat together. He had walked her to her front door, forced his way in and then raped her in the front room. The same room where Finola now lay dying. She had confided in no one and within a few weeks he had gone back to wherever he had come from.

Then Finola had discovered she was pregnant.

'Why didn't she go to the police? Get the bastard arrested?'

'It was different back then.' Sam had looked away into the distance as he talked about the time he would rather forget. 'No one would have believed her and even if they had, they would have thought it was her own fault for letting him know where she lived, for letting him walk with her, for letting him befriend her.'

'Why did she let him know where she lived? How did he know there was no one in the house?'

'She chatted to him on the bus and he was a neighbour of Gran's, she knew his landlady and she knew who he was. It never occurred to her that he intended anything. Anyway, by the time I got back from Nigeria she was four months pregnant and hiding it under tight girdles and baggy dresses so it was decided that it was for the best to keep quiet. Your mother went to stay with Gran for the last three months and then we just pretended we had adopted you.'

'Why didn't she have an abortion? It could have been over and done with before you got back and no one would have been any the wiser.'

Sam had looked at her and for the first time a small smile played around the edge of his mouth. 'Can you really imagine that ever being an option for Finola? She couldn't have lived with herself, we both know that.'

'So she chose to have me and make me suffer as well. She rejected me and took her shame out on me. Why not have had me really adopted instead of pretending?'

When Sam didn't answer Maria had thought about it for a moment. There were so many questions and they were popping into her head at random.

'What about the paperwork? How did you get round that? Forgery?'

'Sort of but not really.'

'Supposing I had been interested in my birth family, supposing I'd wanted to go searching, what would you have done?'

'It would have depended on how old you were. As an adult I would grudgingly have had to tell you but when you were a child?' Again the half-smile. 'I'm sorry, Maria, but I have to say I would have lied. I couldn't have told you the truth, could I? Whatever happened, whatever we did wrong, there is one thing that I want you to know, Maria. You are my daughter. I love you. I wouldn't change you for the world. You are my daughter and I've never once thought of you as anything else.'

Maria stared hard at her father. 'Why? I don't understand this at all, why did you let her carry out that charade? Why did you let her persuade you to keep me?'

Sam chewed his bottom lip as his eyes surveyed the room almost as if he was looking for an escape route. 'It was the other way round, I persuaded her. You don't have to understand, sweetheart, not everything in this life is logical. The moment you were born you became *my* daughter and you still are. Regardless of absolutely anything.'

'No I'm not. Sophie is your daughter. I'm the daughter of a rapist.'

As the daylight started to flicker through the gap in the curtains Maria was still as wide awake as when she had lain down the night before. She desperately wanted to get up and make a cup of coffee but she didn't want to wake Ali and Merlin. She wished she was in a separate room where she would have been able to pace the floor all night and get her thoughts into some order.

Did she hate Sam? No, but she was angry with him for deceiving her.

Did she hate Finola? Yes, but the woman who had denied her all her life was dying.

Should she tell Ali? No, she knew he wouldn't be able to accept that the mother of his son was the result of a rape.

Should she tell Patrick and Joe? No. The pleasure of telling them that Finola really was her mother would be outweighed by the mileage they would get out of the circumstances of her conception.

Then there was Ruth. And what about Sophie?

'Mummy, Mummy.' A small but weighty body landed on top of her and then scrambled under the covers to cling to her like a young monkey. 'Are we going to see my nana who I've never met today? And are we going to see old Granny Bentley?'

Maria smiled and hugged the warm little body to

her. Never had he been as important to her as at that moment. Her son. The only person in her life who she was one hundred per cent certain of. With everyone else there were secrets and lies, half-truths and deceptions. Nothing was as it seemed.

'Yes, my little man, we're going to see both of them but I want to talk to you about them both first. Nana Harman is very, very poorly so she's in bed and sleeps a lot. She has to take lots of medicines so she may be a bit muddled about you and me. Do you remember Granny Bentley? She is really old now and talks a lot.'

'Is Daddy coming with us?'

'No, he's got to get back to the salon before mad Uncle Ollie wrecks the place. But Granddad Sam will be with us.'

'Yeesssss.' Merlin gave a whoop of delight. 'And Nana Ruth?'

'No, she's got to go to work as well.'

'And Sophie?'

'Enough!' growled a voice from under the covers of the other bed. 'This isn't a bloody holiday.'

Maria snatched Ali's mobile phone from the bedside table and lobbed it in the general direction of his head, following it quickly with two pillows. 'I can do without you being so bloody bad-tempered and snapping and snarling. Now just bog off back to your precious salon. This is hard enough as it is without you being a frigging prima donna.'

The covers flew off the bed and Ali shot upright.

'What's up with you, you temperamental cow?' He frowned at Maria.

'What do you think?' Jumping out of bed she ran straight into the bathroom, locking the door firmly behind her.

A few minutes later there was a tentative knock on the door.

'We're both out here with our legs crossed, are you going to be long? We'll swap the bathroom for a cup of coffee?'

She could hear Ali and Merlin giggling on the other side so she swiped a damp flannel across her face, pushed her hair behind her ears and forced a watery smile on her face before opening the door.

'I wish you'd let me come with you.'

'No, Ali.' Maria panicked at the thought of Granny B revealing all to Ali. 'I've decided it's best to keep it low-key. Anyway, the bathroom is all yours. Quick dip in the shower for Merlin and then let's get going. I just want to get today out of the way and then go back home to normality.'

But even as she said it, Maria knew that it would be hard for her to be 'normal' ever again.

Chapter Twenty-four

'You've kept something like this from me all these years?' Ruth screamed, her face a combination of fury and puzzlement. 'How could you? And how could you do that to Maria? Jeez, I can't believe it, how could you and Finola do that? And then to go and tell her the stark truth in one fell swoop now? When her mother's on her deathbed? You're nuts, absolutely fucking nuts! That poor girl must be off her head.'

On the drive over, Sam had mentally prepared himself for the onslaught and it was no worse than he had anticipated and certainly no worse than he deserved but still it hurt to hear Ruth going for him quite so hard.

It had been a stressful day from the beginning. After making sure Finola was comfortable he had waited for the nurses to arrive and then gone with Maria and Merlin when they visited Finola and Granny Bentley. Straight after, before he lost his nerve, Sam had driven over to see Ruth. To tell her everything. Well, almost everything.

'You're absolutely right and I can't excuse myself, I

should have told you but it was so long ago it was actually easier to play mind games and believe the story we were telling everyone else. I'm sorry. That's all I can say.'

She just stared and shook her head in disbelief before turning her back on him and gazing thoughtfully out of the window at her beloved gardens.

Ruth had moved three times since their daughter Sophie had been born nearly twenty years before and home now was an old country house on the borders of Essex and Suffolk. The square, stone house sat atop a hill but was invisible from the road. Even access via the long narrow drive was hidden by the surrounding hedgerows. But despite the ageing, listed exterior, the inside had been tastefully renovated to include all the necessary mod cons without taking out the original features.

Sam loved the house and spent as much time there as he could with Ruth and his daughter Sophie; he called it his haven of tranquillity, but at that moment the atmosphere was anything but tranquil.

'Ruth, there's nothing you can say to me that I haven't said to myself already. The only excuse I can offer is that it seemed like the best solution at the time, for everyone.'

'But why go and tell her now? Couldn't you have lied and pretended Finola had a one-night stand?' Ruth's leather-soled shoes clicked back and forth across the flagstoned entrance hall that was so large and high it doubled as another reception room. 'Her mother's not going to be here much longer but now Maria has the rest of her life to live with this. It's not fair.'

'I know, and to be honest I thought about being a tad economical with the truth, but the loose cannon in all this is Finola's mother who has the beginnings of dementia, just enough to lose her inhibitions a little. I didn't know how much more she'd say to Maria.'

Ruth shook her head and marched through to the kitchen. She slammed the lids on the Aga in frustration and picked up a damp cloth.

'Where's Maria now?'

'They're probably en route back to London, that's what she said they were going to do, anyway. I'm sure she'll phone you. I think you're the only person she trusts at the moment.' As Sam spoke the words he realised how much he envied the easy relationship between Ruth and his daughter. Maria got on really well with Sophie, too, and it gave him an insight into how the Harman family could have been if only Finola had let them.

Suddenly Ruth stopped wiping the cloth across the massive stripped pine table that took up half the kitchen and lobbed it into the sink. 'Oh hell, I'm sorry, Sam,' she blurted. 'I've just realised, I should be giving you credit for taking Maria on under the circumstances and doing everything you did for her. It must have been hard. You shocked me and I wasn't thinking. But you should have told me!'

Sam breathed in and out deeply and felt himself start to relax a little and feel free to open up about it for the first time to anyone.

'The whole thing was a nightmare made worse by Finola beating herself up every single day of her life. Instead of making the best of it she just had to keep picking away at Maria, constantly looking for something evil in her, a piece of her genetic father.'

'Is that why she hated Maria so much?'

'I think so, but I also think that in a way she wanted Maria to make her life difficult, that way she could feel she was being punished. And punishment was what she was searching for, some pain and suffering that might absolve her in the long run.' Sam shook his head sadly. 'It was the same when she blamed herself for Eddie's death, which she did even though she pointed the finger at Maria. There were no boundaries to Finola's guilt.'

Ruth snatched her jacket from the coat rack by the door. 'I'm going to London, to see Maria. She'll need someone to talk to.'

'Then I'm coming with you,' Sam said quickly.

'Sorry, Sam, but you're not. This is women's talk. Don't worry, I won't leave you out of the loop. And anyway you need to get back to Finola, you'll be the next one beating yourself up if you're not there when she goes.'

Sam put his arm out and gently pulled her towards him. 'I love you, Ruth. More than you can ever imagine, even after all this time. You are such a nice person. Be careful and call me if you need me.'

After he had waved her off, Sam wandered aimlessly out into the grounds and looked about. He wanted to stretch his legs before the drive back and it was so peaceful with no one around. Much as he adored his daughter, he also enjoyed the quiet when she was at college.

Ruth had had the grounds landscaped but there was nothing regimented about it. The lawns were nicely trimmed but the rest of it was organised chaos, a jumble of wild flowers and grasses and two large ponds stocked with almost tame koi that would poke their noses out of the water whenever they heard footsteps. Further down were the stables. They had all liked the idea of horses but none of them fancied the work so they remained empty.

With his hands in his pockets Sam walked down to the pond and sat on the semicircular concrete bench that overlooked it.

Over the years his loyalty to Finola had been tested to the limits. Many a time he had been ready to walk out and go to Ruth permanently but his guilt had stopped him. When he had persuaded his wife to keep the baby, Maria, he had promised that he would always be there for them all.

'Guilt is a terrible thing,' he told the large carp that was hanging around the edge of the pond, eyeing him up and waiting for a hand to chuck him a few pellets. 'I felt guilty about Nigeria, Finola felt guilty about Maria, Ruth felt guilty about me, I felt guilty about Ruth, Finola and Maria felt guilty about Eddie. Guilt, guilt, guilt, everywhere I turn there's guilt. Now I feel guilty about Maria and Maria feels guilty about Finola.' Sam laughed out loud as the fish moved its mouth greedily. 'No good blowing kisses at me, mate, it won't get you anywhere. I'm already spoken for.'

The trilling of his mobile phone in his pocket stopped his conversation with the fish. It was the priest.

'I think you need to come home, Sam, Finola has taken a turn for the worse. I called the doctor but Finola wouldn't let him call an ambulance, she wants to stay in her own home. I've phoned the nurses also.'

'Do whatever Finola says, Father. It will take me about an hour to get home.'

'I'll tell her you're on your way.'

Sam sped back to Colchester; he even resorted to a few prayers that he hadn't used for many years.

Pulling into his driveway he scraped the length of the car on the concrete post before stopping sharply outside the garage doors. The front door was open and he ran into the room. There were about ten people around the bed, some kneeling but all with their hands clasped in prayer.

Sam could feel his angry frustration reach boiling point at the sight of comparative strangers grouped around his wife's deathbed.

'I'd be grateful if you would all leave and let me

say goodbye to my wife in private. Father, Patrick and Joe, just give me a few minutes. The rest of you, if you feel you've got to pray then I'd sooner you went to the church.'

The expression of surprise on their faces was quickly replaced by one of pious irritation but when none of them moved Sam lost patience.

'Get out! Let Finola die in peace with her family.'

Patrick opened his mouth to protest but the priest shook his head very slightly and hustled them all out, pulling the door to behind them.

'Can you hear me, Finola?' he asked her but there was no response. There wasn't a sound in the room bar the dying woman's slow, laboured breathing.

Without warning tears started streaming down Sam's face and he could feel the sobs growing deep in his throat.

'Oh Finola, why did this happen to you? You deserved to live longer, long enough to exorcise your demons and be happy just for a while.' He knelt by the bed, not in prayer but just to get close to his wife of over forty years. The woman he understood better than anyone.

'We'll miss you, we'll all miss you, including Maria. She knows everything now. Your mother told her some of it and I told her the rest. She knows and she doesn't blame you so why did you always blame yourself? It wasn't your fault.' Sam took her cold and bony hand in his and, bringing it up to his mouth, kissed it gently, his lips barely glancing her knuckles as the tears dropped down onto it. 'I'm sorry, maybe I should have tried harder, perhaps if we'd moved away, let Maria be adopted . . .'

He felt a slight fluttering inside his hand and knew that she had heard and understood him.

'You'll be OK, you'll be with Eddie again and your dad and it won't be too long before Mum is up there with you. You'll be happy, especially now you've had the chance to see Maria and Merlin. He's a lovely little boy, isn't he? So much like Maria, though I can see you in him, I think it's the eyes.'

Again the fluttering.

As he reached up and touched her face, her eyes moved in his direction and her mouth relaxed. Suddenly she looked at peace for the first time in so long, and with her lips no longer pursed in constant anger she looked almost young again.

Without moving from the beside he turned his head and spoke quietly in the direction of the door.

'You should come back in now, Patrick, Joe, Father.'

In the end, considering her suffering of the previous few weeks, Finola's passing was gentle and peaceful. Just another flutter in Sam's hand, a long sigh as she breathed out and that was it.

As soon as he could, Sam slipped out of the room to call Maria and tell her; he was relieved to hear that Ruth was there with her.

*

Later in the evening and within a few minutes of Finola's body being taken away by two respectful young men in the shiny black undertaker's van that everyone recognises but no one acknowledges, Patrick and Joe started bickering and Joe's wife Leanne joined in for good measure.

Without warning it suddenly hit Sam and he lost his usual control. He wanted to lash out at them, to batter them, anything to stop them.

'Shut up, the lot of you, just shut up. Your mother has only just died and already you're bickering like children over her funeral. Well, listen hard. I am arranging everything.'

Sam grappled with his emotions, determined that they wouldn't take over. He knew he had to assert himself right away before Patrick got a firm grip on it all.

'I know exactly what your mother wants and how she wants it, so it is between me and Father Dermot. I'm open to suggestions but if you think you're going to hijack this to score points off me, you're wrong.'

Patrick and Joe exchanged knowing glances across the same kitchen table they had sat at all their lives.

'Yeah, well, we have a say in it all whether you like it or not,' Patrick said nastily.

'I don't like, and you have a say in nothing. One wrong word or move and you'll be looking for some-where else to live. This is my house you're living in, remember.'

Patrick stared at his father. 'This is where I live and it's where I'm staying and there's absolutely nothing you can do about it.'

'Wrong. This is my house, always has been and always will be. Now, if you're going to act like five year olds then go and do it elsewhere. I have phone calls to make.'

Patrick and Joe looked at each other and shrugged their shoulders. They didn't say anything more because at that moment Father Dermot appeared in the doorway with a suitably sombre expression on his face.

'Will your Maria be coming home for the funeral?' he asked curiously. 'I'm surprised she didn't make it here today, knowing how sick her mother was.'

'She's probably dancing a jig of joy as we speak, Father. She never had any appreciation for our mother, the woman who took her in and brought her up as one of the family. She ran off donkey's years ago.'

Deliberately ignoring Patrick, Sam focused his gaze on the priest who was looking surprised at the display of family disunity.

'It's OK, Father, Maria's seen her mother to say her goodbyes. They made their peace with each other yesterday, in a manner of speaking.'

'You what?' The chair fell backwards as Patrick jumped up. 'You brought that bitch into my house? How dare you?'

'My house, Patrick, and Maria came because your

mother asked her to and for once you weren't around to sabotage it all.'

'She's not coming to the funeral, we won't have her,' Joe joined in.

'Oh, I think you'll find she is.' Sam looked at the priest. 'I'm going out for air now. I'll be in touch.'

Chapter Twenty-five

'What do you think I should do?' Maria asked her sister Sophie as they sat side by side in the apartment over the salon, drinking white wine. 'I'm so bloody confused. The funeral's tomorrow at three o'clock and I still don't know what I'm doing.'

'You're asking the wrong person here, I haven't got a clue. Whatever you want to do, I suppose. Do you really want to go?'

'Yes I do, but if I go I'm going to upset so many people, it'll cause such bad feeling. I suppose I don't want to cause Dad any more problems than he's already got. The golden boys will be on his case twenty-four seven now.'

Maria had thought long and hard about going to her mother's funeral and still couldn't make up her mind. Ever since Sam had told her about her mother's rape, Maria had had to review her feeling towards the woman she now knew to be her blood relative, her true mother. She wished she had had time to talk to her about it, to try to get some answers to all the questions that kept whizzing round in her head.

'Oh, stuff the brothers Grimm and their bad feelings, and Dad can stick up for himself.' Sophie smiled. 'You don't really give a toss about your stupid-ass brothers, do you?'

Maria thought about it for a few seconds. 'Not really, no, but if they disrupt the funeral, which they're perfectly capable of, it'll be my fault.'

'If they disrupt the funeral it'll be their doing, not yours. You can stand back and look serenely aloof and let them make complete assholes of themselves.' Leaning forward, Sophie picked up her wine glass from the oval glass-topped table they both had their feet up on, and clicked her sister's glass. 'Here's to you and the right decision.'

Maria smiled and drank.

At nineteen Sophie was the spitting image of her mother, in fact Maria could see nothing of Sam in her at all and she was strangely grateful for that. She often wondered if she would have taken to Sophie if she had looked like the golden boys, but she was small and curvy with masses of fair wavy hair and skin that tanned golden at a glimpse of sun. She also had a strong personality and a sharp sense of humour.

'Doesn't all this family stuff bother you?' Maria asked curiously. 'The golden boys are your relatives as well. Aren't you even a little irritated that they don't even know you exist?'

'Well, a bit, I suppose, but I know the situation and if I thought I had a couple of adorable big brothers who would love to meet me then that'd be different but from what you've said they're more twin dickheads than golden boys and nothing to write home about!' Sophie tossed her hair and giggled, then suddenly clapped a hand over her mouth. 'Oh God, I'm sorry! I'm so busy taking the piss I keep forgetting it's your mother who has died. I'm really sorry.' Sophie looked mortified. 'I suppose it's because she's been out of your life for so long I've never really known much about her. I always think of Mum as being your mother as well.'

Maria felt hugely comforted by Sophie's remark. 'It's OK, I know what you mean. Ruth has always been there for me and for so many years even I forgot Finola was my mother. Or rather my adoptive mother.'

Unintentionally and without thinking Maria automatically clarified the role that she had always thought was the true one. As she spoke she felt a shiver run down her spine.

She could almost hear Finola laughing her signature humourless, sarcastic laugh. Now she herself was perpetuating the lies and deceit because it was the easy option. But for the time being at least she couldn't imagine telling anyone the true story. Not Sophie, not Merlin and certainly not Ali.

'Shall we sneak out past Ali and go shopping down Stratford market? I really, really need some new, strappy, really high shoes. I've got a hot date tomorrow and he's over six foot, I don't want to be dancing with my head up his armpit.'

'No chance.' Maria shook her head and smiled. 'I wouldn't do that to Ali. We're so short-staffed I shouldn't even be up here but I tell you what, why don't you come down and help out on the reception desk? I'll pay you and then you can toddle off and get an even better pair.'

'Have I got to wear the dreaded uniform?'

'Of course, but luckily it suits you and there are plenty of spares in plenty of sizes to choose from in the back staff room.'

'How much?'

'The going rate for as long as you can stand it.'

'OK, so long as I get enough for a pair of fuck-me heels.'

'Sophie!'

'Ooh, you sound just like Mum!'

As Sophie expertly manned the reception desk, flattering and humouring the clients waiting expectantly for their appointments, Maria sneaked back up to the apartment alone. Much as she loved her sister she found it increasingly difficult to be with anyone who didn't know what she knew. Especially Ali.

She knew she was pushing him away but she couldn't help herself. They had been together a long time both professionally and personally but Maria knew that their relationship was on the wane.

Ali had come into Maria's life when she was at her lowest ebb and had pulled her onwards and upwards.

They were a great team and together they had built up the business to what it was; they were on the verge of opening another in the West End. And of course there was Merlin, their son; but marriage was out of the question because Ali already had a wife and five children in Birmingham.

Maria had ignored it in the beginning but lately she found herself feeling increasingly guilty and unsettled. She had somehow managed to get caught up in the same situation as her father and Ruth – except for two big differences. Unlike Sam, Ali was separated from his wife who knew all about Maria and Merlin. But because she didn't want her family to know, Ali and his wife pretended they were still a married couple at family functions. The rest of the time Ali lived with Maria and Merlin. And unlike Ruth, although Maria loved Ali and was infinitely grateful to him, she was not in love with him, and never had been.

Maria sat quietly assessing her life and the route it had taken. It has been simpler when she could lay the blame for her screwed-up childhood and adolescence on Finola but all of a sudden the goalposts had been moved.

With a scream Maria jumped up and with one hefty swipe cleared the shelf of all the photographs that were displayed higgledy-piggledy in different frames. They flew across the room in all directions, some remaining intact, others shattering.

She wasn't who she'd thought she was. Apart from

Sam, no one in her family was who she'd thought they were and it was all down to one person: Samson, the rapist.

As Ali came running up the stairs to see what all the noise was about, Maria swung her leg back and kicked the debris before dropping to her knees and sobbing her heart out.

'For fuck's sake, Maria, what's the matter with you now? I thought you hated the old bat.'

Maria looked up at him and shook her head. He didn't understand and she couldn't explain.

Chapter Twenty-six

Slipping into the back of the church at the very last minute, Maria saw Sam look round and beckon her forward but she shook her head and settled into the corner of an empty pew, well out of the line of vision of the golden boys should they also look round.

She had arrived at the church with plenty of time to spare but had deliberately stayed out of sight in the obsolete graveyard, watching the slow and dignified arrival of the hearse and cars. Sam had tried to persuade her to go to the house and leave with the family in the funeral cars but she refused, she couldn't face the thought of having to listen to her brothers complaining and bitching about her presence.

As the cortège pulled up, Sam had been first out of the car and Maria felt for him as he chewed his lips and unsuccessfully tried to smile at the waiting group of mourners standing outside to welcome them.

The previous few months had taken their toll and he looked old and careworn. For the first time Maria contemplated his mortality. His hair was sparse to the point of disappearing and the touch of arthritis in his joints gave him a leaning gait that was compounded at that moment by his sadly drooping shoulders.

Sam stood aside as they moved the coffin out of the hearse and onto the waiting shoulders. Maria watched from a distance, feeling completely detached; she felt as if she was watching a movie. She simply could not equate the ornate wooden box with the fancy brass handles being carried forward on the shoulders of four sombre young men with Finola Harman. Her mother.

Once the procession was inside and everyone was safely seated, Maria had slipped in unnoticed.

It was the first time she had been in this church since she had rebelled against religion all those years ago and she looked around curiously, studying it closely as if she had never seen it before – studying everything except the oak coffin that stood high and proud at the top of the aisle in front of the altar, with just one small spray of white lilies on top.

She wondered who they were from. Sam? Patrick? Joe? And who had chosen those particular flowers to take pride of place?

Throughout the service Maria was aware of her father constantly looking over his shoulder at her but she refused to even look in his direction let alone meet his eye. Instead she focused fiercely on the distorted rays of sunlight shining through the stained-glass windows high above the altar. But despite looking here, there and everywhere, she couldn't keep her mind away from the fact that the coffin contained the body of her birth mother.

More than anything that had happened in her life, Maria resented having been in her mother's company just once with that knowledge, and at a time when it was too late for either of them to talk about it or make amends.

Everyone stood, and the bearers took up their posts again and hoisted the coffin up onto their shoulders.

Maria had already decided against going to the cemetery but she followed the procession outside with the rest of the mourners and then moved through to the front to watch the cortège move slowly away. As it turned out onto the road, she stepped forward to watch it go, just as Patrick looked round.

Her last sight of the funeral procession carrying her mother to the cemetery was of Patrick, his face distorted with hatred, sticking two fingers up at her.

Holding her head up and ignoring the surprised expressions on the faces of Finola's friends and acquaintances, Maria turned and started to walk away.

'Maria, wait. Maria! Hold up, will you . . .'

Slowly and against her better judgement, she stopped and turned to look back.

'Annalise! What are you doing here?' Maria was stunned to see her friend running up to her, arms open ready to hug her.

'Oh, it's such a nice day that I thought to myself, I know, I'll go and search out a funeral.' Annalise pulled a face and flung her arms round Maria and hugged her tight. 'I came to support you, you silly beggar. I guessed you'd be in there hiding away under a pew somewhere but I couldn't see you.' Pulling back, she slipped her arm through Maria's.

'I wasn't hiding, I was sitting at the back away from trouble. I was with the professional mourners. I just didn't want to upset the proceedings, for Dad's sake.'

'Well, looking at that ignorant swine in the back of the car, I'm not surprised. I'd have opened the car door, given him a kick and let him roll out into a stinking ditch somewhere. That was just so disrespectful, especially at his mother's funeral.'

'Yes, well, that's Patrick,' Maria shrugged, 'and the worst part is that it was his own mother who made him like that. So sad.' Maria tightened her grip on Annalise's arm for comfort.

'What are you going to do now?' Annalise asked.

'Go home, back to London and back to work. That's the trouble with having your own business, there's no excuse good enough for not being there.'

'Well, bugger the business for today, I've got an excuse for you. You're going to come home with me and we can be all girlie. Dom is working in Scotland this week so we can put our feet up and catch up. How does that grab you?'

'I'll have to ring Ali and let him know and ask him to look after Merlin.'

'Well, go on then, I'll wait. Are you in your car?'

'Yes, I drove myself straight here, I didn't want to go to the house and set the golden boys off.' Maria raised her eyebrows and rolled her eyes in towards her nose, making Annalise grin. 'And I certainly wasn't going to the cemetery. I can just imagine Patrick giving me a sly shove.'

'He's a pig and not worth expending words on so let's forget about all that now and go and grab your car. I came on the bus. How's that for dedicated support of a friend?'

Maria smiled tearfully. At that moment she really needed a friend to confide in and Annalise had always been a good listener.

Arm in arm they walked through the churchyard to the small car park at the back. There were still a few stragglers wandering about and just as they were turning out under the archway, a figure walked out from between the trees and cut quickly across their path. They hesitated to avoid bumping into him, and the man turned, ducked his head and broke into a jog.

'Wow, he left his manners at home today.' Annalise laughed but Maria looked hard, her antennae twitching.

'I recognise him . . .' Maria's voice rose. 'That's Davey Allsop! I swear that's Davey.'

The man's step faltered but he didn't look round.

'Davey Allsop! Stop, I know it's you. Stop!'

He quickened his pace and ran round the corner out of sight.

'These fucking stupid heels,' Maria puffed as she ran

after him with Annalise not far behind. 'If I had my trainers on he wouldn't have got away from me.'

They stopped at the back gate and looked up and down the road but he had disappeared.

'How do you know that was Davey? You couldn't see his face. I didn't recognise him.'

'Well, you wouldn't, he didn't kill your brother! Anyway, did that look like a jogger to you? He had a suit on, for God's sake. He only started running when he saw us.' Maria was suddenly on edge. The thought that she had come so close to Davey Allsop made her pulse start racing in anger.

At that moment the thought that had been niggling away at her for days took off. She had to find him, challenge him, do something. She didn't know exactly what she wanted or why she wanted it, but she knew she had to find him again.

'Come on, let's go home. We can stop and pick up a takeaway en route.' Annalise frowned. 'Maria, you're not thinking what I think you're thinking, are you? You're never going to look him up?'

'Of course not. Anyway, I haven't a clue where to find him. Granny Bentley said he never came back here after prison.' Maria knew she didn't sound convincing but she carried on anyway. 'Mind you, I'd like to know why he was here and why he ran off like a frightened rabbit. I would never have imagined him doing that in a million years. Not Davey.'

'Maybe he didn't recognise you, maybe he was just

in a hurry, who knows? Come on, today isn't the day for any more high emotion. Let's go.'

Maria's enduring and easy friendship with Annalise was ideal for both of them. Sometimes they went for many months without any contact but they could always pick up where they left off.

Although cleared of her cancer, the prolonged treatment had left Annalise infertile. It was one of the first things she had told her husband Dom about herself. Together, they had decided not to try to adopt or attempt treatment but simply to concentrate on each other.

'How's everything with you?' Maria asked her now. 'Still happy as Larry and travelling like crazy?'

'Oh yes.' Annalise laughed. 'We've been away three times already this year. Dom works hard and we don't spend much on anything else, we love travelling and also all the planning beforehand. It's a full-time hobby for us.'

'Why don't you buy somewhere abroad? You could rent it out and subsidise your own visits. That's what Ali wants to do, he's after a villa in either Spain or Florida.' Carefully Maria backed her car into a space outside the pizza house just around the corner from where her friend lived.

'That's what Mum suggested but we don't want the commitment. We like to take off as and when. We're going to Singapore next. You know what, Maria? My illness has given us a completely different take on life.'

Annalise smiled as she glanced at Maria. 'We don't buy many things, we don't value belongings as such. I know it sounds a bit yukky but really we just value our time together and make the most of each day.' Without warning Annalise started laughing. 'But enough about me, this is a bad day for you so I'm going to molly-coddle you and make you feel better. I'm also going to force feed you the pizza and ice cream that you promised me all those years ago. You're far too skinny. I'm going to fatten you up before you disappear in front of me.'

'Come on, we'll eat inside. My treat.' Maria smiled. She had no intention of being fattened up and she always found it easier to pick at her food in a restaurant than when a friend had put it on a plate in front of her.

It had taken a lot of dieting to get to her ideal weight and the thought of putting any of it back on horrified her.

Chapter Twenty-seven

Going to look at Finola Harman's funeral had been a spur of the moment decision for Davey Allsop. Seeing the familiar name of his old adversary in black and white in the local newspaper had brought back so many memories, both good and bad. *Finola Harman, beloved wife and mother . . . sadly missed . . .*

Yeah, right, he'd thought. Strange how death always seems to affect people's memories.

After Eddie's accident and the court case, he had thought of Maria every day at first, especially after he'd been sent down, and when his father had visited him in prison and gloated about Karen beating her up, his guilt had soared to an all-time high. But as time had gone on and he had successfully got his life back together, the memories had gradually faded and been tucked away in the part of his memory marked history — until the visit to his father in the local hospital when he had flicked through the local paper and the name had jumped off the page at him.

Finola Harman. The woman he had wasted so much energy on hating was dead.

It was straightforward curiosity that had drawn him to the church on the day of the funeral but the unexpected sight of Maria and her friend appearing just in front of him had sent him scuttling away to hide like a nervous schoolboy. It had never occurred to him that she wouldn't be well away in the funeral car along with the rest of the Harmans en route to the cemetery.

As soon as they had looked the other way he had made a run for his car, knowing that Maria would never have expected one of the dreaded Allsops to be behind the steering wheel of a low-slung classic Jaguar E-type. Then, wryly, Davey had smiled to himself as he watched the two women turn into the car park and get into a classy new car which Maria drove. It hadn't occurred to him that Maria would be behind the steering wheel of a top of the range BMW.

Maybe they had both veered away from the expected route.

Despite common sense telling him not to, he hadn't been able to stop himself from pulling out behind the car and following it at a distance, first to a nearby pizza parlour and then, after a couple of hours, on to a small terraced house round the corner. It would have been impossible for him to loiter unnoticed in the narrow street full of parked cars on either side so he had made a note of the address and Maria's number plate and reluctantly driven back to his own home.

With his mind far back in the past, Davey walked

across his lounge, pulled open the cabinet and took out a bottle of brandy and a glass. Seeing Maria had made him feel far more emotional than he could have imagined.

He had recognised her instantly despite the fact that the last time he had seen her she had been a school-girl and was now even taller, considerably thinner and dressed and groomed to perfection. But she was still the Maria he had fallen for all those years ago in the school playground.

Taking a slug of the brandy, Davey walked over to the large gilt-framed mirror that hung over the imitation Adam fireplace and looked at himself closely. It had taken him by surprise that Maria had recognised him so easily because he thought he had changed out of all recognition. He turned his head sideways and studied his profile before stepping back to take in the longer image.

His once long dark hair was cut a lot shorter and groomed neatly; fashionable rimless glasses perched on his nose and his expensive suit hung perfectly on his wide shoulders. No longer was he Davey Allsop, the tinker's no-good son, he was David James, the successful businessman.

Yet still Maria had recognised him. He wondered if that was good or bad.

As he continued checking himself out, he heard the front door opening.

'Is that you?' he shouted.

'Well of course it's me, darling. Who else would it be or am I missing something? Were you expecting someone else?'

Still looking in the mirror, Davey watched the reflection of the woman who sauntered over and air-kissed him in the general vicinity of his cheek.

'And where have you been all afternoon? You should have been at the restaurant with me,' she gave him a warning glare in the mirror, 'as you well know. Darling, if you want me to continue keeping you in the manner you seem to wallow in, then you really must play the game. I don't come cheap and you can't bum around all day at my expense.'

'I haven't ever bummed around, thank you very much. I work bloody hard. But that's irrelevant, something important came up, something I had to deal with.'

She laughed. It was a gentle tinkling laugh that in the beginning he had found so beguiling. Now it just irritated the hell out of him.

'I sincerely hope it didn't,' she murmured suggestively. 'That wasn't part of our agreement. Something only comes up when you're here with me.' Her dark green eyes made contact with his in the mirror and held his gaze for a couple of seconds before turning away.

In one fluid movement she threw her coat on the back of the armchair, sank onto the suede sofa that was positioned to look out over the river, crossed her legs elegantly and smiled. 'Don't I get a drink as well, darling?'

'Just about to do one for you, gin and tonic coming up.' He smiled back, trying to lighten the mood and distract her from giving him the third degree. 'Have you got a cigarette? I've run out, I was just about to go and get some more.'

With a heavy sigh she reached down into her handbag and pulled out a new pack. 'Here, catch. You can have the packet, save you having to go out to wherever yet again for whatever reason.' With a flick of the wrist she threw the pack at him.

Ignoring her jibe with a quick grin, Davey expertly caught the pack in one hand and handed her the glass with the other. As she took it, he perched on the arm of the sofa and kissed the top of her head.

'Now tell me all about your day, Paula.'

'No, David,' Paula's voice was clear and clipped, 'you tell me all about yours. I was exactly where I said I would be, doing what I was supposed to do. You weren't. I was waiting for you and you'd turned your fucking phone off.'

He stood up and looked out over the murky river water as he spoke. 'I went to a funeral. I'd forgotten about it, it was an old family friend I hadn't seen in years. I went to the church to pay my respects but I didn't stay. I didn't even talk to anyone. It was strange really, I don't think anyone recognised me.'

'Mmm,' she murmured. 'I suppose I'll have to take

your word for it though I'm not sure I believe you. This, however, is the last time I'll give you the benefit of the doubt. I don't take kindly to being made to look stupid.'

After Davey had been released from the detention centre on parole, a goon connected to the Farrells had soon approached him and passed over an envelope containing five thousand pounds. It was the payment he had been promised for keeping the brothers' names out of the frame for the ram raid. He knew it was blood money and was all too aware that it was tainted, but the temptation to accept it had been too great.

Five thousand pounds in cash was a fortune for someone of his age who owned nothing and had nothing going for him, but rather than go crazy with it Davey had bought an old classic car and, with the help of the skills he'd learnt inside, set about restoring it.

It had been the start of a legitimate and successful business venture that had eventually seen him reinvent himself, away from his family, his old haunts and the Farrells, as David James, the businessman with a thing about old cars. And then he had met the newly widowed Paula Wellbeck.

Glamorous, wealthy, and an astute businesswoman, Paula had set her sights on the handsome young man from the very first moment she'd gone into his showroom to look for a restored MGA. She had eventually offered to invest in the business. Using a mere fraction of the money she had inherited from her late husband, Paula had slowly but surely reeled Davey in both financially and emotionally and by the time he realised exactly what she was doing, it was too late. She owned him and most of his business and he was inextricably tied to the woman who was twenty years his senior.

'We're going to the Holdens' barbeque tonight. Seven thirty for eight. Not too casual, this is important. It's some sort of charity nonsense but it could be useful. I'm hoping they'll hold the next one at the restaurant.' Paula Wellbeck put her cigarette to her lips and inhaled deeply. 'The car's coming for us at seven. Be ready.'

Dave felt himself bristle. It irritated him when she treated him like a minion but he knew his situation was all his own fault. He had, without giving it too much thought, let himself be seduced by Paula's cash and had badly underestimated the woman herself. He now had everything he could possibly want except his self-esteem.

Before he could stop himself his mind was back with Maria. He wondered what she was doing at this moment.

'Are you listening to me, David? I want you to sort out the holiday cover for the showroom and the restaurant. We're going to be away for three weeks.'

'Where are we going? Or aren't I allowed to know that?'

'Don't be petulant, darling, it's not an attractive trait.

You know full well we're going to Barbados, I told you about it weeks ago. Don't tell me you've forgotten already . . .'

As Paula chattered on and on, Davey didn't bother to answer. He switched off from Paula and let his mind stay with Maria Harman.

Chapter Twenty-eight

A couple of glasses of wine combined with the trauma of the day and Maria was past tipsy. Annalise had eaten with gusto but Maria had, as usual, picked half-heartedly at her meal and pushed it back and forth across the plate, so as soon as they got home and opened the wine, it went straight to her head.

'You're going to have to stay here for the night, you can't possibly drive now,' Annalise said as she topped up their glasses.

'It's OK, I'll get a taxi. Ali can bring me back tomorrow to collect the car.'

'A cab all the way back to London? That's plain daft. No, stay here, I want you to, it's been ages since we've really caught up.'

'Thanks, I'd like that; you're a really good friend.' Maria smiled, suddenly feeling emotional again. 'You've been there for me through it all.'

'You helped me when I needed it. That's what friends are for.' Annalise put her head on one side and spoke out of the corner of her mouth in a silly cowboy accent, 'In sickness and in health, for richer for poorer . . .' She faked hesitation then theatrically smacked her head with the palm of her hand. 'Oops, wrong relationship. That was Dom!'

The effects of the wine sent them both into a fit of stomach-holding giggling that was way out of proportion to the joke. When they calmed down, Maria looked affectionately through tear-filled eyes at her friend.

Annalise had changed little over the years; her body was more rounded and her hair had grown back coarser and a slightly darker shade of blonde but she was still the laughing, ever-optimistic girl she had been way back before her illness. It fascinated Maria that none of it appeared to have got her down.

'Annie, there's something I want to tell you. It's not that I want to lay any more of my problems on you, but I have this really big secret and I'd like you to help me get it all in perspective.'

'Fire away then, I'm all ears but the brain may not be in perfect working order.'

'You have to promise me you won't tell a soul, no one, especially Ali.'

Wearing a pair of Dom's pyjamas and with her make-up from the day before streaking her face, Maria staggered into her friend's kitchen holding her head and moaning.

'Oh God, my head hurts, why didn't you stop me?'

'Now that would have been a bit like trying to stop

a speeding train with a gentle wave. Fancy a fry-up?'

'God, no. I've got some strong painkillers in my bag, they cure anything.' Maria looked at Annalise and sighed. 'I gave you chapter and verse on my latest crisis last night, didn't I? I always seem to get the urge to talk when I'm with you. You really should be a professional counsellor, you know, you're such a good listener.'

'Well, thank you kindly, ma'am, but I think the alcohol played a part as well.' Annalise bowed as she poured the coffee.

'No, seriously, I mean it, I'm grateful to you for listening. Dad and Ruth are too close to it, Granny Bentley is happily confused and oblivious to the chaos she's caused by telling me about it and Father Richard is tucked up in the old priest's home with a bottle of Scotch to replace old Ma Callaghan.'

'You really should talk to Ali about it, I'm sure he would—'

'Out of the question,' Maria interrupted. 'I know just how he'd feel about it and I don't want to spoil his relationship with Merlin. And it would.'

'I can't believe he'd hold that against his own son.'

'Trust me. He wouldn't mean to but he would. I know him. For all his trendy appearance and liberal talking, he's quite conservative at heart.'

'Dare I say that's a bit rich coming from a man with two families up and running alongside each other.' Annalise stopped. 'Maria, I'm so sorry, I shouldn't have said that.'

'But it's true, and one day Merlin will have to know all about it, along with all this other crap.'

'Not if you shut it away in the past where it belongs. Sam is Merlin's granddad and a terrific one too.'

'I know, but I have to do this. I have to find out if Samson is still alive. I want to look him in the eye and ask him—'

'Maria, Maria.' Annalise grimaced. 'Isn't it better to let sleeping dogs lie?'

'Maybe, but I'm not going to. Now what was the name of that programme you mentioned last night? The daytime telly chat show thing?'

Annalise raised her eyes towards the ceiling and sighed. 'I was talking crap last night, I reckon. I was a bit pissed and talking nonsense.'

'Go on, tell me,' Maria pleaded. 'I can always watch it for myself now. I've never really had the chance to watch daytime TV, maybe it's time I got out of the rat race and relaxed. Your life seems so much happier than mine.'

'Your life could be exactly the same if you let the past go. You can't change it so just tuck it all away in the done and dusted file and enjoy the present. It's easy once you start. I've done it, remember.'

'Maybe I might give it a go eventually but first I need to find Samson.'

Shaking her head, Annalise plopped a plate in front of her friend with a fat, warmed croissant in the middle of it and a blob of jam on the side.

'You are such a masochist, Maria Harman, your life would be so much happier if you'd just accept that the past is part of who you are, you really can't change it whoever you talk to.'

'Maybe, but I can't accept it until I've put all the pieces together.'

'OK, but in the meantime eat your breakfast and do something about that phone of yours that's been vibrating and bouncing all round the room.'

Maria loved Annalise dearly but she knew she didn't really understand the issues that plagued her. Although she had struggled with serious illness she had always had the support of her close and loving family to help her through.

Snatching up her mobile phone she skimmed her missed messages and then chucked it in her handbag.

'They can all wait. Now come on, tell me again about the programme, please? It's got to be worth a try.'

At just before two o'clock that afternoon Maria arrived back home and, after pleading a stomach bug to Ali, ran straight up into the apartment over the salon and perched in front of the wide-screen plasma TV that was Ali's pride and joy, waiting for *Tallulah Talks* to start.

Annalise had jokingly planted the seed of the idea in her mind and although they had laughed about it the night before, in the cold light of day it seemed on

the surface to be a brilliant short cut to finding Samson.
When she had told Maria that the show did all the
donkey work involved in finding lost relatives in
exchange for the reunion being shown on the programme, it sounded like the perfect solution.

As soon as the intro music played and Tallulah
bounced down the steps towards the camera, Maria
was riveted to the TV screen.

Annalise had described the programme as 'car crash
telly, you know you shouldn't be looking, you don't
want to look, it isn't nice but you can't help yourself'.

Playing to the camera, the effervescent presenter,
dressed in a black suit that would have looked sombre
except that she wore nothing under the jacket apart
from a Wonderbra, seductively encouraged the guests
to bare their souls and their lives to the fired-up and
baying audience mostly made up of younger women.
Invariably the female guests were received sympathetically, however shocking their confession, while the
males were booed and hissed almost before their feet
hit the stage. It was glaringly obvious that the programme had been carefully put together to provide a
shocking snapshot of the most sensational relationship
problems they could find to slot into one hour.

At the end of the credits there was a web address
and Maria rushed to her computer and logged on to
the website. Clicking through, she found exactly what
she was looking for. *Are you looking for a long-lost
relative? Are you prepared to be reunited in front of the*

audience? Contact our helpline . . . Maria made a note of the number and then grabbed a notebook from her desk to write down everything she knew about Samson. The man who, with one single act, had both directly and indirectly ruined so many lives.

Meticulously listing everything that Sam and Granny Bentley had told her, Maria chewed over the best way to approach the programme. She could hardly say she was looking for the man who raped her mother, so she decided she would pretend that she knew nothing about the circumstances other than that he was her birth father and she desperately wanted to get to know him. Maybe someone would recognise him and call.

Nothing ventured, nothing gained, as Sam, her true father, would say.

Sam! Maria suddenly felt guilty as she remembered the missed messages on her phone. She knew she would have to phone him, and also Ruth, but she wanted to plot her course of action first.

Chapter Twenty-nine

'Things have changed between us!' Ali suddenly blurted out with an angry edge in his voice as he stood in the doorway to the salon. 'It's just not the same any more. Are you seeing someone? Because if you are, I want you to tell me. I don't want you taking the piss out of me behind my back. I need to know.'

'Don't be ridiculous, Ali, do you really think I'm that much of a hypocrite?' Maria snapped, turning slightly and hiding her face behind her hair so that she didn't have to meet his eye. 'If I was seeing someone else I wouldn't still be here, would I?' This much was true but he was spot on about the rest of it.

Things had changed dramatically over the weeks since Finola's death and she was finding it hard to pretend that everything was fine in her life. Their easy personal relationship had gradually become so strained it seemed as if only their professional partnership, and of course Merlin, held them together.

Forcefully she shoved past him back into the empty salon and briskly started buffing the already sparkling mirrors.

'Well, why are you being like this to me then? Why won't you even look at me?' he asked, chucking combs and scissors into the steriliser. 'It's been like it ever since your mother died, and I don't see why. I mean, let's face it, you couldn't stand her. You've been distant and distracted and you jump six foot every time that fucking mobile of yours rings.' He looked at her face in the mirror. 'I need to know if it's anything to do with the night you spent with *your friend* after the funeral?'

The bitter sarcasm in his voice was hard to miss but Maria chose to ignore it because she understood why he was doing it. She knew she was being unfair to him but she couldn't help it, she just didn't want to be near him.

Ever since she had found out about the circumstances of her conception she hadn't been able to think about anything else. Every person who spoke to her and every minor event felt like an irritating distraction from her obsession.

'Ali, just leave it, will you? There is no one else, I promise. You know I was with Annalise. I've just got a lot going on, my mind is mush right now with it all. I need to work through it on my own.'

'You're giving me crap!' Ali slowly shook his head. 'Give me one good reason why I should believe you when you won't tell me what's going on? What exactly am I supposed to think?'

'It's just all the shit surrounding my mother and the funeral and everything,' Maria said, frantically wielding the duster. 'It's got to me, that's all. I've got issues that I need to resolve by myself. Sometimes things happen that don't actually involve you, believe it or not. I'm sorry if that's not what you want to hear, but you're irritating me with all this nonsense.'

'I'm irritating you?' He glared. 'Well, sorry! And like I'm supposed to believe all this shite about issues! Now there's a meaningless soundbite if ever I heard one, a great excuse for you to behave like a sulky five year old for nearly three months.'

Angrily Maria whipped round to face him. 'OK, Ali, you want honest, you'll get honest. I don't give a flying fuck about what you do or don't believe so just don't push me too far, right? I'm trying to be nice here but you keep on and on, push, push, push.'

'Trying to be nice? So sleeping in the guest room is being nice, is it? Avoiding me all the time is being nice? I want to know what it's all about, Ria. We can't let this fall apart, we've both got far too much to lose if our relationship goes belly up.'

'Aha, of course.' Curling her lip, she shook her head slowly. 'Now we're getting to the crux of it. You don't actually give a toss about me personally, just the good old business.' She spat the words at him venomously. 'I'm not that goddammed stupid, I know where your priorities are and I know how far down your fucking list of priorities me and Merlin perch. Numero uno, the salon, numero dos, the wife and kids, numero end of the line, me and Merlin.'

'Don't twist what I'm saying.' Ali swivelled his eyes at her. 'You know exactly what I mean, the business is our livelihood.'

A tight, humourless smile flashed across her face. 'Yep, unfortunately I do know exactly what you mean, Ali. If we split up then it might screw the business. Well, right now, I don't really give a toss about the precious business so if it's all right with you, I'm going to have a shower.'

Once away from him, Maria quickly dismissed Ali and his questions from her mind, as well as her anger at him. As the fierce jets of water pummelled the back of her neck, her mind was again back with the image she had built up in her mind of Samson.

Granny Bentley had dragged a description from the back of her confused mind and although Sam had warned her about taking it too seriously it had helped her build a picture in her mind.

Tallish with muscles, Granny B had said, tanned looking, short, dark, curly hair, too many teeth for the size of his mouth, about twenty and with either a scar or a dimple on his chin. However hard she tried to jog her grandmother's failing concentration, Maria hadn't been able to find out anything else.

Ever since she had learned the truth, it seemed that no matter what she was doing, a part of her mind was constantly in that place where Finola Harman, a deeply religious mother of three young sons, was raped in her own home. Attacked by a young man, possibly a lot younger than her, who she had thought was nothing more than a friendly travelling companion. A friend of a friend, certainly not someone to be scared of, certainly not someone who would attack a lone woman.

Maria gritted her teeth as she thought about the circumstances once again. Running her soapy hands over her body she wondered about the anonymous man's genes that formed part of her own make-up. A rapist's genes.

As the shampoo ran down her face into her eyes she almost savoured the stinging pain that distracted her from her mental torment.

Every time she closed her eyes she could see the image of her mother as a young woman walking from the bus stop with the man, unaware of what was about to happen, and every time her mobile phone burst into life she jumped, hoping that it was the call she was waiting for. The call from *Tallulah Talks*. The call that just might lead her to the confrontation she wanted more than anything she had ever wanted in her life before.

Wrapping herself in an enormous bright yellow bath sheet Maria wandered over to the mirror and studied herself closely, her features, her colouring, her hair texture. All too aware that she looked nothing like Finola, she wondered if she resembled Samson. She guessed that she probably did. Her skin tone definitely came under the heading of olive.

When she was with the naturally blonde Annalise she looked quite dark but alongside Ali she looked quite pale.

Suddenly her mind was back with Ali. So much had changed for her recently that she wasn't sure of anything any more. Annalise was convinced that she should confide in Ali, that she should tell him everything, but Annalise didn't know him like she did.

Ali was a mass of contradictions where his traditional upbringing clashed with his modern way of life. It was all very similar to Maria's own background and she could see that that was why they had been drawn to each other in the first place.

Frustrated by Maria's intransigence, Ali Shah crashed around in the empty salon. Much as he wanted to go upstairs and continue the argument, he realised it would be a waste of time with her in the mood she was in. The same mood that had enveloped her ever since the day Finola Harman had died.

Snatching up a broom he meticulously swept the shiny tiled floor before, pushing it ahead of him, he went into the small kitchenette at the rear of the salon and absent-mindedly clicked on the kettle.

He wanted to believe Maria and deep down he did because he knew her so well, but at the same time he couldn't work out what it was that had made her so distracted and distant with him, and even more bewildering was the way she was with Merlin who seemed to spend more time with Sam and Ruth than he did with his mother.

Ali had been born and bred in London and loved it there. He loved the buzz of excitement that went with living and working in the capital and he also loved the fact that he had a flourishing business and could enjoy life to the full. Unless of course Maria wanted out and expected her share back in hard cash.

Leaning against the tumble dryer which was humming loudly and vibrating against his leg, he wondered how best to keep the business whole without showing him in a bad light. He was a good businessman and had ensured from the start that the legalities were all in order and in his name but he knew that for the good name of the salon he would have to keep Maria onside in the event of a break-up.

Once again he wondered exactly what it was that was making Maria behave as she was.

On the spur of the moment and watching furtively over his shoulder in case Maria returned to the salon, he picked up the phone and punched in a number.

'Sam? It's Ali. I'm sorry to trouble you but I'm worried about Maria, there's something really wrong but I don't know what it is. I really need your help.'

Sam's reply made Ali frown. He pressed the receiver close to his ear and cupped his hand round his mouth.

'What do you mean how much has she told me? Told me about what? She's told me nothing about anything since she came back after the funeral. I've asked and asked. Can you talk to her? I'm really worried.'

Ali listened intently to everything Sam was saying. It was all too apparent that something was going on that he didn't know about and that infuriated him. With so much at stake he was determined to find out everything by fair means or foul.

Chapter Thirty

Davey very nearly turned and walked away from the door at the last moment; that was what his common sense told him to do. But while his brain told him to go, his emotions screamed at him to stay.

Hesitating on the step, he tried to reason himself out of it and wondered again if he really wanted to open up old wounds, to catch up with and be reminded of the traumatic past that he had spent so long burying.

Common sense lost out and he gave in to his impulse and pressed sharply on the doorbell. He waited, his professional smile fixed in place.

'Hi, Annalise. It is Annalise Carson, isn't it?' Apprehension bubbled away in his stomach as he stood on the doorstep face to face with Maria's old school friend.

At first he had thought it was probably Maria's home, but a quick investigation of the electoral roll the next day showed that it was the home of Dominic and Annalise O'Leary. It had taken him several days of mind searching to remember who she was but eventually it had come to him. Annalise Carson. The pretty little thing who had been seriously ill. The one all the boys had been desperate to get off with; all the boys, that is, except for himself who, from his very first day, had only ever had eyes for Maria.

'Well I never! Davey Allsop! What are you doing here? How did you know where to find me?' The words were staccato but her expression was friendly. 'That's assuming of course that this isn't all one great big coincidence. Maybe you're really here to sell me some manky old dusters.'

'No coincidence at all, Annalise, and I certainly have no dusters.' He smiled. 'It's you I want to see and I feel you're not actually that surprised. Have you got five minutes? I'll explain as briefly as possible.'

'Yes, I've got five minutes, and of course I'm prepared to listen to what you want to say,' she smiled slightly, 'but be aware, I have a memory. I remember Eddie Harman.' She stood aside and motioned for Davey to enter. 'And it's not Carson any more. I'm married now.'

'Who's the lucky man?' Davey flashed his amiable smile at her.

'That's not really anything to do with you, is it?' Annalise smiled back equally amiably but it was a put-down nonetheless.

'You're right of course. I'm sorry but I'm really quite nervous.'

Davey watched curiously as Annalise led the way down the compact hallway through into a small con-servatory that had been added on at the back of the terraced house and which encroached drastically on the already minute back yard.

Out of the schoolmates he could remember, Annalise would have been the one person he would confidently have predicted being successful in her life. He would have imagined her as a model or an actress with a financially successful husband on her arm. He would certainly never have pictured her still living in her old home town, let alone ensconced in a tiny railway worker's cottage.

'Well, Davey, what exactly is it that you want from me? Not that I can't guess.' Annalise sat down at the small rattan breakfast table and inclined her head to the opposite chair. 'It's Maria you're after, isn't it?'

'Well, you believe in getting straight to the point, don't you?' Davey looked at her and raised an eyebrow. 'Yes, you're right, I do want to meet up with Maria. I want to talk to her and I want to explain about Eddie. I still think of him and regret being so recklessly thoughtless.'

'I don't doubt it but I don't think she'll be very receptive,' her voice was gentle as she spoke, 'because whatever else, he's still dead. I don't think Maria will want to hear your version of events. Most of it came out in court, after all.'

Davey stood up and looked out of the window at the paved courtyard dotted with enormous plant pots and centred with colour-washed benches around a small table.

'I did write to her, you know, to apologise as best I knew how, that was all I could do. I couldn't turn the clock back. I wish I could have but I couldn't.'

'No, I know that. But neither could Maria or her family. You know they blamed her, don't you? Her mother and brothers? In fact I think her mother poured more hatred in her direction than in yours. Which was strange considering how they were all so mean to Eddie when he was alive.'

For the first time since he was released from prison, Davey could feel tears prickling at the back of his eyes as the guilt washed over him again. Suddenly he was back in the courtroom with all the eyes staring at him with open loathing. He focused hard on the furthest corner of the high fence that enclosed the small court-yard and gritted his teeth.

'How is she now? It's been such a long time.'

Annalise didn't answer so Davey turned to look at her.

'Please tell me. It's not an unreasonable question, is it? I just want to know how she is. When I saw you both at the funeral I panicked and ran. I know it was stupid but I didn't know what else to do. And then, like a bloody stalker on the loose, I followed you both back here.'

Annalise shook her head and grinned. 'I guessed that the second I saw you on the step. But tell me, why were you at the funeral anyway? Finola Harman wasn't someone you cared about and I'm sure you would have anticipated the reaction from the Harmans if you'd been seen.'

'Honestly? I don't know. I saw it in the local paper when I was visiting Dad in hospital and curiosity got the better of me. I wanted to see Maria from a distance. I stayed out of sight until the hearse pulled away. I expected Maria to be in the car. You can't imagine the panic I felt when I realised she was about to walk into me.'

Annalise laughed drily. 'Maria wasn't even welcome at the funeral, believe it or not, and as for going to the cemetery, can you imagine her in the same vehicle as the golden boys? She's not seen them since Eddie died; she'd not even seen her mother until a few days before.'

Davey rubbed nervously at his lips first with his knuckles and then with his fingertips. 'I caused her so much damage, didn't I? Do you think she'll see me? Would you ask her?'

'Of course I'll ask her if you really want me to but I want you to go away and think about it for a few days first. Be sure it's what you really want. Maybe this particular can of worms is best left closed. Maria has her life and from what you've told me, you have yours and you seem to have made the most of it.' She stood up and touched his arm gently. 'Davey, I don't want to be judgemental, I'm the outsider and this isn't my call but Maria is having a hard time right now with one thing and another. I don't know if she can handle seeing you.' Annalise looked at him for a moment and then said brightly, 'Now, would you like a drink? Then you can tell me everything you've been up to. You have an air of success about you now, you're certainly not the same little ragamuffin that I remember!'

Davey laughed loudly. 'I've been called most things in my time but never a ragamuffin, or not to my face at least. Yes please, I'd love a drink and a catch-up. I've spent so long trying to forget the past and yet now I want to know all about it. Very strange, huh?'

An hour later Davey held out his hands and took both of hers in his. 'Well, I can't believe how quickly the time has gone, especially after I was expecting you to send me packing at the off!'

Annalise smiled widely. 'Davey, you wouldn't believe how happy I am that you've got your life so well in order. I am so impressed, it makes me feel quite emotional.'

'If anyone else said that I'd think they were being sarcastic but you mean it and that's so nice to know. So, about Maria, will you speak to her?'

'Of course. If you think it over and still want me to do that then I shall, I'll tell her exactly what you've told me and then leave it to her to make her own decision, but as I said, she's in turmoil right now. Now give me your mobile number and I'll call you.'

Davey sat in his car outside Annalise's house for several minutes before pulling out and heading slowly back to his car showroom, hoping Paula wouldn't be there. The thought made him feel guilty because he knew he wouldn't be where he was without her, but she was beginning to drive him crazy with her constant checking up on him. Her insistence on knowing exactly what he was doing every minute of the day and who he might be doing it with was making life very wearing. For all his faults, Davey had never once cheated on Paula and he resented living under a constant cloud of suspicion.

In the beginning he had been perfectly content to be in a relationship with Paula and to be dependent on her. Straight out of prison and deliberately away from his home town, Davey had been emotionally lost until she came into his life and took control of all aspects of it. But now he felt suffocated and didn't know how to deal with the situation.

Chapter Thirty-one

Paula Wellbeck sat at her overly cluttered dressing table, studying herself critically in the ornate triple mirrors. Moving her head, she studied her face from every angle but no matter what she did there was no getting away from the fact that she was starting to look old. She pulled back on her hairline, drawing her skin taut. The effect was instant and she could see that it took a good ten years off. Ten years that would bring her a little closer in age to David. As she relaxed her hands she watched her face sink back down and the wrinkles reappear around her eyes and across her forehead.

Shaking her head in frustration she reached out for her pack of cigarettes among the anti-ageing lotions and potions and vast range of cosmetics that she had been experimenting with. Angrily lighting a long slender cigarette she inhaled deeply and was horrified to see the wrinkles around her thinning lips fan out top and bottom. Just like a cat's arsehole, she thought to herself in horror as she quickly looked away. Inhaling again, she imagined the disgust David must feel at seeing her looking more like his mother than his lover.

She reached out again but this time for the phone. She needed the reassurance of hearing David's voice but once again she couldn't reach him. His phone was switched to the messaging service.

'David, it's me and you're missing once again. Call me back the instant you get this message. You're fucking me about again.' Her voice was strong and assertive but underneath she wanted to cry, she was convinced David had found someone else, someone nearer his own age.

She dialled another number.

'Rupert darling, what are you doing with yourself today? I'm so completely pissed off with everything and in need of cheering up, can you escape for a drink with your old mother?'

Although Paula Wellbeck had had three children during her marriage, only Rupert, the eldest and her only son, still lived in England. Both her daughters lived abroad and had their own lives and successful careers but Rupert had gravitated home after university and lived a mere ten minutes away from her and David's apartment. Luckily for Paula, Rupert was his father's son and had an easy-going nature so he had never taken offence at his mother's choice of partner who was only a few years older than he was.

Paula had just finished getting dressed when the doorbell rang.

'Rupert. That was quick, I take it you're at a loose

end. I've just got to finish layering on the old slap and I'll be with you. Where shall we go? Somewhere nearby then we don't have to worry about driving.'

The young man leaned forward for a hug and kissed his mother on both cheeks affectionately.

'I have this feeling that you need to relax over a glass of chilled something or other. How about the Riverside? We can sit outside, watch the river and ruminate on life.'

'Sounds good. There's something I want to discuss with you.'

'Aha, Mother suddenly sounds serious.' Rupert pulled a face and crossed his eyes. 'Am I in trouble? "Something I want to discuss with you" used to be Wellbeck speak for an imminent bollocking.'

'Of course not.' Paula smiled. 'I'll tell you when we get there.'

'No, no, you'll tell me now, I can't wait that long.'

'OK, I want some advice; there's something I want to run by you.' Pausing, she looked at her son. 'I've decided that as I look like such an old hag I'm going to sneak off abroad for a few weeks to have a secret facelift and I want you to cover for me with David. I don't want him to know.'

'Oh, Mother.' Rupert held up his hands. 'Honestly, don't be so daft, you don't need anything lifted; you're gorgeous and you know it, you don't look anywhere near your age. A facelift? Come off it!'

'Thank you, darling, I know you mean well but I

also know you're lying through your teeth. Look at this turkey neck.' Paula tugged at the skin under her neck. 'Yuk! While I look old and haggard and ready to retire, David is young and good-looking and in his prime. I have to do something.' Paula looked at her son affectionately as she spoke, aware that he loved her regardless.

Rupert Wellbeck certainly didn't look like the millionaire he had become after the death of his father. Tall and lanky, he still wore worn-out jeans and baggy T-shirts with weird slogans and logos spread across them. But his angular face, framed by unkempt dark brown wavy hair, was devastatingly handsome and he was never short of female company.

'Mother, I think you're nuts but if that's what you want then go for it but I don't know how you're going to keep it secret, I don't even know why you want to keep it a secret for that matter. David's not like that.'

'Maybe not now but he might be in a couple of years and I don't want to take the chance.'

'OK,' suddenly Rupert was serious, 'but I want you to promise me that you're going to do this properly. You have to go to your doctor and get a recommendation. You can afford the best so make sure you get it.'

Arm in arm they left the apartment and for once Paula wasn't worrying about where David was.

Chapter Thirty-two

Maria concentrated on counting her steps as she walked across the salon to where her phone was ringing in the drawer; she forced herself to feign a nonchalance she didn't feel in an attempt to show that she wasn't desperate to answer it. Ali was watching.

The suspense of waiting for the all-important call was driving Maria towards breaking point and her nerves were in shreds.

'Yes? Oh, Annalise, hi there. How are you?' Her shoulders slumped as she tried to disguise her dismay at yet another false alarm.

'Tonight? Oh, I don't know, I'll have to ask Ali, we don't close until eight and there's Merlin. Tell you what, I'll have a chat with him and call you back in five minutes, he's with a client right now.'

Despite her overwhelming disappointment because it wasn't the call she was hoping for, Maria was all too aware of Ali trying to listen in on what she was saying while at the same time trying to look interested in the client in front of him at the mirror.

'Ali, honey, Dom is working away again so Annalise

has invited me to a meal tonight at her place. Is it all right with you if I go?' Maria called across to him, aware that it would look churlish in front of the clients if he refused. 'I won't drink and then I can drive home. I won't be late and I promise I won't leave opening up to you again, I'll hurl myself out of bed tomorrow like a tornado.'

'Yeah, sure, but I've got a better idea, why don't we both go? That way I can drive and you can have a drink. I don't mind spending the evening sat between two gorgeous women.' Ali grinned and winked, playing up to the full salon, trying to make it sound as if it was part of the usual banter and leaving Maria with no choice but to join in.

'No way, Casanova,' Maria retorted, with a forced grin. 'We're talking a girlie night, you'd be bored witless, but thanks for the offer, I'm sure I can lay off the old vino for a night.'

'I don't mind,' he said lightly. 'I'm sure Sophie will babysit. I'll phone her in a minute, it'd be nice to drive out of London and clear out the lungs.'

Maria gave it a few minutes to avoid giving the staff and clients any cause to gossip before going through to the utility room and then calling to him.

'Ali, have you got a minute? I need some help, I think this sodding dryer is playing up again.'

Ali excused himself from his client and followed through. Maria shut the door gently.

'Ali, will you stop pressuring me, you're acting like

a fucking jealous juvenile. I am allowed to go out for the evening without you. I'm not going out on the shag, I'm going to see Annalise at her house.' Maria's expression was venomous. 'We're not even going out. I don't want you with me so do yourself a favour and stop play-acting in front of the whole salon.'

'Why don't you want me to go with you? What have you got to hide this time, Maria? What's going on?'

'Oh, shut up! I'm not going through this again. Read my lips, I am not having an affair, I'm going to have a meal with Annalise!'

'Why don't I believe you? Why don't I believe that it was even Annalise on the phone?'

'Because you're a suspicious asshole, that's why. Why won't you give me some space? Just leave me alone, I'm so sick of all this.'

As they glared at each other, the phone she was still grasping in her hand started ringing again.

'Yes?' she snapped into it, her eyes still furiously locked on Ali's.

'Is that Maria Harman?'

'Yes, it is,' she replied, feeling her heartbeat increase.

'Hi there,' the voice bounced back. 'I'm Hattie, one of the researchers from *Tallulah Talks*. Is this a good time to talk with you, Maria? Is it OK for me to call you Maria?'

Maria's heart started to palpitate with such force she felt dizzy. 'I can't hear you, can you hold on a minute while I go outside? The reception is really bad.'

Ignoring the bad vibes from Ali, Maria rushed through the salon and out into the street.

'What do you think I should do?' Maria frowned fiercely as she discussed it with Annalise later that evening, but then, just as quickly, she smiled. 'No, don't answer that, I already know what you think I should do. Nothing!'

'Well, that's all academic now, isn't it? You've already done something, you've told them you'll do the stupid show. I wish I'd never mentioned it to you.'

'Well, I'm glad you did and yes, I have sort of agreed. I mean there are still some things to discuss, someone is coming to see me next week, but in principle . . .' Maria looked sheepish as she moved forward to the edge of her chair and leaned towards her friend. 'It'll be OK, I'm sure. I'm actually looking forward to it, it'll be an experience if nothing else.'

Annalise shook her head, concern written all over her face. 'I don't know about that. What did Ali say about it?'

Maria glanced away guiltily and didn't answer.

'You have told him, haven't you? Oh Maria, you must have told him.'

'I haven't told him and I'm not going to. I can't, we both know what he'll say. It's best this way.'

'So let me get this straight.' Annalise spoke slowly and emphatically. 'You're going to appear on national television appealing for the father you never knew existed, the man who raped your mother, to come forward, and you think no one you know is going to see it? That no one is going to tell Ali? Or Merlin?'

'Well, I suppose I'll have to tell Ali after it's happened but by then it'll be too late for him to stop me, and I don't see why anyone would tell Merlin.'

'Oh, for God's sake, Maria, you have to think this through a little better than that, you're not being logical.'

'I have thought it through, I haven't thought of anything else for weeks and weeks, ever since I found out all that shit about myself,' Maria snapped. She jumped up from the chair and started pacing around the furniture. She wasn't used to hearing Annalise be so assertive. 'I don't have to explain anything to Ali or anyone else. This is something that I have to deal with.'

'But Maria, you have to consider him and especially Merlin, you have to think of him in all this, and anyway, you've always told me how much you have to be grateful to Ali for.'

'Way back when maybe, but I've paid him back tenfold. Without me, Head Start wouldn't even exist let alone be the money-making machine that it is. The ideas were all mine.'

'Maybe, but without Ali, there would be no Merlin.'

For a few seconds the two women stared at each other. Annalise cracked first and looked away with a wry smile. 'Come on, Maria, we've been friends for so long, we don't want to fall out now. Tell me about the programme. Did they give you a date for your appearance on the show?'

Maria sank back into her chair and both women sighed and relaxed.

Maria pulled a face. 'No, I've got to have some sort of arty-farty counselling first. For fuck's sake, don't they think I know what I'm doing? I'm a big grown-up who walks and talks all by herself, I don't need some do-gooder investigating my intentions and making judgements.'

'Mmm, I have to say I think it's a good idea. At least you have to think through what you might be doing before going ahead with something that could change your whole life and mess up your head at the same time.'

'But my life has already changed. Surely you'd do the same thing in my situation.'

'No, I don't think I would, seriously I don't. And what about your dad? Sam, I mean. Doesn't he deserve some consideration in all this? I'm so scared you're going to end up regretting this.'

'Maybe. But it's something I have to do. No one else seems to give a toss about justice. The man's a rapist, he could have done it before and maybe since.'

'Don't try and convince me you're doing this for the good of the world. You're doing this for you, which would be fair enough if I didn't think that you're going to do yourself so much damage in the long run.'

'I only want to see him, to talk to him, to find out why . . .' Maria lied easily to her friend because she knew that if she told her the truth then Annalise would definitely stop her. 'Same as I want to ask Davey Allsop why. I think Finola's death has made me look at everything differently.' Maria moved the conversation away from Samson as smoothly as she could.

'Ah! Davey Allsop! Well, I might be able to help you there, if that's what you really want.'

'How do you mean you can help? Do you know where he is?'

'He came round here.'

'Davey Allsop? Came to see you? Why?' Maria couldn't keep the incredulity out of her voice.

'Well, it was him at the cemetery and he followed us all the way back here. Anyway, he came to see me because he wanted to find out about you, to see how you are. He wants to see you.'

'What do you mean he wants to see me? The murdering bastard's got more neck than a fucking giraffe.' She paused and frowned when Annalise burst out laughing. 'Well, he has. I can't believe he'd say something like that. What are you laughing at?'

'You tell me you want to ask him why he did what he did and when I tell you you can because he wants to see you, you go off the deep end. What is it you really want?'

'I want you to tell me everything.'

'Do you want to hear that Davey Allsop has turned

his life around? 'Cos he has. He's a successful businessman in a regular relationship. He didn't go back
home after he was released from prison because he was
eaten up with guilt over Eddie. He still is.'

'Successful businessman? More like career criminal,
and like he ever gave Ed another thought. Once a
murdering bastard, always a murdering bastard.'

'Oh, come on. You asked and I'm telling you as I
saw it. The rest is up to you.'

Maria pursed her lips. 'Give me his address.'

'I don't know it and even if I did I wouldn't give
it to you in your current frame of mind. I've only got
his mobile number.'

'Give it to me.' Maria held out her hand and wag-
gled her fingers at Annalise.

'There are conditions.'

'Whatever.'

'No, I mean it, Maria. If you intend anything bad
then I'm telling you nothing. You're my best friend
and I love you dearly but I can't be party to that, I
can't let you hurt yourself.'

'I won't do anything. God, you're making me sound
like some sort of black widow woman walking around
plotting and planning and muttering, "Come into my
web, little man."' She laughed. 'What do you think I'll
do to him? I only want to talk.'

'OK, what I'll do is call Davey and arrange for him
to come round here when both of us are here. It'll be
easier to break the ice that way.'

Maria thought quickly. She knew if she gave Annalise any cause for concern then she could lose her chance to get to Davey Allsop.

'OK, if that's how you want to play it. Call him now.'

'Oh no,' Annalise snorted. 'I'm not going to do it while you're here. You have to trust me on this, Maria. I'll be piggy in the middle but only if you both play it my way.'

It took all Maria's will power to sit tight and smile receptively at her friend.

'OK, I'll leave it to you. I'm sure you'll do the right thing for me.'

Chapter Thirty-three

Maria swung her car off the road and roared up the drive, leaving wide tyre tracks in the gravel.

'Mummy, why are you driving so fast? Daddy always says you're a maniac behind the wheel and Grandpa will get so cross if you mess up his drive.'

'Give it a rest, Merlin.' Maria sighed. 'I'm not a maniac and Grandpa doesn't give a toss about his drive. I'm in a hurry, I've got things to do and you said you wanted to come with me.'

'I did want to come with you, but I don't want to die before I get there.' Merlin laughed at his own joke and started making strangling and gurgling noises.

Maria clenched the steering wheel ferociously. She loved her son with a passion but he was a very bright child, way ahead of his years, and he had an uncanny knack of making her feel stupid. And she hated that because it was the way Finola used to make her feel.

On the spur of the moment she pressed her foot on the accelerator while simultaneously snatching on the handbrake. Smiling, she watched Merlin's expression of horror in the rearview mirror as the wheels spun alarmingly on the gravel before she stopped the car expertly outside Sam and Ruth's front door.

'That'll teach you to criticise my driving, you little tyke.' Maria laughed as she jumped out of her car.

Before Merlin could move, Sam and Ruth appeared from the side of the house and each hugged Maria in turn before Sam opened the rear door of the car and let Merlin out.

'What was that all about?' Ruth asked. 'We heard the screech from round the back. I was expecting to find the SAS out here.'

'Merlin said he thinks I drive like a maniac so I thought I'd show him what the word means.'

'No I didn't say that.' The boy sighed. 'I told you it was Dad who said you drive like a maniac.'

'That's even worse.' Maria reached out and grabbed him in a stranglehold. 'How dare your father, who has a licence full of points and who truly thinks his surname is Schumacher, criticise me? Grrrrrr.' She pulled him from side to side, laughing as his feet left the ground. He started to giggle uncontrollably which Maria enjoyed.

Merlin Harman-Shah was a very serious child. Tall for his age with a mass of floppy dark hair and a pair of metal-rimmed glasses that magnified his already large brown eyes, he looked as intellectual as he actually was. He was also very good-looking and people frequently said, 'That boy will be a heartbreaker when he grows up.'

'So,' Sam put his head on one side and raised an eyebrow, 'to what do we owe the pleasure? We don't usually see you during the week, busy working woman that you are.'

'Is Sophie about?' Maria responded as if she hadn't heard the question. 'I thought she might like to take Merlin for a walk down the lane to the shop. Give him some fresh air after the oh-so traumatic drive that I've just put him through.'

Merlin looked down and kicked his feet through the stones but grinned mischievously. 'I think I might need some sweets to raise my sugar levels after the shock.'

Ruth smiled and held her hand out to him. 'Sophie's just popped over to see the, quote, *fit lad* next door. She'll be back in a few minutes.' She ruffled Merlin's hair affectionately. 'And then I know she'd love to spend some time with her favourite nephew.'

The group walked slowly into the house and headed, as they always did, straight through to the enormous but cosy farmhouse-style kitchen that Maria loved. The apartment over the shop in London where she and Ali lived was minimalist and modern and in keeping with the impression they both liked to create for the business but Maria yearned for the day when she could buy a big old house in the country exactly the same as the home that Ruth had created.

Whenever Maria visited Easter Lodge she had to stifle her feelings of envy for her half-sister's life and undisputed parentage; she had tried from the day Sophie was born to block it out but whenever she was feeling down she would try and imagine what it would have been like to have had Sophie's idyllic childhood.

She had lived with Ruth after leaving King's Crescent the day Eddie died but she had already moved to London by the time Ruth bought Easter Lodge. Ruth had insisted that she have a room in the new house and she would spend the occasional weekend there but it was never her home.

Sitting round the large pine table in the centre of the kitchen the group chattered inconsequentially, the three adults all aware that there was an agenda to this visit. No one said a word until after Sophie had appeared and whisked an eager Merlin off to the village shop.

'Dad, Ruth, I thought I should tell you, Davey Allsop has been in contact with Annalise, he wants to meet up with me,' Maria said without preamble. 'He wants to talk about Eddie. I want to meet him, to talk to him, but I'd like to know what you think.' Maria leaned back and folded her arms slowly and defensively before continuing. 'I've also decided that I'm leaving Ali. It's no big deal, we just don't get on any more and I want out. I'm leaving at the weekend.' The familiar feeling of detachment washed over her as she watched Sam and Ruth staring at each other in dismay. She knew what they were thinking before either of them spoke.

'I don't know which to comment on first, Maria.'

Ruth spoke gently. 'Maybe it's not for me to comment on any of it. Sam? What do you want to say?'

'I don't know.' He looked from Ruth to Maria. 'I just don't know what to say. Ali has phoned me a couple of times because he's so worried about you. You still haven't told him about the other business, have you? It certainly made it a little difficult for me.'

'No, I haven't told him any of it.' Maria glared defensively from Sam to Ruth. 'I mean, what do I say? "Oh, by the way, Ali, did you know your son's mother is the end result of rape? How do you feel about your son having rapist genes in him?" Yeah, right, I can just imagine how he'd react to that. You know how traditional he can be about some things.'

Sam looked directly into his daughter's eyes and held them. 'I'm sure he'd understand if you worded it correctly instead of being so flip, if you told him how it really happened. I think you're being unfair to him, he really is worried about you, you know.'

'Worried about the bloody business more like. That was one of the first things he said when he sussed all was not well chez Maria and Ali. He actually said we can't afford to have problems, it's bad for business. Well, stuff the business, I'm out of there.'

Maria noticed Sam and Ruth exchange nervous glances as if they knew what was coming next.

'OK, I can see you know what I'm going to ask so I may as well get it out of the way. Can Merlin and I come and stay for a short time? Just until we find somewhere else. I don't want to start dragging Merlin around from rental to rental but I don't have any cash until Ali buys me out.'

Sam stood up and walked nervously over to the window. 'I don't think you've thought this out and I can see you haven't talked it through with Ali. You can't just take a son away from his father without discussing it, it's not right, Maria, you know that.'

Maria looked at her father and tried to judge exactly what he was thinking. A part of her realised that she was being childish but she desperately wanted Sam to support her unconditionally, to reassure her that he would be there for her even if she was in the wrong.

'How come you're more interested in me leaving Ali than you are in Davey Allsop? This is the same person who killed Eddie. Remember Eddie? Your son? Don't you care that he's still around?'

'Don't be so facetious, Maria.' Ruth's voice was uncharacteristically sharp. 'I know exactly where your father's coming from and he's absolutely right. You and Merlin are the present and the future, Davey Allsop is in the past and of no consequence to any of us any more. That's where he should be left,' and she slammed her hand on the table, making both Maria and Sam jump. 'It's ridiculous and I'm surprised you're even entertaining the idea of meeting him after all this time, especially now. Surely you've had enough of old wounds?'

Maria was stunned. She had thought that Sam

wouldn't be happy about it all but she had never for a moment thought that Ruth wouldn't support her as she always had.

'So what you're saying is that you don't want me and Merlin here?'

'Oh, for heaven's sake, Maria. Your father and I both love you dearly and unconditionally but that doesn't mean we have to agree with everything regardless. We're allowed to say if we think you're wrong, and this time you are. You've gone the wrong way about deciding Merlin's future; surely Ali has as much say in it as you?'

Maria shook her head. 'Do you really not see what will happen? If I discuss this with Ali he'll not look at it from every perspective, he'll think belongings. Salon first and then Merlin. Before we know it, Merlin will be spirited away to his family in Birmingham and I'll be cut out of the salon.'

'Oh, come on, that's a bit dramatic, isn't it? Ali isn't like that. He wouldn't—'

'He would. I just know he would. Ali is obsessed with appearances both in business and in his personal life. He'd be mortified at the thought of someone finding out.'

Sam moved round the table to his daughter and put his arm round her shoulder. 'I'll say what I always say, think about it. Really think. Is this the right time to be making decisions like this, life-changing decisions, when you're not on an even keel?'

Maria again felt detached from the situation as they

tried to persuade her against leaving Ali. She wondered what they would say, how they would react, when they saw her on *Tallulah Talks*.

She knew she was being unfair but she was determined to do it all in the right order. She had to find Samson and get some answers, some revenge, before she went completely mad but she also knew she had to get Merlin away from Ali before the storm broke, otherwise she might lose him.

'If I promise to think about it a little longer, will you agree to us staying here if it comes to it? I'll think about talking it through with Ali and I'll try and be rational in—'

The roar of a car racing up the drive made them all look at each other and then there was a frantic hammering on the cast-iron door knocker.

Sam jumped up and headed out to the hall, Ruth and Maria close behind. He pulled the heavy door back but before he could say anything Ali was in the hallway.

'I want to know what the fuck is going on here and I want to know now. Maria? Tell me what this is all about. Why isn't Merlin at school?' Ali pushed through into the hall, shouting, 'Merlin? Merlin? Get here now, we're going home. Merlin?'

When there was no response he turned towards Maria, his face a mask of frustrated anger, raised his hand and slapped her hard across her cheek. The force made her stumble backwards into a large wooden cabinet. The back of her head cracked against it and she fell to the floor.

Ali looked alarmed. He leaned forward and stroked her face. 'I'm sorry, I'm so sorry, Maria. I didn't mean it, Maria. Where's Merlin?'

'Get out of this house!' Sam suddenly bellowed. 'No one lays a finger on my daughter for any reason. Now get out!'

Ruth, meanwhile, sneaked back into the kitchen and called Sophie's mobile phone. 'Get into a shop and stay out of sight until I call you again. Don't let Merlin out of your sight!'

Chapter Thirty-four

'Are you really sure you want to go ahead with this?' Annalise asked her friend in the moments before the researchers from the show were due to arrive. 'This is your last chance, once you've taken this step it'll be nearly impossible to go back. I bet they make you sign some sort of agreement so you don't screw up their bleeding-hearts show.'

'I'm sure and don't be such a worry guts,' Maria said with a smile. 'I'm definitely going ahead with it – in about six weeks' time, all being well. I can hardly wait. What do you reckon the chance is of someone telling me where to find Samson?'

'I don't know.' Annalise shook her head and turned down her lips. 'I mean, he's not going to come forward himself, is he? And if they find him and he doesn't want to meet you, there won't be anything you can do about it. The show won't be able to give you any information without his permission. I'm so worried you're setting yourself up for major disappointment.'

'Oh, I'll find him. One way or another, I'll find him.'

They were sitting opposite each other in Annalise's cosy sitting room which overlooked the pavement outside. They were trying to relax after Maria had spent most of the morning panicking as she prepared for the interview. Carefully dressed in well-cut light brown trousers and a pale blue shirt, and subtly made up with her hair pulled back in a pony tail, she hoped to achieve the right balance between appearing sad about her situation and looking striking enough to be good television. She crossed her legs and checked out her natural leather boots for scuffs, breathing deeply.

Maria had found it easy to lie to the researchers from *Tallulah Talks* when they had asked to visit her the week after the break-up with Ali. She had asked for the meeting to be at Annalise's because, she told them, she felt she might need a friend's support.

In the run-up to their arrival she had purposefully blanked her mind to everything but Samson. Her thoughts were so taken up with him that she had a positive mental picture of him that was constantly in the forefront of her mind. Her desire to meet him and confront him was overwhelming. So much depended on her appearance and presentation on the programme that she was determined not to do anything to jeopardise it; she knew she only had one chance to convince them that she was one hundred per cent honest about her intentions.

'I do appreciate you letting me meet them here,

really I do.' Maria smiled at Annalise. 'You're a good friend to me.'

'I'm not at all sure I'm doing right by encouraging you but Dom said it should be your decision to make.'

Maria's face registered her shock. She sat up straight and glared at Annalise. 'You told Dom? Shit, I didn't know you'd told him, why did you do that? I didn't want anyone to know until afterwards, until it was too late for them to stop me.'

'Maria! How could you? I've never kept anything from Dom and likewise him with me. He wouldn't dream of telling anyone and I'm surprised you're surprised!'

Maria opened her mouth to respond but right at that moment the doorbell rang.

'Oh my God, they're here. OK, OK, calm down,' she muttered to herself. 'Deep breaths and smile, deep breaths and smile . . .'

She grabbed Annalise by the hand and pulled her to the front door with her.

'Are you Maria Harman?' the taller of the two young women asked with a smile.

'Yes, I'm Maria, and you are?'

'I'm Hattie, and this is Agnetha, we're the researchers from *Tallulah Talks*.'

Maria held out her manicured hand and smiled widely. 'Would you like to come in? This is my best friend Annalise, this is her house. She's been such a support to me over this, which is why it was nice for me to meet you here so that she can hold my hand, metaphorically speaking.' Maria giggled lightly, aware that Annalise was looking at her quizzically, but she wouldn't meet her eye.

Everything about her appearance and mannerisms was designed to get her on the show. For weeks she had sat in front of the television every afternoon, single-mindedly studying the format and the guests, and analysing the dynamics that worked best. The dynamics that she was going to put into practice for the benefit of Hattie and Agnetha.

As they walked through, Maria clasped her hands and put her head on one side. 'I do so hope you can help me, that I'll get the opportunity to make my appeal on your programme. It's so important to me that I get to meet the man who fathered me. It'd be a dream come true to be able to see him, to get to know him.' Again the winning smile. 'You wouldn't believe how much this means to me!'

After the researchers had left, Maria sank back into her chair. 'God, I need a drink. How did I do? Do you reckon I swung it?'

Annalise looked at her friend. 'I didn't realise you were such a good actress, you nearly had me convinced that you were a helpless little girlie who wanted to find her long-lost daddy and be happy ever after.'

'Was I really that good?' Maria's eyes were alight

and she laughed excitedly – until she realised that Annalise was almost sombre.

'Yes you were and frankly, Maria, you scared me. Look, I need to know if you're lying to me about this Samson stuff. Somehow it doesn't ring true any more. If your father raped your mother then how can you possibly build a relationship with him? How can you not hate him on sight?'

'That's not fair. You know I want to meet him to find out what happened and why, I just had to lay it on a bit to make sure I get through. They only want interesting and over the top. Mousy wouldn't hack it, that's for sure. I had to make them want me on their poxy show.'

Annalise didn't answer and suddenly it was Maria who was disconcerted.

'You're not intending to say anything to them, are you? Annalise, please don't sabotage this for me, you know how important it is. I only want closure, to find the answers and to get it done and behind me so that I can get on with my life.'

'I won't sabotage it but from now on I'm staying on the sidelines. I felt really uncomfortable sitting there smiling while you were at the very least economical with the truth. I don't want the psychologist coming here, Maria, or those two creepy, smiling stick insects again.'

'But where else can I go?'

'Sorry, Maria, you're on your own.'

Maria didn't want to fall out with Annalise, they had been friends for such a long time and Annalise had supported her through thick and thin over the years, so she shrugged sheepishly.

'Fair enough. I suppose I can understand where you're coming from. But trust me, I only went through all that crap to get on the show, I think the end justifies the means so I wasn't lying as such. Still friends?' Maria smiled and held out her hands to her friend.

'Oh, you are such a pain,' Annalise smiled gently, 'but how could I possibly fall out with you? Just don't go on about that bloody show all the time! Come on, let's go out for lunch. We could walk to Purple's Wine Bar in town, it's not new, just a name change. I know you've not been there and it shouldn't be too busy on a weekday.'

Maria agreed immediately. She wanted to get her friend and confidante back to being just that.

The fashionable wine bar was small and friendly and set back from the main road in an alleyway. The inside had old-fashioned four-seater booths along the walls.

'Wine?' Annalise asked as Maria glanced around the bar, which was almost empty.

'Please. This is really nice, sort of trendy meets traditional in one room.'

'Dom and I often come in here, it doesn't encourage the lager louts and vino quaffers, it even does coffee.'

'Oh bugger, I'd better go now then before they

chuck me out. I'm a vino quaffer, or at least I will be very shortly!'

Both women laughed as they collected their drinks and then settled down in one of the cosy booths tucked away at the far end of the room.

'So, I know you don't want to talk about the show but can we have just a teeny bitch about the short and tall clones Hattie and, er, what was it? Agnetha? She's no more an Agnetha than I am, more like Aggie from Bethnal Green. Honestly, they were so far up themselves I bet they can see their own tonsils . . .'

Maria was still in full flow when Annalise, laughing so hard she was crying, held up her hand.

'Stop! That's enough. I want to tell you something before it's too late.'

Knowing her friend well, Maria stopped laughing and instinctively felt her senses sharpen. 'What do you mean too late? Too late for what?'

'I've arranged for Davey Allsop to meet us here. He'll be here in . . .' Annalise paused and looked at her watch, 'a few minutes so you have to decide now if you want us to stay or go.'

Chapter Thirty-five

As the words sunk in Maria felt so faint and sick with dread that she couldn't have got up and run away even if she'd wanted to.

'Why the fuck didn't you tell me before we got here?' Leaning forward she closed her eyes and rested her forehead on the table. Annalise reached over and rubbed her shoulder soothingly.

'Because I thought this was the best way. You said you wanted to meet him and this way you haven't had time to stew on it for days and get yourself in a state.'

'How could you do this to me? I thought we were friends. You should have told me . . .' Maria muttered angrily through the teak veneer of the table.

'OK,' Annalise responded lightly. 'I'll go outside and catch him, tell him not to come in. It's no problem.'

Maria's head shot up. 'Oh no, I'm not running away from the bastard . . .'

As she was speaking a figure approached the table and stopped beside it. Without looking she knew it was him but she found she couldn't turn her head to look, something inside her froze and she couldn't move or speak.

Annalise jumped up and kissed him affectionately on both cheeks.

'Hi, Davey. Ooops, sorry, David. I'll get you a drink. Maria has had a bit of a shock, I didn't tell her you were coming until about two minutes ago.'

'No, it's OK, I'll get the drinks . . .' His voice tailed off and he moved closer.

The shock that surged through her at the sound of his voice took Maria completely by surprise. The old aggression had gone and the intonation was different but the Allsop twang was still there, albeit muted and deeper.

Slowly she raised her eyes and looked directly at the once familiar face.

Davey Allsop. An older, more refined and definitely gentler version but there was no denying that it was him. Despite being dressed down in jeans and a casual white shirt, he exuded an air of affluence and grooming. And sexuality. He fitted into the wine-bar setting perfectly.

'Maria? Are you OK?' Annalise's voice broke through into her distracted thoughts. 'Maria? This is Davey . . .'

'Well, I did manage to figure that out for myself, thank you very much, Annalise. I was just a bit surprised, that's all.' Slowly she looked from one to the other and then focused challengingly on him. 'Well? Are you going to join us?'

'Would you mind?' He didn't smile, he just leaned his head slightly to one side and raised his dark, groomed eyebrows. 'I can understand if you tell me to piss off.'

'No.' She almost snarled the word. 'There are questions I want answers to.'

'I'll do my best.'

Annalise smiled. 'I'll get this round then. What would you like, Davey?'

'Brandy please, with ginger ale.' He smiled at her and she walked over to the bar.

Maria watched warily as Davey sat down opposite her. In an instant the years dropped away and she was sixteen again. Maria and Davey, the two teenage rebels, united against the world, hugging and giggling and vowing to be together forever.

'I hear you're doing OK for yourself now.' Maria looked him up and down. 'Quite the trendy businessman, according to my mate over there. Brandy and ginger ale? Who'd have thought it! I'd have predicted a pint of lager and a roll-up for Pikey Allsop!' As soon as the words were out she wished she could take them back but her initial instinct had been to wound him.

A sad smile played around the corners of his lips and he gently shook his head. 'I certainly wouldn't say trendy but I'm doing OK. I promised myself when I came out of prison that I'd be as straight as a poker from that moment on.'

'Eddie never had that chance.' Maria fixed her eyes on him angrily.

'I know that and for that reason alone I wanted to have a worthwhile life. OK, I don't volunteer for soup kitchens at weekends and I don't go trekking up mountains to raise cash but, trust me, I do my bit on his behalf. Even us pikeys have consciences, you know.'

Before she could answer, Annalise was back at the table with a tray of drinks.

'Do you want me to join you or shall I go?' she asked. 'I don't mind, you know, you can wander back home when you're done.'

'No!' they both answered in unison.

'Oh, OK then.' She smiled. 'How could I possibly resist an echo like that?' She shuffled along on the seat, propped her chin on clasped hands and looked from one to the other. 'So. Where are we at?'

After the initial stunted conversation the three of them settled down and superficially caught up on everything that had happened during the intervening years but all the while Maria was aware that the charming man entertaining them with edited highlights of his life was the same young tearaway who had killed her beloved Eddie all those years ago, the same person she had vowed to take revenge on one day. Yet she could feel the same tingle of sexual attraction that she had felt back then, although this time her feelings were far less innocent. She was sure that he felt exactly the same because every time their eyes connected, it was there between them like a flashing beacon. An animal magnetism.

After about an hour Annalise jumped up from her seat. 'Right, I've got things to do so I'm going to trot off to town and leave you two to it.' She delved into her handbag and produced a single key on a ring. 'Here's the spare key in case you're going to be late but can you give me a ring if you are? Just so that I don't worry. Sorry if I sound like a mummy!'

'Just hang on a bit and I'll come with you.' Suddenly Maria could feel herself panicking like a teenager at the thought of being left alone with Davey Allsop, but Annalise wouldn't play.

'No way. You two have a lot to catch up on and I've got to go to the bank and pay a couple of bills. Boring stuff but it has to be done. We can catch up in the morning before you go back to Suffolk.'

She almost ran out of the bar, leaving Maria and Davey sitting in an uncomfortable silence.

'Would you like another drink?' he eventually asked with a smile that Maria could see was the grown-up version of his old cheeky grin.

'Yes please.'

'Same again?'

'Please.'

As he leaned on the bar waiting to be served, Maria studied him carefully and tried to analyse exactly how she felt at seeing him again.

Imagining such a meeting over the years, she had often anticipated feeling uncontrollable anger; she had fantasised about slowly slipping a carving knife between his ribs or blasting his brains out at close range with a twelve-bore. But she had certainly never considered that within such a short time of setting eyes on him again she would want to rip his clothes off and drag him straight off to bed. Watching him, she couldn't help feeling pleased that she had dressed and done her make-up extra carefully that morning because of the *Tallulah Talks* interview. She knew she looked good, but Davey looked fantastic.

As he turned back to the table, Maria quickly looked down and pretended interest in the menu.

'Would you like something to eat?' he asked as he put the glasses down. 'I don't know what the food is like here. Or we could go somewhere else.'

'No, it's OK, I was just looking to see what they did. Just curiosity.'

Maria felt her face warming as she reached for her third glass of wine on an empty stomach. The excitement of the morning followed by the unexpected meeting with Davey Allsop had pushed her to such a high that the flush of alcohol was spreading rapidly over her face and neck and she was starting to feel quite light-headed.

'Maybe we should at least have a sandwich as we're drinking,' Davey suggested. 'I don't drink very much so it affects me quite quickly. You're not driving today, are you?'

'No, I'm staying the night at Annalise's. Her husband is away and I had an important meeting here this morning so it seemed logical to stay over but I hadn't realised that she'd pulled you into the equation.'

'Tell me about your life, Maria. Annalise gave me only a very brief précis. I know you had to leave home after Eddie, that your mother blamed you. I'm so sorry.'

'Yeah, well, she'd have soon found some other reason to get rid of me, she hated me so much. For so many years I didn't understand why and I hated her back and then, when it was too late to put things right, I found out why.'

'What reason can anyone have to hate their child? I know you were adopted but that shouldn't make any difference.'

Maria looked at him steadily and the years slipped away.

'I wasn't adopted, Davey, that was all a big fat lie that Mum and Dad fed me.'

His eyes opened with surprise. 'Not adopted? What do you mean? Wasn't it made official then? Have you found your real parents?'

Maria hesitated. Apart from Annalise she had confided her secret to no one outside the family and yet here she was with Davey Allsop on the verge of telling him everything. She wondered whether she could trust him but the doubt lasted only a moment; there was something between them that the intervening years and events hadn't destroyed.

'I suppose I have in a manner of speaking. Well, I know who they are. Sort of.' Hesitating again, she looked into his eyes so that she would be able to see his true reaction. 'Finola Harman wasn't my adoptive mother, she was my birth mother, she gave birth to me after she'd been raped by a young thug when my dad, Sam, was working abroad. Now I'm going to find the bastard who fucked up our lives and rip his balls off!'

Chapter Thirty-six

As they left the bar several hours and drinks later, Maria and Davey started to head in the general direction of Annalise's house. It seemed so natural when he put his arm round her shoulder that after a few minutes she looped her arm casually round his waist. They walked together the way they had all those years before.

'Did you say you brought your car with you?' she suddenly asked. 'What are you going to do about getting home?'

'It's OK, I'll leave it here. It should be safe in the car park. I hope. I'll get a cab home and collect it tomorrow. I certainly hadn't anticipated spending as long as this with you. I expected to be whacked within a few minutes, with my remains floating in the river.'

Maria studied his face as he smiled. The well-defined outline was the same although nicely fuller and his expression wasn't aggressive, but the sparkle was still there, as well as the sexual attraction.

Definitely the sexual attraction.

She smiled back at him and decided that time had been exceptionally kind to Davey Allsop.

'I think I've got enough going on without wasting time and energy hating you. Samson is my sole focus now, I have to find him, I really have to find him if I'm going to stay sane. I want to get my hands on that bastard so much it hurts.'

'As I said, I'll do all I can to help. Anything you want, just ask.' He pulled her tight towards him. 'I'll owe you forever, Maria Harman.' Suddenly he stopped and turned towards her. 'Stay the night with me, Maria.'

She felt her heart stop pumping for a split second before thudding so hard she was sure Davey would hear it.

'I can't. What about Paula? You're in a relationship you said, a long relationship. I can't be responsible for wrecking it.'

'It's already wrecked, I told you. My relationship with Paula was over long ago but I still feel an obligation to her. She helped me after prison, when I'd moved away from my no-good family and had no one. We're in business together which makes it more complicated.'

'A bit like me and Ali except that I did have Dad and Ruth and of course my little sister Sophie, but Ali came into my life when I was at an all-time low and that was it. Now we're in business together and we've also got a son together, but at least I've jumped ship. You haven't.'

'Is your split permanent? Will you go back to him? You do have a son.'

'Ali would never be able to accept the rape element in my background, I know it. But more important than that, I don't love him and don't want to go back to him. Same as he doesn't love me, he's just worried about the salon.'

Despite being in the middle of the pavement, Davey pulled her towards him and kissed her. Gently at first but then more fiercely and Maria couldn't help responding. They backed towards a shop doorway, completely oblivious of passers-by who were all pretending not to notice, but then suddenly she laughed.

'Oh dear, just look at us, Davey. We're acting like a couple of dopey teenagers again, kissing and groping in a doorway. For fuck's sake, let's be grown up and go and find a hotel!'

After pausing for a second as if to check that she was serious, he grabbed her hand and pulled her along the street, laughing and skipping, just the way he used to when they were teenagers.

When they got to the main road they linked arms and walked the short distance to an anonymous travel motel set back from the road on the edge of a boring industrial estate.

Neither of them noticed the shadowy figure that had been close to first one, then both of them, all day, and was only a few steps behind as they walked into the motel and booked a room.

The ordinary looking young woman, dressed in run-of-the-mill blue jeans, a charcoal sweatshirt and scuffed trainers, her mousy hair pulled back in a band at the nape of her neck, stopped and watched from the car park then pulled out a mobile phone and clicked on a number.

'Hello? It's Margaret, from the agency, calling in again. I've got a result for you. You were right. They've just checked into the Travel Motel at the crossroads by the main road. Do you want me to wait and get pix or are you going to drive over yourself?'

The woman cupped her hand over her other ear to hear better over the sound of the traffic.

'OK, I'll try for the pix and then I'll gather as much info as poss. I'll use my charms on the receptionist first then follow when they leave.'

Barely had they shut the door to their utilitarian room than Davey and Maria fell into each other's arms and simply hugged each other tightly. For a few seconds they just stood and savoured the moment before frantically tugging at each other's clothes and throwing them all round the room in their urgency until they were both standing naked. As they wrapped their arms round each other again they sank back onto the bed.

Without any foreplay Davey quickly pulled himself on top of Maria and, propping himself on his arms, entered her hard and fast. She wrapped her legs round his back to draw him closer inside her.

After a few short thrusts it was over.

'Oh God,' he sighed as he rolled back and tried to catch his breath. 'I'm sorry but I couldn't wait.'

Maria smiled. 'Me neither. We've got no self-control, either of us, have we?'

'Seems not.' He smiled and gently moved his fingers round the outline of her lips. 'As soon as I saw you again I knew I was still in love with you. Those eyes, it's those eyes. In all these years I've never forgotten them. If you weighed twenty stone, were grey as a badger and hadn't got a tooth in your head I'd still have instantly recognised those eyes and been drawn back into them.'

'Ah, but would you still have fancied me?' Maria smiled in the half-light that signalled the setting sun through a crack in the curtains.

'Yes, I would. It was always you I loved, Maria, the whole person, but I was young and stupid and thought I knew it all. If I hadn't been so pig-headed we wouldn't have fallen out and the stuff with Eddie wouldn't have happened.' He held her face gently and kissed her nose. 'If you knew how many nights I lay awake regretting everything, wishing I could turn the clock back, wanting so much to see you and explain.'

'Me too.' Maria sighed and snuggled up closer, wrapping her arms round his neck. 'Maybe we've both paid our dues now.'

'What do we do next?' Davey asked without looking at her. 'I shall have to tell Paula and try and come to some agreement over my showroom, you have to deal with Ali and the salon. How long do you think it will all take?'

Quick as a flash and with eyes wide, Maria was sitting up in the bed, clutching the sheet to her chest. 'Hang on, hang on, hang on. You're going too fast here. How can we start making plans so soon? We don't know each other, not really, we were friends as kids but we don't know each other as adults. We might have just shagged but we don't actually know each other.'

Quickly and silently Davey got out of the bed and snatched up the small plastic kettle which he took into the adjoining bathroom. Maria listened to the sound of running water and wondered if, once again, she'd overreacted.

'Davey, I'm sorry, I didn't mean it quite like it came out,' Maria called, backtracking and feeling guilty about her blunt response. 'All I meant was let's take this slowly. I've got so much baggage that needs sorting out, especially this *Tallulah Talks* thing and Samson. I have to find Samson and deal with him, I can't settle to anything until I've done that.'

Davey walked back and plugged the kettle in. Still with his back to her, he fiddled about with the cups on the stained plastic tray.

'Tea or coffee?' he asked casually over his shoulder.

'Coffee, black no sugar.' Maria smiled. 'You see what I mean? We have to get to know each other all over again, all our little habits and foibles. I'm sorry, really

I am, I still have this habit of speaking first and thinking after. I just want us to be realistic.'

He turned towards her and with a small smile gently nodded his head. 'Maybe you're right but there's a time and a place for being realistic and it's not when we've just made love in ten seconds flat.'

'Then come back to bed and we can do exactly as I said,' Maria laughed, 'take things slowly.'

Davey managed a grin before turning back and making the drinks. 'Do you reckon they do room service here? A bottle of Bolly? A tub of beluga for me to feed you from a silver spoon? What do you reckon?' He laughed as he handed her the small cup of instant coffee.

'I reckon we might be in the wrong hotel. Maybe a can of Coke and a bag of crisps out of the vending machine?' She smiled and then looked at him curiously. 'Would you rather we went somewhere else?'

Davey studied Maria seriously for several seconds.

'What?' Maria asked with a smile. 'What's wrong? Why are you looking at me like that? Does my bum look big in this sheet?'

'Nothing's wrong,' Davey replied, 'absolutely nothing. I was only thinking that I don't care where I am so long as I'm with you. I know that sounds trite but I mean it. So you choose the pace but just remember, I want to be with you, however long it takes.'

Leaning over, he took the cup from her hand and kissed her gently on the lips before pulling the sheet away from her.

'And just to get the record straight, your bum doesn't look big. In fact everything about you is just perfect, Maria Harman, and I love you.' Davey pulled her towards him before sliding back onto the bed and pulling her over on top of him.

It all felt so right to Maria that she couldn't bear to think past that moment.

Chapter Thirty-seven

The next morning Maria and Davey checked out of the motel together. Hand in hand and standing so close together they looked joined at the hip, both of them seemed down in the mouth as they waited for the taxi that would take them back to the real world. Neither of them spoke and they were so engrossed in themselves and their feelings that once again neither of them noticed the rather ordinary dark blue hatchback that was parked a couple of rows away.

The car followed the taxi.

'I'll call you,' Davey murmured, kissing her very gently as the cab pulled up outside Annalise's house. 'Later. I'll call later.'

Maria smiled as she clambered out. 'You'd better. As soon as you can.'

Standing on the pavement, she watched as the taxi pulled away with Davey's hand waving at her from the rear window.

Rather than use the key, Maria rang the bell and then hung her head in mock shame as Annalise flung it open.

'I don't suppose I need ask where you've been, I almost expected you two to jump on each other in the wine bar. The air was electric!' Annalise laughed as she let Maria in. 'But some not so good news. Ali has been calling virtually nonstop, he's left loads of messages, reckoned he needed to speak to you urgently but your phone was turned off.'

'Not turned off, just on silent. So was Davey's. Oh, Annalise, I can't stop grinning. I feel like a silly little teenager again.'

'And you look like one. Come on, spill!'

Maria smiled distractedly as she checked her phone for the first time since she and Davey had left the bar. 'Ooops, seventeen missed calls and eight text messages! Give me a minute, I just have to check that there isn't a problem with Merlin.'

'Merlin's fine, Ruth rang here this morning but I said you'd gone to get me some milk. No probs other than an irate Ali who was demanding to know where you were. I think Sam or Ruth had fobbed him off and I was next on the list.'

Maria walked over to her friend and hugged her tight. 'You do so much for me, I really do appreciate it.'

'How much do you appreciate me? Is it lots and lots?' Annalise shrugged her shoulders up tight and, eyes wide, giggled girlishly.

'Of course.' Maria giggled as well. 'Love you lots and lots and lots in fact. Why?'

'Because I want chapter and verse on whatever is going on between you and Davey Allsop. Assuming of course that he's still alive. You haven't just spent the night weighing his body down in the river, have you?'

'That's exactly where Davey himself thought he was heading apparently.' Maria slumped into a chair with a grin on her face. And then suddenly she felt the overwhelming impact of the events of the previous night. A part of her was convinced it had all been a dream but no, she had just spent one of the happiest nights of her life with the man she had spent so many years of her life hating. The man who now wanted to make a life with her. Or so he said.

In the cold light of day a twinge of doubt crept into her head for the first time. Maybe it was all talk to appease her over Eddie. Maybe he had just wanted to get her into bed as his own form of revenge.

'We spent the night together at the motel up the road, he says he loves me and wants to be with me. What sort of shit is that to lay on me right now?'

Annalise's mouth dropped open. 'Wow. That's sudden. I knew he was desperate to see you. How d'you feel about it?'

'Worried.' Maria pulled a face and shook her head. 'I'm suddenly worried that it's all a game, that maybe he's manipulating me. I hasten to add that I didn't feel that last night but now, back in the real world . . .'

'Never in a million years, you're just being your usual neurotic self.' Annalise's tone was emphatic. 'I like to think I'm quite shrewd with people and Davey struck me as genuine right from the start. I mean he could have just laid low and left it all in the past.' Hooking her hair behind her ears, Annalise pinned her friend with her eyes.

'Mmm. I suppose so. In the meantime I need to call Dad and Ruth and I should also call Ali but really all I want to do is sit and think about the past twenty-four hours. I can't believe what's happened. I must be absolutely barking mad.'

As she spoke, her mobile started trilling. She looked at the screen.

'Oh shit, it's Ali again. Why can't he leave me alone?'

'Maybe because you've got a son together? Maybe because he doesn't understand why it's suddenly all gone south?'

Maria didn't respond, she just kept looking at her phone, willing it to quieten. She didn't want to answer it because she knew that would bring her back to reality but her conscience agreed with Annalise.

She sighed and took the call. 'Hello. What's with the panic again? It's no good ringing me thousands of times and then not leaving one coherent message, is it?'

She rolled her eyes at the ceiling. 'Ali, please don't shout and carry on. Just don't harass me like this, I don't need it. I've told you, it's over.' She clicked the phone off and turned back to Annalise. 'Well, come on, you started all this, what should I do? Why did you have to bring Davey Allsop back into my life at this moment in time?'

Ali finished his cup of coffee in one gulp and then threw the mug full force across the kitchen in frustration. He was at a complete loss to know how to deal with the situation he had unexpectedly found himself in. When Maria had verbally laid into him a few days previously he had promised himself he would pull back, ignore her for a while and wait for her to come to him. A few days out of his life wasn't too much to sacrifice if it brought Maria to her senses.

But she hadn't. She had just avoided him completely.

He thought back to when she had first hinted that things weren't right between them and he had brushed it aside by putting it all down to the death of her mother and the surrounding problems. But then, instead of trying to resolve their problems, she had switched off completely and pushed him to the limit by constantly taking off and staying out all night. Despite her bad-tempered reassurances that she was only with Annalise, he didn't believe her. He wanted to believe her, he tried to, but he just couldn't.

Crossing his arms tightly over his chest, Ali sank down the wall into a crouching position and tried to analyse his feelings about the situation, the strange feelings that had crept up on him and caught him by surprise.

Up until the moment Maria had kept Merlin off

school and gone to Sam and Ruth's, he had been so sure it would all resolve itself in time that he had been instinctively dismissive. He had even convinced himself that he was mainly concerned about the business until she had actually gone, and then it had hit him like a speeding bullet. He didn't want to lose Maria. It wasn't only the salon and it wasn't only his son Merlin. Suddenly he had realised that he loved his whole life exactly as it was. That he loved Maria more than he could possibly have thought.

But then he had made his biggest mistake and charged after her like Rambo, pushing, shoving and shouting like an out-of-control adolescent.

Born and brought up in London in a large, traditional, Indian family, Ali had always carefully trodden the path between the two cultures that made up his life. While he was still at home he had conformed to his parents' traditional expectations but as soon as he had gone away to university he had become increasingly dissatisfied with the direction his life was taking. He had no ambition to be an accountant as everyone expected, he knew he wanted to capitalise on his artistic skills and do something creative.

For years he had darted back and forth between his two families, his wife and adolescent children from his arranged marriage, who had moved to Birmingham, and his mistress and illegitimate son who lived with his alter ego in London.

As he was trying to make sense of it all he was

interrupted by the voice of one of his stylists, Antonio, calling up the stairs from the salon.

'Ali? Can you hear me, Ali? There's someone here asking to see you. Are you available?'

Ali's instant reaction was to say he wasn't available but after a few seconds' hesitation his professionalism took over.

'OK. Give them a coffee and a magazine. I'll be down in five.'

As he walked into the salon, Antonio indicated a woman who instantly walked over and held out a graceful hand. Quickly taking in her appearance and bearing, he made his usual spot judgement. Wealthy middle-aged divorcee. Self-confident but bored. A lady who lunches and shops as a hobby. Probably recommended to the salon and now expecting preferential treatment.

'Ali Shah, I presume?' With her hand still outstretched she looked him up and down.

'Yes, I am.' He smiled his widest, most professional smile and took her hand in both of his. 'And you are?'

'Is there somewhere we can talk?' She pulled her hand back and looked around the salon.

'We can talk here, my staff do not gossip.' Despite his irritation, Ali kept a welcoming smile on his face.

'No, I mean somewhere really private. This is a personal issue.'

Ali's smile faded. 'We'd better go upstairs then.' He looked over to Antonio. 'I'll be upstairs for a few minutes and I don't want to be interrupted. If it's urgent then text me.'

Wondering what this was all about, he led the way up the spiral stairs.

He pointed to the sofa. 'Please, take a seat. Would you like tea or coffee?'

'Nothing, thank you.' The woman perched gracefully on the edge of the nearest dining chair and stared directly at Ali. 'This isn't exactly a social visit so I'd like to get straight to the point, Mr Shah. Did you know that Maria Harman, your partner, is having an affair with David James, my partner?'

Chapter Thirty-eight

Maria was sitting cross-legged on the floor in front of the television with Merlin in front of her, her arms wrapped tightly round his skinny little body. Ever since they had gone to live temporarily with Ruth and Sam, Maria had been trying to find the right words to tell him that they would not be going back to live in London with his father. She also wondered when she would have to tell him about the siblings he had in Birmingham that he knew nothing about.

For a while now Ali had been strangely silent and Maria was feeling edgy and unsettled. Something was going on and she didn't know what it was but instinctively she sensed trouble ahead; from experience she knew only too well that the man she was in partnership with in both her business and personal life could be quite ruthless when crossed.

'Merlin darling, how would you like to go on holiday with Ruth and Sophie? They're going down to the villa in Spain for a couple of weeks and they'd like you to go as well, it'll be in the half-term.'

'What about Daddy? He said he was going to take

me on holiday, to Florida to Disneyland.' Merlin paused and then looked over his shoulder at his mother. 'Daddy said you'd try and stop him taking me away. He said that you won't let him come and see me, he said you're being difficult.' His aggressive tone and piercing stare made Maria freeze instantly.

'When did he tell you that? I didn't know you'd spoken to him lately.'

'I talk to Daddy every day. He phones me on my new—' He stopped and looked away, his face reddening.

'On your new what, darling?' Maria tried to keep her voice calm despite her bubbling anger. 'Did Daddy give you a mobile phone that you haven't told me about?'

'He told me not to tell you because you'd be cross but I can phone him whenever I want and he phones me all the time.'

'How come I've never seen it or even heard it ringing?'

'Daddy said to turn it off when you're around, or Grandpa, or Ruth or Sophie, and I hide it under my pillow at night and then keep it in my pocket.'

'OK, OK, I get the picture.' Maria tried to keep the anger out of her voice. 'I know you're a clever little boy so I also know that you know that's being a bit deceitful. You shouldn't keep secrets like that from Mummy.'

Merlin's face grew pinched and his expression was

like his father's. 'Daddy said you'd say that but he said that it isn't bad because he's my dad and I'm only doing it because you're trying to stop us from seeing each other.' Merlin spoke faster and his voice got higher until he was just one step away from tears. He pushed himself from his mother's arms, stooped down to pick up a book and threw it directly at Maria. She managed to duck just in time. She jumped up and grabbed him by the arm.

'Hey, hey!' she snapped. 'What on earth is going on here? Do you really think I'm trying to stop you from seeing Daddy?'

'Yes!' he screamed at her. 'Daddy said you're going to stop me from ever seeing him again, that's why we're out here living in the sticks instead of in London! That's why you've taken me away from all my friends.'

'Not true, darling, that's just not true. Daddy must have misunderstood something I said, I'd never stop you from seeing your father.' When he didn't look at her she pulled him back towards her. Quietly steaming, Maria knew she had to regain her son's trust.

'Now listen to me.' She turned him round to face her. 'Daddy and I both love you. We might be cross with each other about things but neither of us is cross with you. But there mustn't be secrets, do you understand?'

'Can I see Daddy tomorrow then?'

'Not tomorrow, it's a busy salon day, but we'll sort something out. Now, do you want to go to Spain?'

'Why aren't you going?'

'I've got some work to do. I thought it would be nice for you, but you don't have to go if you don't want to.'

'I'll ask Daddy if it's OK. He's all alone now without us there, he told me he misses us both.' Merlin sighed dramatically.

Maria knew that her biggest challenge was going to be dealing amicably with Ali. She sent Merlin off to seek out Sophie and the dogs, her mind in turmoil. She had no idea how best to approach Ali.

Her thoughts were cut short by a phone call from *Tallulah Talks* with a date for her appearance. She hadn't been summoned to see the psychologist and Maria had expected it to be still several weeks off but a change of schedule had moved that particular show forward.

It was the news she had been waiting for, the news she desperately wanted to hear but instantly she started palpitating at the thought of it. Almost immediately the problems with Ali and Merlin dipped out of her mind. She dialled Davey's number and arranged to meet him. He was the only person who understood exactly where she was coming from.

Although deep down Maria knew that she was behaving irrationally she couldn't help herself. Awake or asleep, busy or bored her mind constantly flitted back to Samson, the obsession that was ruling her life. In her mind she had a picture of him and he was as much a part of her life as if he was actually in it.

She snatched up her jacket and bounded down the wide staircase.

'Sophie? Are you there, Soph?' She ran from room to room until she found her sister down in the summer-house alongside Merlin who was deeply engrossed in a computer game. 'I've got to go out, I've got some business to deal with. Do you mind if I leave you two together? I'll only be a couple of hours.'

Merlin looked at her suspiciously. 'Are you going to see Dad? I've already told him you've found the phone, I phoned him on it.' His tone was challenging and Maria could see that he was spoiling for an argument.

'No, I'm not going to see Dad, I've got a business appointment.' She smiled and looked at her sister. 'Is that OK with you, Soph? I'll have my phone with me.'

'Yeah.' Looking at Merlin, who had leaned back with his shoulders hunched and his arms folded across his chest, Sophie raised her eyes to the ceiling. 'I'll just about survive an afternoon with the sullen little git before I strangle him. You go and do what you have to do.'

As she walked into the pub and saw Davey leaning on the bar talking to the girl serving him, Maria felt an unexpected surge of jealousy wash over her. She had only seen him once since their reunion and that had been a snatched half-hour in a pub but they had talked constantly. Now as she watched his animated hand and body movements she just wanted to grab him and race off to another hotel and stay there forever.

'Hi there.' She smiled as she approached him. 'How's it going?'

He spun round and she was pleased to see a wide, happy grin spread across his face as he looked at her.

'Hi there you too.' He touched her fingertips with his and she felt her hands tingle and a shock run straight through her. 'Shall we sit over there where it's quiet?'

Maria didn't answer, she just smiled and walked over to a small table by the window, aware at every step that Davey was close behind her.

'I've missed you so much,' he whispered as he leaned forward with his elbows on the table and his hands clasped in front of him. 'I know you won't believe me, but I've never felt like this before. I feel like an obsessed adolescent, I just want to touch you all the time.'

Maria laughed. 'That's exactly how I feel. Perhaps it's because we were teenagers when we last met and now we're caught up in an emotional time warp!'

In unison they lifted their glasses and clinked them together gently.

'So, give me the latest on Samson and Tallulah. I've watched the show a couple of times since you told me about it and I was stunned, I have to say. The people on it reminded me of the Allsop family in action. They all hate each other but as soon as anyone else suggests the same they go straight for the jugular.'

He laughed and she joined in as she suddenly realised he was right.

'I suppose that's why the format works, and it really does. When they have the reunion specials the viewing figures are phenomenal, as you can imagine. Everyone loves a happy ending.' Maria shook her head gently as she thought about the irony of it all. 'I just hope they can find that bastard for me. I want to get up close to him, I want to feel his discomfort and I want to look him in the eye and ask why. I want to know if he ever gave a thought to my mother and the consequences of his actions after he'd moved away.'

Reaching out he took her hand and rubbed it soothingly between his palms. 'Maria, are you really sure about this? I've thought about it and I'm scared it's all going to implode on you. Even if someone does come forward, Samson isn't going to want to be found so he's certainly not going to agree to go on the show, is he?'

She was about to snap at him but the concerned expression on his face stopped her. She realised that he actually understood what she was going through.

'Oh Davey, do you think I haven't thought this through myself? First there'll be the appeal and then they'll put their investigators onto it. Then, if the target agrees, they arrange a meeting. All I want to know is that he is alive and contactable, preferably in this country.'

'But why on earth would he come forward?

Wouldn't you be better off hiring an investigator yourself?'

'Huh,' she snorted. 'It would cost a fortune considering how little information I have. If I take as much as I can for free, even if they don't find him the groundwork will have been done and I can go on from there.'

'I'm not sure about that. I mean, aren't you setting yourself up for public humiliation if it all goes pear-shaped?'

Maria opened her mouth to respond but, smiling, he held a hand up. 'I'm just playing devil's advocate here, so don't jump down my throat, missus.'

'Don't missus me,' Maria shot back. 'I'm not anyone's missus, never have been, never will be.'

Davey threw back his head and laughed. 'It's just an expression, as you well know. All the same, don't you think it's strange that neither of us has married? I mean, considering we both desperately wanted to escape home, isn't it surprising that we didn't get married young? To other people, of course.'

'I suppose so,' Maria said thoughtfully. 'The odds must have been pretty high that we'd each have half a dozen kids by now and be living on some rundown estate with either the Old Bill or the Young Bailiff banging on the door at regular intervals. That's what Finola would have expected.'

'Instead we've done OK, considering, although we both wound up with much older partners who took us under their wings. Looking for role models because of our history maybe.'

'Maybe. Or maybe we were each lucky enough to meet the right people to pull us back from the brink. And that, Davey, is why I feel so guilty. We're both betraying basically good people who have really done nothing wrong.'

Silently they locked eyes as they both thought about how they were going to resolve the situation they found themselves in.

Again, neither of them noticed the woman at a nearby table who seemed completely engrossed in the broadsheet newspaper spread out on the table in front of her, open at the crossword page. 'Samson. Tallulah. Davey,' she wrote in the squares before carrying on chewing her pen.

Chapter Thirty-nine

Paula Wellbeck had always been a natural planner, someone who invariably plotted her path in advance, and to a large extent it was this focusing that had made her life such a success. She never usually made spur-of-the-moment decisions and had always been good at keeping her problems close to her chest while at the same time working out the best way of dealing with them.

This time, however, with hindsight she could see that she had made a serious error of judgement in going to see Ali Shah and sharing her information with him. She had hoped that they would team up and, between them, crush the relationship between their respective partners. Instead Ali Shah had shown complete lack of interest in the news she had shared with him. It had never occurred to her for a moment that he wouldn't want to join forces with her.

In order to regain the equilibrium in her life she had already decided that as soon as possible she would marry David and, with a considerable cash incentive, ensure that he wouldn't stray again. But Ali had been distant and aloof. He had politely listened to everything she had to say but that was about as far as it had gone. Paula had tried hard to read him but his face had closed down and his body language betrayed nothing of his feelings.

'Why are you telling me all this?' he had asked her quite calmly after she had given him chapter and verse on her investigator's report. 'Shouldn't you be talking to your boyfriend? The same as I'll talk to Maria if and when I want to know anything. This is too personal to be bandied about between all and sundry.'

'No, not all and sundry, just the investigator, you and me. Aren't you interested in putting a stop to this affair? Between us we can do that, you know, we can each get our partners back and return to normal.'

'I have to think about this before I make any decisions. Unlike you I have a child to think of. Leave me your number and I'll call you.'

After she had left she realised that she had told him all about David but she knew no more about Maria Harman than when she had gone in. What she did know, and it bothered her more than she liked to admit, was what Maria looked like.

The photographs Paula had seen when she went to the private investigator's office for her initial report had unsettled her. The young woman standing affectionately beside David outside the motel was not a classic beauty but she was really quite striking. Despite the long lens shots, she had a presence that emanated from the photographs, and Paula's heart had sunk. Tall and lithe with long thick hair and large features, Maria was everything she herself used to be but no longer was. Her decision to undergo cosmetic surgery suddenly seemed urgent if she was to ensure David stayed exactly where she wanted him.

When she got home she had studied herself critically in the mirror. She knew she looked good for her age but the lines were now past being described as 'laughter lines', her heavily highlighted hair was far thinner than when she was young and her neck seemed to become more turkey-like by the day. Her body she could, and did, cover with expensive and well-cut clothes but her face was there on display for all to see and no amount of potions and lotions could turn the clock back as far as she would like.

It was with a mixture of distaste and apprehension that she made her second visit to Margaret Mann's office.

Good manners made her knock on the door but then she walked straight in without waiting for a response.

'Mrs Wellbeck!' Smiling, Margaret jumped up from behind her cluttered desk and held out her hand. 'You're earlier than I expected. I still have to get my file in some sort of order for you, I've just been working on it so I'm in a bit of a pickle.'

'Don't worry, I'll wait.' Paula sat in the chair facing Margaret Mann's desk. 'I'm not in any rush, I have a feeling you're going to tell me lots of things I don't really want to know.'

She watched curiously as Margaret, perched on the edge of her tatty grey fabric office chair, shuffled and collated the paperwork and photographs and then placed all the listed information inside the folder.

'How did you get into this business, Margaret? I have to admit I wasn't sure about a woman doing the job but you've come up trumps. You're very professional.' Paula smiled at the young woman in front of her. 'And young of course.'

Margaret didn't look up as she responded. 'I'm used to being professional and I'm not that young. As you know from my credentials, I was a police officer for ten years but I was invalided out after an incident.'

'What sort of incident?' Paula raised an eyebrow curiously.

'The sort that's part and parcel of police life.' Margaret laughed drily, 'I was injured during an arrest. I got in the way of a thug with a knife and got myself stabbed. I was off work for ages and now only have one kidney and no spleen. Quite rightly the police force didn't want me out and about and I didn't want to be on permanent desk duty so I changed career. This suits me down to the ground.' She patted the file straight and stood up. 'Now, how do you want to do this? Do you want to take a copy of it away to study or shall I go through it with you? There's much more information here than when we last met, and some background on both David and Maria.'

'I'd really prefer it if you didn't refer to them as a couple.' The flicker of annoyance that crossed her face was quickly replaced with a polite smile. 'Perhaps you could give me an outline first while I have a quick look, and then I'll take a copy. I'm actually going to be away for a couple weeks but I will be contactable. I have some business to attend to in South Africa.'

Paula studied the latest batch of photographs.

'She's so very attractive, isn't she, this Maria woman? And so much nearer David's age,' she murmured rue-fully. 'This can't be allowed to continue. Methinks drastic measures are called for to put a halt to this nonsense . . .'

'You're not going to do anything stupid or illegal, are you, Mrs Wellbeck?' Margaret asked quickly. 'I don't get involved in anything like that. I did explain that to you in the beginning. I'm strictly above board here, as legal as legal can be. I never even bend the law, let alone break it.'

'I don't do illegal either. I'm far more subtle than that.' Paula laughed hunourlessly. 'Now just update me and then I'll give you my instructions for while I'm away. I don't want to be caught with my eye off the ball again so you're going to have to be even more vigilant on my behalf. I want to know absolutely every-thing about Maria Harman so that I can deal with her appropriately on my return from Cape Town.'

'Appropriately, Mrs Wellbeck?'

Paula smiled. 'Yes, but don't worry, I don't have to resort to criminality. There aren't many problems that can't be disposed of by throwing the *appropriate* amount of money at them. I feel sure Maria Harman can be bought off quite easily.' She paused and looked at Margaret Mann. 'And then it will just be a matter of pulling David back into line, also with the appropriate amount of money, I'm afraid.'

As Margaret looked back at her, her expression professionally vacant, Paula laughed again. 'What's the matter? Don't you approve? I tell you what, come and see me when you're my age and see if you still think I'm a crazy old woman with no morals. Sometimes the means justifies the end. I can afford to buy him back and keep him back so why shouldn't I?'

After Paula had been updated on the latest meetings with Maria and had left the office looking grim, Margaret Mann checked once again through her own office file on Maria Harman and David James and then laid out the papers in two piles. In one was the basic, confirmed information and photographs she had shared with Paula Wellbeck; the other pile contained less specific information that still had to be checked out and verified before she passed it over to her client.

If she passed it over.

Margaret was a thoroughly modern private investigator. She had heard every gumshoe joke going and had suffered no end of teasing from her ex-colleagues, especially the one about 'Margi Mann who wasn't a man, the private dick without a dick', but she also knew that they all respected her and that her successful business had been built on integrity.

Integrity was something Paula Wellbeck seemed to be lacking in.

Margaret chewed the end of her pen thoughtfully as she pondered where exactly the case was going to take her before Paula, or she, called a halt.

She looked down at her checklist and added ticks and question marks in the margin. She may not like Paula Wellbeck but that was beside the point. She was employed to do a job and she would do it to the best of her ability unless, or until, it compromised her integrity.

Chapter Forty

By the time the moment came to get ready to leave for London to appear on *Tallulah Talks* the following day, Maria had started to feel exactly the same way she had when she was a young teenager.

As she packed her carefully selected new outfit into an overnight case, she had to keep stopping to breathe deep and long. It was the same panicky feeling in her chest from the past, the fluttering that used to creep up on her when she instinctively knew that she was going to get caught out by her mother, the familiar combination of butterflies and sickness bubbling just under her ribcage. But this time she knew it wasn't only nerves because of the impending television appearance; it was also a large attack of guilty conscience.

Despite managing to convince herself that she had no need to feel guilty about Sam because he had deceived her all her life, she knew Ruth and Sophie would be devastated when they found out about it. And Ali, and of course Merlin. But she also knew that if she had discussed it with any of them they might have succeeded in talking her out of it.

She had also managed to push to the back of her mind the invasive thought that she was betraying her mother's lifelong guilty secret; but she justified that with the thought that if she could find Samson and pay him back for what he had done then it would all be worthwhile.

The timing of the show couldn't have been better from her point of view. Sam, Ruth, Sophie and Merlin were all at the villa in Spain and Maria knew that Ali never watched television during the daytime, or certainly not what he called 'women's crap'.

Maria was staying in a hotel in the West End at the show's expense and she was looking forward to a long lazy bath with a glass of wine but before she had a chance to even slip her shoes off there was a knock at the door. Maria cursed as she looked through the spyhole and saw the dreaded Hattie wearing her widest smile and holding a bouquet of flowers.

'Hi!' She held out her arms with the flowers in one hand as Maria opened the door. 'These are for you, aren't they just gorgeous? How are you? All ready for your big moment? I am so looking forward to seeing it and I really, really hope it works out for you.' Hattie leaned forward and kissed her on both cheeks as if she were an old friend. 'I just popped up for a teensy check of the running order. We have so many guests staying here at the moment it's completely mad.' Laughing, she bounded into the room and looked round. 'Mad, mad, mad! Did you say your partner was coming with you?'

'Yes, I did, and no, he's not. He doesn't want to be in the limelight so I don't want either him or my son mentioned on the show. I did say that right from the off.'

'Yes of course you did and it's all agreed, so no need to be tetchy, you're letting your nerves get the better of you and it's not good. Chill, darling, chill. I just wondered if he'd come along to give you support in the background.'

Hattie's uniform of the day was khaki combats, designer trainers and a skimpy but obviously expensive T-shirt that clung to her braless boobs and bared about an inch of flesh round her slender tanned hips.

Still smiling widely, she settled down on the pink padded stool at the end of the bed and pulled a screwed-up piece of A4 out of her pocket. 'Right now, let me think.' She sighed dramatically and straightened the paper out on her leg. 'You do remember this show is pre-recorded, don't you? It won't air tomorrow, we don't take chances in case of punch-ups and swearing. Been caught out like that before, but it is almost live so, after we've edited it just a teensy bit, it will air the following day which will be . . .' She looked up at the ceiling and grimaced. 'Yep. Wednesday. All the days roll into one on this show! Now, let's go through all this one more time and then I'll leave you in peace.'

When Hattie had left in the same whirlwind fashion as she had arrived, Maria kicked off her shoes and lay back on the bed with her hands under her head. In spite of her nervous excitement she made herself think long and hard about what she was embarking on. She chewed over the fact that the moment her name was announced on *Tallulah Talks* there would be no going back. No putting the genie back in the bottle and certainly no keeping her background a secret any longer. Everyone would know everything about her. Or rather they would think they did. She wondered how she would react to the sympathy that would come her way from strangers. Hattie and Agnetha had warned her that an appearance on the show would be a nine-day wonder but in those nine days she would be approached in the street by perfect strangers who would each have an opinion on her situation, and she would have new friends and enemies in equal parts.

She knew that she had about twelve hours before she would be whisked to the studio, twelve hours in which to make up her mind whether or not she wanted to go ahead. Although her obsession with Samson was still as strong, she now had someone else in her personal equation. Davey Allsop. Or David James as he called himself in his new life.

Maria had wanted to see him again, she had wanted to punish him but it had never occurred to her that the second she set eyes on him again she would feel the same about him as she had when she was fifteen. She could have imagined wanting to physically harm him but as it turned out all she wanted was to be with him, to talk with him and to make love with him.

Now she wished she had never found out about Samson, that she was free from all her emotional baggage just to be with Davey.

But she wasn't and she couldn't so she mentally shook herself and set about double-checking her prepared speech for the programme the next day.

The trilling of her mobile on the bedside table interrupted her thoughts. As she reached out for it, her eyes glimpsed the clock. She was shocked to see that she had been asleep for over three hours.

'Hiya, sweetheart. How's it going up in the big smoke?' Davey's voice laughed down the phone. 'Are you out on the town yet?'

'Believe it or not I was asleep. I don't know what happened, I just put my feet up about three hours ago and that was it. Don't remember a thing. How's it with you? Are you going to be able to come up?'

'I'm really sorry, I can't. I want to so much, but as you know Paula has buggered off to South Africa on some business venture and left me to deal with the restaurant. I've tried to get cover but I don't think it's fair to just leave it to the staff.'

The disappointment that swept over Maria took her by surprise.

'That's OK, don't worry about it,' she replied as nonchalantly as she could. 'It's going to be hectic anyway and probably best if we don't take any chances. We are talking national telly here!'

When he didn't answer she continued, still keeping

her tone light, 'What's going on in South Africa then? She's not going to take you off there to live, is she?' The words were jokey but there was an underlying panic in her voice.

'I don't know what she's up to. I guess it's one of her latest business ventures. Paula has always kept her investments secret from me. Not that I care. As long as I can extricate my car showroom and business from it all, I'll be cool. Then we can really plan for our future.'

'After Samson,' she murmured into the phone.

'Of course. After Samson. I understand that. I love you, Maria, very much.'

'And I love you too, I'll call you tomorrow.'

Deep in thought, Maria held the phone in her hand for several minutes before deciding against going down to the restaurant and socialising with the other participants of the show, as arranged. Instead she rang Hattie, pleaded a headache and ordered room service before checking out the mini bar and clicking on the wide-screen TV.

Ali Shah stared morosely into the glass in front of him and thought back over the previous few months during which time everything in his life had been unexpectedly turned back to front.

The surprise visit from Paula Wellbeck and the information she had shared with him had shaken him to the core but, irritated by her overbearing arrogance, he had forced himself to stand his ground with her. Instinctively he had put on his neutral mask and heard her out without commenting, but inside he had been fuming and desperate to rip the anonymous David James's head straight off his shoulders.

But despite his feigned disinterest he had listened and taken mental note of everything she had told him, everything that confirmed his fears. Maria, the woman he thought of as his wife, was having an affair despite all her protestations to the contrary.

The implications of losing her to another man, as well as possibly his business and maybe even Merlin, flashed through his brain constantly as Paula was imparting her news to him and he determined then and there that it would not happen. He would use every weapon he could to maintain his hard-earned life.

To that end he was sitting with his shoulders hunched and his head down in the furthermost corner of the bar of a London hotel waiting to see who Maria was there to meet. With his shoulder-length hair pulled back into a band at the nape of his neck and wearing a dark suit with a plain white T-shirt he looked fashionably smart and certainly not out of place.

Out of his usual clothes and definitely out of his environment he knew that even if Maria saw him, the chances of her registering him were slim.

Unlike Paula, Ali didn't intend to pay a private detective to find out what he wanted; he had his own sources and was more than capable of doing his own sleuthing, but it was purely by chance that he had followed her to this particular hotel today. When he had phoned Merlin in Spain and the boy had innocently repeated that 'Mummy's going to stay with Aunty Annalise for a few days', Ali's ears had instantly pricked up. To him the name Annalise was code for David James so he instantly staked out the Suffolk house in a borrowed anonymous white van and waited impatiently.

Now he could feel his anger rising as he glanced furtively through to the reception area hoping to spot David James so that he could confront them both. Together. Paula Wellbeck had shown him the photographs of Maria with David so he knew exactly who he was looking for but despite seeing Maria check in, there had been no one resembling David James and no sign of Maria coming down.

He stood up and headed over to the sweeping rosewood reception desk. He smiled flirtatiously at the efficient-looking young woman flitting busily about, clicking keys and shuffling folders.

'Hi there, I wonder if you could help me. I'm supposed to be meeting some friends here and I'd like to know if they've checked in yet. Maria Harman and David James.' His smile was wide and friendly as he looked the woman straight in the eye.

She only hesitated for a moment before returning his infectious smile. 'I'll just check for you.' She clicked some keys. 'Maria Harman is here but she's with a party of eight, there's no David James booked.'

'Isn't he in a double room with her? They're usually joined at the hip, those two.' Again the winning smile, a gentle shake of the head and some direct eye contact worked wonders.

She looked at the screen again and scrolled through. 'No, sir, Ms Harman is booked in alone.'

'OK, thanks. I'll wait in the bar, I'm sure she'll be down soon, I can't wait to find out if they've had a row.' He turned to leave and then spun back round. 'I'm so dumb, I completely forgot. Have you got a room for tonight? I may as well stay in town as we're having a big night out tonight.'

He checked in but didn't go upstairs; instead he went back to his vantage point in the bar. Not for one moment did he believe that David James wasn't in the hotel and he reckoned it was just a matter of time before one or other or both of them appeared, and he wanted to be waiting.

Chapter Forty-one

A tattoo of banging on the door woke Maria with a start and it took her a few seconds to get her bearings and remember where she was and also why. It had been nearly 4 a.m. before she had dropped off and her body clock was completely out of sync.

'Who is it?' she shouted, knowing there was no way anyone outside the door would hear her. Dragging herself to the door she looked through the spyhole to see Hattie, once again wreathed in smiles.

'Wakey wakey, rise and shine.' Hattie smiled as Maria pulled the door back wide. 'We're all going to have breakfast together and then the cars are collecting us at nine.'

'Sorry, Hattie, I don't do breakfast. I just—'

'No choice today, Maria,' Hattie tutted, 'we can't afford to have you feeling sick and faint in the studio under all those lights. It's incredibly hot and sticky and also very, very boring hanging around. The order of filming puts you last on the list so, boy, have you got a long wait.'

'I'll get something later,' Maria said curtly, feeling

almost childish. The ball of activity that was Hattie was irritating the hell out of her. 'Right now I'm really not hungry and I'm certainly not into group break-fast bonding.'

Hattie raised her eyebrows and shook her head in silent reprimand. 'OK, if you insist. I'll see if they'll put some bits in a takeout box for you. We leave at nine on the dot, be in the lobby by eight forty-five at the latest.' With a cheery wave Hattie was gone, leaving Maria feeling irritated and edgy.

After a strong cup of tea and several cigarettes she pulled herself together and quickly showered so that she could spend as much time as possible making her-self look her very best.

A part of her wished Davey was with her to give her some support but another part was grateful for the chance to gather her thoughts and get ready alone for the event that she had spent so much time and energy thinking about.

This was her one chance to find out something about her birth father, her chance to persuade someone, somewhere in Britain to come forward with enough information for her to then carry on and find him herself. And to do that she knew she would have to act her heart out, she would have to pretend that she wanted a relationship with the man who had raped her mother.

She had told the researchers that she had found her father's name among her late mother's belongings. And she had then taken a grain of the truth that Granny Bentley had told her and embroidered on it to make just the sort of story the show would like. And she had succeeded. Now all she had to do was follow through and hope for the best.

She shook herself back to the mirror and then, with a final straightening of her skirt and a quick glance over her shoulder, she marched purposefully down to the hotel lobby to meet up with the rest of the staff and guests for *Tallulah Talks*.

Ali had been just about to storm up to Maria's room when he had seen her walk nervously out of the lift, looking like an older version of herself in a smart two-piece suit and high heels. With his eye for fashion he could see that her outfit was expensive but it was very traditional and unlike anything he had ever seen her in before.

For a few seconds he watched open-mouthed. He couldn't understand it. Maria was almost directly in front of him, dressed like one of the boring middle-aged women who invaded his salon for a shampoo and blow dry, but there was no sign whatever of David James.

As she started walking across the lobby, Ali ducked behind a group of Japanese tourists who were milling around. Out of the corner of his eye he saw two shiny black stretch limos pull up under the awning.

Casually he slipped over to the concierge's desk.

'Interesting–looking group of tourists that, what are they up to?' He leaned one elbow on the desk and smiled at the elderly man who he could see was looking in the same direction.

'That's the motley crew that are going off to spill their guts on some TV talk show,' the man whispered conspiratorially. 'We often have them in here. They're off to film the show at the studios not far from here. Then they'll all get tanked up in the green room and fall back here and beat each other up.' He looked at Ali, suddenly aware that he might be speaking out of turn to the wrong person. 'Still, it's not for me to judge. What can I do for you, sir?'

Ali relaxed. The group was obviously nothing to do with Maria. He smiled amiably at the man. 'I could do with a map of London. I've got quite a few business calls and I left my A to Z on the train.'

Leaning down, the man pulled out a map book and some photocopied sheets. 'Now where exactly is it you would you like to go?'

Trying not to look impatient with the game he was playing, Ali glanced over his shoulder just in time to see Maria climbing into one of the limos, followed quickly by the two women who were so obviously in charge.

'What the fuck is she doing with them?' He hadn't realised he had spoken out loud until he noticed the suddenly wary expression on the concierge's face.

'I'm sorry, sir, what did you say?'

Ali managed a vacant expression. 'I said, do you know where it's filmed, the programme you were telling me about? The one you said that group were going to?'

'No, sir.' The concierge shook his head, obviously on his guard. 'I'm sorry, I don't know. They'll all be back tonight, you could ask someone then. Now where is it you're wanting to go?'

The music faded along with the applause and Tallulah smiled beatifically.

'And now our next guest is someone who is desperately seeking information about her birth father. Adopted at birth, she has never seen him and knows very little about him so she needs our help. Ladies and gentlemen, please welcome Maria!'

The atmosphere in the studio was electric as Tallulah made her format announcement and smiled endearingly into the camera.

With the applause echoing in her ears, Maria straightened her shoulders and walked down the few short steps to the stage where Tallulah was standing with her cue cards in her hand and smiling sympathetically in her direction.

As Maria approached her seat, she breathed in deeply and then exhaled as slowly as she could to try to dull the sparking nerves in her body. This was it. Her one and only big chance and she didn't intend to blow it.

'I'm here because I really want to find my father . . .' She spoke to the camera using the exact same words and intonation she had practised.

Her moment passed in a flash, all those weeks of practising in front of the mirror, of training herself to act out the part without so much as a glimmer of anger, and suddenly it was over. She had said her piece and made her appeal and suddenly she felt incredibly deflated. Sinking back into her chair she was close to tears and bit deeply into her bottom lip.

Tallulah smiled victoriously. 'Who could fail to be moved by Maria's story? We are all entitled to know everything about ourselves.' Her voice was kind and caring and the audience were one hundred per cent focused on her words. 'Our genes are what make us what we are and if we don't know our heritage then we don't really know ourselves. Whether we know them or not, our parents make us what we are, what we look like, the colour of our skin, our hair colour, our temperament. Everything is dominated by our genes.' She smiled at Maria. Her perfectly capped teeth, set off by scarlet painted lips, shone under the lights.

'So, Maria, to sum up, tell us once again, tell our viewers out there, what it is that you want most in the world.'

'More than anything I want to meet Joseph Samuelson, Samson, my birth father. I want to get to know him, to make up for all the lost years . . .' As she spoke she heard a gasp ripple so loudly through the audience it made her hesitate and glance nervously towards Tallulah who was smiling broadly.

'Well, Maria,' she said quickly, 'I'm going to make your wish come true because on this show we really can perform miracles. We've been working away secretly on this and we've found your father . . .' She paused dramatically. 'Maria, turn round and meet Joe, your birth father. Joe, come and say hello to Maria, the daughter you never knew you had.'

Chapter Forty-two

Maria felt as if she had been punched in the stomach. This wasn't how it was supposed to be. The lights above her head started to spin and she could taste the bile rising up towards her mouth, but amid the bewilderment a small part of her was still aware that she had to continue to play the game even if she didn't understand the rules any more.

Turning in her chair, she followed the direction of Tallulah's eyes and tried to focus on the man heading towards her from the wings at the back of the stage.

She had thought of him for so long that she expected to recognise him but nothing about him connected even remotely with her mental image of him. He was almost nondescript, slightly taller than Maria and bordering on fat, his dark wavy hair going grey around the temple and ears.

He was just an ordinary, overweight, middle-aged man who didn't appear in the least bit intimidating.

Maria registered that he was smiling broadly as he walked towards her. She didn't understand why. Why was he smiling? Why would a man who was about to be unmasked as a rapist be smiling? Why was he holding his arms open as if to welcome a prodigal daughter back to the fold?

As the thoughts flew through her mind he reached her and, as if on autopilot, Maria stood up and looked directly at him.

Somewhere in the distance she could hear the studio audience going wild, clapping and stamping their feet in a frenzy of voyeurism, all of them willing the woman on the stage to throw herself into the arms of her long-lost father.

But he acted first and wrapped her in a bear hug.

After a pause Maria heard Tallulah's voice again. 'Maria, Joe, take your seats and we can talk about this. Maria, you look so shocked, understandably of course. How does it feel to see your father in the flesh for the first time?'

Using up all her reserve of self-control, Maria smiled at the man and then at Tallulah.

'It's unreal. I really can't believe it. I didn't expect this today, I didn't really think you would find him, that he would want to be found . . .' She grasped the arms of the chair tightly and stared at him, looking for some reaction to her veiled words but there was none. He was smiling and to her surprise he appeared genuinely happy to be sitting next to her but as his hand reached across the chair towards her, Maria's resolve failed. She snatched her hand back before he could touch it and wrapped her arms tightly across her chest.

'Now, Joe,' Tallulah carried on happily, 'tell us your side of the story. We'd all like to know how this happened. How come you didn't know about the existence of this beautiful young woman here?'

He looked at Maria but she couldn't bring herself to meet his eye. The whole thing was getting out of hand and all she wanted to do was run off the stage and carry on running as far away from him as she could. It passed through her mind that they had found the wrong man, that maybe there were two Joseph Samuelsons. The man on stage beside her didn't look like the man she had been so completely focused on from the minute she had found out.

'I had no idea.' The man's gentle Welsh accent took her by surprise. 'I wasn't told. I don't want to go into too much detail in public like this, but the circumstances at the time were difficult and I left the area. I never knew your mother was pregnant, I never knew. She told me to leave and never contact her again, she was insistent, so I did. I promise, I never knew about you.'

'I don't believe this,' Maria started to shout. She jumped to her feet but suddenly Tallulah, ever aware of the mood of her guests, was there in front of them, talking into the camera.

'And that's it for today, folks, another success story from the production team at *Tallulah Talks*. See you all at the same time tomorrow.'

The programme quickly wound down and Maria

and Joe were hustled from the stage by Hattie and led directly into a small room with several armchairs, a coffee machine and the show's resident counsellor.

'Take a seat.' The counsellor smiled at them both. 'I'm sure you can both do with a little help here. That would have been a shock out there, especially for you, Maria. How do you feel?'

'Honestly?' Maria glared around the room. 'Completely and utterly fucking betrayed. It wasn't meant to be like this, this was only supposed to be the appeal. I don't want this film to go out, I want it stopped. You stitched me up!'

Hattie moved forward and held out her hands to Maria. 'I can understand you're feeling over-emotional right now, sweetie, but we've actually done exactly as you asked. You phoned us and asked us to find your father and we've found him for you. That is what you asked for, isn't it?' Taking Maria's hands she tried to lead her to one of the chairs. 'I know how you feel, this has happened before but as soon as you think about it rationally you'll thank us.' Hattie's voice took on the tone of an understanding adult trying to calm a recalcitrant child. 'You will, really.'

'Yes, but . . .' Maria realised that the hole she was in she'd dug for herself. She looked across at Joe who had quietly taken a seat beside the counsellor and was looking completely bewildered.

'I want to leave now,' Maria stated firmly, pulling herself away from the limpet-like Hattie. 'I want to go and think about all this, it's too much for me to take in at once.'

'I don't understand.' Joe suddenly spoke. 'I was told you were desperate to meet me. What's gone wrong? I thought you'd be pleased. Is it something I said?'

Maria looked again at the man and tried to figure out how she felt. He was her father but she felt nothing towards him. The hatred that had kept her going for so long had been focused on the young man whom Granny Bentley had described, the violent young man who had forced his way into the house in King's Crescent and raped her mother. Not the very ordinary, bewildered-looking man who was face to face with her, unaware of her hidden agenda.

'This isn't how I wanted it to be, I wanted to find you and talk to you in private, not in front of half the goddammed country. They've conned me and you as well probably, can't you see that?'

Joe shook his head. 'No, not really, I can't see that, but right now I don't want to argue with you. I want to spend some time with you.' His lilting voice was kindly and hypnotic. 'I want to introduce you to my family, I want you to be part of my family, you're my daughter, I'm your father, you have sisters and a brother, nephews and nieces.'

Maria started laughing and once she started she couldn't stop until the tears flowed. Hattie and the counsellor both tried to calm her but she was hysterical beyond reason.

'Take me back to the hotel, I want to collect my stuff and go home. This isn't what I want . . .' Her body juddered as she stuttered the words.

'You can't, not like this. Stay here and talk it through.'

'Oh, I think you'll find I can go wherever I want and if you don't arrange it right now I'll call the police and not only that, I'll call the newspapers and totally wreck your stupid programme.'

As Maria, make-up streaked down her face, was hurried through the hotel lobby by Hattie on one side and the counsellor on the other, she didn't notice Ali watching and frantically trying to read the situation. He was almost sitting on his hands because he wanted to go over to her, to confront her, but there were just too many people milling around generally.

'Oh, for fuck's sake, stop following me!' she screeched at the man and woman running along beside her. She jumped into the lift and pressed the button. Hattie blocked the closing doors with her body.

'Tell me what's wrong,' she pleaded. 'We don't understand.'

'You're what's wrong! Stop chasing me around like you think you're in some third-rate made-for-TV movie and mind your own business,' she shouted before banging on the button again to close the doors.

Chapter Forty-three

Maria stuck aggressively to her guns. After throwing her belongings into her case she marched out of the hotel and called for a cab to take her all the way back to Suffolk.

Her mind was in such turmoil that all she wanted was to get back to her home territory as quickly as she could and be alone to think.

She had achieved exactly what she had set out to do and found Samson, but everything was wrong. He was wrong, his words were wrong; it was completely wrong that he had actually turned up at all. He should have been hiding away, shaking in his boots at the prospect of being outed as a rapist in front of the whole country. Instead he had been up there on the stage, smiling and hugging her.

As soon as she got back and dumped her bag on the floor, she felt a strong urge to talk to Sam and Ruth. She wanted to check that Merlin was OK but more than anything she wanted to speak to her father and reassure herself that nothing had changed. Yet. But there was no answer and as she slowly replaced the receiver, she hated herself for going ahead with her stupid plan; it could so easily ruin her relationships with every single member of her family.

It was as if she had been living in a dream for the past few months and today's events had brought her back to the reality that had been absent ever since she had found out about her conception.

She could imagine the family all on the beach. Her family. She could see Merlin running around and swimming in the warm Mediterranean while Sam tried unsuccessfully to keep up with the lively seven year old. She could picture Ruth stretched out on a sunbed, watching and laughing as Sophie strutted her stuff in front of an admiring audience, wearing the tiny pink and purple bikini Maria had bought her sister for her birthday.

Whatever he had said to the contrary, the man she had come face to face with in the studio wasn't her father, Sam Harman was her father. The stranger who had sat with her on the stage was the rapist who had ruined Finola's life and subsequently her own. Yet he had expected her to be pleased to see him, to become a part of his family as if it was the most natural thing in the world.

Something wasn't right.

Walking around in a daze as if it was her first time in the family home, Maria saw things she had never noticed before. She took in the scents of the enormous house plants that Ruth had lovingly dotted around, the gentle gurgling of the water tanks and miles of pipes that echoed from attic to basement, and the rheumatic creaking of the old house as a summer breeze entered through the open windows upstairs and wafted down the polished wooden staircase.

As she stroked the banister that curled gently upwards, she wondered if, after the show had been aired, she would ever be welcome in the house again.

Roaming nervously and feeling quite nauseous, she was aware of phones trilling constantly in the background but she ignored them; instead she wandered about and then sat on the bottom stair, pulled a crumpled piece of card out of her pocket and studied it carefully.

'Joe Samuelson' it said, in large easily legible handwriting, along with three numbers. Work, home and mobile. She read the words over and over again. He obviously wasn't trying to keep her a secret or he wouldn't have gone on *Tallulah Talks* and he certainly wouldn't have agreed to them giving all his personal information to Maria. She had been fuming when Hattie had given her the index card at the hotel after the show but she had taken it nonetheless.

She wondered exactly how much Hattie had told him of her story, the mixture of truth and fiction that she had woven for the researchers. She also wondered how much he thought she knew.

The hammering on the front door shook her back into the moment. She didn't want to answer it but then she heard a voice shouting through the letterbox and realised it was Annalise.

When she opened the door she saw that Davey was standing a step behind her friend.

'What's this? The cavalry to the rescue?' she asked but at the same time she smiled. 'I bet I know where you get your info from, I bet the mad Hattie rang you, Annalise, didn't she? My supportive contact?'

'She certainly did. You've sent her into a tailspin. I think she thinks her job's on the line because she lost a guest.' Annalise laughed gently and reached her hands out to her friend. 'So, come on then, tell all. Dom is working in Scotland this week so I had to ring Davey for a lift as you weren't answering any of your bloody phones.' She hugged Maria tight and kissed her on both cheeks affectionately. 'Honestly, Maria Harman, you'll be the death of me, and yourself if you keep trying to function at this level of stress.'

Davey touched her lightly on the arm and kissed her forehead.

'Come on through then and I'll tell you all about the biggest fucking fiasco of my life. I've really blown it this time, really, really blown it, they're all going to freak.'

Annalise and Davey looked at each, both aware that, despite the bravado, Maria was a whisker away from breaking down.

'Hattie told me you were upset but she didn't go into details, gave me some sort of confidentiality spiel because of the show going out tomorrow. To be fair she sounded genuinely worried about you.'

'I suppose I did go for her,' Maria laughed tearfully, 'and it wasn't her fault, it was mine. I am just so stupid. I should have listened to you.'

Davey held his hands up. 'The suspense is killing me. What happened?'

'You won't believe it.'

'Yes we will. Come on, tell all.'

'They found Samson and he was actually there as a *big surprise*. I just never anticipated that. He came out on stage in front of everyone and treated me like some sort of long-lost fucking daughter that he was desperate to meet.'

'No! Oh my God.' Annalise gasped and put both hands up to her mouth. 'Whatever did you do? You didn't have a go at him on telly? Oh Maria, what's going to happen?'

'No, I didn't do anything to start with, then I threw a wobbly and insisted on leaving. I went and grabbed my gear from the hotel and here I am.'

Davey frowned. 'How about I put the kettle on and you start at the beginning. This is getting more outrageous by the minute.'

'Yeah, well, if you want outrageous then wait for this, he wants to take me home to meet his family, sisters, brothers, nieces and nephews. He laid the whole lot on me and then had the cheek to look quite hurt when I pissed off out of it.'

Completely bewildered, Ali had also returned home. He knew there was no way he was going to get to the bottom of it all on his own so he swallowed his pride and dialled the number that Paula Wellbeck had given him. Margaret Mann's mobile phone number.

'My name's Ali Shah, I was given your number by Paula Wellbeck to ring if I wanted information . . .'

The woman at the other end of the phone was polite and businesslike but it was soon apparent she wasn't going to just hand over everything he wanted to know.

'It's not really that simple, Mr Shah. If you want me to share information with you then I have to discuss it with my client Mrs Wellbeck first. Tell me what it is you want to know and I'll contact her.'

Suddenly Ali felt not only irritated but also out of control and that was the one thing he hated most. He liked his life to be ordered and understandable.

'I tell you what, Ms Mann, I'll employ you myself at whatever your going rate is and then you can tell me everything I need to know. I need you to do something for me. Maria spent the night in a London hotel and it had something to do with some talk show, Tallulah something. I need to know what it was all about.'

There was a few seconds' pause on the line before Margaret Mann responded, her tone formal and businesslike.

'I'm sorry, Mr Shah, but it doesn't work like that.

Now if you'll just be patient, I'll do as I said and contact my client who is abroad right now and then I'll get back to you.' Without any further niceties Margaret Mann switched her phone off, leaving Ali even more angry and frustrated.

After thinking about it he clicked on the internet and keyed in *Tallulah Talks*. He knew there had to be a connection between Maria and the show but he hadn't got a clue what it could be. He studied the website for the show and looked at his watch. It was too late for that day's programme but he decided he would watch the next one.

Chapter Forty-four

Despite feeling strangely discomfited by the idea, Maria had agreed to let Davey stay the night with her so, after driving Annalise back home to Colchester, he had returned, only to find himself deposited in the guest bedroom.

Now, the next morning, they sat together at the scrubbed farmhouse table, comfortable in each other's company; it felt right that they were together.

Davey was washed and dressed but Maria was wrapped in a fairly worn bathrobe and her hair was mad and unbrushed. As they shared a plate of chunky cold toast she became aware of Davey looking at her and, feeling strangely self-conscious, she pulled the robe tighter across her chest and tugged at the belt, making Davey smile. Leaning across, he gently pushed a tendril of hair behind her ear.

'Do you realise that we've known each other for over twenty years and yet this is the longest time we've ever spent together in one hit? Alone?'

'Yes, I had realised, and you were supposed to stay in the guest room, not come creeping along the corridor like we were still fifteen.' She managed a nervous smile as she spoke. 'Still, we didn't do the deed in the parental home so I don't feel so bad. Somehow I just couldn't, not here. I suppose it's all this talk about Finola again. I could imagine her ghostly image standing there, huffing and puffing and shaking her head in sad disapproval at thee and me together.'

'I can understand that, I told you last night. You really don't have to explain.'

'Yes, but it was so stupid, this house wasn't anything to do with her, this is Dad and Ruth's home and it's a happy one . . .' In an instant Maria was on her feet, fired up and pacing the floor barefoot.

'But the connection is still there with your dad.' Davey's voice was soothing and low as he reassured her. 'I know exactly how you feel, really I do.'

Suddenly Maria laughed, a deep and humorous laugh. 'Can you just imagine if my mother really was still around and had come in and caught us? I remember when she found us in the alleyway holding hands. Jeez, hellfire and damnation nothing. That one ran for weeks. According to her we were both doomed from that moment on. Maybe we were – or maybe I was.'

Davey smiled at the memory and Maria felt her chest surge with the same strong emotion that his smile had always been able to evoke in her.

After Eddie's death Maria had sworn off the opposite sex completely and apart from a couple of dates that went nowhere she had stuck with it until she had taken her first step away from home and applied for a job in a small but trendy salon tucked away in a soon to be regenerated part of London's East End. Until she had met Ali Shah.

In the intervening years she had often thought about her situation and smiled to herself. If anyone had told her back then that she would end up in a longstanding affair with Ali, and also have his child, she would have laughed herself silly. But because he had offered her the job that she desperately wanted, Ali, without realising it, had been instrumental in helping her make the break with the past that had haunted her for so long. Together they had worked hard to build the salon into a successful business.

Their personal relationship was almost secondary, something that had just happened as time went on. It suited her. She had known from the beginning that he already had a family that he would always have to support, and it hadn't been an issue with her. In fact it had helped because she didn't have to deal with her own insecurities about commitment.

And then Davey Allsop had reappeared in her life and reminded her exactly what love really felt like.

Davey reached up and caught her hand and gently kissed her fingertips. 'Today's the day,' he murmured. 'Is it a bit of an anticlimax as it's already happened?'

'Too right it is. I really wish I could make them pull the programme off. I can see now it's going to hurt so many people. How could I have not considered that? Why didn't I listen to Annalise and let the past rest?'

'You did what you thought was right at the time, and even if it was wrong, it was done for the right reasons. How about just not watching the programme? You could record it and watch it when you feel better about it.'

'Sounds sensible.' Maria reached for her coffee mug. 'I wish I could do that, but I can't. I'm going to have to watch it and torture myself.' She paused and looked hopefully at Davey. 'Unless you can think of a way I can get the programme pulled off.'

'I was thinking about that for half the night but I really can't see a way out of it. You signed a disclaimer and anyway they haven't done anything wrong. I think you're going to have to bite the bullet and hope that no one who knows you watches it.'

'Sam and co. are in Spain, Ali will be working . . . Anyone else and I suppose I'll just have to lie and pretend she's an imposter! Oh fuck, what am I going to do? What am I going to do about Samson? It was all so clear in my mind and now . . .'

'Please tell me you're not thinking about doing anything stupid.'

'*Moi?*' she drawled sarcastically. 'Do something stupid? Nooo, all I want to do is kill the bastard stone dead, I want to stab him straight through his cowardly gut, I want him to know exactly what pain he caused, I want him dead.' She could see that Davey was alarmed by her outburst but she was past caring. 'That fucker ruined my whole family because of what he did. Everything that was wrong in our family can be traced straight back to him. He single-handedly made the Harmans into the dysfunctional family they, we, are.'

She was so angry and frustrated she wanted to cry. Just at that moment the phone rang.

'Hi, Maria, just calling to see how you are this morning, and to pass on a message. Your father wants to see you again. Can you call him at his hotel or shall I give him your number? He's so pleased to have found you. I'm hoping you'll both get to know each other now. Tallulah wants to do a follow-up show in a few months.'

In your dreams, Maria thought. He'll be long dead by then and I'll no doubt be locked up. The words flashed through her head but she heard herself say instead, 'Tell him I'll call him after the show this afternoon, I want to see how it pans out. When is he going back to Wales?'

After she put the phone down she glared at it for a few seconds before turning to Davey.

'Samson's itching to see me again. How much do you bet he wants to warn me off saying anything? Don't you just love it when a plan comes together? I've been wrong-footed once, it won't happen again. This time I'll screw the bastard. I shall call him, I shall be sweetness and light and then—'

'Don't do anything, Maria,' Davey interrupted

sharply, shocked by the hatred in her voice. 'Trust me, you'll regret it for the rest of your life. Think about what happened to me because I wanted revenge. Have you got any idea what it's like in prison?' He went over and pulled her close. 'Look at me, Maria. Is that what you want for your son? Surely you don't want him to spend his childhood visiting you in some scummy prison at the other end of the country?'

It was the most vehement that Maria had seen him but it was still not enough to dissolve her feelings of vengeance.

'I'm sorry, Davey, I'm going to do what I have to do. I don't have a choice really now I've gone this far. I can't make it go away now I've dug it all up.'

'Choice is the one thing you do have, Maria my darling. He doesn't know where you are so you can choose to walk away from it all. Forgive and forget and get on with your life.'

Maria stared at him but didn't answer and neither of them mentioned it again.

Later that day as they sat together in front of the television impatiently waiting to hear the signature tune, neither of them was aware that there were others watching just as keenly. Ali Shah had set the alarm on his watch for five minutes before the start and as soon as it beeped, he raced up the stairs from the salon to the apartment and clicked on the plasma screen TV that dominated the lounge.

Margaret Mann was also seated in front of her TV, curiously watching to see what it was about the show that had caused the deep conversation between Maria and Davey in the pub. She had only heard bits of the conversation. As a show that was notorious for successfully drawing out the worst in people, she had thought it an unlikely talking point between two new lovers. Her investigative antennae had instantly twitched.

Another person sitting and waiting for the programme was Leanne Harman, Joe's wife.

Leanne was once again feeling depressed and neglected; she hated her boring life with her uninterested husband. Joe was hardly ever there and their children were independent enough to not need her any longer, other than as a cook and cleaner and free taxi service.

The only real passion she felt in her non-eventful life was her hatred of her brother-in-law Patrick. She called him 'the sleazeball' because he eyed her up and down lasciviously at every opportunity, and had, on occasions, actually tried to grope her. He had justified it to Leanne by saying that he and his brother had always shared everything.

Patrick still lived alone in the old family home nearby and he made several visits a week allegedly to see his brother and his nephews but he would usually turn up when no one else was in, safe in the knowledge that his brother Joe would never dare take Leanne's side against him. She hated Patrick so much that the ring on the doorbell made her feel physically sick.

As usual Leanne had called in at the supermarket on the way back from the school run and then quickly skimmed the top layer of housework before settling down on the sofa with her feet up. A finger buffet of crisps and chocolate was balanced on the arm, along with a large glass of strong cider, the only alcohol that was on special offer at the supermarket that week.

In Suffolk the television in the corner flickered and blared then suddenly the adverts were over and the music had started and the viewers were alert as Tallulah, the presenter, bounced into camera shot with a confident smile, ready to start the show that regularly pulled in more viewers per episode than any other daytime show.

Maria knew that her part of the show was going to be the climax and as such would be on in the final segment of the hour, but she still watched the whole programme in morbid fascination. She wanted to see how the other guests that she had shared the green room with would come across on the screen after Tallulah and her helpers had edited the programme.

Guest after guest appeared on the screen, each one happily baring their souls and their secrets to millions of viewers, before Maria's moment arrived.

'And now,' Tallulah's familiar hypnotic voice wafted into several million homes, 'our next guest, Maria . . .'

As Maria walked across the screen, several people sitting in front of their televisions sat up and stared, unsure whether to believe what they were seeing.

By the end of her slot the phone lines were buzzing.

Ali to Sam.

Margaret to Paula.

Leanne to Joe.

Joe to Patrick.

And an assortment of all their friends and customers.

The tentacles of gossip quickly reached out across the country, but although the word was spread within a few short minutes of the programme ending, Maria had no idea how far it had gone because she resolutely ignored the ringing of the phones.

Chapter Forty-five

'I'm going to have go back home for a while, sweetheart. I don't want to leave you alone but I really have to go and put in an appearance.' Davey pulled her to him and kissed her softly on the lips several times. 'I'm sorry, but whatever else is going on, I have to keep a check on Paula's businesses. I've been off the radar for over twenty-four hours and the police will be called if I don't reappear soon.'

Gently, and almost with relief, she pushed him back and turned away so that he couldn't see her face.

'It's OK, Davey, I'm fine on my own. I've got a lot of thinking to do.'

'I'll get back as soon as I can, probably in the early hours, but please promise me you won't do anything mad while I'm gone. It really wasn't so bad and it was shorter than I expected so maybe no one saw it.'

Maria forced a laugh. 'And what exactly do you think I can do to the bastard Samson in leafy Suffolk?'

But as soon as his car crunched off down the drive, Maria snatched up the phone and dialled one of the numbers she had memorised from the piece of card.

'Hello. It's Maria here. I'll meet you again but I want it to be on my territory. You can come to my father's house, that's where I'm staying. No one else will be here, we'll be able to talk alone. Make sure you come alone.'

To her surprise Samson agreed without hesitation, promising to drive up early the following morning. She gave him directions and then sat back and thought about it for a while. She wondered for a split second if she was taking a risk by inviting a rapist to the house but she dismissed the idea just as quickly.

Sitting back, she chewed it all over again. She couldn't figure out why he had so readily accepted paternity, especially in public. Maybe he had truly forgotten about the events surrounding Finola Harman all those years before. Maybe he had unknown children all over the place and his male ego enjoyed having them seek him out. Maybe he had heard she was doing OK and thought he could get some money out of her.

Maybe, maybe, maybe . . .

Her brain went into overdrive with all the ifs and buts she could rustle up until she could think no more.

After the trauma of the previous few months, Maria suddenly felt surprisingly calm as she soaked in the bath before pulling on a pair of jeans and an old sweatshirt. She tugged her hair back into a band, slipped her feet into her old bedroom slippers and went back downstairs.

Without checking any of the messages she unplugged

the house phone, switched her mobile to silent and slid it into her pocket. She had one last thing to do before settling down to wait the night out.

Down the side of the sofa where she intended to sit with Samson the next day she hid a voice recorder that Ruth used for her letters, along with the thinnest, sharpest kitchen knife she could find in the rack.

Then she poured herself a large neat brandy and took a sip. As it hit the back of her throat, she coughed and spluttered as she always did when the liquid burned but she took another sip, and then another, before perching on the edge of the sofa to watch the recording of the show once again.

Still in Spain, Sam and Ruth were completely bewildered by the unexpected phone call from Ali who was so hysterical and angry he didn't make an awful lot of sense. 'How could she do that without telling me? She has made me and my son a laughing stock going on TV and telling everyone she didn't know who her real father was. She is not going to get Merlin, I'm going to seek custody. She is mad, completely mad . . .'

Through his ranting and raging one thing became clear to Sam: Ali didn't know the full story behind Maria's parentage. As far as Ali was concerned, Maria had simply been adopted by Sam and Finola.

Suddenly Sam could see what Maria had meant when she said Ali would not be able to accept the truth.

As quickly as he could he got Ali off the phone and tried to call Maria but she wasn't answering any of the phones.

'Annalise,' Ruth suddenly said. 'Try calling Annalise. If anyone knows what's going on, it'll be her. She and Maria have been as thick as thieves lately. And of course there's Davey Allsop. I wonder if he's got something to do with all this. We have to get to Maria before she does something to that man, she's so unpredictable she's an accident waiting to happen right now.'

Feeling his age, Sam leaned forward and put his head in his hands. 'This is all my fault, I shouldn't have told her about the rape. It was better for her to be angry at Finola for having an affair than for us all to have to go through this. We've ruined her life all over again.'

'Too late for that now,' Ruth snapped sharply. 'We have to check out the flights home and get going as soon as is humanly possible.' With that, she snatched the phone from Sam. 'You go and tell Sophie and Merlin that we have to go home, say it's business or something, I'll explain to Sophie when she's on her own.'

Sam didn't move from his seat.

'Sam! Go! Now! This isn't the time for deep and meaningful reasoning, we have to get back to England right away before Maria snaps.'

Her voice spurred Sam into action and he hurtled out onto the terrace and ran down the stone steps to the pool where Sophie and Merlin were swimming happily.

'Mrs Wellbeck, there's been a rather strange development in my investigation. I don't understand the significance yet but I thought I should let you know anyway.'

Paula listened carefully as Margaret Mann told her about the show and Maria's part in it. It all sounded quite bizarre and she could understand Margaret's curiosity.

'What's David's part in this? Is he still seeing her?'

Margaret explained that although there was nothing to connect David to the programme, the same day she had followed him to Suffolk where Maria was staying.

'You carry on finding out what you can,' Paula instructed her. 'I'll be home tomorrow anyway. My business here is complete and my flight is booked although I intend to try to get an earlier one if I can. I really need to see David as soon as possible.' Paula kept her voice calm and reasoned but underneath she couldn't wait to get back and show herself off to David, to seduce him all over again and, if necessary, propose to him.

The spectre of Maria Harman was dismissed from her mind as she peered into the mirror and studied herself from every which way.

The bandages were off and all the stitches were out.

The bruising was subsiding and she could now appreciate the artistry of her surgeon. He had lifted her face and neck just enough for her to look many years younger without appearing too enhanced. During her recovery she had called in an expensive hairdresser who had trimmed and highlighted her collar-length hair into a much softer style. A make-up artist had worked carefully around the bruising.

Looking in the mirror was a pleasure once again and Paula was thrilled with the results. There was no doubt in her mind that this was all that was needed to pull David back into line – and of course some hard cash.

For the first time in years Leanne Harman was feeling quite high with pleasure. She loved the fact that she had successfully sent her brother-in-law into a fury by telling him about Maria's appearance on *Tallulah Talks*.

As soon as she had realised it really was Maria on the screen she had jumped up and pushed a tape into the VCR before phoning Joe, her husband. But she didn't mention she had the tape. She wanted to tell both him and Patrick all about the programme herself. It would be her moment of glory as she recounted every detail. But not in her wildest dreams could she have imagined the white fury that Patrick would display. Now he was in her kitchen, ranting and raving like a madman, and it took all of Leanne's will power to keep her face straight.

'How dare that bitch bring the whole family into disrepute like this? I told Mum over and over again, adopting her into the family was the worst thing they could ever have done. She killed Eddie and now she's spitting on Mum's grave. I'll break her fucking little illegitimate neck with my bare hands if I get hold of her, appealing on fucking trash television for the lowlife who dumped a cuckoo in our nest.'

'Where do you think Maria is now?' Leanne asked innocently, fully aware that he didn't have a clue or he would already have been on his way. 'Do you reckon she's with her new dad? Although I suppose I should say her real dad, shouldn't I? 'Cos that's what he is, isn't he? Perhaps they're having a father-daughter reunion. It's quite romantic really.' Leanne opened her eyes wide as she looked at Patrick.

'Romantic? Romantic my arse, you thick bitch, you always did talk total crap,' he spluttered, unable to contain his fury.

Suppressing a snigger, Leanne made all the right noises as she made him a cup of tea. Over the years Patrick had eaten himself into gross obesity and everyone remarked, behind his back, that he looked like a heart attack waiting to happen. As his weight had soared so had his blood pressure and his temper. Although he still managed to go to work most days, his spells of illness were becoming more frequent and he had taken to sleeping in the downstairs room where Finola had spent her last days.

'Cake, Patrick?' Leanne offered him an enormous slice of creamy gateau. She really hoped that when the day came that he collapsed clutching his chest, she would be there to witness it and laugh her socks off.

Leanne had realised long before that there was nothing she could do about the power Patrick wielded over his brother Joe so she had ignored it as best she could and concentrated on her children. For many years it had worked but now the children were more independent she resented Patrick's interference in their lives. She despised Joe for being weak and she hated Patrick for being the vicious bully that he was.

Greedily he gobbled the large slice of cake and slurped at his mug of tea while at the same time continuing to lambast his estranged and absent sister.

'I'm going to get out there and find her,' he suddenly snarled, as damp crumbs escaped onto his chin and shirt. 'I'm going to find her and break her fucking neck. Bitch!'

'Perhaps she's with your dad at the villa in Spain?' Again Leanne's tone was both innocent and eager to please. 'Although maybe she's staying at Ruth's. You've always said those two are thick as thieves, she could be there now with her new father. Or I suppose they could still be in London, I know the show is filmed in London 'cos it says so.'

With a grunt Patrick rose to his feet like an ungainly hippo, knocking his plate and cup across the table with his vast belly. Without saying anything more he lumbered out of Leanne and Joe's house.

Leanne smiled widely. It was so satisfying to see the fat bastard steaming mad about something he had no control over.

'Would you like me to drive you?' Leanne shouted after him, suddenly realising that she could be part of the fun. 'Two heads are better than one and you'll be able to spread out and relax in the people carrier.'

Chapter Forty-six

After a few more neat brandies and several hours watching and rewatching the tape, Maria went up to bed, but after tossing and turning sleeplessly for a couple of hours she gave up and ran back down again at around 2 a.m. After making a hot drink she snuggled down on the sofa in the television lounge with the big fleece comfort blanket that usually lay on top of her bed.

Once again she clicked on the VCR and watched Samson. She studied his body movements and every expression on his face. Every time he looked directly at the camera, Maria hit the pause button so that she could study him and look for any familiar features that linked him to her genetically.

She could see that he would probably have been quite good-looking when he was younger although hardly the tall, dark and handsome seducer that Granny Bentley had described; his jawline was strong and well defined, with a permanent dark shadow from years of shaving a heavy beard, and his long neck settled nicely inside the collar of his silk shirt. Although there was a definite suggestion of a large belly, it was concealed by the well-cut suit that hung off his shoulders and shouted, 'I'm expensive.'

But any doubts Maria might have had about her connection to him were dispelled by the dark eyes framed by deep laughter lines and thick black lashes that curled upwards.

Maria had often been told that she had 'come-to-bed eyes' and as she looked at Samson she wondered if her mother had noticed them during that fateful conversation on the bus. And if she did, was she reminded of Samson every time she looked into her daughter's eyes?

For the first time the thought flashed through her mind that maybe her mother, as a young naïve woman, had given him innocent signals that he had misread. But as soon as the thought bounced unbidden into her brain, a wave of guilt enveloped her.

However it had happened, Samson had raped Finola Harman.

She replayed the tape yet again, this time concentrating on the soundtrack and mentally noting everything said by him or about him by Tallulah, but there really wasn't much. Joe Samuelson had spoken a lot but had revealed very little. He'd said he was a businessman but hadn't elaborated on what sort of business and now, as she mused over every word, Maria wondered about it. Did he mean businessman as in having his own business? Or businessman as in working in a bank? He had also told Tallulah that he had a wife and three grown-up children and lived on the outskirts of a village not far from Cardiff. He had been reticent about the events surrounding Maria's conception but had insisted he had left Clacton not knowing that Maria's mother was pregnant, and had gone straight back to Wales where he had stayed ever since. He had resolutely refused to go into any intimate details on air – which was hardly surprising, thought Maria bitterly.

She dug her fingernails deep into the palms of her hands with fury. With hindsight she wished she'd been brave enough to publicly out him, to stand up and denounce him then and there on camera, but the shock of his presence had completely thrown her.

Eventually she forced herself to switch the tape off. She stretched all her limbs alternately and glanced at her watch: 6 a.m. Plenty of time to get ready for the showdown.

As she made a strong pot of coffee she felt her mobile phone vibrate again in her pocket. It was Davey so she clicked the button to answer. His tone was light but Maria could sense his unease.

'Annalise has rung me, she's been trying to get you. Your dad has been on to her because you're not answering your phone, also Ali. I get the feeling that everyone knows. What are you going to do?'

'To be honest I don't really give a toss at this

moment. I've had a bad night.' Maria kept her voice calm but his words made her heart race. Everyone? Ali? Sam? Merlin? How could everyone know so soon?

'I'll come over later,' Davey continued casually. 'There are things we need to deal with. Paula is due back and Ali is on the warpath, I think this is crunch time.'

Maria suddenly felt panicky, she definitely didn't want Davey, or anyone else, interrupting her meeting with Samson.

'You're right, we do need to talk, but can you leave it to this afternoon? I've had a really bad night so I'm going to have a big slug of brandy and go back to bed for a few hours. If we're going to be sorting out our future then I'll need a clear head. But can you do something for me? Would you ring Annalise? I don't want the phone buzzing away and disturbing me for a while. I'm sure she'll ward everyone off for a few hours more if you ask her really nicely.'

After making some more of the right noises Maria was content that no one would be turning up during the morning. Smiling to herself, she went upstairs to get ready.

Because she had been nervously listening and looking for over an hour she heard his car the second it turned off the road and onto the long gravel drive but she forced herself to stay where she was and not fling open the door in advance.

She wanted to make him ring the bell and wait on the doorstep. She wanted him to have time to absorb the grandeur of the house she was living in but mostly she wanted to start with a psychological advantage.

'Do come in.' She didn't even pretend to smile as she finally opened the door then stepped back out of reach of any possible bodily contact. 'We'll go through to the sitting room.'

Joseph Samuelson looked slightly bewildered and that instantly empowered Maria. Glancing past him she saw the navy blue family saloon he had come in parked tidily over by the garages. His clothes were more casual and certainly not new but again they managed to look expensive but not in a deliberate way.

He didn't fit her mental picture in any way.

'Maria.' He stopped abruptly, forcing her to turn towards him. 'I'm really pleased to see you but I feel something has gone wrong, something is different to what I was expecting and I wish I could understand it. I was looking forward to meeting you as soon as they found me.'

Maria backed away from him instinctively but kept her voice cool. 'Come and sit down and we'll talk. There are things I want to know, things only you can tell me. As you well know. Things about my mother and you—' She stopped herself. The last thing she wanted was to warn him off. She had to remember that he thought she had been adopted at birth by strangers, that he didn't know she knew anything about anything.

He smiled and visibly relaxed. She pointed to the large sofa that dominated the room.

'May I smoke?' he asked.

'Of course.'

'I keep trying to quit, in fact I hadn't smoked for several months when I got the call from the show. Now I'm so nervous I'm almost chain smoking, the inside of my car is a fug.'

'It's no problem. I smoke also. Do you think bad habits are hereditary?' Her smile was wide as she looked at him.

He shrugged as he proffered the packet. 'Possibly, but then I have two other daughters. Theresa smokes but Antonia doesn't and neither does Colin. Though I've always tried not to smoke at home.' Leaning back comfortably he crossed his legs. 'What about the rest of your family? Was it a good family that brought you up? This is a lovely home.'

Maria forced herself to be calm and although her instincts told her to feign some sort of emotional attachment she couldn't bring herself to actually touch him. Instead she tried to soften her expression.

'Tell me more about yourself first. I want to know absolutely everything about you. After all, you're my father, aren't you? I want to know all about you and, of course, my mother.'

'I know that I'm your father but I didn't know that before the show contacted me, I swear I didn't, yet somehow I don't think you believe me. Maria, do you really think I would have gone off and never kept in touch if I'd known? And remember, I agreed to go on the show. Would I have done that if I didn't want to know you?' He looked pleadingly at her and she was stunned to see real pain in his eyes.

'I don't know, but that's not the issue really. I want to know about how you met my mother, how it happened. You've been very vague so far.'

'Of course I've been vague, I was protecting you. Did you really want me to bare all on television?'

'I wanted you to but of course I didn't expect you to.' The sarcasm was thinly disguised and again Samson looked perplexed.

'Tell me all about your adoptive parents and I'll tell you everything I can about your mother. Have you been looking for her as well?'

Maria could feel the slow burn inside her and was aware she was teetering on the brink. She perched herself nervously on the edge of the sofa and let her hand slide down between the cushions to where the recorder was hidden. And the knife.

Touching the smooth stainless-steel handle was strangely comforting; for the first time she felt totally in control. She would listen to him, she would let him dig himself into a great big hole and then she would confront him.

She smiled at him encouragingly, moved her hand to the sensitive recorder and gently pushed the record button.

Chapter Forty-seven

'No, I haven't looked for my mother.' Maria didn't elaborate or explain; it seemed safest to keep her response to the basic truth. 'It's only you I was looking for. Please tell me what you can remember about my mother and how it all happened.'

To Maria's surprise, Samson smiled quickly. It was a wide, genuine smile and his whole face lit up in obvious pleasure. Now that Maria had erased the mental picture of him that Granny Bentley had drawn for her, she could see he was actually very attractive for his age.

'She was a lovely woman, she would often come into the holiday camp and have a drink with some of her friends, friends who worked there whom she had met in the town. That's how I met her.'

Maria gritted her teeth; she really wanted to hurl herself across the sofa and stab him then and there. He was doing exactly what she had expected. Exonerating himself at her mother's expense, pretending that it had all been her fault.

'She was good company,' he continued, unaware, 'and she was also very intelligent and well educated, whereas I had run away from school and home at fifteen. I trailed around some squats in London before ending up in Clacton and working at the holiday camp there.' He paused and looked into the middle distance as he reminisced. 'It was really great fun at the camp, I had a fantastic time there and made so many friends, and of course I met Finola.'

'Yeah, right, just like that!' The biting words were out before Maria could stop them but Samson didn't react, he carried on as if she hadn't spoken.

'I was attracted to her the moment I saw her, she was so . . . I don't know, she was just so different, mysterious even. She was older than me, so mature and knowledgeable, but sadly she was married although I didn't know that in the beginning, and by the time I did know, it was too late.'

'Too late for what?'

'Too late not to fall in love with her.'

'In love?' Maria shrieked, starting to lose self-control. 'In love? She was a happily married woman with three young sons, how do you expect me to believe falling in love could even come into it?'

Samson's head swung round and he stared at her. His expression told her that a big red warning light had started flashing in his brain. She had dropped a clanger and she had to think quickly.

'How do you know that, Maria?' His voice had an edge to it. 'You said you knew nothing about her. How do you know how many children she had?'

'I was told about it.'

'Who by? Who could have told you that? Do you know where Finola is? Have you found her already?' The rapid questions caught her by surprise and she looked down at her feet. 'Maria, there's something wrong here. In my business life I'm used to making snap judgements about people and I can tell you're not being honest with me.'

Maria took a deep breath and tried to pull herself back. Her hand stroked the smooth steel of the knife as she talked herself back from the edge of hysteria.

'I'm sorry, I'm just confused. I don't mean to be judgemental, it's just that this is so emotional for me, I'm at a loss. I know something about my background obviously, but please tell me more. I want to know what you know, more than anything I want to know how I came to be.'

Samson relaxed slightly but Maria found she couldn't breathe properly. She realised she had nearly blown it. The last thing she needed at this point was for Samson to find out too soon what was going on because he could just get up and go. He could disappear and she might never find him again.

'I've got a lot to thank Finola for, you know,' he said suddenly. 'She encouraged me to go to college and do something with my life. It's because of her I am where I am.'

'And where's that?' Maria forced herself to ask calmly.

'Happy, successful. Satisfied with my life on the

whole. And you? Are you happy? Are you married? Do you have children?' He smiled again. 'You see? I know nothing about you. You're my flesh and blood and I don't even know your surname.'

Maria avoided his gaze and stared at his unexpectedly long and slender fingers which he was twisting together furiously.

'I was in a relationship,' she continued, still fascinated by the hands, 'and I have a son. Now I live with my father and his second family. But you were telling me about yourself. What do you do for a living?'

'I work with computers. I have my own company but I don't work as hard as I used to, I just don't have the same hunger any more.' He smiled wryly at her. 'I'm getting too old to be an entrepreneur.'

'My stepmother is a business woman, she loves working and is very successful at what she does.'

'Your stepmother? What happened to your mother?'

'She died a few months ago but my father has been with Ruth for most of my life. Ruth has been my mother for longer than the other one was. I adore her, she's always treated me as a real daughter.'

'You know, I can see your real mother in you,' he suddenly blurted out, 'when you smile, and the way you look at me out of the corner of your eye. But then I think I can see me in you. My father was Egyptian and I can see that in you, you are really an exotically beautiful young woman. A credit to the parents who brought you up.'

Maria gritted her teeth tightly as she looked at him through a red mist of anger. How dare he? Again her hand caressed the knife but she didn't want to use it until he had told her everything she wanted to know. Until she had it all preserved on the silently revolving tape that was recording every word.

Chapter Forty-eight

'You stupid thick bitch, what are we going to do now, stuck in the back of beyond?'

Patrick was steaming mad and Leanne was suddenly scared. She knew full well that it was only because he was inherently idle that he had agreed to let her drive him to search out Maria, but now they were stuck on a country B road in Suffolk with a puncture.

'Don't shout at me,' Leanne snapped, putting on a display of bravado in front of her loathsome brother-in-law. 'I was doing you a favour. We'll just have to wait for the AA. They won't take long and in the meantime I'll ring Joe and let him know what's happening. He'll be worried if I'm too late back.'

Patrick leered nastily at her. 'Joe? Worried about you? He doesn't give a rat's arse about you. You're the thicko with the big hips he chose to have his sprogs, that's all. All his women know that.'

The jolly jaunt to watch Patrick lock horns with his sister had suddenly lost its appeal. 'He needs to know where I am . . . and who I'm with . . . and why.'

'Joe is a dickhead. He won't give a toss.'

Leanne looked sideways at her brother-in-law for a second before jumping out of the car and running round to the back to look at the flat tyre. She flipped open her phone but then snapped it shut again before opening the back door and pulling out the roll of tools.

Patrick and Joe could both go hang. She could change a tyre if she had to. She would prove herself to the ignorant pig slouched in her car and his lily-livered brother who had never stood up to him in his life. Although Patrick was being deliberately nasty, Leanne also knew he was only really confirming what she already knew about her philandering husband, and at that moment Leanne realised that she had had enough of her life as it was.

For the sake of her own sanity she intended to get out of her marriage and her old life just as soon as she could.

'I've tried to figure it out but I really don't understand what's going on,' Sam whispered over a sleeping Merlin as the taxi made its way round the gridlocked M25 from Gatwick airport. 'I think she's having some sort of breakdown, cracking up. I just hope she's at the house when we get there.'

'Don't bank on it, love.' Ruth sighed. 'She could be anywhere if what Ali told us is correct. I'm really worried about her, I wish she'd pick up the goddammed phone. I don't for a second believe that "catching up on sleep" nonsense that Annalise told us.'

Sam's face was grim. 'I think if we find Davey Allsop we'll get to the bottom of this. I think he's got a lot to answer for. And Ali. He's showing his true colours now. They've confused Maria at a bad time in her life and now she doesn't know what she's doing.'

'Maybe not but that doesn't make it any easier to deal with, does it? We can only work with what we know and really that isn't an awful lot. Just a heap of mixed messages and rumours.' Looking out of the window, Ruth watched the landscape flash by and felt very sad that Maria, whom she thought of as her own daughter, hadn't been able to confide in her about her search for her birth father. More than anyone she was aware of Maria's vulnerability and despite never having met Finola Harman, she felt incredibly bitter towards the woman on Maria's behalf. Even knowing that Finola had been raped by Maria's birth father didn't take away the anger Ruth felt at the woman who had treated her own flesh and blood so very harshly. She just hoped that they would be able to get to Maria in time.

While Paula had been away her thoughts had been concentrated on her new face and she had been convinced that David would fall back into her arms, but arriving back in England had been a reality check for her.

She had arranged for Margaret to meet her at Heathrow airport but as they drove off she had suddenly decided to confront Maria face to face and deal with her once and for all, and Paula had instructed Margaret to take her straight to Suffolk.

'Are you sure you really want to do this?' Margaret asked the calmly furious woman sitting behind her on the beige leather seat that closely resembled a comfy armchair.

'Of course I want to do this. All I need to do is pay the slut off and she'll be gone. The only mistake I made was not doing it sooner. I really thought I'd given him enough to do while I was away to keep him occupied and away from her but I was wrong. I won't be wrong again.'

Margaret looked at her in the rearview mirror. It hadn't taken her long to realise that Paula had had a substantial facelift and, as she watched her fussing around with a dollop of concealer and a huge blusher brush, she felt a wave of sympathy.

Under instructions, Margaret had carefully observed Maria and David together and it was glaringly obvious that the two of them were hopelessly in love and she doubted very much if either of them would snatch an infusion of cash from Paula Wellbeck. But she was being paid by Paula so she did as she was told and headed back to the house on the Suffolk border.

Margaret's eyes flicked from the road to the mirror and back again, watching as Paula clicked numbers into her phone and barked orders at everyone. But on the last call her tone was different.

'Hello again, Mr Shah. This is Paula Wellbeck. I'm

on my way to your girlfriend's cosy love nest in Suffolk. You've not kept her on much of a rein, have you? They've been at it like rabbits apparently, her and my David. I'll be there around midday if you're interested in watching how a professional deals with infidelity.'

'Was that a good idea?' Margaret asked as she realised who Paula was talking to. She watched Paula's eyes narrow in anger.

'Just remember your place, Ms Mann, and get on with driving my fucking car safely!'

His mind weirdly confused by the whole situation, Davey was once again having a heated debate with Annalise on her doorstep.

'Please listen, I know you're really pissed off with the way I keep turning up and whisking you off on missions of mercy but something isn't right about this. I was stupid this morning, I let her fob me off with some crap about going back to bed. Tell me if you know anything, please!'

'Davey, I've told you. If anything, you know more than I do. I promise, if I knew I'd tell you.'

'Will you come with me? She'll go mad if I just turn up ahead of time but if you're with me . . .' He paused. 'I wish she wouldn't keep turning that fucking phone off. The more I think about it the more I'm convinced she's planning something, something to do with Samson. Please come with me.'

Annalise smiled wryly. 'What you mean is will I

come with you and stand in the firing line when Maria kicks off. OK, I suppose I have to. It's a good job I don't have children, you and Maria and your ongoing traumas keep me busier than a clutch of kids.' She walked inside, leaving him to follow her. 'I'll just get ready. I won't be long but I also can't be away long. Dom is due back today and we're off on our hols again in a couple of days.'

'Thanks. You're the best!' Creeping up on her with a loud growl, he put one arm round her shoulder and pulled her close in a tight, affectionate hug.

'Yeah, right. Just don't push it any further than you already have, sonny.'

Chapter Forty-nine

Maria's fingers kept tightening round the handle of the knife but she still made no attempt to pull it from its hiding place. Her mind was confused as all her nightmares of the previous few months blended together and roared loudly around her brain, bringing down a dark red mist of fury.

She knew Samson was still speaking but she couldn't hear the words; she felt as if she was out of her body and looking down on the scene. She vaguely wondered if that was what the moment of death felt like. Would Samson feel like that when she forced the sharp knife through his ribcage into his lying heart? As his chest tightened with pain and his life slipped away, would he look down at his daughter and assailant and regret his attack on Finola Harman all those years ago?

'Maria? Maria, are you OK?' Samson's voice penetrated through the fog of her rage.

'No, I'm not OK, of course I'm not fucking OK, you arrogant bastard. Why did you rape my mother? Tell me, why did you do it? Couldn't you just have screwed some willing slut from your precious holiday camp? Why do what you did?'

'Maria, I—'

'Don't Maria me,' she snarled, jumping to her feet like a scalded cat with the knife clasped to her chest but with the blade pointing towards Samson. 'You fucked us all up. It wasn't just the one day, the day you did it, it was all of her life, all of my life. The whole family paid for what you did, my father, me – especially me, she hated me because of you.'

Watching the hand with the knife, Samson stood up very slowly and cautiously made his way round behind the oversized sofa.

'Maria, listen to me. I don't know where you got that idea from but that certainly isn't what happened. Your mother and I were in love with each other, we had an affair. I know it was wrong, she knew it was wrong but we couldn't help ourselves.'

'You're lying!' Maria screamed across the room, then she started to shake as her hysteria rose. 'You're a dirty, filthy, lying rapist and I'm going to kill you for what you did.'

'Maria, please listen to me. Why don't we just find your mother? She'll tell you what really happened. You found me through the show, now let's both look for her. I loved Finola.'

Instantly a wave of deadly calm swept over her and, stretching out the hand holding the knife, she looked him in the eye triumphantly.

'I don't have to find my mother. I know exactly where she is but you're wasting your time if you want to apologise to her. She's dead and buried and hopefully at peace after the miserable fucking life you brought down on her. Can you imagine what it was like for her carrying a baby that was the result of rape? Can you imagine how she felt every time she looked at me? She hated me and rightly so.'

'Maria, stop this right now.' For the first time Samson's voice took on an authoritative tone. 'Do you really think that I would have responded to that ridiculous Tallulah show if I'd raped your mother? Good Lord, it was hard enough having to go on that show for the best of reasons. Think about it.'

'I don't have to think, I know. She said it herself, to her husband, the man who brought me up as his own. She told Sam and her mother, she said she was pregnant because she had been raped – in her own home by a virtual stranger.'

Samson shook his head. 'So this was only ever about revenge, was it? Nothing to do with finding your father and getting to know him. Boy, you did well on that ridiculous show then. That appeal would have had the nation in tears.'

Laughing manically, Maria started towards him with her arm outstretched. 'I don't want to know you. I want to kill you, I have to avenge my mother.'

With one quick vault Samson was over the sofa and had Maria's wrist firmly in his grip.

'Drop the knife, Maria, come on now. Just drop it and we'll talk. I don't want to hurt you but I do want to explain and I want you to listen. Come on, let go of it.' His voice was suddenly low and gentle as he tried to persuade her rather than force her. 'I swear to you on my children's lives that the only thing between your mother and myself was love, we were in love and you were the product of that love. I promise you it's the truth, Maria.'

Slowly her fingers loosened under the hand that gripped her wrist and as she let go of the knife, her body started to judder uncontrollably. The knife hit the carpet with a gentle thud and Samson kicked it away under the sofa. He pulled her tight into his arms and hugged her close to him.

'Sshh, sshh. Now let's talk properly. We can get through this, I'm sure. I promise you I didn't rape your mother. I loved her, truly I did. She was my first love and I've never ever forgotten her. I could never have hurt her. I'd have stayed with her, I wanted to be with her but she sent me away. She wanted to do the right thing by Sam and the boys and she never told me she was pregnant.'

Maria could feel herself wavering with uncertainty. She wanted to believe him but if she did that then what did that make her mother? Surely that was a lie too far to have to live with.

'But why would she have lied? Why would my mother have perpetuated something so horrible? I can't believe it of her, she made my life a misery.'

'Guilt I imagine, my dear, she felt guilty because she had betrayed her husband and her religion, both of which were important to her. She did what she thought was the right thing but went the wrong way about it.'

At that moment the door flew open and, puffing and panting, Sam hurled himself across the room.

'Leave my daughter alone! Get your disgusting hands off her—'

'It's all right, Dad,' Maria said quickly. 'We're just talking. Dad, this is Samson, my birth father.'

Sam's face was screwed up with anger and hatred. 'Well, I guessed that. How could you do this to us, Maria? How could you bring this . . . this . . . this creature into our home? This isn't King's Crescent, this is a happy home and I thought you respected that. Now this house has been sullied by him, by the man who—'

'Dad, listen to me, I didn't want to be friends with him, I wanted to ki—'

'Don't, Maria.' Loudly to cover her words Samson interrupted her. 'There's no need for that, it's forgotten already but I'm going to leave now and let you sort this out with your family.'

'But . . .' Again she was wavering. Suppose what he said was true, suppose he walked away and she never saw him again?

'No buts, my dear. You have to talk this through with your family. You have my numbers if you want to keep in touch. I really would like us to get to know each other but I leave it to you to decide what you want to do.' Leaning forward he kissed her on the cheek. 'This man here is your father, he deserves you far more than I do.'

As he walked away, Sam and Maria looked at each other. She could see the hurt and disappointment on his face and in his slumped shoulders. She came to her senses with a jolt and realised that she had betrayed the one person who had supported her and loved her unreservedly all her life.

'Dad, I am so sorry, I don't know what I was thinking of. I was going to kill him. I really could have done it, I had the knife in my hand, I was just about to do it, but he stopped me. I wanted to kill him for what Mum had said he did. But it wasn't true, it was all a lie . . .' For the first time since Finola's death the tears started as the full impact of what she had so nearly done hit her. She couldn't stop. Slumping down onto the sofa she sobbed until the door flew open and Ruth ran in.

'You'd better get yourselves outside, Patrick's collapsed in the drive. I've called an ambulance. We think he's had a heart attack. Davey Allsop is giving him heart massage.'

'Patrick?' Maria murmured incredulously. 'What the fuck is he doing here?'

'I don't know, Maria, you tell me what Patrick is doing here,' Ruth snapped angrily. 'He turned up with

Leanne, of all people, at the same time as that man marched out of the house without a care in the world and Annalise appeared with Davey Allsop in tow. Patrick hurled himself across the drive at someone or other like a raging bull and then just hit the floor. Suddenly my home is a drop-in centre for all the local nutcases.'

'That's not fair.'

'Don't you tell me what's fair, ask Merlin what's fair. He's your son, if you remember. He doesn't have a clue what's going on but he's getting used to being pushed from pillar to post. Right now I've had to send him off with poor Sophie once again.' Ruth glared at Maria in exasperation. 'Come on. We'd better get outside and see what's happening with Patrick. We can argue over all this later.'

As they all ran outside, the sound of an ambulance siren echoed in the distance but it was still quite a way off. Patrick was on the ground unconscious with a group around him. Leanne was standing back watching with a gentle smile playing on her lips as Davey tried to breathe life back into Patrick's still body.

'What exactly is happening? How come you're all here?' Stunned, Maria looked around the forecourt of the house at the flurry of people. It was all too much. Turning on her heel she ran back indoors and up to her bedroom.

Chapter Fifty

Maria continued to watch the events from her bedroom window. It was like watching a television drama unfold in front of her eyes. The ambulance crunched its way up the drive with two more cars following behind. One she recognised as Ali's but the other she didn't have a clue about until an immaculately dressed older woman stepped regally from the back seat and walked over to where Davey was sitting on the ground, trying to catch his breath.

'Get in the car now, David,' she ordered imperiously. 'We're going home.'

Maria guessed it was Paula, the woman she had heard so much about from Davey. Mesmerised she watched, wondering first how the woman knew where she lived and secondly whether Davey would do as he was told.

'No, Paula,' she heard him reply softly. 'I'm not going home with you. I'm staying with Maria.'

'Do that, my darling, and you'll lose everything.' Paula smiled through gritted teeth. 'If you walk away from me now it'll be with nothing. Stay with me and

426

we'll marry, we'll split everything fifty-fifty, I'll even change my will in your favour.'

'No, it'll be if I stay with you that I'll lose everything. I'm sorry but this is the end of the line, I've danced to your tune long enough. I'm in love with Maria and we're going to be together.'

'The fuck you are!' Suddenly Ali was beside them. 'Maria is coming back with me, she's the mother of my son, we belong together.'

Maria shook her head as she watched and listened. It reminded her of an episode of her favourite soap. She looked over to where the paramedics were working on Patrick. They were pulling equipment out of the ambulance and attaching it to her brother, the brother she hated and despised and had wished dead on many occasions. But then she saw Sam, ashen and scared, and she pulled herself up. For better or worse, Patrick was his son. As they stretchered him into the vehicle, Maria saw Sam hesitate, obviously unsure whether to go in the ambulance or not.

In an instant all the anger she had felt for them left her and was replaced by an overwhelming sadness that spread through every pore in her body. Slowly she walked away from the window and over to her bedroom door. She turned the key forcefully; it was a gesture more to herself than anyone else, a sign that she wanted to be left alone with her thoughts and her guilt.

She stripped off her clothes and on auto-pilot went

through to the bathroom and turned on the shower. She held her hand under the shower head until the water was just the right temperature and then stepped into the large cubicle.

Maria felt the water on her shoulders before putting her head under and turning her face to the steaming water and savouring the almost painful beating down of the jets onto her cheeks.

She was aware of knocking on the door but ignored it, she didn't want to see anyone. Not anyone. All she wanted to do was purge her mind of the thoughts that had raced back and forth for so long. She wanted to sleep. Forever.

Reaching out to the shelf she grabbed a disposable razor and carefully snapped it in two before removing the blade from its casing. Carefully she ran the blade across first one wrist and then the other. She stepped back and held her hands out to the water.

Light-headed and weak, she slipped to the cold tiled floor and sank into oblivion.

Sam had known something was wrong. His instincts about his daughter were finely tuned and he knew every turn of her personality. As the chain of events unfolded that morning he realised that Maria was missing. The central character around whom the whole scenario revolved had gone up to her room. Racing up there he had knocked gently at first, then harder, and then he tried the handle.

Using all his strength he shouldered the door. Unlike in the movies, it had taken him several attempts before the door flew open and he fell through. He heard the water in the bathroom and felt the steam on his face and he had known before he ran into the bathroom what he would see. Watery blood had settled in a pool behind the backs of Maria's buckled knees and her head rested on her chest as she leaned almost gracefully into the corner of the cubicle.

Then Sam had started to scream.

'How are you feeling?' Sam asked his drowsy daughter who lay in her hospital bed looking the same shade of white as the over-boiled linen under her head.

It was two days later, and Sam felt as if he'd been to hell and back as Maria had drifted deliriously in and out of consciousness.

'I'm sorry, Dad.' The words were slow and slurred. 'I'm sorry, really sorry, I'm so sorry for everything. I've been such a bitch to everyone, I hate myself.'

Reaching out for her hand, Sam blinked fiercely to hold the tears that threatened. The doctors had told him it had been a close call. Another few minutes and Maria would have bled out.

'No, Maria. It's me who is sorry. We weren't very good parents to you, were we? Any of us. Samson has told me briefly what happened and suddenly there's a new history for us all.' He clutched at her hand. 'This is such a mess. We should never have done what we did, Finola and I, we shouldn't have lied to you. None of this need have happened, none of it.'

Maria blinked rapidly to get her focus back and turned her head to the other side of the room where she could see an outline that she recognised as Davey Allsop.

'Davey . . . You're here. After she tried to make you choose I thought you might have gone back to her . . .'

'Never.' He smiled gently. 'I've been here all the time. You can't get rid of me that easily. Anyway, rumour has it that she's found herself a new beau already. A successful businessman who goes under the name of Ali Shah. He's just what she's been looking for.'

Although Davey was trying to lighten the atmosphere it didn't work. Maria didn't even seem to hear him.

'Where's everyone else? Are any of them still talking to me?'

Maria saw Davey glance briefly at Sam before answering and she noticed the subtle shake of Sam's head that he tried to cover up with a stretch of his arms.

'Of course, but they only allow two at a time by the bedside. You'll see the others in due course. They all wish you well. Ruth and Sophie will be back later, they've been here as well.'

Maria tried to remember exactly what had happened, her mind was still foggy but she could recall looking out of the window and seeing everyone bunched around her brother.

'Patrick,' she murmured. 'How's Patrick? What happened to him?'

Again, a look passed between the two men on either side of the bed.

'Tell me what happened? I can see it's bad news.' Maria struggled to sit up but fell weakly back on to her pillow. 'He's dead, isn't he?'

Sam chewed his lip and looked away, unable to say the words.

'I'm sorry, Maria,' Sam stroked her forehead gently. 'He didn't make it. He suffered a massive heart attack. It was instant. He got himself so worked up and he was so overweight.'

Maria looked down at her heavily bandaged arms and instantly the fog started to clear. 'Oh God, I'm so sorry. How could I do something like this to you all? I've fucked up big-time, haven't I? First Eddie, now Patrick, two of your sons gone . . .'

Sam stood up quickly and ran his fingers through what little hair he had left on his head. 'I know that, Maria, and I'll beat myself up over it for the rest of my life, but it's not your fault. Somehow Finola and I managed to fail all our children.'

'Is Merlin outside?' Maria asked suddenly.

Again the exchange of glances across her bed.

'I'm sorry, love, but he's with Ali. There was nothing we could do, he is his father after all and Merlin wanted to go with him. You can sort it all out when you're feeling better. I've spoken to him on the phone every day though and he sends his love.'

'It's probably the best place for him right now. Ali's a good father.' Maria forced a smile. 'And you've been a wonderful father to me and I love you so much. Can you forgive me for raking up the past like that? It was so stupid, I should have left well alone.'

'No, sweetheart, it was a natural instinct. You had to do it. But I hope you won't forget me amid it all. I love you so much.'

Maria smiled and felt her eyes close.

As she drifted off to sleep, she felt Davey's breath on her face. Gently he kissed her cheek.

'I know the timing isn't great, but I love you so very much also, Maria. Will you marry me?'

'Mmmmm . . .' she murmured drowsily. 'I think I probably will, but first we have to resolve so many things . . . Patrick must be buried with Finola, they have to be together, she'll be so pleased to look after him again . . .' Her voice faded as she fell asleep.

Davey looked at Sam. 'Can we talk? I mean really talk. I need to explain about Eddie, I need to know if you can ever forgive me.'

'Forgive you?' Sam shook his head slowly and sighed. 'I guess I can forgive you, I probably did a long time ago but that doesn't mean I'll be able to forget. Same as I'll never forget Patrick.'

Sam looked into the middle distance. 'So many lives

ruined. I have to bury another son and then make amends to my remaining children, Joe and Maria. So, yes, I can forgive you, but you have to understand that if you ever do anything to hurt Maria or Merlin then I certainly won't forgive you again.'

'I'll never hurt either of them, I swear.'

'Then we should get along just fine.'

Epilogue

On the balcony of a luxury hotel room that looked out over the dark blue waters of the Red Sea, Maria stretched her legs out on the sunbed and sighed loudly. But it wasn't an unhappy sigh, more a long sigh of satisfaction.

Maria's recovery had taken longer than expected and she had also had the ordeal of another funeral to go through, but as soon as she had started to heal, Davey had whisked her off to a secluded resort in Egypt. After just a few days of warm sun on her back, Maria had been able to let the relaxed atmosphere wash over her.

It had taken many weeks for her to get to grips with what had happened but her psychiatrist had helped her analyse at least some of it and she knew she would be forever grateful to her patient family for their non-judgemental support.

Here in the bright sun of Egypt, Maria could almost convince herself that the previous few months had been nothing more than a bad dream.

'You do realise I'm a quarter Egyptian?' she said.

'Somewhere in this country I have family. Maybe grandparents, uncles, cousins. I wonder why Samson never kept in touch with his family. I must ask him why he simply left and never went back. It seems so strange not to know them.'

Davey sat forward and reached for a bottle of water. 'Not so unusual. I did the same although as far as I know the Allsops are all still in the same country. Anyway, *Tallulah Talks* wouldn't have you on there again, not after the way you traumatised those poor researchers.' Davey laughed and reached his hand out to her from the adjoining sunbed. 'You've found Samson even if it wasn't quite the result you expected. You still have Sam and Ruth and Sophie, and of course Merlin. In fact you have more family than I have. Leave it at that, eh?'

'I suppose you're right.' She squeezed his hand and looked thoughtfully into the middle distance. 'It's so strange, all this. I never thought I was the cracking-up type. I went completely off my head, didn't I? I'm still surprised you stayed around. Looney Tunes has got nothing on me.'

'Don't talk like that, Maria. Anyone would have cracked under those circumstances. In fact in a way I think many of us went a bit potty. Patrick, Leanne . . . It was like some sort of crazy sitcom with everyone on LSD, all running around.'

'And me upstairs slitting my wrists. Too crazy.'

'It's over now.'

'Not really. There's still Merlin. I'm so scared I've damaged him for life. It kills me that he prefers to live with Ali at the moment. I can understand it but I can't accept it. The rest of you understand what happened to me but Merlin . . .'

'Merlin will understand in time. He just needs to find his own level in it all. You said yourself that Ali is a good dad and you see him more now because he's with you at the weekends instead of weekdays when he's in school. And it's good for him to know that both his mum and his dad love him.'

'Mmmm. I hope it'll all be OK eventually. The nutty professor seems to think so anyway.'

Davey laughed. 'How to win friends and influence people, call your psychiatrist the nutty professor.'

'I quite like her actually. She's really helped me to get my life into perspective. She thinks that Merlin is strong and has made a good decision for his age. Weekdays with his dad and back at his old school and weekends to do fun things with his crazy mother.' Maria stood up. 'Sometimes you have to laugh so you don't cry.'

She looked at Davey; her mouth smiled but the sadness was still in her eyes. 'I've cried so much and been so angry. Now I have to move on and accept that the past is gone. It's sad that Finola spent the whole of her life after Samson swathed in sackcloth and ashes when she could have been with him and me. Sam could have then gone to Ruth way before he did; and Patrick and

Joe might not have turned into such assholes. Now Eddie and Patrick are gone and Leanne has left Joe. So many lives screwed up by my mother's guilt.'

'Maybe, but now's the time to break the chain and we're the ones to do it. You and I. The first of the happies!'

Maria leaned towards him and took his hand. 'I love you so much, David James Allsop.' She held out her other hand and grinned. 'Isn't it strange that I never knew your middle name? Always just Davey Allsop. You don't look like a David James! Now, let's go to bed. I need some more TLC if I'm to recover fully in time for the wedding.'

With a quick glance over her shoulder at the setting sun, Maria smiled. It would all be all right in the end. She was sure.